DREAM'S END

Book Five of the Dream Waters Series

Erin A. Jensen

2021 Dream's End
Text copyright © 2021 Erin A. Jensen
All Rights Reserved
Dream Waters Publishing LLC
5"x8" Softcover
ISBN: 1-7336504-3-1
ISBN 13: 978-1-7336504-3-4

To Chris for always believing in me and my dream, especially on the days when I didn't.

To Katie, Amy, Penny, Al, Stacy, Tara, and Pat for all the time and effort you devoted to beta reading this story.

To my Wegmans family for supporting my writing career since the moment I first announced that I'd written a book.

And to every reader who has ventured into my Dream World and joined me on this journey. I wouldn't be here without all of you.

The colossal waters rear their heads above us like demons of the deep, but like demons confined to simple threats and forbidden to destroy.

—Edgar Allan Poe, "MS. Found in a Bottle"

1

CHARLIE

I sat in a booth near the back of the pub nursing my single malt, with the Darkness cloaked in shadow beside me. Every now and then, Benjamin would curse and mutter something about being at the end of his rope. Under normal circumstances, I might've been equally pissed that the man we were there to meet was almost an hour late, but I was enjoying myself too much to care. It wasn't every day that I got to travel to Glasgow for a top-secret meeting with the commander of an allied kingdom's army.

I sunk back against the booth's buttery leather upholstery and swirled the rich golden liquid in my glass. Despite the hushed grumblings of the invisible buzzkill sitting next to me, I was perfectly content to sit back and people watch until the commander showed up.

Honestly, a part of me still couldn't believe that I'd been chosen for such an important task, no matter how sound the logic behind the decision was. If the Sarrum—or any of his usual delegates—had met with the commander of the Light army in Draumer, it would've drawn too much attention. If the Sarrum had been the one to fly to Scotland to meet with Commander Mackendrick, that still would've raised too many eyebrows. But despite the fact that I was Godric's son, I was still enough of a nobody in the waking world to hop on a red-eye flight to Scotland without anyone questioning who I was, or what I was up to.

Benjamin had flown to Germany on a private jet five days ahead of my departure from the States. After that, he'd made his way to my hotel in Glasgow almost entirely under the cover of shadow.

After a day of sightseeing with Benjamin cloaked in shadow beside me, we'd arrived at the Fox's Den Pub and Scullery promptly at six o'clock when our meeting was set to begin. Now the minute hand was inching its way toward seven, and the commander had yet to make an appearance.

"Exactly how long do you want to sit here like a jackass waiting for Mackendrick to show?" Benjamin grumbled under his breath.

"I've got nowhere else to be," I said, hoping nobody would notice me striking up a conversation with myself. "Come on, where's your sense of adventure?"

"Schlepping around as your shadow all day isn't exactly my idea of an adventure."

"I love you too, Benji," I whispered with a smirk.

"You know," he said, closer to my ear, "I could dump your body in Loch Ness, and nobody would ever be the wiser."

"Yeah? And what would you tell the boss?"

"That you fell out of the boat during our tour of the loch, and despite all my efforts to save you, you disappeared—never to be seen again."

The Darkness in his tone sent a shiver down my spine, but I answered him with a carefree grin. "Sounds like you've given that a lot of thought."

"A shadow has to pass the time somehow while he's following you around like an asshole all day."

Before I could fire off a clever comeback, the bell above the front door jingled and a fragrant gust of evening air wafted in, chilling the room as a middle-aged man stepped inside. He was smartly dressed in a black wool topcoat over his suit and tie. His reddish-brown hair and beard were precisely trimmed, and despite appearing to be in perfect health—and walking in steady purposeful strides—his left hand gripped a decorative wooden cane that he wasn't using. As he approached the bar, the man flashed the bartender a charming grin.

Still slouched in my incognito people-watching mode, it caught me off guard when the bartender nodded and pointed to our table as he handed the man his drink. The man's grin widened as he placed his money down on the bar and said something that the bartender responded to with a boisterous belly laugh.

The guy we were there to meet had been appointed commander of the Light army by Emma's grand-mother, the last true fairy Queen of the Light Kingdom. I wasn't pissed off that the commander had kept us waiting; but for him to keep us waiting only to have some other stooge show up on his behalf—that was just plain rude. Benjamin and I had traveled across the globe to meet with Mackendrick, and the guy couldn't be bothered to drive a few hours to talk to us?

"Who the hell is this guy?" I muttered under my breath.

"That's him," Benjamin whispered.

"That's who?" I asked as the commander's delegate approached our booth.

"Lochlan Mackendrick, at your service," the man replied, his charming grin widening as he extended his hand for a handshake. As he shook my hand, his gaze shifted to Benjamin. "Sorry to keep you gentlemen waiting for so long. The traffic is murder this time of day."

I turned my head to see if Benjamin had slipped out of the shadows. My dragon-vision could just barely detect the blurry edges of the Darkness's outline. *So how the hell could this guy see him?* "Are you here on your grandfather's behalf?" I asked as Mackendrick Junior slid into the opposite side of the booth.

The twinkle in his sea-blue eyes as he chuckled made it damn near impossible to dislike him. "No," he said, leaning over the table. "I am the fellow you came here to meet."

I sat my drink down on the table and studied him through narrowed eyes. "*You* were the love of Emma's grandmother's life? Your plastic surgeon must be one hell of a miracle worker."

He chuckled again, but the grin slipped from his face as his attention shifted to the man cloaked in darkness beside me. "You didn't prep him very well for this meeting, did you, shadow?"

"I didn't want to detract from his grand adventure," Benjamin muttered.

A hint of disapproval glinted in the commander's eyes as he stared at my invisible friend, but his expression softened as he turned back to me. "Tell you what, why don't you ask that selfish child whom you work for to give you a history lesson when you get back home?"

"Huh?" It wasn't exactly an eloquent response, but I was at a loss.

"David," Mackendrick replied, spitting the name from his mouth like a chunk of rancid meat.

"David Talbot?" I muttered. "Am I missing something?"

"Apparently," he replied, his grin a bit more forced. "But this isn't the time nor place for a history lesson, now is it?"

"Are we going to have a civil conversation?" Benjamin asked in a hushed growl. "Or did we come all this way just for you to bore us with a bunch of pointless grumbling and name-calling?"

"Why don't you tell me what we are here for?" Mackendrick replied in a clipped tone. "Because I find it a bit odd that this boy takes offense at someone standing in for me, when he is only here because David doesn't dare meet with me face-to-face."

Feeling more like a clueless bystander by the minute, I asked, "What's happening here?"

Mackendrick frowned at me as he slid to the edge of the bench on his side of the booth. "I'm afraid you have wasted a trip, Mister...?"

"Oliver," I said, "Charlie Oliver."

He was just starting to rise from his seat when I said my name. The instant he heard it, he sat back down. "You're Godric's boy?"

"I'm afraid so, but I hope you don't hold that against me."

"Henry Godric never broke a promise to us," Mackendrick replied. "The same cannot be said of David Talbot."

Now at a total loss, I asked, "What exactly did my boss do to piss you off so much?"

"That is a discussion for another time," the commander replied, "in another world. Let's get down to business now, shall we?"

2

DAVID

The air was so thick with the scent of blood that its telltale metallic tang coated my tongue the instant Tristan, Mia, and I emerged from the Water portal at the edge of the forest. The sun had already begun its descent, drenching the evening sky—and the Waters that mirrored it—in such a vivid mix of bloodred hues that it seemed as if even the elements had not escaped the massacre unscathed. Despite the waning light and our distance from the shore, it was clear that the nomadic tribe's encampment along the fringe lay in ruins.

Ribbons of blue smoke escaped my nostrils, unfurling in the air like silent snarls as we stepped from the trees and moved toward the smoldering remains of the elves' makeshift shelters. The Purists' attacks along the fringe had become an almost daily occurrence at this point, but there was still no discernable pattern as to how they were selecting their targets. This made it all but impossible to prevent the attacks, since we couldn't very well station the royal guard along every stretch of Waterfront without making our presence known to the Unsighted inhabitants.

The call from the hospital had come early that morning, informing Tristan that Beverly Mason had passed away unexpectedly in her sleep. Although Brian was her biological son, and Tristan was the by-product of her incubus husband's infidelity, Beverly had raised both boys as her own since the day Tristan's birth mother died of a drug overdose when he was seven. Despite his unsavory origins, Tristan was her favorite, and she had never made any attempt to hide that fact from either child. I had hoped it'd simply been Beverly's time to go, but the timing was suspicious enough to warrant a trip to her encampment.

The carnage amidst the smoldering wreckage we were walking toward confirmed what Tristan had suspected since he'd received the call—the Purists had murdered his Unsighted mother, along with the rest of her elven tribe.

Mia muffled a gasp as a demonic scavenger appeared, scurrying on all fours from one scorched shelter to the next with a charred limb dangling from her mouth.

As we moved closer, the scavenger imps flitting amidst the smoldering corpses bolted and took flight, filling the airspace above us with a fluttering canopy of tiny silhouettes as they ascended into the darkening sky as one morose entity.

Tristan barely seemed to notice the demonic scavengers poking around in search of scraps. His attention was solely fixed on locating his mother's remains. After identifying her body in the waking world, he had tucked a rosary into her hand and charmed the coroner into leaving it there so he could track her in Draumer. Now he followed its pull on him with trancelike determination, seeking what remained of the woman who'd raised him.

Thankfully my eyesight was keener than his deceased mother's pull on him. I stopped short as I caught sight of her and blocked his advance with my forearm to prevent him from moving near enough to see.

Grief-stricken rage flashed in his eyes as he turned toward me, but the look on my face was enough to deter him from asking why I'd stopped him.

I answered his unvoiced objection with an apologetic frown. "You should head back now, Tristan."

"With all due respect, Sarrum, she's my—"

"This is not the last memory you want to have of her," I said, without waiting for him to finish. "Leave this to me."

His muscles were coiled with fury and he was clearly itching to barge past me; but as Mia took hold of his hand, he let out a defeated sigh. "You'll bring her remains back, so we can give her a proper burial?"

My eyes drifted to what was left of Beverly Mason as I nodded. "Yes, of course. Trust me. It's best this way."

"Fuck," he said, shaking his head. "All right. We'll go wait inside the forest."

"No, I want the two of you to head back to the palace now."

Tristan opened his mouth to argue, but there was no fight left in him. So he tightened his grip on Mia's hand, and they turned and started toward the trees.

I stood there watching to make certain he wouldn't change his mind and turn back. When they reached the trees, I reopened the Water portal and watched them step in hand in hand. Then I sealed it shut behind them.

In the absolute silence that followed their exit, I turned toward the wreckage, sunk the sun below the horizon, and started toward Mrs. Mason's remains beneath a starless sky. Every living creature and natural element in the vicinity seemed to be holding its breath in mourning for the tragedy that'd befallen this nomadic tribe.

The only sounds as I drew near were the euphoric moans of the berbalang who was feeding on Mrs. Mason's disemboweled corpse. The ghoul's dark leathery wings were tucked back as his humanoid body crouched over her, tugging her entrails loose with his teeth and gulping them down with shameless groans of pleasure. Silent as my approach was, the ghoul did not sense my presence until I was almost near enough to touch him. The instant he caught my scent, his ravenous moans ceased and his head jerked up.

"**Step away from her, berbalang,**" I growled, both aloud and inside his head.

The ghoul's feline eyes flashed like fireflies in the darkness as he lowered his head and bit off another chunk of the elf's intestines.

Astonished that his hunger was vehement enough to surpass his fear of my wrath, I unmasked and stepped toward him in dragon form. "**You shall come to regret that bite.**"

Still, his head remained bent over Mrs. Mason's corpse as he continued to tear off such massive chunks that it was a wonder he didn't choke on them.

I knocked him back from her body with a claw to his left flank. Yet he shook it off, pushed himself to his hands and knees, and started to scurry back. When I struck him again, he unfurled his wings and took flight.

I plucked him from the air by his leg, flung him to the ground, and pinned him beneath my claw. **"Your mindless appetite astounds me. You act as if you haven't fed in years."**

His catlike eyes widened as he shook his head. "Haven't."

"With all the carnage along the fringe recently, how is that possible?"

Blood-tinged drool trickled from the corner of the berbalang's mouth as his feral gaze drifted to Mrs. Mason's body. "Kept caged. Released here."

I tightened my grip on him. **"Caged and released by whom?"**

"Would-be-king's soldiers," the berbalang replied. "Feast is gift. From him."

My stomach dropped at the implication of his words. **"Was this entire spread of carnage the gift, or just this particular kill?"**

"This one. Mine. Feast." The ghoul started to turn his head in her direction again, but I squeezed him to draw his attention back to me.

"No, I'm afraid it isn't," I replied as I summoned the Waters, opened a portal to the palace, and tossed him in.

I unmasked with a heavy sigh and scooped Mrs. Mason's body into my arms as gingerly as I could, hoping Tristan would be elsewhere when I stepped into the corridor with his mother and the ghoul I'd found feasting on her.

3

EMMA

I yawned and stretched my limbs as I stepped out into the fairytale splendor of the massive courtyard to the Queen of the Light Realm's palace. Technically, I suppose I should've considered it *my* palace, but this place didn't feel like home to me. *My* home was at the center of the Dark Forest, and that's where my heart was too.

I only made it a few steps out the door before Freya—the Queen's chief attendant—rushed up to me, dropped to one knee, and bowed her head. "Good morning, my Queen. Shall I bring your breakfast out here for you?"

Breakfast in the Light Realm was nothing like the meal I was accustomed to starting my day with. Their traditional morning beverage was a bubbly pink drink they called nectar. It tasted like cotton candy in carbonated liquid form, and I couldn't take more than a sip or two before it turned my stomach. Their breakfast foods were all sugar based too. In fact, it seemed as if a five-year-old had devised the Light Realm's entire food pyramid, which seemed to consist of nothing more than various forms of sugar.

I smiled at my pixie attendant as she tilted her head to look up at me, her dewy violet eyes squinting in the morning light. "We talked about this, Freya. You don't have to bow every time you see me."

"Right," she chirped, hopping to her feet. "Sorry, my Queen."

"Please call me Emma, and I would love some coffee."

A grimace contorted her delicate features for a split second before she realized what her face was doing and forced a smile. "Of course, my Qu...Emma—although, I don't know how you can stomach that dark, bitter stuff."

"I grew up surrounded by Dark and bitter. It's like a little taste of home."

"Thank heavens Commander Mackendrick was able to provide us with a plentiful supply of it then," Freya replied, as if she truly did consider it a blessing.

"I hope he keeps it coming," Brian chimed in as he stepped out into the courtyard. "Not all of us are morning creatures."

Freya's cheeks flushed a deep shade of pink at the sound of the half-incubus's velvet voice. She started to greet him with a bow, but thought better of it when she glanced back at me. "Good morning, Sir. Shall I bring you some coffee too?"

"Yes, lots," Brian said, sitting down on a white marble bench a few steps from where I stood. He shook his head and combed his fingers through his perfectly disheveled locks as he watched the pixie rush off to fetch our coffee.

I flashed him an affectionate grin and sat down on the bench beside him. "Please tell me the troops are almost battle ready. I'd really like to get on with this war, so we can go back home."

"If only," he said, slouching toward me. "What I wouldn't give to slip between the black satin sheets on my own bed and see the Dark Realm's pitch-dark sky outside my bedroom window."

"Tell me about it. I'd give anything to spend a night beneath the stars in my clearing."

Brian let out a throaty chuckle. "I'm guessing that has a lot to do with the Dark guy who keeps you warm beneath that starry sky."

I shook my head as I tucked my legs up on the bench. "Is it that obvious I'm missing him?"

A devilish grin spread across his handsome face as he extended a hand to me. "Hi, I'm Brian. I'm half incubus, and I'm pretty perceptive when it comes to desires."

"You don't say," I said, placing my hand in his and smiling as he shook it. "Careful with those observations, unless you want me to start commenting on what I've noticed about you lately."

His grin widened as his dreamy lost-puppy-dog eyes locked with mine. "You know, you're awful damn grouchy in the morning when you haven't had any coffee or..." Brian's voice trailed off as Freya stepped outside carrying two steaming mugs of coffee, but his expression got the point across.

"Well, at least Freya can satisfy one of my desires."

"I'm pretty sure she'd be happy to satisfy both," he said as we watched her move toward us.

Freya blushed the instant she noticed Brian's eyes were on her, and I let out a laugh. "Yeah, I don't think I'm the one she's interested in."

"See, that's where you're wrong," he whispered as Freya handed me my coffee.

I nodded a thank you to her, then narrowed my eyes at Brian as she handed him the other cup.

He winked at me, then fixed his heart-melting gaze on her. "Thank you, Freya."

Freya's blush deepened. "You are most welcome, Sir. May I be of further service to either of you?"

"Nah, I think we're good for now," Brian said. "Thanks."

She dipped her head with a breathy, "Of course." Then she turned and headed back toward the door.

I savored my first few blissful sips of coffee in silence, then turned to Brian as Freya slipped inside the palace. "Why are you so naughty this morning?"

Brian let out a hushed chuckle. "I'm an incubus, remember? I don't know. I think all this Light just brings out the Darkness in me."

I took another sip of my coffee, then dropped my head to his shoulder. "I'm glad you joined me out here. I needed a bit more Darkness this morning. There's way too much Light around here."

He clinked his cup against mine. "Amen to that, sister."

"You get used to it," Lochlan said as he stepped outside with a cup of coffee cradled in his hands. The commander flashed me a charming grin as he crossed the courtyard, but the grin slipped from his face as his eyes moved to Brian. "I seem to recall you criticizing me for being too familiar with the Queen the day we first met, Mason."

Brian wrapped an arm around my shoulders to irritate him. "Yeah? Well, you'd just met her, Mackendrick. She and I go way back."

"How nice for you," Lochlan said, raising an eyebrow. "Don't you have some soldiers to train?"

"Not before coffee," Brian muttered.

Grinning, the commander sat down on my other side. "Well, I cannot fault you there."

I leaned back against Brian's arm and shifted to face Lochlan. "How did your meeting go last night?"

"Fine. Your dear husband sent your friend Charlie in his stead."

"What is it with the two of you?" I asked, searching the commander's oceanic blue eyes. "Why won't either of you tell me why you hate each other so much?"

Lochlan shrugged. "I believe that is a question for your husband."

I would've scowled at him, but I was too comforted by the beating of his dragon heart to even pretend to be annoyed.

4

BRIAN

Finished with pairing up my trainees to work on the moves I'd taught them, I winked at Emma as I headed toward the stairs to join her. While I climbed the steps of the open-air amphitheater, I had to make a conscious effort not to roll my eyes or shake my head. The gleaming marble sculptures lining the walkways, the white satin cushions on the spectators' benches, and all the other opulent details looked more like they belonged in a cathedral than a military training facility.

Emma smiled as she slid over on the bench to make room for me. "You've definitely got your work cut out for you."

I sat down, wrapped an arm around her, and leaned back against the bench cushions. "Good thing I'm brilliant at what I do."

"You are brilliant," she said, dropping her head to my shoulder. "I'm not sure anyone else could whip them into shape in time."

I gave her an affectionate half hug with the arm around her shoulders. "Don't forget, these are just the new recruits. Most of them had never even held a weapon before you took the throne. They volunteered for this because they were eager to serve their rightful Queen."

"And I appreciate their loyalty, especially since most of them knew nothing about me until I showed up here. I just don't want to send them into a battle they aren't ready for. It's my job to keep them safe."

I cast her a sideways glance, grinning at her without fully taking my eyes off the trainees. "Have you ever known me to miss a deadline?"

"No, never."

"They'll be ready. Trust me."

"I do trust you," she said, "with my life. I always have."

"If you want to get a better feel for how the troops are doing overall, you should stick around and watch Zeke's trainees practice, and Addison and Bob's group after that, and the commander's former soldiers from before the imposter Queen disbanded the Light Realm's army. You'll feel a hell of a lot better after observing all of them."

She nodded without turning to look at me. "Does it frustrate you, working under Commander Mackendrick?"

Down below us, one of my trainees took a nasty blow to the head. Wincing, I muttered, "What makes you ask that?"

Emma leaned forward—watching the injured trainee shake it off and go right back to sparring—with a faint smile on her lips. "It's been a long time since you took orders from a higher-ranking military officer. Benji and David trust your judgment without question. Doesn't it feel odd taking orders from the commander?"

"Once a good soldier, always a good soldier," I replied with a shrug. "It hasn't been so long that I've forgotten how to follow orders. Besides, this is the perfect job for me. I'm used to training new recruits, and I'm damn good at it. And for the record, technically I outrank Mackendrick since the royal guard is the Sarrum's army and the Light regiment reports to us. It's just professional courtesy to let the commander call the shots on his playing field."

"I wouldn't expect you to follow any order that went against your good judgment. I trust you with my life, and the lives of everyone in this kingdom, for good reason."

I turned my head to look her in the eye. "You know, I have orders from the Sarrum to protect you above all else."

"That's irrelevant," she said, holding my gaze, "since I know darn well you'd do that anyway."

I grinned and turned back to watch the training floor. "Once your bodyguard, always your bodyguard, and it'd be an unforgivable crime not to guard a body like yours with my life."

Emma let out a laugh. "You are in serious need of some female companionship, my friend."

Before I could fire off a flirtatious response, Zeke came sauntering into the arena with his sister beside him. Davina's eyes searched the stands while they crossed the training floor, and a grin spread across her gorgeous face the second she spotted me. "That's not happening anytime soon," I muttered, smiling at Davina despite my words.

Emma let out a heavy sigh. "Why does it seem like everybody in this realm has secrets they don't want to share with me?"

"I'll tell you anything you want to know," I said, watching Davina take a seat near the spot where Zeke's trainees were beginning to congregate. "Dinner tonight?"

"It's a date." Emma's smile took a downward turn as another recruit took a hit that knocked him on his ass. "Looks like you should get back down there."

"Yup," I muttered, standing up. "See you at dinner."

By the time I reached the training floor, the fallen trainee was already back on his feet throwing punches. So I took the nearest empty seat to watch them up close for a few minutes. These Light creatures had a lot of heart. There wasn't a doubt in my mind that they'd lay down their lives for their Queen if it came to that.

Across the arena, Zeke's soldiers were limbering up so they'd be ready to take the floor when my recruits hit the showers. Although his soldiers were far more battle ready, most of them were renegades or former marauders as opposed to trained militia. That was exactly why this particular ragtag bunch, who'd all spent time outside the Light Realm, had been assigned to Zeke's command. Davina's half-incubus, half-giant brother had never had a day of official military training, but you sure as hell wouldn't want to go up against him in battle. Zeke had learned to fight for survival. You had to when you grew up in an orphanage and got carted off to a work camp before you were even old enough to shave.

Zeke was a good man who'd defend a brother to the death, and I loved him for that because he and I shared a brother. Zeke wasn't Tristan's brother by blood like I was, but the two of them had been thick as thieves since their early days in the orphanage for Sighted kids whose parents never claimed them. When the two of them turned twelve, and were no longer considered children by Draumer's standards, they were sent to the same work camp on the outskirts of the Dark Forest. I was glad the big guy had always had my younger brother's back, since my path didn't cross Tristan's till much later on in Draumer.

My life had started off in another orphanage on the opposite side of the Dark Forest from the one Tristan and Zeke grew up in. The fact that I was Walter Mason's legitimate son in the waking world made no difference whatsoever to him. In Draumer, Tristan and I were both bastards our father had no interest in claiming. Hell, if it weren't for my mother, he probably wouldn't have taken responsibility for me in the waking world either. My mom may not have doled out much affection when it came to me, but she'd taken care of me in the waking world—keeping me fed and clothed—and I was grateful for that. Unfortunately, since she was Unsighted, my mother kept to the fringe along with the rest of her tribe of Unsighted elves in Draumer. So my life had begun in an orphanage, just like my brother's. Although when I turned twelve, my life took a very different path.

After showing my trainees a few moves to work on and giving them a quick pep talk, I dismissed them and settled back in my seat to watch Zeke's soldiers take the floor. Observing Zeke and his group's streetwise fighting style got me thinking about the alternate turns my life could've taken, and eventually my thoughts drifted to the point where my path diverged from the one Tristan and Zeke had taken…

…I was two weeks shy of my twelfth birthday when Nick told me about the recruiters who were in the area searching for able-bodied men to join the nomadic knighthood. Nick was a teen from the village who worked at the orphanage, tending to the livestock. Like every other kid at the orphanage, I'd been assigned a daily chore at the age of ten; and since my job was to clean the barn and muck out the stalls, I spent a fair amount of time around Nick.

Having spent my whole life at the orphanage, I knew almost nothing about the knights who watched over the Unsighted inhabitants of the fringe. But I was painfully aware that my days were numbered. The orphanage had limited resources. So when I turned twelve, I'd be relocated to a work camp to make room for younger orphans, and that's where I'd remain until I was old enough to be out on my own in the world. I'd heard enough from Nick and the other teens from the village who worked at the orphanage to dread the move I'd soon be forced to make. Those camps were dangerous places, and not everyone made it out of them alive.

When Nick confided that he planned to sneak off after curfew and head to a pub where the recruiters were setting up for the day, I asked if I could tag along. Nick said he was confident that the knighthood would accept him because they were an order of elves and he was of pure elven blood, but he warned me that they might not be interested in a half-breed like me. Still, I figured it was better to take my chances there rather than sit around waiting to get carted off to a camp. At least this way, I'd have a shot at a better life.

As I stood in line outside the pub, watching the elf with coarse silver hair and shaking hands size up potential recruits and turn away strong men with no explanation, this seemed like a much less promising venture. Still, I squared my shoulders and did my best to quiet my nerves.

"You're not what we're looking for." The recruiter's harsh voice yanked me from my thoughts as he dismissed Nick without any more explanation than that.

Eyes full of tears, Nick turned to me. "Good luck, mate." With that, he took off toward the woods without even waiting to see how I'd make out.

"And who might you be?" the weather-beaten elf at the front of the recruitment line asked as I stepped up to him.

"My name is Brian Mason, Sir," I replied in a voice that conveyed much more confidence than I actually felt.

"Mason," the elf muttered, "any relation to Walter Mason?"

My throat tightened. I knew being associated with my dad wouldn't do me any favors. Still, it seemed important not to lie to this knight I'd come to prove my worth to. "Yes, Sir. He's my father in the waking world."

The crease on the elf's leathery forehead deepened as his brows knit together. "But not in this one?"

"No, Sir. I was raised in the orphanage nearby."

The man sized me up through narrowed eyes. "How old are you, boy?"

"I'm two weeks shy of twelve."

He sneered at my answer and shook his head. "Ah, so you're just looking for an easy escape from the work camps."

"I'm looking for an opportunity to do something noble with my life," I replied without shying away from his judgmental glare.

"There's no room for a lazy half-breed like you in our order," he said, dismissing me with a flick of his hand.

I stepped out of line with a heavy heart, debating whether to head for the woods and catch up with Nick or try my luck somewhere else.

As I passed by an open window of the pub, the hearty aromas of roasting meat and freshly baked bread came wafting out amidst a jumble of rowdy conversations. I stopped to savor the smell for a second, and my stomach growled.

Behind me, a very proper-sounding deep voice asked, "Are you hungry, young man?"

I turned around and found myself staring into the inquisitive ice-blue eyes of a noble elf. He was dressed all in black, and his long blond hair was tied back from his face, accentuating his regal features and pointed ears. "Yes, Sir, I am."

The elf smoothed a hand over his perfectly straight hair. "Then would you care to come inside and join me as my dinner guest?"

I hesitated, unsure what to make of this nobleman inviting a young boy he didn't know to dine with him.

The elf grinned at my perplexed expression and extended a hand to me. "I am sorry. Where are my manners? I haven't properly introduced myself. I am Sir Jacob Harris, commander of the Nomadic Knighthood of the Northern Shore."

"Brian Mason, Sir," I replied as he shook my hand.

"Well, Mr. Mason," he said, releasing my hand, "now that we've been properly introduced, will you accept my invitation?"

I couldn't imagine why he would want to dine with me, but he was the man in charge of the order I'd come to join;

my only other option was to head off to the woods and slink back to the orphanage. "Yes, Sir."

Without further discussion, he walked up to the side door of the pub, pulled it open, and motioned for me to go in ahead of him.

As I stepped inside, a delicious combination of smells enveloped me, and my stomach rumbled again.

The commander smiled at me and started across the floor. "Follow me."

I fell into step behind him, and we weaved our way through a boisterous crowd of Dark creatures to a door at the other end of the room. We stepped through the door and entered a private dining room, where an assortment of food like I'd never seen was spread out on the table.

The commander pulled out a chair for me, motioned for me to sit, and then sat down across the table from me. "Our hosts have been most generous, but there is no possible way for me to eat this much food." He started to fill his plate and signaled for me to do the same.

"Thank you," I said.

The commander nodded. "May I ask you a question, young Mr. Mason?"

Eager to make a good impression, I sat up a little straighter. "Of course, Sir."

"You are half incubus, are you not?"

"Yes, I am," I said, holding his gaze despite the urge to drop my eyes to the table.

"My recruiter dismissed you because an incubus lured his older sister away from home and led her down a rather dark path when he was a boy," the commander confided as he cut into a baked potato.

I nodded because I didn't know what to say to that.

"You could have easily changed his mind by charming him," the commander mused, lifting a forkful of potato to his mouth. "Yet, you chose not to?"

I watched him stick the potato in his mouth, wondering whether to start eating or wait for permission. "Yes, Sir."

"And why is that?" he asked around a mouthful of potato.

"I just don't think it's right to charm somebody into doing what you want them to," I said, picking up my fork. "Every creature deserves to be free to make their own decisions."

The commander motioned for me to start eating as he swallowed the food in his mouth. "Your mother is an elf, is she not?"

Figuring it must be okay to talk with food in my mouth since he'd done it first, I muttered, "Yes, Sir," around a mouthful of the most succulent meat I'd ever tasted.

The commander nodded and placed his fork on the edge of his plate. "How does she treat you in the waking world?"

"Sir?"

"I assume you do not charm her either?" he asked, picking up his wine glass.

"No, I don't."

"But your father does?"

"Yes."

"I must confess, I am familiar with your father." As the commander paused to sip his wine, my stomach dropped. "You look very much like him."

Cheeks burning, I muttered, "Yes, Sir."

The commander dropped his eyes to his glass as he set it down on the table. "So tell me, how does your mother react to you?"

"She's not too fond of me," I admitted, setting my fork down on my plate. "When my dad goes away on business, she realizes all the faults that he charms her into overlooking while he's home. And since I look so much like him, she treats me the way she would treat him if he didn't charm her into loving him."

A sorrowful smile spread across the commander's face. "That is quite unfair to you, don't you think?"

"I don't look at it like that," I replied, my voice little more than a whisper.

"How do you look at it?"

"She needs to be herself and let out what she's feeling some of the time. If I keep quiet and let her do that, it's the one way that I can help her."

A grin spread across his face. "You are far more elf than incubus, Mr. Mason."

"Thank you, Sir."

"The order would be honored to accept you as one of our trainees," he replied with a nod. "Of course, I do not mean to sugarcoat things. My recruiter will be your sergeant during your training, and I doubt he will go easy on you, given his past. He will accept you because I order him to, but I imagine he will be much harder on you than he is on the other recruits."

"I can handle that, Sir," I said, picking up the glass of water beside my plate. "I'm pretty used to that already."

The commander smiled at me as he raised his glass and clinked it against mine. "Welcome to the order, Mr. Mason."

5

CHARLIE

Benjamin was adamant that we show up late for our second meeting with the commander of the Light Kingdom's army. He wanted to let Mackendrick sit and stew for at least a good forty-five minutes.

I suggested we get there ten minutes late, and in the end we compromised and agreed to show up twenty-five minutes past our arranged meeting time. Despite the fact that the commander had kept us waiting for almost an hour the first time we met, this secretive military-collaboration-between-kingdoms stuff was still new to me, and I didn't want to earn a reputation for being a spiteful asshole right off the bat. Sure, the commander had done it first, but he seemed to think he had a pretty good reason to hate David Talbot. I was still waiting for somebody to fill me in on the details— or hell, even the Cliffs Notes version—of what the boss had done to make Mackendrick despise him so much. So far, Benjamin had sidestepped the question every time I brought it up. He, like the commander, said it was the Sarrum's story to tell.

I raked a hand through my hair as I stepped inside the pub and did a quick visual scan of the room. The Fox's Den was a lot more crowded than it'd been the night before. Apparently, the place was a mecca for day drinkers and travel-weary tourists on a rainy Thursday afternoon.

"If you ask me," Benjamin grumbled as he followed me inside, "this is a colossal fucking waste of time." Tired of lurking in the shadows as my invisible sidekick, he'd chosen to pose as a fellow tourist, albeit a far more menacing one than the pub's other jovial patrons.

I shook my head as we approached the bar because so far Mackendrick was nowhere to be seen. I could already picture myself trying to explain to the Sarrum why Benjamin had killed the guy we'd traveled all this way to meet. Making a mental note to start working on a cover story, I turned to Benjamin. "What do you say we sit and share a drink like a couple of regular guys, and enjoy the time to ourselves?"

"What do you say we drink in silence, and I try to refrain from killing you?" Benjamin growled as he flagged down the bartender.

There was a time when a sentence like that from the Darkness's mouth would've chilled me to the bone. *Now, I practically considered it an expression of endearment.*

"Endearment my ass," Benjamin muttered as he handed the bartender a wad of cash that was at least twice the cost of the two whiskeys he'd placed on the bar in front of us. "Keep the change."

The bartender shot him a lopsided grin that suggested he'd been sampling the stuff behind the bar. "Thanks, mate."

Tipping his cap to the bartender, Benjamin picked up his drink and headed toward the only empty table in the room. I grabbed the other drink and followed him, waiting while a waitress with a head of disheveled curls wiped down the freshly vacated table Benjamin had plopped himself down at. Giving her an appreciative nod as she finished, I sat down across the table from the Darkness.

Benjamin glared at me over the rim of his glass as he took a slow sip of his whiskey. "The bastard's still making us wait on him."

I held his stare as I took a drink and savored the mellow burn as the rich liquid slid down my throat, warming my insides. "All right, you win. We should've shown up forty-five minutes late. Tomorrow we—"

"Tomorrow the commander can go fuck himself," Benjamin growled, "if he thinks we'll be wasting another day sitting around waiting for him to grace us with his presence."

"What exactly do you expect to accomplish with these meetings, while you're being so hostile to each other?" I asked, turning toward the door as the jingling bell above it announced the arrival of another customer.

I breathed a sigh of relief as the commander stepped inside, brushing the rain from his overcoat. With a nod to us, Mackendrick headed for the bar.

"Well, halle-fuckin'-lujah," Benjamin muttered as we watched the rosy-cheeked bartender greet the commander.

While Mackendrick started toward us with a drink in one hand and that fancy cane he didn't seem to need in the other, I turned back to Benjamin. "You didn't answer my question."

The commander grinned at us as he stepped up to our table. "Good afternoon, gentlemen. It's a bit crowded out here to have a proper conversation. Would you care to join me in a private room in the back of this establishment?"

"Sure," Benjamin growled. "You go ahead. We'll be there in an hour or so."

Instead of snarling something hostile back, the commander turned to me. "Is he always this much of a cheeky bastard in the daylight hours?"

I bit my tongue as I stood from the table, hoping Benjamin would take the high road and just let that go. "Why don't you lead the way? If Benjamin wants to sit out here and drink by himself while we talk for an hour, that's his prerogative."

Mackendrick's grin widened as he clapped me on the shoulder. "I am beginning to see why David sent you in his stead. You clearly have yet to undergo their stick-up-the-arse initiation ritual."

A low growl rumbled in the base of Benjamin's throat as he stood up from the table, locking the commander in a bone-chilling death glare.

Mackendrick just shook his head as he turned and started to lead the way. As we passed the bar, he flagged the bartender's attention. "Better send a bottle of your finest back to us, mate. I suspect we might need it to break the ice."

The bartender dipped his head. "Will do, Mr. Mackendrick."

With that, the commander headed down the back hall without turning to see if the two of us were still behind him. I followed him with Benjamin behind me, staring daggers at Mackendrick that I could practically feel piercing through me. When we reached the end of the hall, the commander stopped to tuck the cane in his left hand under his left arm, and switched the drink in his right hand to his left. Then he opened a door to the right and ushered us in with an elegant flourish of his hand that brought to mind the Sarrum's regal movements. I stepped through the door and took in my surroundings while Benjamin followed me into the room. Mahogany trim. Metal leaf-patterned ceiling. Expensive leather chairs. The room was just as charming as the rest of the pub.

Benjamin and I settled into two seats on the far side of the table, and Mackendrick shut the door and sat down across from us. Then we all just sat there awkwardly staring at each other till a knock on the door broke the silence.

At the commander's invitation, a server slipped in the room and placed a bottle of top-shelf whiskey and three glasses on the table between us. "On the house, sir."

Reaching into his coat pocket, Mackendrick pulled out a handful of shiny gold coins and handed them all to the server. "Well, thank you, lad. That is most generous."

The server's eyes widened as he stared at the coins in his hand. "Thank you, sir," he muttered. Then he dipped his head and left the room.

I raised an eyebrow. "How much money did you give him?"

Mackendrick shook his head, then leaned back in his chair and cracked open the bottle. "That is a rather bold question, isn't it?"

"Sorry."

"No need to apologize," the commander replied as he filled a glass for himself. He raised a questioning eyebrow, looking to us as he tilted the bottle. We both pushed our glasses forward, and he filled them with a carefree grin. "I appreciate a bloke who doesn't beat around the bush. There's no time for that sort of nonsense, given the current state of things."

"Maybe there would be if you didn't keep us waiting so fucking long," Benjamin growled as he picked up his glass.

"You know perfectly well that it's difficult to gauge time whilst traveling through the Waters, Darkness," the commander replied, setting the bottle down on the table.

"Maybe you should take that into account and allow yourself extra time for the trip," Benjamin said without missing a beat, "so you don't keep everybody else sitting around waiting with their thumbs up their asses."

"What a charmingly colorful suggestion," Mackendrick replied, smiling to himself.

Benjamin was about to snarl something back when his phone started ringing. He fished it out of his jacket pocket and grumbled as he glanced at the screen. "I've gotta take this."

"Is that my old friend David, perchance?" the commander asked, his voice dripping with sarcasm.

"Sure is," Benjamin said, answering the call. "Hey, boss. It's not—"

I didn't catch the Sarrum's words, but the urgency of his tone was enough to wipe the smile off Mackendrick's face. He and I both stayed quiet, studying Benjamin's tight-lipped expression while he listened to the boss.

"On my way," Benjamin said, ending the call as he stood from the table. "I've gotta go back to the hotel and head through the Waters to the palace."

"Trouble at home?" Mackendrick asked, his unreadable expression making it impossible to gauge whether the question was meant to be sarcastic or serious.

"Yeah," Benjamin muttered. "The Purists attacked another encampment along the fringe. Brian and Tristan's mother's tribe. There were no survivors. The Sarrum brought back the berbalang he found feeding on Mrs. Mason's entrails, and he wants me to help interrogate the son of a bitch. Sounds like these attacks might not be as random as we thought."

The commander nodded. "Well, that certainly takes precedence. Charlie and I can continue this on our own."

I shot Benjamin a quizzical glance because I still wasn't entirely sure whether I could trust this guy who loathed my boss for reasons I still knew nothing about.

"You're Emma's best friend," Benjamin said, in answer to my unvoiced concern. "The commander wouldn't dream of harming a hair on your head."

I narrowed my eyes at Benjamin. "What are—"

"That is the first thing to come out of this shadow's mouth that I'm in complete agreement with," Mackendrick said. "I'd never dream of doing anything that would cause our Queen pain."

Benjamin gave me a nod. "Talk things out. You'll probably accomplish more without me anyway. I'll call when I can fill you in on the details."

"Yeah, all right," I muttered after Benjamin, who was already rushing out the door.

"Emma's primary guard is a good man," the commander mused as Benjamin closed the door, shutting the two of us in together. "I do not relish having to inform him that his mother passed when I return to the Light Kingdom."

"I don't blame you." I paused to take a gulp of my whiskey, pondering which of my questions to ask first. "So, why does me being Emma's best friend make a damn bit of difference to you?"

A wistful smile spread across Mackendrick's face as he picked up his glass and took a drink. "Emma's grandmother was the love of my life. I treasured her with all my heart, and I love that girl with every bit of the love I had for my Violet."

I took another sip of my whiskey, considering his response. "Okay, so why doesn't Godric feel the same way about David Talbot? I mean, that's something I've never understood. David's mom was Godric's sister, and she was his greatest treasure, wasn't she?"

The commander dropped his eyes to the bottle on the table between us. "Aye. She was, but Emma is my beloved's granddaughter; she had no part in my Violet's death. Lilly Talbot, on the other hand, died giving birth to David. So in Godric's eyes, David killed her. To him, the Sarrum is a living breathing reminder of all the ways that the Talbots wronged him and his dear sister."

"How can Godric be so irrational? None of that was David's fault. His family made those decisions before he was even conceived."

Mackendrick let out a sigh as he picked up the bottle and topped off both our glasses, without asking if I wanted more. "I don't know how much of your birth father's story you've been told, but the Talbot family decided to pass the crown to David's dad after Henry Godric murdered his own father. The patriarch of the Godric family was a bitter, wicked old creature, and the world was fortunate to be rid of him. But as the light left his father's eyes, Henry drained the magic from him—taking it into himself to gain more power—and all the malice that polluted his father's blood poisoned Henry's mind, turning him into an unpredictable, vicious version of his former self. I knew him, before and after he corrupted himself with his father's tainted magic, and the difference was astounding. The Talbots couldn't very well let a monstrosity like him take control of the world. So they came up with a plausible excuse—that Godric's intended bride, Louise Talbot, had become infertile as the result of an illness—and they passed the throne to her brother, Alexander."

"How old are you?" I asked, lulled into a comfortable state of boldness by the whiskey. "I mean, how can you be old enough to have been the love of Emma's grandmother's life and still look like you do today? I realize an old creature can retain his youthful appearance in Draumer, but how the hell do you still look this young in the waking world?"

The commander leaned back in his chair, studying me with an inquisitive eye. "You really don't know a damn thing about me, do you?"

"Obviously not, but I'd sure appreciate it if you enlightened me."

"Come now, Charlie. Give it some thought. You know there is more to this world than most of its inhabitants are aware of, and there's only one explanation that makes any sense. I can tell you are a clever lad, so why don't you tell me what the answer is."

"How the hell am I supposed to know that?"

"Can you fathom a rational explanation that'd make sense in this world?" the commander asked in an encouraging tone, like he really was rooting for me to puzzle it out and prove my intelligence.

I raked a hand through my hair. "There's *no* explanation that makes any sense in the waking world."

"Then that only leaves one logical conclusion, doesn't it, lad?"

I sat up a little straighter, staring into his sea-blue eyes as if they might provide the answer. "I don't know."

"Come now, Charlie. You know the answer, you're just not willing to voice it aloud. So tell me, what rational explanation can there be?"

"You're…" I picked up my glass and chugged the rest of its contents, despite the fact that alcohol had no effect on me other than warming me up a little. Narrowing my eyes at the enigma that was Commander Lochlan Mackendrick, I set my empty glass down on the table. "You're not of this world, are you?"

An ear-to-ear grin spread across his handsome face. "There it is, lad. I knew you were brighter than that stubborn son-of-a-bitch cousin of yours."

"So, how old are you?"

Ancient wisdom glinted in his oceanic eyes as he took a moment to think it over. "Well, you tend to lose track after a time. But by my best estimate, I reckon I am somewhere in the neighborhood of three thousand years of age."

6

LOCHLAN

I took my time in the Waters, in no particular hurry to report what I'd learned during my second meeting with Charlie and the Darkness. The Sarrum's shadow had taken his leave after receiving an urgent call from David, and Charlie had left a few hours after that to return to his hotel and check in with them. We planned to meet at the pub again the following day, presuming the two of them had not made arrangements to return to America by then. With no other business to attend to in the waking world, I'd headed back to the Waters to return to the Queen I had pledged my life in service to long before she was born.

By the time I emerged in the Light Kingdom, a full moon hung low in the lavender sky—the closest the realm ever came to darkness. I took the path through the Light Forest at a dawdling pace, quieting my mind and collecting my thoughts.

As I neared the palace, snippets of conversation carried to me on the breeze told me the Queen and her primary guard were sharing a candlelit dinner in the courtyard. Despite the dire news I'd come to deliver, I couldn't help grinning at the sound of their laughter. It'd been ages since the Light Realm's court had been filled with such genuine merriment.

Emma's laugh—like her smile, and her voice—were so like her grandmother's that I stood there outside the gate for several heartbeats, allowing myself to imagine it was my Violet dining out there in the moonlight. It felt like a thousand lifetimes since I had seen her smile, yet I remembered it as if it were yesterday. When I'd first answered that unexpected knock at the front door of my cottage to find Emma standing on my doorstep, my world had tilted on its axis. Then I realized who she was, and I thanked my lucky stars that the rightful Queen had come home to us at last.

As I stepped out into the courtyard, they both turned their heads and grinned at me. Such contented, carefree smiles. The two of them shared a history and a bond that warmed my old heart. For all the grief I gave the Queen's half-incubus guard, I had no doubt that he would lay down his life to protect her, and I had no desire to deliver such sorrowful news to him, but this couldn't wait.

Emma beckoned me nearer with a wave of her hand, her porcelain skin luminous in the light of the full moon. "Back so soon?"

I nodded and pulled up a chair, joining them at the table.

"You don't look like you've come with good news," Brian said as he poured me a glass of wine.

I didn't normally drink the stuff, as it had no effect on me and it was far too sweet for my liking, but I accepted the glass with a nod. "I'm afraid I have a somber message to deliver."

Perceptive as usual, Brian picked up on the fact that I'd directed that statement more to him than the Queen. "What is it?"

I shook my head and took a sip of wine, regretting the momentary stall tactic the instant its syrupy sweetness assaulted my taste buds. "I'm sorry to inform you that your mother's life was taken last night, Mr. Mason."

Tears filled the young warrior's eyes as he pushed his chair back from the table. "Purists?"

I set my glass down with a heavy sigh. "I'm afraid so. The hospital called yesterday to inform your brother of her untimely passing, and he tracked her down in Draumer after identifying her body in the waking world."

Brian nodded and ran a hand through his hair, but said nothing.

"When your brother and the Sarrum found her tribe's encampment along the fringe, it'd been laid to waste. I'm sorry to say there were no survivors. However, the Sarrum did bring a witness back to the palace for interrogation."

Brian dropped his eyes to the table. "Have they questioned him yet?"

"The Darkness left our meeting rather abruptly to return to the palace and assist with the interrogation."

"Have they learned anything more?" Emma asked, her lovely eyes glistening with tears.

It pained my old heart to hear the sorrow in her voice, especially since my words had caused it. "They have reason to suspect that the attacks along the fringe are not random."

Emma slid her chair closer to Brian's and took his hand in hers. "Why is that?"

I hesitated a moment before replying, "Isa's Unsighted son has slipped into a coma. They have been unable to locate him in Draumer thus far, but it cannot be coincidence."

"Poor Isa," Emma whispered. "First Rose, and now this."

"We need to meet with the Sarrum," Brian muttered.

I raised an eyebrow. "How? The two of you are under sedation in the waking world."

Emma's gaze shifted from me to her guard. "Maybe it's time to undo that."

Brian wiped a tear from the corner of his eye as he cleared his throat. "Absolutely not. It'd be too dangerous for you to travel back and forth between worlds, and I'm sure as hell not going anywhere without you."

Emma gave his hand a squeeze. "You have to go back for your mother's funeral."

"My mother's already gone," Brian muttered. "There's nothing I can do for her now. All going back would do is put you at risk."

"I can stay in the Light Kingdom," Emma whispered. "I've got the commander, Bob, Addison,

Zeke, and the entire Light regiment here to protect me."

"Forget it," the half-incubus replied. "I'm not leaving your side with everything that's going on."

Emma answered with a sympathetic frown. "I know you weren't as close to her as Tristan was, but she was still your mother. You'll never forgive yourself if you don't go and say goodbye."

Brian brushed his thumb over the back of her hand. "You did all right without going to your father's funeral."

"There was a lot more to that," Emma said, dropping her eyes to their joined hands.

"I know," Brian whispered, giving her hand a squeeze, "but I said goodbye to Beverly a long time ago."

Emma let out a sigh as her eyes met mine. "So, what do we do now?"

I picked up my glass, and set it back down without drinking from it. "I think we ought to meet with the rest of your allies who are stationed here in the Light Realm. I suspect all of their loved ones may be at risk."

"Fuck," Brian muttered. "If they are, this has got to be Rose's doing. Emma, your mother…"

Emma shook her head. "I parted ways with her a long time ago. What happens to her now is no concern of mine."

"Emma," he whispered.

"She never stood up for me," Emma said, "not even when my father wrapped his hands around my neck and tried to choke the life out of me, the night he found me and David together. She let me walk out the front door for good, and didn't even try to stop me."

"You would still grieve if you lost her." David Talbot smiled at his wife as he stepped through the gate into the courtyard, as if it were a perfectly ordinary occurrence for him to pay us a visit.

Eyes welling with tears, Emma rose from her chair and hurried to meet him halfway across the courtyard.

A fire erupted in my belly as I watched his arms wrap around her. I couldn't be certain whether the flames were fueled by anger over the fact that he'd endangered her by coming, or jealousy, or fury that he dared saunter into our midst as if he'd done no wrong. All I knew was that if I stayed, Emma's reunion with her husband would end in bloodshed.

As much as I wanted to make that bastard bleed, it would gut me to hurt Violet's granddaughter. So I pushed my chair back from the table and walked away, ignoring the Queen's request for me to come back.

7

DAVID

I hugged my wife a bit tighter as Mackendrick stormed out of the courtyard. If that old Water dragon expected me to cower in his presence, he was going to be sorely disappointed. I had no intention of shying away from the kingdom that was keeping my wife from me.

As Emma called out to Mackendrick, imploring him to come back, my thoughts drifted to the first time he'd stormed away from me like that...

...Plumes of aquamarine smoke escaped the commander's flared nostrils, tainting the air in my home with his saltwater scent as he emerged from the Waterfall entrance and stormed across the floor of the great hall. "Have you no honor, you thankless bastard?"

A warning growl rumbled in the base of my throat as I stood from my throne and descended the steps. "I kept the promise my father made to your Queen."

"Not in spirit," he snarled as I walked toward him. "You had no right to take the Princess."

"She is not your child."

"Where is she?" Mackendrick demanded, his eyes darting from one Waterfall to the next. "I need to see that you have not harmed her. You owe me that much."

"I owe you nothing," I snarled as our paths collided. "The agreement was for me to orchestrate the marriage of the Queen's Unsighted son with the female fairy he was meant to wed. I did that, and their union produced the heiress to the Light Kingdom's throne. However, as the Unsighted couple's closest friend, I have every right to appoint myself as her guide and raise her until she is old enough to take her place in the Light."

"You have no right at all! It was the Queen's intention that I raise her grandchild and watch over her in the Light Kingdom until she came of age."

Ribbons of blue smoke wafted from my nostrils as my eyes filled with flames. "You must think me a fool."

"And why is that?"

"The child is the spitting image of her grandmother. I will not stand back and let you raise her to take her grandmother's place in your bed."

A surge of Water came rushing in from every Waterfall that lined the walls of the great hall as the commander let out a venomous growl. "Do you honestly believe your intentions are pure? If that is the case, you're a much bigger fool than I thought."

"The Princess will not leave this palace until she comes of age," I snarled, narrowing the gap between us. "If you wish to take her now, you shall have to declare war against the Dark Realm."

The Water flooding into the hall continued to rise, rushing over our feet as Mackendrick shook his head. "You are actually stupid enough to think you'll be able to give her up once she's grown, aren't you?"

"I am done discussing this. Take your leave now, or I shall consider this a declaration of war."

"This is not over," the commander growled as he spun on his heel and stormed toward the nearest Waterfall.

The instant the commander was gone, Benjamin stepped out of the shadows. "Do you really think it's wise to start a war this early on in your reign?"

"Mackendrick has no right to wage a war with the Light Queen's army," I said, watching as every last drop of Water that'd flooded the hall receded with the commander's exit...

..."You shouldn't be here," Emma said, drawing my focus back to the present.

I flashed her a devilish grin. "It's wonderful to see you too, my Queen." As my wife and I moved toward the table, I turned my attention to Brian. "You should go back to the waking world to help with the arrangements and attend your mother's funeral."

It was clear from his vacant expression that Brian's mind was elsewhere, but my words still managed to get his attention. "You expect me to leave the Queen's side?"

"Why do you think I risked coming here? I will stay with Emma until your return."

He cleared his throat. "Do you think that's wise, Sarrum?"

A sorrowful grin spread across my face. "Well, it's too bloody late to worry about that now, isn't it? The damage is done. I am already here."

Brian leaned forward, resting his folded arms on the tabletop as he studied me through narrowed eyes. "How can I be sure you and Mackendrick won't kill each other before I get back?"

I raised an eyebrow, a subtle reminder for him to mind his tone. Grieving or not, there was only so much impudence I would tolerate. "I have more self-restraint than that."

"Really?" Emma whispered. "You couldn't stay away from here."

I brushed my thumb across my wife's lower lip, grinning as she shivered in response. Keeping my distance from her was an entirely different matter, and she was well aware of that. "Regardless of the nature of Brian's relationship with his mother, he should go back to be with his brother whilst he grieves."

"Damn it," Brian muttered. "You just had to throw Tristan's misery into the mix, didn't you?"

"You know I'm right."

"Maybe," Brian muttered, "but you may have tipped off the Purists about Emma being here by coming to the Light Realm."

"Perhaps," I said, "but I will not allow Godric and his followers to dictate the parameters of my family's mourning."

Brian nodded as he stood up from the table and planted a kiss on my wife's forehead. Then he left the courtyard without another word.

Emma watched him until he stepped out of sight. Then she wrapped her arms around my neck as her eyes locked with mine. "I know I shouldn't be happy that you risked tipping off the Purists by coming here, but you are a sight for sore eyes."

I bent to kiss her, the taste of that god-awful beverage they were so fond of in the Light Realm warring with the taste of her on my tongue.

A hushed burst of laughter escaped her as she broke the kiss. "I'm trying to acquire a taste for nectar. Freya looks so hurt every time I decline when she offers me some."

I let out a pensive sigh and caressed her bottom lip with my thumb again. "I suspected the inhabitants of this realm would attempt to convert you to their ways. Do you mean to tell me they're succeeding already?"

Her throaty chuckle stoked the fire inside me, further fueling my desire to drench her in my scent and remind those self-indulgent Light creatures exactly whom she belonged to. "When in Rome."

Flames filled my eyes as I pulled her closer. "Well, then I suppose I have no choice but to restake my claim on you. My scent on your flesh has grown far too faint."

A sinful grin lit up her face. "I'm not so sure about that. I catch the Light creatures wrinkling their noses at your scent all the time."

"One can never be too careful," I said, steering her toward the entrance to the palace.

The scent of her arousal flooded the courtyard as she met my gaze. "No argument here, Sarrum."

8

CHARLIE

I smiled at the bleary-eyed woman slouching against the wall outside the lavatory as I stepped out the door. Desperate to stretch my limbs, I took my time walking back down the aisle of the plane toward my seat. The more my dragon nature became an invariable part of my identity, the less I could stand being cramped in small spaces. So for me, spending fifteen-plus hours in the belly of a crowded aircraft ranked somewhere just shy of light torture.

As I slipped past the white-haired gentleman slumped in the seat next to mine, he let out a snore that could've woken the dead. His head lolled in my direction while I settled into my seat, his breath ripe with the mingled scents of cheap whiskey and the cheese crackers he'd scarfed down before nodding off so abruptly that some of the orange powder still dusted his lips. I tucked the travel pillow I'd picked up at the airport around my neck and turned toward the window, feeling a bit jealous of the old man's ability to slip out of consciousness at the drop of a hat.

Benjamin and I had concluded our meetings with Mackendrick earlier than we'd originally planned to, after learning that Brian and Tristan's mother had been murdered by the Purists. Although I wouldn't admit it to the Darkness's face, the commander and I had actually managed to accomplish quite a bit after Benjamin excused himself from our last meeting. Without him there to hike up the tension, the discussion had grown far more cordial. We were finally able to buckle down and talk strategy, discuss the coordination of our troops, and hash out a few issues concerning the soldiers.

Benjamin had taken the boss's private jet back to the States ahead of my departure, after getting word that Isa's Unsighted son was fighting for his life in the ICU—which seemed unlikely to be a coincidence. The way things were escalating, I had no idea what might await me when I got back home. So I didn't want to deplete my strength by summoning the Waters to check in with Benjamin at the palace.

I expected it to take hours to quiet my mind enough for me to fall asleep. Instead, my thoughts drifted off to the past the instant I shut my eyes—only, it wasn't *my* past…

…My vision was failing me. I could only make out the contours of Clay's blurry face as he placed my newborn child in my arms. I wanted to keep my promise to Jack— to fight for my life and find him in the waking world—so we could raise this child together. But my surroundings were growing dimmer by the second, and I could feel the precious bundle in my arms draining the life from me.

I squinted, concentrating on my son's tiny face until his perfect features came into focus. "Hello, Charlie. I'm your mommy."

His eyes filled with orange flames, as if in answer to my greeting.

I stroked a hand over his fine hair, soft as silk and the same vibrant mix of colors as my own. Tears blurred my vision as I whispered, "I wish I could stick around and raise you, but I'm not strong enough."

His tiny flame-filled eyes blinked up at me.

"But don't worry, my precious boy. I'm not leaving you alone. You'll be with your father soon, the father I chose for you. Jack is a good man. I know he'll keep you safe and raise you to be noble like him."

Charlie scrunched up his cherubic face as he watched me, as if he were hanging on my every word.

I let out a faint chuckle at the absurdity of the notion that he could understand spoken language straight out of the womb. "I know you will grow up to be a man I'd be proud to call my son, Charlie. Please don't ever doubt how much I loved you."

My sweet boy let out a cooing sound, and again I couldn't shake the feeling that he understood what I was saying.

"It's all right, Charlie," I whispered. "I know you're hungry for more power, more magic. I can feel how much you need it, but you aren't taking it from me. Why is that?"

The flames in his eyes blazed brighter as I stroked a loving hand over his cheek.

"It's okay," I assured him. "Take what you need from me. Bringing you into this world is what I was made for. You are the purpose I was always meant to fulfill."

I felt an indescribable tug on my soul as Charlie blinked up at me, and I vaguely sensed Clay's hand on my arm, and heard the faint whisper of his voice as everything beyond me and my baby grew dark.

"I love you, Charlie, always and forever..." With those final words, I felt the last of my life drain from me.

And the final thought to cross my mind, was how grateful I was to have survived long enough to see my son's face...

...I wasn't sure whether it was a snore from the neighboring seat, or turbulence, or the end of that vivid memory that jolted me awake. Whatever had caused it, my jarring movement was enough to rouse the old man seated next to me.

He straightened, righting his center of gravity to his own seat as he rubbed a hand over the snow-white stubble on his face. "Won't be long now," he said, glancing at his watch.

It took me a few seconds to find my voice. This wasn't the first of my mother's memories to overtake me without warning, but it was without a doubt the most powerful. "Good," I muttered, forcing a polite smile. "I'm dying to stretch my legs."

Overwhelmed by a flood of emotions—prompted by the memory I'd just witnessed—that was all the small talk I could manage. So I gave up on drifting off to dreamland the old fashioned way. I shut my eyes, summoned the Waters, and stepped through the main entrance into the great hall of the Sarrum's palace.

Benjamin was the only soul there; he was pacing the floor, cloaked in shadow.

My footsteps thundered through the silence of the great hall as I crossed the room to him. "How is Isa holding up?"

"She's tough as hell," Benjamin muttered, letting the shadows slip away. "But this is too much for any mother to bear. Not being there to protect your child from harm is every mother's worst nightmare."

"Yeah, I can imagine."

Benjamin narrowed his eyes at me. "You okay, kid?"

"I'm not exactly sure," I muttered. "I just had another flashback that wasn't mine."

"I wouldn't worry too much about that. It's a dragon thing. You should talk to the boss about it next time you meet with him."

"How soon do you think that'll be?"

Benjamin shrugged. "He's with Emma now, but you and I will be meeting up with him after Mrs. Mason's funeral is over and Brian returns to the Light Kingdom."

"Good. I've got a few questions for him."

The corners of the Darkness's mouth turned up in a hint of a smile. "Figured you would."

I sat down at the base of the black marble steps to the Dragon King's throne. "Do you know the story behind the boss and Mackendrick's hatred of each other?"

Benjamin nodded as he sat down next to me. "Yeah."

"And?"

"And it's still not my fucking story to tell."

"Have they learned anything more about what's going on with Rose?" It had been way too long since I'd seen my soul mate's face. Each day without her, I hated myself a little bit more for spending our last night together in the waking world arguing.

Benjamin squeezed his eyes shut as he shook his head, making me feel like a brainless asshole for asking him about Rose. Consumed by my own anxiety—over what Godric could be mind-controlling my girlfriend into doing—I'd forgotten the Darkness had just as much reason to worry about her. Rose was his soul mate's Sighted child, which basically made her his daughter. He was every bit as sickened as I was over what might've happened to her since she was coerced into joining Godric's side because his blood had polluted her mind.

I just hoped to God Rose still knew how much I treasured her. If it took every last breath in my body, I was going to free her from Godric's control.

9

BRIAN

I stepped into the foyer of the boss's house and immediately shrugged off my suit jacket. I'd been dying to ditch the damn thing since the moment we picked up my mother's coffin to carry it down the center aisle to the front of the church. Funerals always made me feel itchy, like I was trapped in own my skin. I could almost feel it tightening on me—shrinking in and constricting my movements—during the ceremony.

I wasn't fooling anyone. No matter how many times I told myself and everybody else that my mother's death had no effect on me, we all knew it was a damn lie.

Mia smiled at me as she followed Tristan into the foyer and shut the door. Then she turned to Tristan, taking his hand in hers as the three of us headed for the lounge without a word. I was glad my little brother had found someone to share his life with. He'd been so pigheaded about never getting serious with anyone ever again after Nina's death, but he and Mia were good for each other. Tristan was a better version of himself with her. A part of me couldn't help being jealous of what they had.

As soon as I entered the lounge, Benjamin clapped me on the shoulder and handed me a drink. It was pretty much the closest the Darkness would ever come to saying, *I'm sorry for your loss, and I'm here for you.*

It didn't matter if he said the words. I knew the Darkness well enough to get what he didn't say. "Thanks, man. I appreciate you being here."

"Isa sends her condolences too," Benjamin muttered with a nod.

I headed for the leather furniture across the room. The Darkness fell into step beside me, and we parked ourselves on opposite ends of the couch. "How is Isa's son doing?" I asked, setting my untouched drink down on the coffee table.

Benjamin dropped his gaze to the couch cushion between us with a sigh of frustration. "It's hard to decipher much from all the different doctors' contradictory medical opinions. But Mark is as stable as you can expect a guy in a coma to be, I guess."

"Poor Isa. Godric and his goons have caused her more grief than any soul should have to suffer in a lifetime. Thank God she's got you."

Benjamin blinked his eyes a few times as he looked up at me. "I haven't been able to protect her from any of the hurts those sons of bitches have caused her."

I glanced across the room to where Tristan and Mia stood talking by the bar. "But you've always been there for her. That's worth a hell of a lot. Life's a lot tougher without a soul mate to share your burdens with."

A melancholy smile spread across Benjamin's face as he followed my gaze. "You could have that too, if you wanted to."

"Nah, that was never in the cards for me."

"That's not what Tristan says."

"Yeah? Well, my brother should learn to keep his damn mouth shut about other people's business."

"You deserve to be happy too. You know that, right?"

I cleared my throat as I met the Darkness's inquisitive stare. "Defeating Godric and the Purists and getting things back to normal around here would make me plenty happy."

"That's not what I mean," Benjamin muttered, "and you fucking know it."

Thankfully the boss and Emma stepped into the lounge at that point, rescuing me from having to steer the conversation in a different direction. They stopped a moment to pay their respects to Tristan. Then Emma grinned at me as they headed our way.

I stood up from the couch and greeted the Queen with a hug. "I think you're lost. You're in the wrong world."

Emma shook her head as she looked up at me, eyes filled with tears. "You've always been there for me, Brian. There's no way I would skip being here for you today."

I touched my head to hers and found myself fighting back tears as I hugged her a little tighter. "You're a damn stubborn pain in my ass," I whispered, smiling as she chuckled at that, "but I love you for it. Thanks for being here."

Emma smiled at me as we sat down on the couch side by side. "Even a tough guy like you needs a friend to draw strength from every now and then."

The boss regarded me with a sympathetic frown as I looked up at him. "I am truly sorry for your loss, Brian." When I started to stand to shake his hand and thank him for coming, he placed a hand on my shoulder. "No need to get up. My wife insisted on being here for you today. She's all yours. Besides, I have much to discuss with Benjamin."

I nodded as Benjamin stood up from the couch. "Thanks, boss."

As the boss and his shadow rounded the back of the couch together, Benjamin gave my shoulder a squeeze—which was practically a hug and kiss from him. "We're gonna make that bastard pay for all the hurt he's caused."

"Yeah," I muttered, clearing my throat before adding, "Give Isa my love when you get back to the hospital."

"Of course," he said, his voice a bit thicker at the mention of his soul mate, "but I won't be seeing her till later. I'm gonna stick around for a while tonight. We all need to touch base before we part ways."

Emma and I watched the Sarrum and his shadow cross the room to Clay, who was doing his best to remain invisible in the corner.

I turned back to Emma with an affectionate grin. "So you just couldn't stay away from me, could you?"

She let out a hushed chuckle, tilting her head toward me. "Nope. I missed you the second you left the Light. It felt colder without you."

I let out a laugh as I lowered my mouth to her ear. "Liar. You had your husband there to keep you warm."

Emma shrugged. "What can I say? I missed you."

"I know how much you've been missing the boss. It means the world to me that you gave up your alone time with him to come here today."

"I couldn't stand the thought of you going through this by yourself," she said, wiping a tear from her cheek.

I made a show of looking around the room at all the guests who'd come to pay their respects. "What are you talking about? I'm surrounded by people."

"And yet, you still feel alone."

I shook my head as my eyes drifted to Tristan and Mia. "You sure you're not part succubus, sweetheart? You're too damn perceptive for your own good."

"Just shut up, and let me comfort you."

I answered her with a hushed burst of laughter. "Yes, ma'am."

For the most part, the rest of the day passed by in a blur—thanking people whose names I couldn't remember for coming…smiling politely as they told me how much my mother loved me…pretending they weren't full of shit, and they didn't know damn well that Tristan was the son Beverly treasured.

After all the guests had gone home, Emma wouldn't hear of letting me or Tristan help with the cleanup. So Tristan and Mia had stepped out for a walk along the beach. And I sat alone in the living room with a drink in hand and my feet propped up on the coffee table, since Isa wasn't there to give me a loving smack upside the head for it. That sweet woman was more of a mother to me than Beverly had ever been, even back in the days when our mom was still lucid.

Hard as I tried to recall the last pleasant exchange I had with the woman who gave birth to me, all that would come to mind was the last time I'd seen her at the nursing home. Charlie was still our virgin trainee at the time. Since Benjamin was spending the day working with him on unmasking, Tristan had insisted I go along with him for a visit. From what the staff had told us, Beverly was having a rough week and they were hoping a visit from family might help ground her. I don't know why the hell I'd let my brother talk me into it. Maybe if I hadn't gone, I could recall a happier memory of her. There sure as hell hadn't been many, but there were a few.

She'd done her best. The poor woman had spent her entire adult life wed to a man she'd been charmed into needing, both desperately loving him and hating him for trapping her. That's where her mind was the day we visited—stuck in a memory where Dad was off on one of his "business trips" while she was left behind to take care of his kids—aware that he was a selfish bastard she wouldn't be able to live without as soon as he came home and turned on the charm…

…She looked so small and frail, hunched in that chair by the window when we walked in her room. I knew exactly where her mind was. She was staring out the window, waiting for Dad, desperate to see him but furious at him for leaving again.

"Hey, Mom," Tristan murmured in that smooth-as-silk voice of his that always brought the color back to her cheeks.

"Tristan?" she whispered, turning at the sound of his voice and grinning as she watched him shut the door. "How is my beautiful boy today?"

Tristan flashed her a radiant smile as he crossed the room, knelt down in front of her, and engulfed her small body in a loving embrace. "I'm good, Momma, and I brought somebody else here to see you."

"You did?" she muttered, slumping in her chair as he released her from the hug.

I smiled at her as I stepped toward them. "Hey, Mom."

She looked up at me, and her eyes filled with tears. "Walter?"

I cringed at the unintentional insult, but I couldn't blame her. It wasn't her fault that I looked like a younger version of the asshole who'd ruined her life. "No, Momma. It's Brian, your son," I said as I knelt down next to Tristan, hoping she could tell the difference if she saw me up close.

"Brian?" she echoed in a hollow whisper.

"Yes," I said, leaning closer.

She reached an age-spotted hand toward my face. "You're so handsome."

"Thanks," I whispered, forcing a smile.

Tears filled her eyes as she touched my cheek. "Why did you leave me again, Walt?"

I took her hand from my cheek and gave it a gentle squeeze. "I'm not him, Momma. I'm Brian."

"Brian," she muttered. "My son?"

"Yes."

Her grin slipped away as she pulled her hand back and struck me across the face. There was no strength behind it, but her feeble blow stung deeper than any injury on the battlefield ever could. "You're just like him, you good-for-nothing boy."

"No, Momma," Tristan murmured as I stood up and backed away. "Brian is a good son. He came here to visit you because he loves you, just like I do."

Her eyes glazed over as he charmed her into calming down, but her stare remained fixed on me.

"Both of your sons love you, Momma," Tristan said softly. "You should be proud of the man Brian has become. He is the most noble soul I've ever met."

"No," she said, shaking her head without taking her eyes off me. "Brian is a worthless, selfish boy. I hated Walter for leaving me to take care of his little brat while he ran off to fuck other women."

"You don't know what you're saying, Momma," Tristan murmured. "Brian is nothing like Dad."

"Why, Walt?" she asked, reaching a trembling hand toward me. "What did I ever do to make you hate me so much?"

Damn it. Why the hell had I let Tristan talk me into coming? It broke my heart to see her suffering like this, knowing I was the cause of her pain. I'd spent my entire childhood hating myself for looking like the bastard who'd done this to her, loathing the way she looked at me with so much hurt in her eyes. Everything I'd ever done was to prove to this woman that I was nothing like the man who'd wronged her. But I could never escape the undeniable truth staring me in the face every time I looked in a mirror; I was like him. I looked just like him, and just the sight of me was enough to break her heart all over again.

I stuffed down the self-loathing as I stepped toward this frail, senile version of the mother I remembered. For once in my life, I had to ease her pain. "It's all right, Beverly. I'm here now," I murmured, laying the charm on every bit as thick as Dad used to.

Her wrinkled cheeks flushed with color as Tristan backed away, his eyes full of tears.

I knelt down in his place and smiled at her. "I love you with all my heart, Beverly. I'm so sorry I caused you all that pain."

"Walter…" A tear slid down her cheek as she touched my face, gingerly tracing the contours she'd been forced into loving. "You came back to me?"

"Of course, I did," I said, taking her hand from my face and holding it in mine. "You're the love of my life, Bev. I'll always come back to you."

"But I don't deserve you," she whispered, dropping her eyes to her lap.

I lowered my head to meet her eyes. "That's not true. I'm the one who never deserved you. You deserved so much more than what I gave."

"No," she whispered, squeezing her eyes shut. "I'm a horrible person."

"What are you talking about?" I murmured, dialing the charm up even more.

"I've been a horrible mother to our son."

"No, don't say that."

"I hit him, Walter," she whispered, recoiling from me as the words left her mouth. "I hit our son when you were away."

Despite my best efforts to hide what I felt, the pain in her voice and the sob that hiccupped from Tristan brought tears to my eyes. "It's all right," I said, touching her cheek to get her to look at me. "Brian knows that you loved him the best you could."

"No, that's just it," she muttered, searching my eyes. "I never loved him, Walt. I hated our son. He made my life miserable. I always wished he'd never been born."

I wanted to kick myself for showing up and putting her through this all over again. "It's all right, Beverly," I murmured, flooding the room with my charm as I leaned closer and kissed her cheek. "None of that was your fault. There is nothing you could ever do to make me stop loving you, so don't you waste another second of your life feeling bad about what you did." With that, I charmed her to sleep.

"I love you," she said in a groggy whisper as her head lolled back against the chair.

I lifted her small body out of the chair as Tristan drew back the covers on her bed. Then I laid her down, drew the covers up to her chin, and planted a kiss on her forehead. "I love you too," I whispered, "and I forgive you."

As I started toward the door, Tristan put a hand on my arm. "I'm so sorry I dragged you here, Brian. I thought that if..."

"It's all right," I said, forcing a smile. "You should stay, so she wakes up to a friendly face." Then I slipped out of the room, shut the door behind me, and headed for the exit as my eyes filled with tears.

Mom had been right all along. I was just like that son of a bitch who fathered me...

...Tristan smiled at me as he walked into the living room.

I shook my head, banishing that final memory of our mother from my mind as he moved toward me with a slight sway to his gait. "Hey," I said as he sat down next to me on the couch.

A tear slid down Tristan's cheek as he pulled me into a bear hug, his breath thick with the scent of obscenely expensive single-malt whiskey. "Thank you."

I pulled back from him, searching his eyes. "What are you thanking me for?"

"For being such a selfless big brother. She should've loved you more than anybody. I'm so fucking sorry I wasn't strong enough to charm her into seeing that."

"I never asked you to do that."

"No," Tristan muttered, "you never ask anything of anyone. Nothing she ever said or did to you was fair, Brian. You deserved so much better. Do you know how much I hated myself for getting all the love she should've given to you?"

"I never hated you for anything, Tristan. You were the only good part of my childhood, and you deserved all the love she gave you. You'd already suffered more than any kid should ever have to before you came to live with us."

A sob hiccupped from my brother's mouth as he wrapped his arms around me again. "I love you so fucking much, Brian."

"Ditto," I said, hugging him back. "Bringing you into the world is the one thing I'm grateful to Walter for. Can't imagine my life without you in it."

Tristan cleared his throat as we dropped the hug. "Everybody's waiting for us in the boss's office. He wants to discuss what comes next before we all part ways."

"What comes next," I said as we stood up from the couch. "We do whatever we have to do to take down the son of a bitch who had our mother murdered."

10

DAVID

I took my wife's hand in mine whilst Doc fiddled with the medical equipment he'd set up beside our bed. "Have I mentioned how much I detest this plan?" I asked, kissing her lips to distract her from the syringe in the doctor's hand.

She smiled at me as we broke the kiss. "About a thousand times, but I have to go where I'm needed most."

"This is where you are needed most," I replied, "here with me."

Emma's hand twitched in mine as Doc sunk the needle into her flesh. "And this is the only place I want to be. I'm counting on you to end this war as soon as possible, so I can come home to you in both worlds."

I drew a deep breath and slowly exhaled it as her eyelids drooped shut. "I shall certainly do my best."

"I know," she whispered, a faint sleep-drunken smile tugging at the corners of her lips as she inhaled my scent. Then her hand went limp.

I lifted her hand to my mouth and kissed the back of it; then I locked eyes with Doc while I lowered it to the mattress. "My heart is in your hands now, Doctor."

He nodded and unmasked, a skeletal grin spreading across his bony face as I stood up from the bed. "I am well aware of that, Sarrum. Looking after the Queen's well-being is the greatest honor that has ever been bestowed upon me. I do not intend to disappoint."

"Good answer." I bent to kiss Emma's lips once more, and lingered there a moment—inhaling the scent of her deep into my lungs. Then I straightened and left the room.

Ignoring the ache already forming in my heart in response to her absence, I walked to the end of the hall and descended the staircase, smiling at each precious memory of Emma framed on the wall to my left.

I stepped off the stairs on the ground floor, headed straight to my office, and locked the door so as not be disturbed. My eyes drifted to the shore outside my window while I moved to my desk and slipped into the chair behind it. Then I leaned back, summoned a Water portal, and stepped in.

"Took you long enough," Charlie said, looking very much at home on my throne as I stepped from the Waterfall into the great hall of the palace.

As I crossed the room and climbed the marble steps to my throne, I couldn't help grinning at his offhand reference to my words to him on more than one occasion during the earlier days of his training. "Well, I can't say as I'm sorry," I replied, narrowing my eyes at him until he vacated my seat and took the one beside it. "I would much rather be spending my time with

Emma than with you. Besides, you looked rather comfortable up here."

Charlie shrugged. "Just getting a feel for it. I've got to say, I felt totally at home on your throne."

"Is that so?"

"No, I was too busy worrying that Benjamin was going to come in here and kick my ass for it."

"It's a little late in your training to be fearful of shadows, isn't it?"

"Not that shadow," he said with a chuckle of admiration that didn't match his words. "Did he tell you he threatened to kill me and dump my body in Loch Ness when we were in Glasgow?"

"No," I replied, suppressing a grin, "but that certainly sounds like something he would say."

The smile slipped from Charlie's face as he nodded. "Any word on how Isa's son is doing?"

"No change. It has become quite clear that the Purists' Unsighted targets are no longer being chosen at random. You and I have much to discuss before we part ways this evening."

"Part ways?" he muttered. "Where are we going?"

"I shall remain here at the palace to coordinate the war efforts, but you will be setting off soon."

"In which world?"

"This one," I replied, shifting in my seat. "We need to ensure the safety of the Unsighted loved ones the Purists will most likely target next. Benjamin will be leading the operation when you begin, so that everyone may set out under the cover of shadow. Then your team members will be branching off to protect different souls at various points along the way. Benjamin will be extracting Emma's Unsighted mother from the encampment where she's rumored to be staying. You will accompany the Darkness there, and that is where the two of you shall part ways."

Orange flames filled Charlie's eyes as he nodded. "That's where I hook up with the Purists and ask them to take me to my father."

"Yes, just as we discussed."

"I won't let you down," he replied as the flames in his eyes receded.

"I have no doubt that you will accomplish what I am counting on you to do."

"Who else is going on this rescue mission, and who will they be protecting?"

"Bob, Nellie, and Addison will head to the cove along the fringe where Addison's Unsighted husband and children reside; and Brian, Tristan, and Zeke will see to the protection of the Unsighted woman who raised you in the waking world."

Charlie's eyes widened at that. "You're sending three kickass warriors to protect the adoptive mother who made a hobby out of dumping me off at the nearest nuthouse?"

"Think for a moment before you answer this question, and then respond truthfully. How would you feel if you were to learn that she was murdered because of her association with you?"

Charlie opened his mouth to answer but snapped it shut, mulling the question over as I'd asked him to. After staring at the Waterfall entrance across the hall for several heartbeats, his focus shifted back to me. "I would feel like shit because it'd be my fault that they killed her."

"That is debatable," I replied. "In fact, it's simply not true. Be that as it may, I am quite certain you would feel responsible, which is why we intend to see to her safety."

"Thanks."

I nodded. "We shall all sit down together to discuss the specifics of the operation you are about to embark on before we part ways tonight. However, Benjamin said that you have some questions for me. So why don't we address those now?"

Charlie's eyes drifted back to the Waterfall entrance across the room. "Could we get some air and stretch our legs while we talk? I spent way too many hours cramped inside a small airplane today."

I grinned at him as I stood from my throne. "That is the largest aircraft in the world. I don't believe I've ever heard it described as small."

He stood from his chair and descended the steps at my side. "Well, size is sort of relative when you're trapped in a body that's too small for your soul."

"I could not agree more," I said, stepping into the nearest Waterfall.

Charlie stepped out into the palace courtyard a second after me, and a satisfied smile spread across his face as he outstretched his arms and filled his lungs with the sultry evening air. "Oh yeah," he said, expelling the words from his mouth with a rapturous moan that seemed to echo for miles across the silence of the courtyard. "This is much better."

I raised an eyebrow. "Shall I give you a moment alone?"

Despite all his progress with tapping into his full power as a royal dragon and carrying himself accordingly, Charlie's cheeks flushed with color. "Nah, I'm good."

Grinning to myself, I started down the cobblestone path that wove through the center of the courtyard. Interpreting my movement as permission to be at ease, the creatures lurking in the shadows resumed their nocturnal pursuits. A lively chorus—of chirping insects, scampering feet, and the melancholy cries of winged night creatures—swallowed up the silence in the Darkness as they scurried about, whilst being careful to keep their distance from the two dragons strolling in their midst. "So ask your questions."

Charlie drew a contemplative breath as he fell into step beside me. "I've been having a lot of memories lately that I wanted to ask you about."

"Then ask."

"Well, actually they're more like flashbacks," he said, plucking a blossom from the low-hanging branch of a chinaberry tree as we passed beneath it, "only they're not my memories. I'm pretty sure they're my mother's, but none of them are memories that Clay shared with me. I was starting to think I was going insane, but Benjamin assured me it's a dragon thing."

I veered off the cobbled path to a stone wall and sat down on the wrought-iron bench tucked at its bend. "You are not losing your mind."

"Okay," he muttered, sitting down beside me.

I smiled at him, considering how best to explain what he'd been experiencing. "I assume you've witnessed the moments following your birth through your mother's eyes?"

"Yeah, I have."

"I am sure you recall from your lessons that when a newborn dragon enters the world, his mother often does not survive childbirth?"

"Given my history, that'd be kinda hard to forget."

Ignoring his sarcasm, I leaned back against the bench and tilted my head to gaze up at the vastness of the Dark Realm's eternal night sky. "As a newborn dragon's mother fades, he instinctually devours the magic that emanates from her. This strengthens the dragon, rendering him into a far more powerful creature than a dragon whose mother survives his birth. You and I both began that way," I said, turning to face him. "Whilst devouring so much of his mother's magic, the infant dragon inevitably consumes some of her memories as well. Many of them are never consciously recalled, but the memories of childbirth are the mother's last moments. And since those moments are rife with emotion, they are the strongest and most likely to imprint upon the newborn dragon's memory. As we mature and come into our full power, those memories often surface. They can be quite unsettling, but it is our duty to keep them alive. We carry our mother's final breath within us, and there is no greater magic than the purity of a mother's love for her child."

Charlie remained silent for a moment, wrapping his mind around what I'd said. "So those really were my mother's last moments?"

"They undoubtedly were, and she most likely took great care to think and say what she wanted you to retain during her final breaths."

"She said that she knew she'd be proud of the man I'd become," Charlie muttered, tilting his head toward the heavens to conceal the tears in his eyes. "She told me never to doubt how much she loved me, and she said I was the purpose she was meant to fulfill."

"Then it is your duty to make her sacrifice worthwhile." I could tell he had more questions, but he remained uncharacteristically tight-lipped. "What else is on your mind?"

Charlie cleared his throat as his flame-filled eyes met mine. "Rose was angry with me when we set out on our last mission."

"And why was that?"

"She wanted to consummate our relationship in the waking world," he replied in a reluctant whisper, "but I was too afraid to risk her life like that."

"And now you fear that she doubts how much you care for her?"

"Yeah, I guess." He opened his mouth to say something more, but seemed to think better of it before uttering a syllable.

I crossed my arms and prodded his arm with my elbow. "Ask your questions. This is your last chance to do so before you depart."

"How did you…" I could sense Charlie's heart rate accelerating as he stopped to clear his throat. "How can you justify risking Emma's life with a physical relationship in the waking world? I mean, she's a fairy. She'd never survive a dragon birth."

I narrowed my eyes at him as I shifted to face him. "You are an imbecile."

"What? You told me to ask my questions," he said, turning to look me in the eye rather than shying away. "This is the question that's been on my mind the longest. Benjamin waited to be with Isa until she didn't need to worry about getting pregnant. He let another man marry her in the waking world because he loved her too much to risk her life with a sexual relationship. So how can you take that risk with Emma, if you treasure her as deeply as you claim to?"

"What in God's name makes you think I would ever risk Emma's life?"

"I uh…come on," he muttered. "You don't expect me to believe the two of you are celibate? You're practically falling all over each other whenever you're in the same room, and your scent on her skin is strong enough to make another man dizzy. So what am I missing?"

I didn't really intend to laugh, but I couldn't help it. "In your earliest days of training, would you ever have guessed we would one day be having a talk about the birds and the bees whilst we sat beneath the stars?"

An awkward burst of laughter hiccupped from his mouth. "No, but I know all about the birds and bees thanks…and there aren't any stars out tonight."

I grinned at him and flicked my hand skyward. "Look again."

He tilted his head back, eyes widening as he gawked at the star-speckled sky.

"How long must you live amongst us before you grasp the concept that things are not always as they appear in this world, Charlie?" I asked, dimming the stars until they vanished from existence.

"I don't know, but I do know you're having a pretty good laugh at my expense. Care to let me in on the joke before I take off tonight?"

"Who gave you the impression that I would risk Emma's life to gratify my desires, you utter dimwit?"

"Wow, don't sugarcoat your response or anything," he muttered. "I don't know. I guess…it was Godric who first put the idea in my head. But come on, I'm not stupid. You and Emma do not have a platonic relationship in either world."

"I never once endangered her life in the way you are implying," I growled, letting my eyes fill with flames to emphasize my words. "It was never my intention to father the next Sarrum, so I eliminated that risk from the equation."

"Huh?"

"I had a vasectomy long before I ever laid a hand on her."

"Wow, I definitely didn't see that coming. That's a bit…extreme, isn't it?"

"A moment ago, you were asking why I would dare take the risk. Now that I tell you I didn't, you have the gall to question that choice as well?"

"You said you removed the risk *long before* you ever touched Emma?"

"Yes."

Charlie sat up a bit straighter and narrowed his eyes at me. "How long before?"

"The week Emma was born."

It had been a long time since the word *pedophile* sprang to mind when he thought of me. In fact, it had been a while since any unguarded thought had crossed his mind. But I heard the accusation screaming loud and clear in his mind now. "Am I supposed to pretend I'm not disgusted by that?"

"You misunderstand me."

"Then clear up the misunderstanding. What am I getting wrong?"

"I did not take the step because I intended to have a sexual relationship with Emma. She was my child in this world, and I loved her with all my heart. Therefore, the thought of risking the life of any other man's daughter in that way was simply too horrific to contemplate. So I saw to it that I could never be the cause of such heartache."

"Damn," Charlie muttered. "You never stop surprising me."

"I am glad you find my life choices so entertaining, but you have more questions."

"Yeah, one more."

"Well, you cannot get any more personal than your last. So out with it."

"Right." He flicked his hand toward the sky, grinning with satisfaction as the stars reappeared in their previous positions. "Why does Commander Mackendrick hate you so much?"

A wisp of blue smoke wafted from my nostrils, and the creatures in the shadows fell silent the instant they caught my scent. "Mackendrick believes I stole what belonged to him," I growled, my words a thunderous roar in the absolute stillness of the courtyard.

Charlie swallowed a gulp of air. "And what was that?"

"Emma."

11

CHARLIE

All the puzzle pieces that hadn't seemed to fit together quite right slipped into place the moment the Sarrum explained why Mackendrick hated him so much. He felt that the boss had stolen something that belonged to him. *Emma.*

I flicked a hand toward the heavens—banishing the stars from the sky—because this felt like a conversation to be had in the shadows. "Emma's grandmother was the love of the commander's life."

There was a beat of silence before the Sarrum replied, "Yes, she was. Mackendrick intended to raise Emma and watch over her in the Light Kingdom until she came of age."

"So, you *did* steal her."

The Sarrum fixed his flame-filled eyes on me, and the sweltering heat of the Dark Realm intensified until my shirt was plastered to me and my brow was slick with sweat. "I appointed myself as Emma's guide and guardian. There is a difference."

I wasn't about to let a little fiery eye contact dissuade me from getting answers. "Yeah, but what did Emma's grandmother want?"

David shrugged as he stood up from his seat on the bench beside me. "She died before Emma was born, and the commander would not have been a suitable guardian for her."

I stood up beside him. "Why?"

"His intentions were not pure," the Sarrum said matter-of-factly as he headed toward the cobblestone path that traversed the courtyard. "Emma was the spitting image of her grandmother. Mackendrick would not have been able to resist taking her to his bed."

"Says the dragon who kidnapped her, raised her as his daughter, and then *married* her."

David stopped dead in his tracks and glared at me as the flames in his eyes blazed brighter. "Well, it sounds as though you grasp why Mackendrick hates me."

Shit. This was obviously a touchy subject for both him and the commander. "Yeah, I guess that'd do it."

"Not that it is any of your business, but I fully intended for Emma to take her rightful place in the Light Kingdom after she came of age," David said as the flames in his eyes receded. "It is not my fault that she chose to remain in the Dark Realm."

"You mean, she chose to remain *with you.*"

A smug grin spread across the Sarrum's face. "Precisely. Mackendrick resents me because Emma chose to stay in the Dark with me, rather than move to the Light with him."

"Did she even know that he existed?"

The sapphire flames in his eyes flickered back to life, like the last stubborn embers of a campfire, refusing to be snuffed out. "It never came up."

"Well, then it wasn't exactly an informed decision."

"Does she seem dissatisfied with her choice to you?"

"No," I said without a moment's hesitation, "but now she's in the Light Kingdom with Mackendrick. Doesn't that worry you?"

"I will admit, it does irk me to no end," he replied as we started walking down the path. "But there is no safer place for Emma to be during this war. The commander would never allow any harm to come to her because he loves her as deeply as I do."

Unable to sensor myself, I muttered, "You do realize that's all kinds of fucked up, right?"

"I realize that I have no intention of debating the matter with you."

"One more question?"

A wicked grin spread across the Sarrum's face, and I couldn't help noticing that his teeth looked a bit more fang-like. "Do you intend to provoke me into ending your life to spare you from embarking on the mission, Mr. Oliver?"

"No, but I've gotta ask. What the hell is Mackendrick?"

"He is a Water dragon, conceived eons ago by the coupling of a wayward dragon and a mermaid."

"If he was born ages ago, how the hell does he still look so young in the waking world?"

"Mermaids are direct descendants of the Water creatures, and the Water creatures are neither of this world nor the waking world. They belong to the Waters. They exist only in the Water, and their lifespan is so long that they are practically considered immortal."

"If they only exist in the Waters, how come Mackendrick can hop out of the Water and stroll around in both worlds?"

"Mackendrick is not a Water creature," the Sarrum replied. "He is a dragon. However, Water is a tremendous source of power for him because of his mother's origins. The commander is capable of emerging from any body of water and traveling wherever he pleases on dry land—in the Light and Dark Realms, as well as the waking world. I assume you have heard of the Loch Ness monster?"

"Sure."

"That's him."

"Right. How big of a fool do you think I am?"

"I am going to assume that was a rhetorical question because I doubt you want my honest answer. Although in this particular instance, I am being entirely truthful with you."

"How strong is the commander?"

"He's an immeasurably powerful creature," David replied, "because he draws his strength from the Waters."

"Then I guess it's a good thing he's on our side."

"He is on *Emma's* side," the Sarrum replied.

"And what does Emma think of him?"

"She is quite fond of him, for the same reason that she is fond of you. She is drawn to the sound of a dragon's beating heart because it reminds her of me."

We walked in silence after that, long enough for the creatures in the shadows to relax and go back to whatever they'd been up to before we interrupted their evening.

When we reached the Waterfall at the end of the path, another thought occurred to me. "This rescue mission we're setting off on, how can we take that many warriors away from the Light Kingdom? Don't you want to keep them all stationed there to protect Emma?"

"Only a trusted few are aware that Emma has taken her rightful place in the Light Kingdom," he said in a hushed voice, as if the enemy might be listening from the shadows. "She should be perfectly safe with the commander whilst Brian and the others are elsewhere."

I turned away from the Waterfall, searching his eyes. "How can you be so sure Godric doesn't already know Emma is there?"

"If any Purist were to learn of the Queen's whereabouts," he replied in such a hushed whisper that even I barely heard him, "the entire fight would converge on the Light Kingdom's border."

"That's a pretty terrifying *if.*"

"It would be, if I had any doubts that the few who know where Emma is would protect that secret at any cost."

With that, we turned around and headed back down the path to where we'd started without another word. All of my questions had been answered; and regardless of whether or not I liked the answers, the Sarrum had been truthful with me. He trusted me to rescue Rose from the Purists and help him put an end to the war, and he'd chosen me to succeed him on the throne. With no more unanswered questions to dwell on, my thoughts drifted to Rose and what might be happening to her.

By the time we stepped back through the Waterfall into the great hall of the palace, Clay and Mia were there waiting for the Sarrum. Informing me that he was late for a meeting with the two of them, the boss took his leave.

Clay and I exchanged a cordial nod. Then I stood there and watched the satori who'd witnessed my mother's last breath—and my first—follow the Sarrum and Mia through the nearest Waterfall.

I drew a deep breath in the silence that followed their exit, steeling myself for where I was headed next. Then I stepped through the Waterfall, back to the waking world.

I opened my eyes in the guest bedroom at the boss's house where I'd crashed the instant I got back from Scotland. After taking a minute to stretch my limbs, I sat up, raked a hand through my hair, and tossed the covers off. Then I hauled my jet-lagged ass out of bed, shuffled to the door, and let myself out into the hallway.

I started toward the stairs but stopped when I reached the door to David and Emma's bedroom. Emma was under sedation on the other side of that door, and very few souls were allowed in her presence. I kissed my fingertips and touched them to the door, smiling at the fact that my best friend from the mental facility had turned out to be the ruler of an entire kingdom. Shaking my head at the surreality of our current life-or-death circumstances—and their stark contrast to the monotony at the facility where our friendship had begun—I headed downstairs.

The house was still pretty dark and I didn't want to disturb anyone who might be sleeping, so I tiptoed down the dim hallway without flipping on any lights. The doors to the ballroom were shut but not locked. I opened them and slipped inside.

Doc greeted me with a nod from the armchair where he sat reading at the other end of the room.

I gave him a halfhearted wave as I started down the rows of empty hospital beds, recalling the day we'd set off on our last mission. As I passed the beds Bob, Nellie, and Pip had occupied, that horrific image of Rose snapping Pip's neck flashed through my mind for the umpteenth time. I stopped at the spot where our friend had lost his life, touching the pillow on the freshly made bed that bore no hint of its last occupant's tragic demise. A tear slid down my cheek as I pictured the anguish in Bob's eyes as he cradled his tiny sidekick's body in his hands.

Clearing my throat, I squared my shoulders and moved on to the next row, and the only bed that was still occupied. Someone had placed a chair next to Rose's bed, probably Isa. Benjamin said she'd spent most of her time sitting at her daughter's bedside before her Unsighted son ended up in the hospital. Acutely aware that I wasn't the only conscious guy in the room, my eyes drifted to Doc.

He looked up from his book and closed it as he met my gaze. Then he stood up from his chair and stretched, a somber grin spreading across his face as he crossed the room to me. "It's about time for me to go check on the Queen. Why don't I give you a little privacy?"

"Thanks," I muttered, dropping into the chair next to Rose's bed. I watched as Doc walked to the door, stepped out, and shut the two of us in together. Then I turned to Rose and took her hand in mine. She looked so beautiful and peaceful, exactly the way she'd looked when I walked past her on the way to my own hospital bed the day we set out on our mission.

A pang of regret struck me at the thought of how we'd wasted our final chance to be alone together. I'd replayed that fight over in my head at least a hundred times since then…

…I woke up feeling queasy and disoriented from all the glimpses into my mother's past that Clay had just shared with me. I was in my bedroom at the house on Sycamore. The sky outside my window was dark, but the lights were still on in my room. I glanced at the alarm clock on my bedside table, and my heart sank. It was almost three in the morning. Rose and I had a lot less time to spend alone together before setting off than I'd expected we would.

Rose's delicious floral scent still hung in the air of my bedroom. As my scent began seeping from my pores in answer to hers, my first thought was that I'd give just about anything to wake up to that scent every morning for the rest of my life. My second thought wasn't a verbal one; it was a barrage of heart-wrenching images from my mom's pregnancy that I'd just witnessed during my Vulcan mind-meld with Clay.

Giving birth to me had cost my mother her life. How the hell could I justify sleeping with Rose, if there was even the slightest chance that she could suffer the same fate? Dread seemed to weigh me down to the mattress as I rolled over and found myself face-to-face with my soul mate, lying wide awake on the bed beside me.

"Hey," Rose whispered, greeting me with an affectionate smile as she propped herself partially upright on one elbow. "I was beginning to think you were never going to join me."

A lock of hair fell over her face as she shifted position, and I brushed it back with my fingertips. My God she was beautiful. She was also the kindest soul I had ever met. How long would it take her to realize she could do much better than a dork like me? Royal blood or not, I was a hopeless case. It'd taken me forever to figure out how to get off the ground during my flying lessons, and the fact that I'd managed it twice in the heat of the moment was still no guarantee that I could do it again. Rose deserved a fierce, powerful, capable dragon who could protect her from harm without breaking a sweat and making a complete ass of himself. I loved her too much to let her risk her life by losing her virginity to a pathetic excuse for a dragon like me. "Sorry," I muttered. "My final trip down memory lane with Clay took longer than I thought it would."

She glanced at the clock on the bedside table behind me and shrugged. "No worries. We don't need sleep tonight. We'll get plenty of that while we're sedated."

This was our last night together in the waking world before setting off on our mission, and I knew exactly how Rose wanted to spend it. She'd made it very clear that she didn't want to be a virgin when we set off on this mission.

"You know," I said, "there's no need to rush things tonight. We'll have plenty of time to do things right after all this is over."

"Do things right?" she muttered, cringing as if I'd struck her. "What's that supposed to mean?"

"Rose, if you had any idea what I just witnessed—"

"What, Charlie?" she said, cutting me off. "What could you possibly have witnessed that'd make you think it's wrong for us to make love on our last night of freedom for God knows how long? Does it even matter to you that I don't want to risk dying a virg—"

"I don't want to risk you dying at all!" I snarled. "I could literally be the death of you by sleeping with you, Rose. Doesn't that matter?"

The hurt in her eyes hit me like a punch to the gut. Hating myself for snapping at her like that, I wrapped an arm around her to draw her closer.

But she put her hand on my chest and pushed me away. "What the hell are we even doing if we have no future together, Charlie? Our world is at war. Nobody knows what's going to happen to us down the road. We could both die on this mission. So I don't see the point in spending the time we have right now worrying about things that might not matter."

"Might not matter?" I said, sitting up and tossing off the covers. "You're asking me to play Russian roulette with your life, Rose, and I can't do that."

She shook her head as she slid out of bed. "Then there's really no point in me staying here, is there? You know...I honestly can't tell if you're being this stubborn and unreasonable because you truly care about me, or if this is just a convenient way for you to break things off and still come out looking like a hero."

"How can you say that?" I asked, scrambling out of bed after her. Desperate to fix this and show her how precious she was to me, I tried to wrap my arms around her.

But she stepped out of reach as those beautiful doe eyes of hers filled with tears. "What's the point of giving you my heart, if all you want to do is set me on a shelf like *some fragile untouchable doll? I'd be better off spending my last night in a bar looking for an Unsighted stranger who'd be more than happy to make sure I'm not a virgin when we set off tomorrow."*

Her words instinctually lit a fire in my belly, and rage obliterated my common sense. Rose was my dearest treasure. I loved her with all my heart. How could I deny her this when it'd be so easy to just give in, and do what we both desperately wanted? Flames filled my eyes as I grabbed her by the waist and kissed her with every ounce of the desire I felt for her, flooding the room with both our scents.

Her heart was hammering just as furiously as mine, but she pushed me away and took a step back. And the silence stretched out like a widening chasm between us, her eyes searching mine as her chest rose and fell.

I don't know who lunged first, but the next thing I knew she was in my arms and we were falling back onto my bed. She was mine, and I'd be damned if I would let any other man lay a hand on her. Crazed at the thought of some random guy at a bar stealing her from me—taking my treasure to his bed—I grazed her earlobe with my teeth and started kissing my way down her neck as her fingers knotted in my hair. My lips and tongue eagerly trailed lower, inching toward the buttons on her shirt as my hands slipped beneath it.

Then a mental image struck without warning: the heartache in my dad's eyes as my mom asked him to promise that he'd raise me and keep me safe after she was gone. Pregnancy was draining the life from my mother right before his eyes, and there wasn't a damn thing he could do to stop it. But I could prevent that from happening to Rose. All I had to do was find the strength to stop myself now.

The pounding of Rose's heart recaptured my attention, replacing those rational thoughts with mindless feral hunger. The racing of her heart was music to my ears because it was physical proof that she treasured me as passionately as I treasured her. She was obviously bluffing about finding some guy at a bar to sleep with. Aroused all the more by that revelation, I dug my fingers into the smooth flesh of her waist and slid my hands lower as I tore the top buttons of her shirt open with my teeth, desperate to stop thinking and just give in to temptation. Why the hell had we been wasting time fighting? Both of us wanted this. She was mine, and I needed her to know without a doubt how deeply I loved her.

She let out a whimper—and it struck me like a slap to the face, smacking me back to my senses.

I couldn't do this.

I stilled for a moment, breathing heavily, my face still buried in the V of her shirt. An ache flared in my chest as I drank in her hypnotic scent, more delicious than anything else ever could be. Then I lifted my head, slid off the bed, and stepped back. "Rose...I can't."

She got to her feet without a word, stepped toward me, and slapped me across the face.

For one agonizing moment we both stood there staring at each other, the harmonious pounding of our hearts a deafening roar in my ears. Then she pushed past me, and stormed out of my room with the top of her shirt still hanging open, taking those perfect breasts of hers off to be manhandled by some nameless fucking stranger for all I knew.

Heart hammering in my chest, I stood there staring at the door she'd just slammed shut. All I wanted to do was chase after her, tell her how much I needed her, and beg her not to go. But I knew that'd only weaken my resolve to keep her safe and end with me dragging her back to my bed, putting her life at risk to show her how precious she was to me.

It'd be safer to give her time to cool off, then apologize in the morning and try to talk things out when we were both thinking more rationally. Then I could explain how head over heels in love with her I was, and how terrified I was of doing anything that could take her away from me forever.

But when I went to talk to her in the morning, she'd already left for the boss's house. By the time I walked into the makeshift hospital ward in the Talbots' ballroom, Doc had already sedated her.

And I never got the chance to make things right...

..."Sorry it's taken me so long to come visit," I muttered, feeling stupid for talking to her when I knew her soul was elsewhere, but needing to nonetheless. "I can't tell you how much I wish we'd slept together that last night before setting off on the mission. I know I can be a stubborn ass sometimes, but I honestly just treasured you too much to risk losing you. I wish I'd told you how deeply I love you before you left my room that night. I wish I'd thrown you down on my bed and made love to you until there wasn't a doubt in your mind that you are my soul mate and I would do absolutely anything for you. If I had any idea things would end up..." My voice trailed off as my eyes drifted to Pip's empty bed, and I couldn't bring myself to finish that sentence. "I'm going to get you out of there, Rose. None of what happened on that mission was your fault. I know that now, and I hate Godric so much more for what he's done to you."

I could've sworn I felt her hand twitch in mine. *Was it possible for her to hear me?* I didn't think so, but what if I was wrong?

I studied her tranquil expression as I stood up and leaned over her motionless body. "I'm so sorry we couldn't bring you back to the waking world, Rose. Isa, Clay, and Doc were afraid that waking you from this medically induced coma might kill you if the Purists had tethered your soul to Draumer, but don't worry. Your body is safe here with Doc."

I gave her hand a squeeze, hoping she could somehow take comfort in the gesture in the other world. Then I kissed her cheek and kept my lips pressed against her flesh for a second, imagining how things might have gone if we'd spent that last night together in my bed.

A tear slid down my cheek and dripped onto her chin. "Hang in there, Rose. I'm coming for you."

12

ROSE

A sweet summer breeze tousled my hair as I strolled through the grounds of the rightful King's headquarters. The warmth of the wind's gentle caress was a welcome sensation because I'd been plagued by an inexplicable chill since the moment I entered Godric's mirage. For some absurd reason, the feel of my hair brushing against my cheek brought to mind Charlie's kiss. A shiver raced down my spine at the thought. That familiar floral fragrance started seeping from my pores—scenting the air the way it always did in Charlie's presence—and I almost could've sworn I caught a whiff of Charlie's scent.

I was losing my mind. Charlie was nowhere near Godric's mirage, and I would never smell that intoxicatingly masculine scent of his again. He despised me now. My stomach lurched every time I pictured the hurt in his eyes as I fled Zeke's mirage at the end of our nightmarish battle.

There was nothing I wouldn't do to be with Charlie again, and hear him tell me how special I was in that tender voice of his that made me want to believe in happily-ever-after endings...

...I was lying on the floor of a balcony on one of the lower levels of the palace, the stone tiles cold and damp against my back. The rush of the great Waterfall entrance to the Sarrum's lair down below was normally silent; but it could be loud enough to drown out your thoughts if you asked it to speak up, and I always did. Since this was a small balcony that could only be accessed by way of a seldom-used library, it was the perfect spot to sneak off to when you wanted to be alone.

I shut my eyes and focused on the steady rush of the Water, imagining that the sound had the power to erase all the thoughts I wanted to be rid of. I had shown up early for our afternoon training session with Benjamin, and found Charlie already there with Emma. The two of them were smiling, and laughing, and sitting far too close for my liking. No matter how many times Charlie assured me that they were just friends, my possessive dragon instincts immediately took over whenever I witnessed a reminder of just how close the two of them were. I treasured Charlie more than anything, and the thought of another woman holding a special place in his heart filled me with jealousy and rage.

"You know," Charlie said, as he stepped out onto the balcony behind me, "there are other balconies higher up in the palace that actually have furniture."

I opened my eyes and fixed them on the starry sky above. "Whatever. I like this one, and the floor's not so bad."

"Right," he muttered, crossing the balcony and lying down on his back beside me. "It's cold. And wet."

I turned my head to meet his gaze. "But the view is spectacular, and it's a great place to go when you want to be alone."

He turned his head to look up at the stars, breaking our eye contact. "Is that supposed to be a hint?"

"If it was," I replied, directing my gaze skyward too, "would you take it?"

"Probably not."

I almost smiled at that. "What do you want, Charlie?"

"I want you to tell me what I did to make you mad at me."

I let out a sigh, expelling a whirl of lavender smoke toward the heavens. "I saw you and Emma together when I walked into the courtyard for our training exercise this afternoon. The way you look at her...it's like she's the center of your entire universe."

Charlie shook his head without lifting it from the tiles. "No, I look at her like she's a ghost from a nightmare I used to be trapped in. Emma was the first person to ever look at me and see something more than a smartass lunatic. If it weren't for our friendship, I would still be locked up in a mental facility, completely unaware of what I truly am."

"How nice for you," I muttered, making a conscious effort to sound impassive. "Maybe you should go find Emma and bother her."

"Nah, that's the Sarrum's job. I'd much rather stay here and bother you."

Flames filled my eyes as I pictured the adoring way he'd been looking at her when I walked into the courtyard. "You could've fooled me."

For several heartbeats, there was no response but the rush of the Waterfall several stories below. Then Charlie rolled to his side and propped himself up on one arm, resting the side of his head against his fist. In this position, his face was so close that my only options were to meet his gaze or shut my eyes. "I don't want to fool you, Rose. I want to be completely truthful with you."

"Great. Now that you've cleared that up, why don't you go find yourself an unoccupied balcony with some comfy furniture?"

He shook his head and brushed back a stray wisp of hair that'd fluttered across my face in the breeze. "You're mental, you know that? And I ought to know. I'm something of an expert in that area."

"That's not funny." I was painfully aware that I was overreacting, but I couldn't help it. Charlie mattered more to me than any soul ever had, and I wanted to be just as precious to him as he was to me. Seeing him look at another female with such fondness was a massive blow to my already threadbare self-esteem. "Why am I mental?"

An affectionate grin spread across his face, the sort of grin that I wanted him to save just for me. "That's what I'm trying to figure out," he said, taking my hand in his.

"Shut up," I whispered, but I didn't pull my hand away.

"Tell me something, Rose. Why is it that you pay so much attention to how I look at Emma, but you completely ignore the way I look at you?"

I shut my eyes with a weary sigh. "What are you talking about?"

"That is exactly what I'm talking about. If you don't look me in the eye, how will you ever notice the way I look at you?"

I opened my eyes, and the affection in his gaze melted my jealous heart. "And how do you look at me?"

"I look at you like you are the most beautiful creature I've ever set eyes on," he said, giving my hand a squeeze.

"You're also the most remarkable dragon. I mean, you pretty much put me to shame during our training session with Benjamin this afternoon."

I let out a hushed chuckle. "Benji is a lot harder on you than he is on me."

"True," he agreed, cracking a smile, "but he's also confident that you're already totally prepared to kick ass on the battlefield. On top of that, you are way better at potions and spells than I am."

"Great. That's just what every guy wants, a girl who's good at hand-to-hand combat and potions."

"I don't give a damn what every guy wants," he said without missing a beat. And I almost could've sworn I detected a note of possessiveness in his tone, but I was probably just deluding myself. "Personally, I think those skills are a total turn-on."

I shook my head. "You could do a lot better than a mutt like me."

"Now you sound like a Purist. Why are you so down on yourself today?"

I bit my lip, fighting back tears. I'd spent my entire childhood listening to Louise Talbot tell me how inferior I was to all the royal dragons I was raised alongside of. According to her, the best a mutt like me could hope for was that some male might lower his standards enough to use me to make a new dragon. "I'm always down on myself, Charlie. The only difference between today and every other day is that I'm having a harder time hiding it."

Charlie sat up so that he was looking directly down at my face. "You are absolutely perfect, Rose, and you don't even realize it. Do you want to know the truth? My biggest fear is that one of these days, you'll wake up and figure out that you are way out of my league."

"I think you've got that backward. You're the one who has royal blood in your veins."

"Yup, and I've also got gummy bears in my stomach," he muttered, grinning when I laughed at that. "Who the hell cares about what's inside us?"

"Louise Talbot, and every other royal dragon I was raised with."

"Well, Louise Talbot and the rest of those snobbish douchebags can kiss my royal ass. When are you going to stop listening to what she taught you, and start listening to me?"

"I am listening to you."

"Good. Then I'll say it again. You are perfect, Rose Salazar Talbot. You're gorgeous. You're a badass warrior. You're smart as hell; and despite having grown up surrounded by a bunch of arrogant royal assholes, you are the sweetest soul I've ever met."

Tears filled my eyes as I reached up and touched his cheek. "What did I ever do to deserve you, Charlie?"

"I don't know," he said, leaning down to plant a whisper of a kiss on my lips. "But whatever it was, it must've been pretty horrible."

I rose up on my elbows to kiss him back, and he cradled the back of my head in his hands as he lowered his mouth to mine. His kiss was gentle at first, but as it deepened, my scent began seeping from my pores in response.

If he kissed me like this enough times, I might actually start to believe him when he told me I wasn't worthless...

...All of that was gone now. Charlie would never see me as anything but a monster after what I'd done.

An ungodly shriek sounded from inside the house, rescuing me from that dismal train of thought as Louise stepped out the back door.

She smiled at me as if she cared for me—the way a mother ought to care for her child—the way Isa had smiled at me during my brief time with her. It broke my heart, knowing I would never see that tenderness in my birth mother's eyes again.

"Godric and the doctor will be done with the patient soon," Louise said, as if she were a nurse bringing an update to a patient's family member.

My stomach soured at the thought. "How is he?"

Her matronly grin widened as she motioned for me to follow her into the house. "Not well, I'm afraid. The doctor suspects he won't last much longer."

"Good," I muttered, immediately feeling ashamed of my response as I followed her inside.

Louise locked eyes with me as she shut the door, then placed a hand on my arm. "You have no reason to feel guilty, Rose. After all, what is he to you?"

I choked back the urge to vomit. "A half-brother."

As we started down the hall toward the locked room where they were keeping Isa's son, Louise narrowed her eyes at me. "He is Unsighted. He's a worthless soul, and a witless human. Yet that sorceress who gave birth to the both of you loved him and raised him, while she left you—her dragon child—to be raised by strangers on the other side of the world."

"She thought it would be best for me."

"That's rubbish, and you know it," Louise replied as we stopped at the door to Mark's room. "The Talbots have never cared what became of any soul whom they had no use for. Your mother's talent in the art of sorcery was useful to David Talbot. So he kept her when she came to him—pregnant and seeking protection—but what use did he have for her illegitimate newborn?"

Another blood-curdling scream sounded behind the closed door as I stood there staring at Louise.

"David had no use for you," she went on, as if she hadn't even heard his agonized cry, "just as the Talbot family had no use for me after they sterilized me and passed the throne to my brother instead of my intended-husband, Godric. David left you to be raised by me because the Talbots had no use for either of us. You and I are the same, Rose."

"That's a load of crap," I said, wincing as another ear-piercing shriek came from the locked room. "You raised me to believe the most useful thing I could ever do was give birth to a male dragon who could fight for the Sarrum. Don't pretend you ever cared about me or had any kindred feelings toward me."

"I underestimated you," Louise replied, "but you managed to capture the heart of the rightful King's son. That makes you the most valuable creature in the world."

I blinked back the tears that welled in my eyes at the mention of Charlie. Louise Talbot did not tolerate weakness, especially not from a worthless mutt like me. "Charlie will never love me after what I've done."

"Ah, that's where you are wrong," Godric said as the door beside us creaked open. "Would you care to come in and meet your half-sibling, Rose?" he asked, beckoning me into the dimly lit room with a charming grin as the door at the other end of the room clicked shut. Godric's grin widened, the skin around his pale blue eyes crinkling in the most endearing way as he followed my gaze to the door across the room and willed the deadbolt to slip into place. "The doctor has other patients to attend to. As you know, Mark is not the only soul under his care. He is simply the one of greatest interest to you."

As Godric spoke, my gaze drifted to the three gangly demons lurking in the corner of the room, their beady black eyes watching me from the shadows. Their clawed hands were streaked with gore, and blood dripped from their fangs onto full round bellies— bellies that'd been concave with hunger when they entered the room.

I stepped a bit farther into the room, being careful to keep the table to my left out of my line of sight. One of the demons sniffed the air as he licked his blood-streaked lips and stomped closer. Godric let out a growl and a harsh warning in their dialect, and the beast dropped to his knees, bowing his head as I moved closer. I wasn't ready to look Isa's son in the eye just yet, but the sight of his blood smeared across this demon's face brought a perverse smile to my lips.

Godric let out a laugh as Louise pulled the door closed from where she stood out in the hall, shutting the remaining six of us in together. "The sight of this Unsighted human's spilled blood pleases you, doesn't it?"

"Yes," I said, stepping close enough to feel the heat of the kneeling demon's breath on my legs.

The other two demons kept to the shadows in the corner, licking the blood from their hands as they watched their kneeling brother.

"Have you ever tasted the blood of an Unsighted soul?" Godric asked as he stepped up beside me.

I shook my head without taking my eyes off the demon at our feet.

"But you are curious," Godric said as he tapped the kneeling demon's shoulder.

The beast tilted his head up toward his King, his Dark eyes pleading for mercy.

"Rose?" Godric said, holding a hand out to me.

My eyes remained fixed on the beast cowering before us as I took his hand.

"One day you shall be Queen of these Dark creatures, so I have ordered them to bend to your will now," Godric said as he drew me closer. "Penny for your thoughts, my dear. What would you like to command him to do?"

Heat pooled in my belly as I turned to Godric. "I don't know."

"That is because you are still measuring your actions by the Talbots' rules," he replied, wrapping an arm around my waist.

At this proximity to the rightful King, I couldn't help noticing the similarity between his scent and Charlie's. Godric's scent was laced with more Dark spice than his son's, but there was a sameness to it that made the fire in my belly burn hotter. The heady combination of fragrances filling the room—mine, in response to his—roused me with the same sort of thrill that you feel when you plummet from the top of a rollercoaster.

As Godric steered me toward the table I'd been making a conscious effort to ignore, my blood heated at the feel of his arm around my waist, and a warning prickled in the back of my mind. *My body shouldn't react this way to Godric.*

"It's a perfectly natural response," Godric murmured close to my ear, the heat of his breath making me tremble, "but you have nothing to fear, my dear Rose. You are what Charlie treasures most of all, and I do not intend to touch what belongs to my son."

I nodded because I couldn't seem to find my voice.

Godric's intoxicating scent bathed my vision in a wash of violet flames as he led me toward the table. His scent was so familiar that I found myself imagining it was Charlie's arm around my waist, because I was desperate to feel that sense of contentment I always felt in Charlie's arms.

"Look at him, Rose," Godric whispered in my ear, coaxing a hushed moan from me as the arm I desperately wanted to be Charlie's gripped me tighter. "This is the worthless soul your birth mother chose over you."

Godric's words sharpened my focus, and I found myself staring into the dull eyes of an unremarkable human male. He watched me fearfully, the way an abused dog watches someone they're unfamiliar with—unsure whether to plead for help or brace for an attack—but he didn't say a word.

I glanced back over my shoulder at the demons cowering in the shadows. Something in the farthest one's mouth caught my eye, and I realized why Mark wasn't speaking. The demon fixed his beady eyes on me as he gnawed on what remained of our captive's tongue, and I couldn't help laughing at the sight.

"This pathetic soul is good for nothing more than a snack for my soldiers," Godric said, drawing my attention back to my Unsighted half-brother. "And thanks to you, my dear, we shall be feeding my troops well for days. I cannot thank you enough for pointing us in the directions to strike where our enemies are most vulnerable."

Normally my stomach roiled at the mention of the names I'd given him, but this time it just made me salivate. This sorry creature on the table was of no importance. He didn't know why he'd been singled out, or who I was, or even who our mother was. He was just a worthless dog who'd been given all the love that should've gone to me. I was glad he was in agony because it meant that the mother who'd discarded me was suffering.

"Would you like to finish him off?" Godric asked, his deep voice summoning a rush of heat inside me.

I took the remaining steps to the table, and locked eyes with the disemboweled soul strapped to the table. As I swept a fingertip over his bare skin, slick with fresh blood, my stomach rumbled.

"Taste it," Godric whispered, "and savor the delectable flavor of Isa's suffering. I promise you've never tasted anything so sweet."

The flames in my eyes burned brighter as I raised my blood-covered finger to my mouth, and a whimper rose from the table as I licked it clean. A moan resonated in the base of my throat as his dull eyes watched me. "I don't want to finish him off," I said, dipping my whole hand in his open chest cavity for another taste and smiling at his agonized groan.

"Why?" Godric asked.

His voice seemed to sound from a distance as I licked the warm blood off my hand. "Because I don't want this to be over yet. I'd like to enjoy it for a few days."

"Then I shall give you the key to this room. He is yours to do with as you please, and these demons will obey your every command."

I turned to look the rightful King in the eye. For a moment his features morphed into Charlie's, an overwhelming need to feel his hands on me heated me to my core, and the room suddenly felt much too small.

A grin tugged at the corners of his mouth as he planted a kiss on my forehead. "Your needs will be met soon enough, my dear. For now, I'm afraid you must sate yourself with this gift. I will not touch what belongs to my son."

The mention of Charlie broke whatever spell I'd been under, and grief replaced my bloodlust. "Your son wants nothing to do with me after what I've done."

Crystal-blue flames danced in Godric's eyes as he drew me into a hug, lulling me with his scent and the warmth of his embrace. "My son wants you more than anything, Rose. I promise you, he will be running into your arms before you know it."

I dropped my head to his shoulder, letting his scent banish my dread and rekindle my desires. "How can you be so sure?"

"I know better than anyone what lengths a dragon will go to for his treasure," Godric replied, "and there isn't a doubt in my mind that Charlie is desperate to hold you in his arms again."

13

BRIAN

Emma and Mackendrick were seated at a white marble table drinking coffee as I stepped into the courtyard of the Light Queen's palace. As always, every last detail of our surroundings was perfect—the birds were singing, every flower was in full bloom, and there wasn't a single cloud in the sky—but today the fairytale setting felt ominous. I just couldn't shake the feeling that all of this could morph into a nightmare in a matter of seconds while I wasn't there to protect Emma.

I fixed the commander in a death glare as I walked toward them. "For the record, I hate this fucking plan."

Mackendrick sat his cup down on the table with a nod. "Noted."

Emma stood up from her chair and wrapped her arms around me. "Stop worrying, Brian. I'll be safe here with Loch."

Mackendrick's grin widened at the sound of his nickname on the Queen's lips. "Put your mind at ease, Mason. She shall not be harmed on my watch."

"She better damn well not be," I said as Freya came flitting across the courtyard with a fresh cup of coffee for me. "Thanks," I muttered as she handed me the cup. Then I turned back to the commander. "I don't care how old and powerful you are. If anything happens to Emma while I'm gone, I will hunt you down and gut you."

"The Queen will be fine," the commander replied with a grin that suggested he admired my devotion to her. "I care about her protection just as much as you do."

"Good," I said, setting my coffee down on the table as Zeke came sauntering into the courtyard with his sister at his side. Davina smiled at me as our eyes met, and—despite all the reasons I had not to smile—an affectionate grin spread across my face in response. A somber expression replaced my grin as I turned to Zeke. "You about ready to head out?"

The scowl on the half-giant's face would've stopped most creatures dead in their tracks. "Tell me my baby sister will be safe here at the palace. Promise me that, and I'm good to go."

My gaze drifted back to his sister. "I swear to you, nobody will get to her here. I wouldn't have asked you to come on this mission if I wasn't sure of that." Davina's cheeks flushed with color at my words; and for a moment I just stood there, rooted to the spot, paralyzed by an overwhelming urge to take her in my arms and tell her how much she meant to me.

Satisfied with my answer, Zeke nodded. "So where's the rest of our party?"

"We're here," Bob called out as he, Nellie, and Addison entered the courtyard.

I let out a resolute sigh as I took one last look at Davina, drinking in every breathtaking feature. "Then I guess we should be on our way."

Mackendrick stood up from his chair right on cue. He gestured toward the weapons and satchels all packed and ready for our trip, and a massive wave came barreling out of nowhere without a sound. The Water stopped on a dime a few inches from our gear, and a circular portal opened at its center. "Safe travels," the commander said as Bob's group started toward it.

I turned back to Emma to give her one last hug, and she smiled and kissed my cheek.

"Have I told you what a royal pain in my ass you are?" I whispered, wrapping my arms around her.

"Several times," she said as her eyes filled with tears. "I love you too, Brian. Come back safe, okay?"

"Will do, sunshine. See you on the other side of all this."

A tear slid down her cheek as we broke the hug. "See you on the other side."

As I started toward the portal, Zeke released Davina from the bear hug he'd scooped her into. "See ya soon, baby sister."

"See you soon," Davina replied in a hoarse whisper.

While Zeke squared his shoulders and started toward the portal, his sister's eyes locked with mine as her fingertips traced the bracelet on her left wrist. *Promise me you'll come back.*

A jolt of electricity surged through me as I held her gaze. *I promise.* With that, I crossed the courtyard to join the rest of my team. Fighting the urge to look back at Davina, I collected my gear and followed the others into the portal.

As I stepped out into the great hall of the Dragon King's palace, the grave expression on the boss's face mirrored every emotion I was working hard as hell to suppress. Nodding to him, I followed the rest of the team to the base of his throne.

The boss greeted us with a somber smile. "It's good to see you all again." Taking a moment to lock eyes with each of us, he added, "I only wish we were meeting under more pleasant circumstances."

As Benjamin slipped out of the shadows across the room, a thunderous chorus of growls sounded from beyond the Waterfall entrance to the hall. The Darkness gave a quick nod to the boss. Then he stepped into the Waterfall.

The rest of us crossed the room and followed him out without exchanging a word.

As I stepped out into the pool of Water at the base of the Waterfall, the sweltering heat hit me like a tidal wave. Being a creature of Darkness, I was used to the oppressive humidity of the Dark Forest—in fact, I enjoyed its tropical climate—but this was much more extreme. It felt like we'd stepped straight into an oven.

Just beyond the pool of Water we were standing in, Charlie was waiting for us in human form. In stark contrast to him, every member of the militia standing at the ready behind him was in dragon form, heating the atmosphere with every fiery exhalation.

There was no need to exchange pleasantries, and no time to waste on it. So Benjamin waded out of the Water and moved to the center of the pack, and the rest of us followed on his heels. "We're good to go," he said as his shadow descended over all of us.

With that, we started toward the tree line as one monstrous invisible entity.

As I fell into step with Tristan and Zeke, my brother grinned at me. "Beautiful day for an adventure."

"Beautiful day to keep your fucking mouth shut," Benjamin muttered behind us.

I looked over my shoulder and couldn't help grinning at the sight of the Darkness and Charlie marching side by side. My former trainee's time with the boss and Benjamin, while I was in the Light Realm with Emma, had clearly done him good. Charlie now wore his power with a menacing air of confidence that I wasn't sure he'd ever possess the day he'd first walked through the door of our house on Sycamore Lane.

Charlie frowned at the Darkness. "Your shadow keeps any noise we make from going beyond its protective barrier. So there's no reason for Tristan to keep his mouth shut."

"Yeah, there is," Benjamin growled. "I'm not gonna listen to his nonsense the whole fucking trip." As Tristan looked back and shot him a smoldering grin, Benjamin snarled, "Don't test me, incubus. I will kick you outside my shadow and let you fend for yourself in the Dark Forest."

"No, you won't," Charlie muttered under his breath. "You wouldn't risk tipping off any creature who could be out there watching."

A growl rumbled in the Darkness's throat as he narrowed his pitch-black eyes at Charlie. "Who the fuck asked you?"

A mischievous grin spread across Charlie's face. "You know, you might wanna stay on my good side, since I'll be your boss someday."

"Don't count on it," Benjamin growled. "I'd rather go live in the Light than take orders from you."

"I love you too, Benji," Charlie whispered.

After a hushed snicker from Bob, who was marching in the row behind Benjamin and Charlie, everyone fell silent.

As we marched on, I looked over the massive herd of dragons forming a protective barrier around our team. Then I glanced at my brother, and my thoughts drifted…

…I opened the front door of my apartment to find Tristan standing outside with a stack of pizza boxes in his arms. He grinned at me as I stepped back to let him in. "Hope you're hungry."

He followed me to the kitchen and set the boxes down on the table, and I shook my head as I handed him a beer. "That's a lot of food. Did you invite an army of friends to join us?"

Tristan shook his head as he dropped into a chair. "Nope. I wanted you all to myself tonight." He said it playfully, the way he said everything, but something in his eyes told me whatever he'd come to discuss was no laughing matter.

I handed him a plate and sat down across the table from him. "Uh-huh. You didn't want to meet in public, so I'm guessing you want to talk about something that happened in Draumer. You know, you might want to start pacing yourself because one of these days the knighthood is gonna get tired of me taking off to bail your ass out of trouble."

My brother let out an uneasy laugh, then took a swig of his beer. "Who said I was in trouble?"

I raised an eyebrow as I helped myself to a slice of pizza. "Come on, man. Why are you beating around the bush? Just how much trouble are you in?"

Tristan eyed the slice of pizza he'd put on his plate, then took a long pull of his drink instead. "Seriously, I'm not in any trouble."

I let out a laugh, half choking on a mouthful of pizza. "Right," I muttered, stopping to clear my throat and take a sip of my beer. "So you just wanted to come over because you missed me? Shit. Is something wrong with Mom?"

"No, Mom's fine."

"Then spill it, Tristan. I'm a busy man."

"Fuck," he muttered. "Can't you down a couple beers before we get into this?"

I dropped the slice of pizza in my hand to my plate. "Just what the hell do you need my help with?"

"I don't need your help," Tristan said, pausing to take a sip of his beer before adding, "Zeke does."

I put my beer down on the table and pushed back my chair. "Then you wasted a trip," I muttered, turning my back to him as I stood up and grabbed my wallet off the counter. "How much do I owe you for the pizza?"

"Zeke came to me asking for help because his Unsighted sister swallowed a bottleful of pills in the waking world, Brian. When he asked her why she did it, she said it just felt like everything was wrong with the world. So he went looking for her in Draumer." Behind me, Tristan slid his chair back from the table with a heavy sigh. "His sister's

tribe was raided by Purists. They killed most of them and abducted her."

I dropped my wallet on the counter and turned to face my brother.

Tristan's normally playful eyes were glistening with tears. "Just come talk to him. Zeke swears he'll devote the rest of his life to doing good, if you save his baby sister."

"Baby sister." The words seemed to stick in my throat. "How old is she?"

"Sixteen. She's a pure succubus and an innocent, Brian. They'll be selling her at their next auction—that is, if she survives that long."

"Damn it," I muttered. "Tell me where to find Zeke."

14

ADDISON

No matter how hard I tried, I couldn't stuff down the dread that was rising inside me as my eyes wandered over the multitude of dragons escorting us through the Dark Forest. This was taking too long. If we didn't get to my family in time, there'd be nothing for me to do but fall on my sword and die next to their bodies.

I had survived more horrors in my childhood than most souls could ever fathom. Yet, nightmarish as my past had been, being subjected to that kind of abuse again wasn't my greatest fear. Losing my husband and children—failing to protect them from the monsters who could be hurting them while we were marching through the Darkness—was what I feared most. I heard what they'd done to Tristan and Brian's mother, and the thought of anything like that happening to my family was too horrific to bear.

Bob touched my shoulder and smiled at me as I turned my head. "We'll get to them in time."

An ache flared in my chest as I whispered, "How can you be so sure? They already got to Tristan and Brian's mother, and Isa's son."

The affection in Bob's eyes brought to mind all those nights during my childhood that we'd spent beneath the stars on his shore. Life had been so much simpler back then. I'd trusted without a doubt that no harm would come to me while I was with him. "Have faith, child," he said, the fondness of his smile making me wonder if our past was on his mind too.

"Faith in what?"

"In me," Bob replied. "In us. We'll get there in time. I feel it in my gut." I was about to voice my doubts when he whispered, "I'd never let anyone hurt you, Addie. You have my word. I won't allow any harm to come to your family."

Tears welled in my eyes as my gaze shifted to Nellie, marching in silence beside Bob. She knew what a nightmare it was to lose a child, and I could tell by the determined set of her jaw that she was intent on preventing her depraved ex-husband's soldiers from harming mine.

"Do you trust me?" Bob whispered as my eyes returned to him.

"More than I've ever trusted anyone."

"Then believe me when I promise you that we'll keep your family safe."

Afraid that I wouldn't be able to answer without breaking down in tears, I nodded.

After that, we all fell silent as the dryads' voices echoed in our heads. Their threats were muted beneath the protection of the Darkness's shadow, but we could still hear them. If anything, their muffled threats seemed even more ominous—or maybe I was just more susceptible to paranoia because of everything I feared losing.

It's your fault they're in danger, elf, the dryads whispered inside my head. *A broken little thing like you had no business starting a family.*

I did my best to tune them out and focus on watching the Darkness's feet marching ahead of me.

And as if that wasn't reckless enough, you chose dangerous vocations in both worlds. Deep down, you must have wanted to risk your family's lives, or you're just selfish and stupid. Your pathetic need for a normal life will be the death of everyone you love.

Bob took my hand and gave it a squeeze, breaking the dryads' spell. "Ignore them. They pick troublesome thoughts from our minds to weaken our resolve, hoping to make us turn back."

"I know," I said, hating how weak I sounded.

A warning sound hissed from a dragon at the front of our group and all of us stilled, following his lead. Until he drew our attention to it, I hadn't had the state of mind to distinguish the sounds of battle up ahead from the dryads' voices.

A scream in the distance made my blood run cold as two of the dragons at the front of the pack broke free from Benjamin's shadow and bounded toward the commotion.

"Shouldn't we go help?" Nellie asked, gripping Bob's arm.

Benjamin shook his head. "There are battles raging all over Draumer. We're bound to come across lots of them, but we can't afford to get sidetracked on this mission. If we stop to aid our side in those battles, we could be too late to protect your loved ones."

"Everyone is somebody's loved one," Nellie muttered.

"That's why we've come," the silver-scaled dragon closest to Nellie said in a velvet voice that sounded surprisingly gentle for such a fierce-looking beast. "We'll go where help is needed. You must stick to your mission."

Nellie nodded, and we all fell silent as a thunderous roar in the distance shook the ground beneath our feet.

The screeches, and cries, and growls echoing from deep within the forest as we marched on made me miss the dryads' harmless threats. Every now and then, a brilliant burst of flames would erupt from far off within the trees, and agonized shrieks would follow soon after. For hours, we marched in the midst of that chaos. The horrific sounds of battle echoed from every corner of the Dark Forest and with each scream, my fear of what we'd find when we reached my family intensified. The dryads were right; if anything happened to my husband or children, it would be my fault.

The number of dragons surrounding us dwindled as they branched off to join the nearby battles, but the remaining dragons stayed evenly spaced around the perimeter of our group. Our bodies were sedated in the Sarrum's ballroom back in the waking world, so we didn't need to stop for sleep. But our souls grew weary nonetheless. The longer we marched without stopping, the greater my desire to take a break became. At times, the cries in the distance were the only thing keeping me going. The Purists were spreading through the Dark Realm like a virus, attacking wherever they detected weakness.

When the dragon leading us stopped to listen to the surrounding noises, I caught a glimpse of Water in the distance up ahead.

Benjamin turned to us and pointed to the patch of deep blue beyond the trees. "This is where you three get off. Addison's family should be somewhere along the fringe up there."

"Then what are we waiting for?" Bob said, turning to me. "We've got this, Addie. I promise you."

I blinked back the tears in my eyes as Bob, Nellie, and I stepped beyond the protection of the Darkness's shadow. The crashes, and wails, and thunderous roars sounded a hundred times louder now that we were out in the open. I looked over my shoulder toward the group that I knew was only steps away, but I couldn't detect any trace of them.

"Come on," Bob whispered as he started toward the Water beyond the trees.

As Nellie and I fell into step on either side of him, I found myself thinking of the day I met my Unsighted husband in the waking world…

…It was a beautiful spring day, and the campus courtyard was packed with students who were enjoying the sunshine between classes. Since there were no empty tables, I chose one with only one occupant and sat down as far apart from him as I could.

He looked up from the book he was reading, greeting me with a lopsided grin as he nudged his glasses up the bridge of his nose with an index finger.

A hesitant smile spread across my face as I unzipped my backpack and took out my lunch. Although I'd never spoken to him, his face was a familiar comfort. We were in a couple of the same classes, and he always sat in the front row. I'd watched him from my seat farther back in the room on more than one occasion. Something about his nerdy disheveled appearance and timid mannerisms appealed to a part of me that would always be wary of strangers, especially male ones. Daydreaming about what it might be like to spend time with someone like him was the closest I planned to get to making friends.

I assumed he'd turned his attention back to his book when I broke eye contact, but the purposeful way he cleared his throat made me look up from my lunch. "Sociology?" he asked with a timid grin.

"What?"

"We're in the same class," he said, frowning as if he regretted disturbing me, "with Professor Marpley."

"Oh, right," I said, dropping my eyes to my food.

He lowered his head to meet my eyes in the most endearingly hesitant way. "I'm dreadfully lost in there most of the time."

I found myself grinning despite my resolve to remain detached. "Yeah?"

"Yeah," he muttered with a shrug and a crooked smile. "Relationships are something of a nightmare for me."

"Me too," I said, shocking myself with the unguarded honesty of my response, "but I get the concept well enough to do okay in the class."

"Then you're way ahead of me. I'll take a physics exam over a two-page paper on social interactions any day of the week."

I cringed at that without meaning to.

"Is that how you feel about me bothering you while you're trying to eat lunch," he muttered, "or physics exams?"

"Physics," I said, blushing. "And you're not bothering me."

His crooked grin widened. "I'm glad to hear it." When I smiled, he extended a tentative hand across the table. "I'm James, by the way."

I put my hand in his without giving myself time to overthink it. "I'm Addison."

"Addison," he said in a pensive whisper as he shook my hand, "is there any chance you're a Lord of the Rings fan?"

"The books or the movies?" I asked, even though I knew nothing about the story in any form.

"Either one."

My cheeks burned at the stupidity of my last response. "I've never read the books or seen the movies."

"They're having a marathon," he replied with a sweet smile that made me feel slightly less idiotic, "playing all the movies on campus this weekend. I don't suppose you'd be interested in going to the first one with me on Friday?"

"Just the first one?"

"Well, it'd be stupid of me to invite you to all of them."

"Why's that?"

"If you have no interest in going anywhere with me," he muttered, dropping his gaze to the table, "I'd be setting myself up for three times the rejection by asking you to all of them at once."

I smiled at him as he looked up at me. "I thought you weren't interested in social interactions."

"No," he muttered, cheeks reddening. "I'm just clueless about them. In fact, to be honest, I'm shocked you're still sitting here talking to me."

I started to laugh, but stopped when I realized he wasn't joking. "You're easy to talk to."

He tilted his head to one side, studying me. "You are the first person to ever say that to me."

I bit my lip, unsure where to go from there. It was one thing to daydream about being friends with this guy, but I didn't actually know him. Sweet as he seemed, he could be a serial killer for all I knew.

"I'm sorry," he muttered. "I've made you uncomfortable, haven't I?"

Afraid I'd let him see too much, I forced a smile and shook my head.

"We could meet at the theater, and maybe grab something to eat after," he said. "That is, if you aren't sick of my company by then."

Despite my conviction to remain detached, I found myself asking, "What do you like about Lord of the Rings*?"*

"Oh, I don't know. I guess...I like that it's a window into another world where magic is real. I've always loved stories about knights, and castles, and mythical creatures." When I smiled at that, he said, "And it's kinda nice to fantasize about living in a world where a guy like me could go on a quest to save the world, and maybe even turn a pretty girl's head."

"Sounds like a pretty great world."

"Is that a yes?"

"I guess it is," I said, surprising myself with my answer.

15

CHARLIE

It felt like we'd been marching through the Dark Forest for months, but this wasn't my first trek through the Dark Realm. So I knew it was just as likely that we were only a few hours into the journey. No matter how much time had actually passed, Bob, Nellie, and Addison looked exhausted as they made their way to the edge of Benjamin's shadow.

A lump formed in my throat as a vision sprang to mind—of Bob and Nellie bickering during group therapy back at the facility where the three of us had met—and I couldn't help grinning as I recalled how impossible they'd made it for me and Emma to keep a straight face. Bob had been swearing like a sailor, and Nellie was scolding him for cursing in front of her child. *Her child.* Not only had Nellie's daughter turned out to be real, but I'd also discovered that she was my half-sister. Unfortunately, the little girl in old Nellie's care was just an enchantment; the real Lilly died years before I was born.

As Bob's trio reached the edge of Benjamin's shadow, a rush of images flashed through my head: *the first time I met lovely young Nellie in the Dream World…the first time I met the noble knight in Draumer and realized he was the crotchety old man from the facility…Bob carrying Nellie and Lilly to dry land after we emerged from the Waters by his shore…Bob and Nellie sitting together on his shore as I waved goodbye to them, knowing they'd be good for each other…Bob, Nellie, and Addison hunched over Pip's lifeless body.*

Tears filled my eyes as they stepped out from under Benjamin's shadow.

I turned my head toward Benjamin, expecting him to give me hell for it. Instead, I could've sworn there were tears in his pitch-black eyes. He didn't even attempt to hide his emotion as he met my stare. That's when it really hit me, just how grave this mission of ours was. We could all be parting ways for the last time. I turned back to give Bob and Nellie a nod of encouragement, but they were already lost to the Dark beyond the reach of Benjamin's shadow.

The thought of losing them on this mission brought to mind our last mission—*and the way we'd lost Rose*—but dwelling on those painful thoughts wouldn't do me any good now. I needed to focus on a happier memory, back when we were all together and my friendship with Rose was just beginning to deepen into something more. So I thought of the day Rose, Bob, Pip, and I were knighted by the Sarrum, after we'd helped rescue Emma and Nellie from Godric…

…After a full evening of celebrating the Queen's safe return and our induction into the royal guard, guests were

beginning to leave the banquet hall with full bellies and rosy-cheeked grins.

There was even a faint hint of a smile on the Darkness's face as he approached the table where Rose and I sat, tucked away in the corner. "Enjoy the rest of your evening," he said, looking from one to the other of us. "Just remember, your training starts bright and early tomorrow morning."

I smiled at Rose before meeting his stare. "Wouldn't miss it for the world."

Benjamin scrutinized our close proximity through narrowed eyes, but he kept his opinion to himself— probably because his soul mate was right behind him.

Isa stepped up beside Benjamin, taking his hand in hers. "Congratulations to you both. We're so proud of you."

"Thanks," Rose said, blushing as she stood up and hugged them both.

With that, the two of them excused themselves.

Rose and I sat there in silence, watching while they crossed the room and left the banquet hall. As soon as they stepped out, I turned to Rose with an awkward smile. The two of us had grown pretty close while the Sarrum was off searching for his abducted wife, since the task of shouldering the weight of their mirage had fallen to us in his absence. While sharing that enormous burden with Rose, my feelings for her had blossomed into something much more than friendship. But I wasn't quite sure where to go from there.

Benjamin had made his objections to me starting a relationship with his soul mate's daughter abundantly clear—and more importantly, I didn't know how Rose felt about taking our relationship beyond the friend zone. Although my dragon instincts were growing stronger by the day, I was still hesitant to put much stock in what I sensed. At the moment, my instincts were telling me that Rose wanted to leave this crowded room and find a quiet spot to decompress. I also sensed that she wanted me to join her, but I couldn't be sure whether that part was genuine instinct or just wishful thinking.

I leaned a bit closer to her, to make sure she could hear me over the crowd. "It's kind of loud in here. Would you like to step out and get some air?"

She met my gaze with a timid smile. "I'd love to."

Nodding, I stood from the table. She stood up after me, and we crossed the room without saying a word.

I wanted to take her hand in mine, but I didn't have the nerve to. We'd already kissed and held hands a few times while shouldering the weight of the mirage. But I'd been a powder keg of raw nerves and feral urges—desperately trying to figure out how to control my bestial impulses—with my inner dragon finally unleashed after years of suppression. At the time, I'd been sure Rose was into me. But now that I could think rationally, it seemed equally plausible that she'd just been doing what was necessary to keep me on task.

As we reached the Waterfall exit to the banquet hall, Rose turned to me. "Where should we go?"

I took a gamble and held my hand out to her. "I know a place."

She placed her delicate hand in mine, and we stepped into the Waterfall side by side.

Rose tipped her head back as we stepped out, her sweet mouth agape as she looked up at the starry sky. "Where are we?"

My gaze lingered on her lips for a few heartbeats before my brain managed to register her question. But the fact that she hadn't pulled her hand away didn't escape my attention for a second, and I fully intended to hold onto it until she did.

Realizing I still hadn't answered her, I cleared my throat. "I found this place when I was trying to avoid Benjamin after a humiliating afternoon of failed attempts to unmask during a lesson." We made our way across the circular stone floor of the watchtower that was positioned at the highest point of the palace, and I stepped up to the railing with her hand still in mine. "I think it's an old military lookout. Nobody else ever seems to come up here. Just between us, this is my favorite place to come when I want to be alone."

Rose raised her hands to the railing, lifting my hand along with hers, and a smile spread across her lovely face as she leaned over the rail and took in the view. "You can see everything from up here."

"Yeah. But my favorite thing about this spot, besides the solitude, is how close to the stars it feels like you are up here."

She tilted her head back, considering the stars. "It looks like you could pluck one right out of the sky. I can't imagine a more perfect view."

"Me neither," I said, only I wasn't looking at the stars.

She turned her head, and blushed when she realized my eyes were on her. "Thank you for sharing this with me, Charlie."

"Of course. There's no one I'd rather share my secret hideout with."

She started walking with her hand still in mine, bringing me to a stone bench on the other side of the tower. "Since we're sharing secrets," she said, sitting down on the bench, and smiling when I sat down beside her, "can I tell you something?"

I gave her hand a slight squeeze. "You can tell me anything."

"You always know just what to say to me," she whispered, dropping her eyes to the floor.

"I'm glad it seems like that," I said, "because I pretty much feel a complete dumbass whenever I'm around you."

She looked up at me with a bashful smile. "You're just saying that to make me feel better."

I let out a laugh. "Trust me, I'm not that smooth. I just speak the truth, and you always make me want to share what's on my mind."

"That's such a sweet thing to say," she said as she tilted her head back to look up at the stars. "You know...for the longest time, I was sure you thought I was an absolutely repulsive disaster."

"Why?" I asked, taken aback. "What the heck did I ever do to make you think that?"

"Do you remember the day we met?" she asked, lowering her voice despite the fact that there wasn't another soul as far as the eye could see. "I came downstairs that night, and found you in the living room eating popcorn and watching a horror movie."

I smiled, remembering the way she'd curled up on the opposite side of the couch, looking adorable as she wrapped herself up in the blanket I handed her. She was so beautiful, and sweet, and demure; and I acted like a bumbling idiot, saying all the wrong things and choking on my soda when she asked if the Sarrum wanted me to 'put a dragon in her belly.' Hopefully she'd forgotten that little mortifying detail. "Of course. How could I forget?"

Color rushed to her cheeks as she met my eyes. "Well, I'm not sure if you remember this, but I made a complete fool of myself by announcing that I was a virgin, and asking you if the Sarrum meant for the two of us to make him an heir."

Crap. So much for her forgetting that part. "Oh, I definitely remember."

The smile slipped from her face as she nodded and pulled her hand away. "You were repulsed by the thought of being intimate with me. I mean, you were too polite to say that, but you were so put off by my question that you choked on your drink."

"I'm an idiot," I said, hating myself for being so clueless. It'd never even occurred to me how vulnerable Rose must've felt telling me that she was a virgin and asking me about her virginity being arbitrarily taken from her. And what did I do to reassure her? I dribbled soda all over myself, and made her think the thought of having sex with her disgusted me. "I was so busy worrying about not making a fool of myself in front of you—because you were amazing, and everything I'd said to you so far had made me sound like a total douchebag—that it never occurred to me that choking on my drink might've given you the wrong impression. I don't know if you've noticed, but I'm not as smooth as Tristan or Brian. When a gorgeous girl tells me she's a virgin and asks if we're supposed to have sex..." I met Rose's lovely chocolate-brown eyes, and hated myself even more when I saw that they were full of tears. Placing my hand on top of hers, I said, "Well, I guess I still don't know what to say to that. But it's definitely not because I'm repulsed by the thought of being with you. It's because my brain can't even fathom a situation where a beautiful, brilliant, kickass girl like you would ever consider sleeping with an idiot like me."

A tear slid down her cheek as she smiled at me. "Then I guess we're both idiots. You have no idea how much time I spent being too embarrassed to look you in the eye, because I was mortified that the thought of touching me disgusted you."

"Disgust is the farthest thing from my mind." Determined to overcome my insecurities and show her how I felt about her, I took her lovely face in my hands and kissed her softly on the mouth.

For a few pounding heartbeats, I was afraid that might've been the absolute worst thing to do. But as she leaned into the kiss, we melted in each other's arms, and there wasn't a doubt in my mind that we were made for each other...

...An explosion in the distance broke through my thoughts—shattering that precious memory into a thousand pieces—and I realized my cheeks were slick with tears.

Drying my cheeks with my shirtsleeve, I turned to Benjamin. "Who's up next?"

"Those three pretty boys marching ahead of us," Benjamin said in that velvet-soft tone he usually reserved for Isa, Emma, and Rose—his gentle voice, another ominous reminder that this mission could be the end for any one of us.

Grinning, Tristan glanced over his shoulder at the Darkness. "What happened to keeping your fucking mouth shut?"

A thunderous growl erupted in the distance before Benjamin could answer, and the dragon leading us signaled for us to stop moving.

Benjamin tugged my arm, pulling me with him to the front of the pack. "What is it?" he asked the dragon in the lead.

"The battle ahead is too packed with warriors, and the ground is too littered with their dead, for us to pass through without great difficulty," the dragon replied.

Benjamin let out a hushed growl. "Then where the fuck do you suggest we go?"

"Down that embankment," a smaller dragon said, nodding toward the slope to our right.

Climbing down an embankment sounded easy enough, but Benjamin didn't look pleased with her suggestion.

"Fuck," Tristan muttered as he, Zeke, and Brian joined us up front.

I shrugged out of Benjamin's grip and walked over to Tristan, who was standing closest to the embankment. Down below, a minefield of jagged rocks sporadically jutted up from a shallow stream. That, in and of itself, wouldn't have been so bad. But an unending parade of warriors was marching downstream in sparse formation, and the look on Benjamin's face told me they weren't our soldiers.

As we stood there weighing our options, a repeating pattern of thunderous crashes began to echo through the forest—each one louder and more impactful than the one before it—and for a moment my heart stuttered as a mountainous man with a scraggly beard and forearms the size of tree trunks lumbered past us. There was no need to ask anyone if he was a full-blooded giant. The fact that the tops of the forest's impossibly lofty trees barely came up to his shoulders was a pretty dead giveaway.

I turned to the dragon who was leading us through the forest. "You can't seriously expect us to march into the middle of all that?"

Silver flames filled the dragon's eyes as he shrugged his massive shoulders. "That is the only way forward." Without further discussion, he started down the embankment.

The other dragons followed his lead without a moment's hesitation, and my group followed them with enough hesitation for the whole damn lot of us.

As we reached the edge of the stream at the base of the embankment, I turned to Benjamin. "How are we supposed to march through here without any of them sensing our presence?"

"Relax. There are no creatures in this group who are more powerful than you or me," Benjamin said with a confidence that made me feel a little less nauseated about the death sentence we'd just marched into.

Another giant's foot stomped down way too close for my comfort, drenching me with a massive splash. I shook my head as I raked my sopping wet hair back from my face. "I don't suppose your shadow can protect us from getting trampled?"

Benjamin narrowed his pitch-black eyes at me. "Don't be a fucking idiot."

"I'll take that as a no," Tristan said as he dodged a wiry, feral-eyed demon that was headed straight toward him.

The Darkness rolled his eyes at the two of us. "Just stay alert."

As our dragon escorts weaved their way through the endless string of nightmarish creatures up ahead of us, I found myself wondering just how far Benjamin's protective cover could stretch. I inched my way closer to the Darkness as we picked our way from rock to rock, while being careful to avoid colliding with our enemies who were all doing the same thing. "What are the odds of us making it through this?"

Benjamin shrugged. "Maybe fifty-fifty."

"Shit," Zeke muttered, sidestepping a yellow-eyed demon with matted hair and a mouthful of rotten teeth, "I really hope you're joking."

Benjamin raised an eyebrow. "Do I strike you as the joking type?"

As Zeke stood there staring the Darkness down, a massive potbellied beast stomped by, coating the half-incubus's head with a nasty gob of his drool. "Fuck," Zeke growled, falling behind to crouch down and splash the mucous off his head. As he caught up to us, Zeke turned to Brian while we all weaved our way through a cluster of sorrows. "If we die here, you better devote the rest of your fucking life to keeping my baby sister safe, or I'll hunt you down and rip you in half with my bare hands."

Brian shook his head as he sidestepped a green-eyed wolfish demon. "There are so many responses to that idiotic threat running through my head right now, but I'm just gonna let it slide because I know you're scared."

"Damn straight I am," Zeke growled as an ogre with a bowl cut and a nose ring started loping along beside him. "I'm scared outta my fucking mind. We all should be."

"We are," Brian said as a pack of winged beasts swooped past. "The rest of us are just being quiet about it."

"Speak for yourself," Tristan muttered. "I'm seriously close to pissing myself."

The dragon leading our group stopped short on a massive moss-covered rock jutting up out of the stream—demon after demon narrowly missing him, yet somehow never colliding with him—and Tristan was concentrating on his footing so intently that he almost ran straight into him. The dragon lowered his head to Tristan as he pointed a razor-sharp claw toward the steep slope on the opposite side of the stream. "Your path is that way."

"Of course it is," Tristan muttered. Then he turned to me and flashed me a killer smile as he gave my shoulder a squeeze. "It's been a real pleasure, dragon. I know you're gonna make us all proud."

Weak as it made me feel, I couldn't help tearing up. "I'm sure we'll meet up again soon enough. But yeah, it has been a pleasure. Good luck, my friend."

"Right back at ya," Tristan said as we exchanged a quick hug.

As Tristan stepped back, Brian touched my arm. "I'm damn proud to say I was your guide once upon a time."

Too choked up to answer, I gave my former guide a hug. And Brian hugged me back like we were brothers heading off to war—which I guess we kinda were.

After Brian and I dropped the hug, Zeke ruffled my hair. "Give 'em hell, dragon."

"Yeah, you too," I said.

For a moment, I just stood there watching as the three of them crossed the stream and started scaling the steep slope on its opposite bank.

"Won't be long now," Benjamin said as he sauntered ahead.

That's when I realized he wasn't sidestepping a damn thing. Every beast in the Darkness's vicinity instinctively veered out of his way when he neared it. I caught up and narrowed my eyes at him. "We didn't have to dodge all those creatures that were coming at us, did we?"

Benjamin let out a deep-throated chuckle that made the nearest demon shiver in the sweltering heat, even though he clearly couldn't sense our presence. "Guess I do appreciate the occasional joke."

"Fuck you," I muttered, marching straight toward the berbalang scurrying from rock to rock ahead of me. He shook his head and lurched to the side to avoid me, although it was obvious I was invisible to him.

"Did you really just say that to me?" Benjamin asked as a grin that didn't mesh with his menacing tone spread across his face.

I outstretched an arm, and watched with maniacal satisfaction as the troll coming up on my left swerved to avoid it. "Yeah. I did."

"Maybe I'll follow you after all, kid."

"Shit," I muttered. *The only reason he'd say that was if I had zero chance of surviving this mission.*

"Fuck that," Benjamin growled. "You don't get to fail, dragon. You are getting Rose the hell out of there."

His fierce reminder of who I'd come on this mission to save spurred me on with a renewed sense of purpose. "Don't worry. I'll do whatever it takes to bring Rose home."

16

BRIAN

By the time I reached the top of the embankment, my heart was hammering in my chest—and not just because of the climb. There was nothing to stop those soldiers marching down below from spotting us now that we were no longer under the cover of Benjamin's shadow. I leaned over the edge, outstretched an arm to Tristan, and tugged him to the top when he grabbed it. Zeke hoisted himself up a second later and flopped down on his back, his chest heaving and his brow slick with sweat.

We stayed low for a few minutes, catching our breath while we watched the parade of Purist soldiers stomp through the stream down below.

Zeke sat up, turning toward me as he twisted his soggy hair up in a topknot. "So, how do we know where to go from here?"

I shrugged. "The woman who raised Charlie is reported to live in a dilapidated cottage near the fringe. So I guess we look for Water, and we'll find her somewhere nearby."

"Not exactly precise coordinates," Tristan muttered, wiping the sweat from his brow.

I stood up and shot my brother a humorless smile. "Well, it's the best we've got, so we might as well get moving and try to beat the Purists there."

"Sounds like a plan to me," Zeke said, cringing as a thunderous roar sounded in the distance. I'd seen the half-giant fight. He wasn't normally afraid of anything, but the air in the forest was thick with paranoia and worry over his sister's safety already had him on edge.

Anxious to get on with it, I started walking. "I've got a hunch the Water's this way."

A heartbeat later the two of them were on their feet, falling into step beside me without a word. The forest was crawling with demons—most of them Purists—and we were on our own out in the open from here on out. So it was best not to risk alerting the enemy to our presence with conversation.

The menacing expression on Zeke's face as he walked beside me brought to mind our meeting all those years ago…

…I drew a deep breath, then yanked the door open and stepped inside the Dragon's Lair. The scantily clad pixie seated at the piano by the entrance was playing a tune that seemed a little too cheery for most of the tavern's patrons. Although, judging by the dopey looks on their faces as they watched her, her beauty and charm more than made up for it.

The pixie met my eye and batted her long silver lashes as I passed by her piano.

I gave her a polite nod, which only seemed to frustrate her; but I didn't have time to waste on flirting, so I fixed my sights on the bar and headed toward it.

A cluster of nymphs draped in long, flowing earth-toned silks paused their conversation as I passed by them. "Hello there, handsome," the tallest one said, reaching out to touch my arm.

I shook my head. "Sorry, sweetheart, I'm just here on business tonight."

"Well, if you're interested in some pleasure after you've concluded your business," she whispered in my ear, "come find me."

I nodded and kept moving because it was easier than wasting time turning her down.

As I approached the bar, the female troll behind it greeted me with a jovial smile. "Well hello, gorgeous. I'm guessing you're here to see your brother?"

I reached across the bar to shake her hand. "You must be the lovely Aubrey. How did you know I was Tristan's brother?"

"Oh, honey," she said, placing her hand in mine, "you've got the same charming aura about you, the same confident swagger, and a smile that'd melt even the coldest creature's heart."

"Thanks."

She studied me as we dropped the handshake. "But you're the serious one, aren't you?"

"Yeah, I guess you could say that."

Aubrey nodded. "Don't tell him I said this, but Tristan thinks the world of you."

I let out a chuckle. "He'd deny that to his dying breath."

"I don't think so," she said, dropping the smile. "They're out back. Come on, let me show you the way."

She stepped out from behind the bar, and I followed her through a door that led to a dark hallway. As we reached the end of the hall, she grabbed the doorknob of the room closest to the exit and smiled at me. "Zeke's a good guy." When I frowned at that, she whispered, "Go easy on him. He's in pretty rough shape." With that, she opened the door and as soon as I stepped inside, she pulled it shut behind me.

Jaw clenched, I moved toward the table Tristan and Zeke were seated at.

Contrary to his menacing expression, the half-giant's eyes were full of tears as he stood up. When I scowled at him, Ezekiel dropped to his knees on the floor in front of me. "Please," he said in a rough whisper, "I'm begging you. I know you hate my guts, but my baby sister is a good girl. She's never hurt anybody. Help me get her back, and the rest of my life is yours. I'll devote every last breath in my body to doing whatever the fuck you tell me to."

"You're a damn Purist," I said as he looked up at me. "Why can't you go get her yourself?"

"I'm not a Purist," he replied. "I just work for them."

I shook my head and dropped into the chair across the table from Tristan. "Then you might as well be one."

"I didn't think it mattered since the Unsighted don't remember what happens to them in Draumer when they return to the waking world," the half-giant said as he got off his knees and sat down next to my brother. "To them, it's just a really vivid nightmare."

I balled my hands into fists beneath the table. "That's bullshit. Whether or not they remember it, abusing any soul is an unforgivable offense in either world."

"Yeah, I get that now," Zeke muttered, raking his fingers through his long dark hair. "My baby sister tried to kill herself in the waking world because of what they did

to her here in Draumer. Look, I get it. You think I'm a piece of shit, and you have absolutely no fucking reason to help me. But Davina never did anything wrong. She's an innocent Unsighted girl surrounded by a bunch of perverted monsters, and she needs somebody to get her the hell outta there."

"And why can't that be you?"

Tristan put a hand on Zeke's shoulder. "The Purists ward their auction sites with blood magic, Brian. They would recognize a relative of one of the captives and execute him on the spot for interfering in their business."

I sat up a little straighter. "They're using dragon magic?"

"Yeah," Zeke replied in a hoarse whisper. "I'm pretty sure there was a dragon somewhere in the lineage of the asshole who runs the slavers' trade. The heartless son of a bitch is a brilliant sorcerer."

"But your sister's a succubus. Why can't she just charm her way outta there?"

Zeke shook his head. "The bastard uses some kinda spell to mute his captives' charm. Besides, Davina's Unsighted. I doubt she fully realizes what she's capable of."

"So what exactly do you want me to do?"

"Go to the auction," Zeke said. "Pretend you're there to buy, and get her the fuck outta there."

I narrowed my eyes at him. "Just like that? You don't think they'll know what I am? That skilled sorcerer of yours is gonna realize I'm half elf and a member of the nomadic knighthood."

Zeke hunched forward, placing his massive hands on the table in front of him, and I couldn't help noticing his nails were all bitten to the quick. "That doesn't mean you can't be a dirty one. Tell them you've been watching her tribe for years, and you had your eye on her because you were gonna take her for yourself."

The ease with which he came up with that lie turned my stomach. It made me wonder whether some of my brothers actually had broken their vow to protect the Unsighted. "You really think I could pull that lie off?"

Zeke shrugged his broad shoulders. "If it's the only way to save an innocent girl from a fate worse than death at the hands of a bunch of sadistic demons? Yeah. I think you could do it without feeling the least bit guilty."

"Don't tell me how I'd feel," I growled. "You don't know the first damn thing about me."

"That's not true. Tristan talks about you all the time. According to him, you're the most noble son of a bitch he's ever met in either world. So, I get that pretending to be a buyer would make your skin crawl."

"What do—"

"But I also know you'd never let your hatred of me keep you from doing what's right," he said, cutting me off, "and it ain't right what they're doing to my baby sister."

Ashamed of myself for wasting time chastising Zeke while that poor girl was out there somewhere, I shoved my chair back from the table. "Tell me where they're keeping her."

17

ADDISON

We'd been trudging through the forest for way too long, and the silence was too absolute. I had no way of knowing whether it was eerily quiet because we'd arrived before the Purists found my family, or because those monsters had already come and gone. "It's too quiet," I said.

"That doesn't mean we're too late," Bob whispered, but I saw the worry in his eyes.

The thought of reaching the fringe only to find them gone—*or dead*—made me feel physically ill. My stomach was churning, my throat was bone dry, and my heart was pounding, but I pushed ahead, desperate to find my family.

Bob took my hand in his as we marched on, none of us daring to speak as we neared the Water. I squeezed my eyes shut, trusting him to guide my steps while I prayed for a miracle. I had survived unspeakable horrors in my past, but I would never survive theirs. If anyone had hurt my husband or children, it'd damage me beyond repair.

The only way to keep from going stark raving mad was to distract myself, so I let my thoughts drift to our past...

...James and I were in the common room of my dorm watching a film we needed to write a Sociology paper on. I was lying on the couch, and he was sitting on the floor in front of it with his colored pencils in a haphazard pile at his feet as he drew in the sketch pad he always carried.

I shifted on the couch, leaning over his shoulder to look at his drawing. It was a landscape, sketched in tones of violet and gray with a low stone staircase leading up to a small castle on a sandy beach overlooking the water. "It's beautiful."

"Thank you," he said without looking up from his work. "This is the sort of place where I'd want to live in a world where magic was real."

That was no surprise. James was always sketching pictures of castles, but this was the first time I'd seen him draw one by the water's edge in such a serene mix of hues. "Violet is my favorite color."

"I know," he said, his head bent and his pencil sketching away, "and you're happiest near the water."

"What?"

He looked up from his work and smiled at me. "The beach is your happy place."

"It is," I said, mesmerized by the tranquility in his eyes.

A lopsided grin spread across his face as he reached up and tucked a stray piece of hair behind my ear. I flinched at the contact before I could stop myself, and the hurt in his eyes hit me like a blow to the heart.

"I think we both know picking up on social cues isn't my strong point," he whispered with a wounded smile. "I

love spending time with you, and our friendship means the world to me. But sometimes I swear I see more than friendship in your eyes when you look at me. Am I just a complete idiot?"

Determined to keep my eyes from filling with tears, I bit my lip and focused on the drawing in his sketch pad. The last thing I wanted to do was push James away, but I didn't know how to let him in.

"Talk to me," he said in a hoarse whisper.

Before I could second-guess myself, I stood up from the couch. "Not here."

He followed my lead, gathering up his art supplies and removing the DVD from the machine, while I grabbed my pillow and shoes. Then we walked down the hall to my room in silence, my heart pounding at the thought of letting him see how broken I was—or worse, losing him because I couldn't.

I unlocked the door to my room, and he followed me in. While I tossed my pillow on the bed and sat down, he dragged the chair at my desk to my bedside. Most of the time James just seemed to instinctively know when to give me space, but I hated myself for sending him such mixed signals.

"You don't have to sit that far away," I said, sliding over so he could sit next to me on the bed.

He stood up from the chair and positioned my pillow between us as he sat down on the bed with a patient reluctance that suggested he was way more perceptive than he gave himself credit for. "Talk to me," he whispered, "please. I don't want to mess up our friendship by being stupid."

"You're right," I said, dropping my eyes to the pillow between us. "I do have more than just friendship feelings for you, but I'm...defective."

"I think you're perfect."

"I'm not," I said, digging my fingernails into my palms to keep my eyes from tearing, "not even close."

"Talk to me," he whispered again. "Don't let me ruin this."

"How could you ruin it? I'm the one who's broken."

"What makes you say that?"

I looked up and drew strength from the kindness in his gentle gray eyes. I wouldn't be able to take it if he stopped looking at me like that. Nothing could possibly hurt more than pushing him away because I was too scared to open up.

"When I was a little girl," I said, dropping my gaze to the pillow between us, "my brother and I were kidnapped by two men who kept us tied up in an abandoned house for almost two weeks before a detective found us."

I paused a moment, waiting for him to comment. But he was too good a listener to interrupt.

"The detective saved us, but he was shot in the head right in front of me."

I stopped again, but I could barely even hear James breathing.

"I had to stay in the hospital for almost a month after we were rescued because my jaw was fractured, I had broken ribs and a concussion, and my pelvic bone was cracked. And I guess my internal injuries—the mental ones—never really healed because when someone male touches me, my mind slips right back to what they did..." I drew a deep breath, bracing myself for an expression of horror—or maybe disgust—as I lifted my eyes to meet his.

Eyes full of tears, James took off his glasses and cleared his throat. "I had no idea...I'm so sorry. I shouldn't have pushed you to talk."

"I needed you to know," I said. "You're the only person I've ever told."

"I want to hug you, but I'm not sure if that's appropriate. Tell me what to do."

Tears streamed down my cheeks as I pushed the pillow between us off the bed. "I think I could really use a hug."

He slid closer and wrapped his arms around me with a tenderness that made it easy to melt in his arms. "I would never hurt you, Addie. Never."

I wrapped my arms around him, holding on for dear life as I hugged him back. "I know, and I don't want to lose you because I don't know how to stop being broken."

"Maybe we could figure all that out together," he said, tightening his hold on me ever so slightly.

"Just...please don't give up on me."

"Never," he whispered.

In his arms, I shed all the tears I'd been holding back for so long. Then I drifted off to sleep—still clinging to James for dear life—and I felt more whole than I could ever remember feeling...

...Bob gave my hand a squeeze, drawing me back to the present. "Addie."

I opened my eyes and squinted at the shoreline ahead of us. The sun was beginning to sink toward the Water. The sky was a lovely mix of violet hues—its pastel palette mirrored in the tranquil surface of the Waters—and just a few steps from the shore, a stone staircase wound its way toward a small stone castle that stood like a haven on the beach. It was exactly like the picture James had drawn for me that night.

There had been so many times I was tempted to tell my Unsighted husband that the magical world he'd always longed to be a part of was real, so many times

I'd wanted to track him down in Draumer. But it was forbidden—and more importantly, I was afraid it'd hurt too much if I found him and he looked at me like I was a stranger. But I didn't care about that now. I could handle anything, except finding him dead.

As Bob, Nellie, and I stepped from the trees at the edge of the forest, a voice called out from the castle, "It's not safe to be walking around out there." *James's voice.*

Tears filled my eyes as he stepped out the door of that quaint little castle on the beach. He looked just the same as he did in the waking world, except for his pointed ears and the confident elven way that he carried himself as he descended the stairs.

By the time we met at the base of the winding staircase, I was too choked up to speak.

His gentle eyes widened as he studied me with perplexed fascination. "You…"

I couldn't hold back my tears after that.

He reached a hand toward my face, but dropped it without touching me. "I know you."

"Yes."

"How?" he muttered. "I've dreamt of you."

A sob escaped me as I nodded.

"I've dreamt of you a lot," he said. "How is that possible?"

I smiled at him. "Anything's possible in a world where magic is real."

"Do you know me?"

"Yes," I said, "I dream about you too."

Something between a laugh and a sob gurgled from his mouth as he reached up and touched my cheek, and I couldn't stop myself from throwing my arms around his neck.

He responded with a startled gasp and hugged me back even tighter. "It's not safe out here. Come inside with me."

As Bob and Nellie stepped up beside us, James greeted them with a smile. "Your friends are welcome within our walls too, of course."

At that, we headed up the steps to his castle by the shore with his arm still around me and a look of wonder in his eyes. As soon as we were all safe inside, he bolted the door.

A sudden thought turned my stomach. "Are you…is there a woman in your life?"

"No," he said, grinning at me like he couldn't quite believe his eyes, "at least, not until three minutes ago when the woman of my dreams showed up unannounced outside my home."

I let out a chuckle of relief.

"I do have two sons though," he said. "They're not rightfully mine, as there was no woman who could've been their mother. But when the storks insisted they belonged to me, how could I not keep them and raise them as my own?"

I wanted to tell him they were ours, but I'd already said more than I was supposed to. "Do you think I could meet them?"

"Yes, of course," he replied, grinning with parental pride. "I think you're really going to like them." When I nodded, he said, "This is strange, isn't it?"

"No, not really," I whispered.

Bob was Unsighted, and he knew about both worlds. *Would it really be so wrong to tell my husband the truth?*

18

CHARLIE

We'd been marching downstream surrounded by Purist soldiers for hours, maybe even days, or weeks. The Dark Forest had a way of messing with your mind that made it impossible to judge the passage of time with any measure of accuracy. Along the way, our numbers had dwindled until Benjamin and I were the only two souls left under the protective cover of his shadow. Bob's group had gone off to get Addison's family out of harm's way. Brian, Tristan, and Zeke had left to protect the Unsighted woman who'd raised me as her son; and as for the members of the dragon militia who'd been escorting us through the Darkness, they had all taken off to aid our side in battles we encountered along the way.

Exhausted to the point of breaking, I forced myself to think of Rose and remember why I needed to keep going...

...It was early in the morning and not a creature was stirring in the Talbot household, but I couldn't sleep. After

my disastrous first flying lesson with the Sarrum, followed by a night spent reliving tragic moments from my mother's life with Clay, I was a wreck. The last thing I wanted to do was drift off to Draumer and risk running into Rose. If Benjamin had told her about my lesson—the way I took flight when I saw Emma falling from the balcony, and my maniacal attempt to fly off with her after I caught her— Rose probably wouldn't even want to look at me.

Attuned to my girlfriend's needs and worries as I'd become, I knew Rose had always felt jealous of Emma. Fear that I secretly loved Emma more than her was Rose's number-one insecurity, and I couldn't exactly blame her for that. When Rose and I had first met, I was still driven by an irrational need to make Emma mine because she'd inadvertently charmed me into loving her—back when we were both mental patients, and neither of us had any idea what we truly were. On top of that, Rose had been raised alongside a bunch of royal assholes with Louise Talbot constantly filling her head with a bunch of bullshit about how inferior she was to everybody else.

I wasn't entirely sure what'd possessed me to try and take off with Emma, when I went all feral during my flying lesson, but it had nothing to do with loving her in a romantic way. The most logical explanation I could think of was that dragons are just instinctually possessive of everything we cherish, and I treasured my friendship with Emma dearly because she was the first soul to ever truly believe in me. But given Rose's insecurities, I was pretty sure she'd interpret my motives for flying off with Emma differently.

The sun was just beginning to peek over the horizon as I slipped out the back door of the Talbots' house and made my way toward the beach. Eyes fixed on the water, I walked along the shoreline at a meandering pace, letting the breeze wash over me and ease the tension from my muscles.

"If I didn't know better," Rose called out from her perch on the back steps of a guest house on the Talbots' property, "I'd think you were trying to avoid me."

I smiled at my soul mate and did my best to quiet my internal chaos—hoping she wouldn't sense it—as I walked toward the house and sat down on the step below her. "Just taking a walk to clear my head."

She considered me with an empathetic smile. "Judging by your expression, I take it things didn't go so well during your first lesson with the Sarrum?"

"Yeah, you could say that. I'm pretty much the biggest disappointment my esteemed group of badass mentors have ever had the misfortune of training."

"That's not true, Charlie," Rose whispered as she slid down a step to sit beside me. "Benjamin thinks the world of you."

I shook my head and might've laughed, if I wasn't so close to tears. "Yeah, the death glares that he was giving me after my pathetic first attempt at flight didn't exactly convey that sentiment. Trust me, Rose, you should give up on me and go find a dragon you can be proud to call your boyfriend."

"I am proud to call you my boyfriend," she said, resting her head on my shoulder.

I tilted my head toward hers. "Well, you shouldn't be. Hell, Rose, I don't even want you to go on this mission because I'm such a fucking disaster. There's no guarantee I can keep you safe."

"You're forgetting something," she said, lifting her head from my shoulder.

"And what's that?"

She shifted sideways on the step to face me. "I'm a dragon too. I don't need you to keep me safe. I've never asked you for that, or expected it. All I want from you is your love."

I wrapped my arms around her and hugged her tight. "You've got that, Rose. You'll always have that."

"Promise?" she whispered as she hugged me back.

I tilted my head back to look at her. "I promise. I love you with all my heart, Rose."

"Then just focus on that. It's not your job to keep me safe on this mission. It's OUR job to keep the rest of them safe, and I don't have a doubt in the world that you are capable of holding up your end of the deal."

Despite my own doubts, I couldn't help smiling at the affection in those big beautiful doe eyes of hers. "Where would I be without you?"

"Let's hope you never have to find out," she said, planting a soft kiss on my lips. "But there is one thing I'd like to ask you for before we set out on this mission."

"Anything," I muttered. "Just name it."

Her smile turned a bit more timid as she dropped her eyes to the step below us. "I don't want to be a virgin when we set out on this mission. Do you think you could help me with that?"

My heart sank, as surely as if she'd tied an anchor to it and tossed it out into the depths of the ocean. It'd taken me forever to work up the courage to lay so much as a finger on Rose because of Benjamin's warnings that a physical relationship between us could kill her. Plus, I'd just spent the past several hours immersed in Clay's memories of the mother I never got to meet because giving birth to me had killed her. After witnessing what my mom had gone through, I was petrified of taking that risk. "Rose," I whispered, reaching down to lift her chin so I *could look her in the eye, "I thought we agreed we should only be together in Draumer, where it's not dangerous."*

"That isn't enough, Charlie," she said as she met my eyes. "You know our bodies in this world aren't sated by what our souls do in Draumer. What do you expect me to do—stay a virgin in this world forever, or go off and have sex with some Unsighted guy who can't possibly know me and love me like you do?"

Flames filled my eyes at the thought of her in another man's arms. "Now's not the time to get into this, Rose. We should be focusing on getting ready for the mission."

"I'm already prepared for combat, Charlie. But suppose this mission doesn't end the way we want it to? What if one of us dies? I don't want to wait to 'get into this' because I don't want my first time to be with just any man. I want it to be with you."

"Rose…"

"Look, I know you're under a tremendous amount of pressure right now. You're doubting yourself because you're trying to master all the things that you were never taught before you set off on this mission, while also getting bombarded by memories of the pregnancy your mother lost her life to. I get that."

"Good."

"But you're looking at things all wrong, you big dope," she said with an affectionate grin that melted my stubborn heart. "You see yourself as a failure for not learning everything fast enough, so let me tell you what I see. In the short time I've known you, you've mastered hundreds of skills that most dragons take twenty or more years to perfect. Every dragon I was raised with began their flying lessons around the same time they started learning how to read. You are more amazing than every single one of those royals with their overinflated egos, and their nauseating

opinions—about a woman's purpose being only to satisfy their urges, and give birth to soldiers for their armies. You respect me as an equal, and you love me. You're terrified at the thought of having sex with me—even if we take precautions—because of the slim chance that we might conceive a dragon. But even on the off chance that I were to get pregnant, a dragon pregnancy is not an absolute death sentence. My mother survived my birth, and she's not even a dragon. And did you ever stop to wonder why Benjamin is such a moody, brooding old shadow? Personally, I think it's because he spent the prime of his life watching his soul mate marry and raise a child with some other man. Benji isn't the guy you should be taking romantic advice from, Charlie. I love you, and I want to be with you before we set off on this mission because I want to be entirely yours in both worlds. Do you have any idea how remarkable you are? You're funny, and brave, and caring, and brilliant, and I want you to be the first man I sleep with. I want you to be the only man I ever sleep with. So don't you dare tell me you love me, if you're not willing to prove it."

"Wow," I said. "That's a hell of an argument."

"Is that all you've got to say?"

I touched her cheek and brushed her hair back from her face with my fingertips. "You're the remarkable one, Rose. Your faith in me makes me believe I might actually be able to live up to my potential."

"You already have, Charlie."

There was nothing I could say that'd be enough to express how deeply I loved her. Besides, she was asking me for something that I wanted just as badly as she did. "I would do anything for you, Rose. I promise before we take off on this mission, I will sweep you off your feet and carry you off to bed. I only hope I can live up to your expectations."

"You've already surpassed them, you idiot," she whispered, sliding closer to me.

Every worry slipped away as she kissed me. If this amazing woman believed in me, I figured I had to be worth something.

Right then and there, I made a silent vow. Before we set out on our mission, I was going to give her the most magical romantic night I could put together on short notice...

...A roar in the distance jarred me from my thoughts, and my heart sank. With everything that'd been going on in preparation for the mission, time had gotten away from me. I never planned that romantic night, and we set off on our mission without me giving Rose the only thing she'd ever asked me for.

Nauseated by the thought of how colossally I'd failed her, I walked to the edge of the stream and sat down on a flat rock sticking up out of the Water.

Benjamin scowled at me as he sat down beside me. "There's no time for breaks, kid."

The massive foot of a foul-smelling beast stomped down next to me, but I didn't flinch now that I knew other creatures instinctively avoided Benjamin's shadow. "Yeah? Well, is there time for death? Because I can't go on like this forever."

"Enough with the fucking drama. We're close, you know."

"We are?"

Benjamin stood up, as if I'd agreed to start moving again. "Yeah, Emma's mother isn't far from here."

"How can you tell?"

"I recognize the landscape."

If I wasn't too exhausted to argue, I would've called him on his bullshit. As far as I could tell, our surroundings looked exactly the same as they'd looked since the moment we entered the stream. "What difference will a few more minutes make?"

"She could be dead in a few minutes."

I pushed myself to my feet with a muffled groan of protest. "Does Emma even care what happens to her mother? The woman never did anything to stop her father from hurting her."

"Yeah, and the woman who raised you treated you like shit your whole life," Benjamin replied matter-of-factly, "but you'd still feel like an asshole for letting her die."

"Wow, tell me how you really feel."

I'm not sure what Benjamin was going to say back because a blood-curdling scream rang out through the forest, bringing every other sound in the vicinity to a screeching halt.

"What the hell was that?" I whispered.

"That was our cue to exit the stream." With that, Benjamin started scrambling up the side of the embankment.

"Of course it was," I muttered, shaking my head as I followed him.

As I reached the top, the sight ahead made my blood run cold. A gangly bald-headed demon had a fairy—who bore a pretty strong resemblance to Emma—pinned up against the trunk of a rotting tree. In the distance behind them, the rest of her tribe was scurrying off in every direction, fleeing like rats from the predators who'd pounced on their territory.

Benjamin let his shadow slip away as we moved toward the demon, who I realized was holding a knife to the fairy's throat as we got closer. "I would drop that knife if I were you."

The demon's head whipped in our direction, and a grin spread across his grotesquely disfigured face. "Well, fairy, you must be someone of great importance to deserve such a rescue."

The fairy's eyes widened as they darted between us and the demon, as if she couldn't decide who to fear more.

"Let her go, you son of a bitch," Benjamin snarled, flicking his hand in the demon's direction.

The knife slipped from the demon's hand and he dropped to his knees, howling as he pressed his hands to his eyes while a steady stream of blood oozed down his cheeks. "Who are you?"

"You must be someone of no importance, if you don't already know," Benjamin replied.

As we moved closer, the demons in the distance all abandoned their fairy prey and started slinking toward us. I couldn't tell what sort of creatures they were because their forms were cloaked somehow. Only their blurry outlines were visible, even to my dragon eyes. All I knew for sure was that there were lots more of them than there were of us, but Benjamin didn't seem concerned by the odds.

We kept advancing, and so did those blurred silhouettes in the dark.

As I watched the unidentifiable creatures move toward us with my heart in my throat, a row of dragons stepped out of the shadows behind them and began closing in on them. A grin spread across my face as I realized all the dragons who'd gone off to aid other battles were now returning to help us.

Some of the creatures moving toward us began to panic, but the ones in front kept their composure as far as I could tell from their steady movements. A chorus of hissing sounds rose from our dragon friends as they bathed the ground in their fiery breath, forming a ring of flames around our mutual enemies.

Most of the creatures started whimpering like frightened dogs, but the two in the lead kept moving toward us. "All this fuss just for the fairy Queen's Unsighted mother?" the taller silhouette mused from the shadows, his deep voice as indistinct as his appearance.

"This is the part where you stand down," Benjamin said as we stood our ground at the center of the ring of fire.

"No, I'm afraid you were given the wrong script," the one in front replied as he stepped into view.

The sight of the would-be-king made my stomach drop. "Godric."

"Hello, son," he replied, meeting my gaze with a wicked grin. "It's good to see you again."

A puff of orange smoke escaped my flared nostrils. "Wish I could say the same."

"You can," the smaller figure said as she stepped out of the shadows and moved to Godric's side. Rose smiled at me, but her lovely doe eyes were fearful and glistening with tears.

The instant our eyes met, my scent started bleeding through the air. "It *is* good to see you, Rose."

She took a step closer so that I could almost taste that delectable floral scent of hers that I'd been missing so desperately. "Do you mean that?"

"Yeah, I do. I haven't been able to stop thinking about you since you left Zeke's mirage with the Purists. It's not too late, Rose. Come back with us, so—"

"So you can lock her up in a dungeon?" Godric growled. "Tell me something, Charlie. Don't you find it interesting that we're all out here in the thick of things, whilst your Dragon King is sitting safe and sound back at home?"

"You've been in hiding for years," I snarled. "Am I supposed to be impressed that you finally decided to make an appearance on the battlefield?"

A grin of amusement spread across Godric's face. "I take it from your tone that you are not. Tell me then, what are you thinking? Penny for your thoughts."

As soon as those words left his mouth, the ring of fire surrounding our enemies died off and our dragon allies stopped advancing on Godric's soldiers.

I turned to Benjamin. "What's happening?"

"Sorry, kid," Benjamin said, his Dark voice thick with regret. "We can't win this one." He took to the shadows, vanishing from sight before I could respond. An instant later, he drew Emma's mother in with him.

But he didn't take me.

A wave of nausea washed over me as I stared at the spot where he'd been standing seconds ago. I knew that me joining Godric's side was part of the plan, but seeing Benjamin abandon me like that still felt like a gut-wrenching betrayal.

"It's time for you to come home now, Charlie," Godric said as he and Rose stepped closer. "Even the Darkness recognizes that your place is with us."

I could hear Godric talking, but his words sounded garbled and distant. The closer Rose got to me, the harder it was for me to think straight. Her intoxicating scent was scrambling my brain, making it impossible to focus on anything—except how much I'd missed her, and how desperately I needed her. My scent intensified, mingling with hers as she planted a kiss on my cheek. "Penny for your thoughts," she whispered.

Orange flames filled my eyes as a familiar rush of warmth spread through my insides, the way it did each time I'd unknowingly ingested Godric's blood wine— back before I had any idea who he really was. *Penny for your thoughts*: How many times had I heard Godric say those words? That had to be the trigger phrase for Godric's will to take control of the souls who'd been infected with his blood.

I fought through the mental haze, forcing myself to revisit that horrific moment when Rose had turned on us during the mission. *When all hell was breaking loose at the Purists' meeting place, the demon restraining Rose whispered something in her ear. Her eyes glazed over in response,* exactly like the dragons who'd just turned on us to side with the Purists. *Rose snapped Pip's neck because Godric's blood took control of her actions.* Her mind had been poisoned by his venomous intent the instant that demon said the magic words.

"Your place is with us." Godric's voice was just a faint echo as Rose's scent overpowered everything else— until there was nothing else—and the mental fog reclaimed me.

I opened my mouth to tell Godric to go to hell, but then I looked at Rose.

I could *feel* how much she needed me. Rose's desire for me to side with her was screaming at me loud and clear, filling me with an overwhelming sense of urgency. Flames filled my eyes as a feral need, to provide whatever my soul mate desired, consumed me.

I had chosen the rest of our team over her on our mission, and the hurt in her eyes had gutted me. *What the fuck had I been thinking?*

Rose was my dearest treasure. She was more important to me than anything else ever could be. I would never betray her like that again.

Godric was right. My place was with them.

My place was with Rose.

19

ROSE

Charlie and I were sitting on a loveseat in front of a roaring fire in the parlor of Godric Manor, safe and sound within the mirage that concealed the rightful King's headquarters. Louise and Godric were in the armchairs on either side of us discussing strategic matters—at least, I think they were. To be honest, I don't think either of us were paying attention to them.

Thankful as I was to have Charlie with me again, a seed of dread had been steadily taking root inside me. Godric was right. He'd assured me that my sway over Charlie was more powerful than his control over every soul who'd been marked with his blood, but I never would've believed him if I wasn't witnessing it with my own eyes.

I turned toward Charlie, wondering how long it would take him to come to his senses. If I could, I would've begged him to get me out of there. But Godric's hold over me was too absolute. No matter how hard I tried to break free, my actions were beyond my control. So I'd been desperately praying for someone to come and free me from this hellish nightmare. Instead, I'd dragged the soul I treasured most into the flames with me.

Charlie smiled at me as he wrapped an arm around my waist and drew me a bit closer.

Was this just an act? Maybe he was waiting for the right moment to tell me this was all part of the plan to rescue me. "It's been a long day," I whispered to him. "I think I'm going to head upstairs and get some rest."

Louise stopped talking midsentence and narrowed her eyes at me. "You've no need to rest, Rose. Your body is sedated in the waking world."

I feigned a sheepish grin. "Fine. You caught me. I'm just anxious to bring Charlie upstairs and have him all to myself for a while."

Louise opened her mouth to object, but Godric shushed her with a subtle gesture of his hand. "These young lovebirds have been apart long enough, Louise. I think they deserve some time alone."

Flames filled Louise's eyes as she glared at the rightful King, but she held her tongue.

I smiled at Charlie as I stood from the loveseat, and the affectionate grin he responded with sent a thrill through me in spite of our dire circumstances. "Would you like me to show you upstairs?"

Charlie's smile widened as he stood up beside me. "I thought you'd never ask." He took my hand in his, and we left the room without another word to the rightful King and Queen.

We made our way up the stairs with our fingers entwined, and the burgeoning sense of dread inside me intensified as I led him down the hall.

"This is my room," I said, stopping at the door. Then I opened it and tugged him inside.

A wicked grin spread across his face as he shut the door. "Alone at last."

I watched him—studying the handsome features I'd been so desperate to see again—as I waited for him to drop the act. I would've asked him outright if I could, but I was physically incapable of doing or saying anything that went against Godric's wishes. It was as if someone had flipped a switch inside me that horrific day at the Purists' headquarters, making it impossible for me to control my own actions or even my own desires.

Unlike me, I knew Charlie was strong enough to resist Godric's control. I'd watched him fight and overcome it, the day we rescued Emma and Nellie from Godric. So I waited for him to let me in on the plan, but he just smiled and pulled me into his arms. "I've missed you like you wouldn't believe," he said, kissing my lips between words.

Tears filled my eyes as I whispered, "I've missed you too." All I could do was pray that he'd see my tears and sense what I wasn't strong enough to say.

An apologetic frown replaced Charlie's smile as we moved deeper into my room; and for a moment, the dread within me subsided because I assumed he was dropping the act—until he spoke. "I'm so sorry I fought against you at the end of our mission, Rose."

"I killed Pip," I muttered in a broken whisper. *Surely reminding him of that would be enough to break whatever spell he was under?*

He shook his head as he maneuvered us closer to the bed. "None of that matters now."

I searched his eyes, desperate to find some hint of the Charlie I knew. "How can you say that?"

"You and I can rule as we please after we take control of Draumer," he said, stopping to brush my hair aside and kiss his way down my neck. "Anything that happens along the way to that end is just unfortunate collateral damage. Pip's death wasn't your fault, Rose. I know that now."

For a few trembling breaths, I just stood there speechless. "I thought you hated me."

"I thought so, too, but I was wrong."

Struck by the oddest sensation that I was drowning in the torrent of dread steadily rising within me, I drew a ragged breath. "I don't understand."

"Nothing matters but the two of us," Charlie said as he slid my collar aside and brushed his lips along my collarbone, sending a warm shiver down my spine. "I was such a fool for not realizing that sooner." He lifted his head to meet my stare as his fingers worked their way down the buttons of my blouse, and the heat of his gaze was like a beacon of light to my drowning soul. "You have no idea how many hours I've spent wishing I could go back to our last night together in the waking world, Rose. Instead of arguing, I'd show you just how much you mean to me."

His words—and the feel of the air, chilling my flesh as he bared it—made my breath catch in my throat. "All I've ever wanted was for you to love me," I whispered as his hands slipped inside my unbuttoned blouse, replacing the chill with his warmth.

"I do love you, Rose." He pulled me closer, pressing my body against his, and his Dark scent flooded the room until it was so intense that it made me dizzy.

The dread inside me ebbed away as I rose up to my tiptoes, aligning our bodies so that I could feel how much he wanted me. This was all I ever needed, *him*—Dark, and intense, and undiluted. Nothing mattered but the heat radiating from his body, and my need to feel his flesh against mine.

"I treasure you above everything else, Rose," Charlie said, lifting me off the floor and holding me exactly where he wanted me as my legs wrapped around his waist. "This war doesn't matter. All that matters is that you and I are together again."

"But we need to end this war so we can go back to the way things were," I said as he sat down on the bed with my legs straddling his muscular frame. "I want us to go back to the waking world and make love there, so I can be yours entirely," I whispered as he peeled off my blouse and tossed it to the floor. "We need the fighting to end, Charlie."

Flames filled his eyes as I tugged off his shirt, and the flames leapt higher as I arched my back, pressing my chest against his. "Then let's end it," he growled as he unclasped my bra, tore it off, and tossed it to the floor.

"How?" I asked as his hands moved over the flesh he'd exposed while his lips brushed their way down my neck.

"We keep doing what you've already started doing," he said, breathing the words against my flesh as his mouth traveled lower, "striking where they're most vulnerable."

His mouth stopped as he reached my breasts—his lips and his tongue dominantly staking claim—and when his teeth grazed over my flesh, I stopped caring about our conversation.

This is wrong, a voice in my head whispered. *Charlie should hate me for helping Godric devastate our friends.* I wanted to remind him of that. Instead I said, "We've already sent the Purists after all of their loved ones."

"Not all of them," Charlie growled as the palm of his hand slid down my stomach at a torturous pace that made it almost impossible for me to keep still.

I wanted to ask him to stop talking like that and beg him to get us away from these monsters, *but I couldn't.* "If there are more targets," I whispered as I watched him unfasten the button on my pants, "we should go tell Godric."

"Godric can wait," Charlie snarled as his hand dove inside my panties, drawing a breathless gasp from me. "I've waited long enough."

The room around us spun as his fingers caressed my flesh—driving me to the point of desperation, and then slipping inside me—setting my insides on fire.

A devilish grin spread across his face as he flipped us both over in one swift movement that landed me on my back with the weight of his body between my legs. When he pulled back, peeling the rest of my clothing down my legs and tossing it to the floor, I forgot all about wanting to escape. The only thing I needed was to stay like this…with him…forever.

"This is all I've been able to think about," he groaned as he drank in the sight of me, naked and wanting beneath him. "I've been desperate to taste you, since the very first time your scent hit the air in my presence."

As he kissed his way up my inner thigh, I forgot how to breathe; and with one broad masterful stroke, the heat of his tongue erased every concern from my mind.

A carnal moan escaped me as I sunk my hands in his hair, holding him exactly where I needed him.

Both worlds could burn and it wouldn't matter, as long as Charlie and I never left this bed.

20

ADDISON

We were seated at a massive oak table eating dinner in my husband's quaint little castle by the Water's edge. James was sitting beside me, staring at me with a look of wonder in his eyes. Bob was seated on my other side with Nellie next to him, and our boys—Bob and Danny—were across the table from us. Our sons had no memory of me, but they seemed to sense our connection on some level because they'd welcomed me into their home almost instantly. I couldn't remember the last time I had felt so utterly at peace.

James smiled at me as he watched me eat. "Tell me you plan to stay with us."

I set my fork down on my plate with an apologetic sigh. "I'm afraid I can't stay, and neither can you. We came to get you out of here."

He lowered his eyes to his plate with a nod. "Because of the gabble ratchets."

When he looked up at me, I frowned at the knowing expression on his face, feeling as though the tables had somehow turned. "The what?"

"Gabriel hounds," he said, and when I responded with a blank expression, "Hell hounds?"

My heart sunk because I was familiar with them.

James studied me with a somber grin. "Judging by the look on your lovely face, I take it you know what those are."

"I do. How long have they been in the area?"

"I've lost track," he said as he stabbed a piece of meat with his fork, "but it's been long enough for me and my sons to be the only remaining members of our settlement."

"There were more of you?"

"Lots more," he whispered. "Some made it to safety—at least, I hope they did. It's become quite clear that the hounds are here for me and my boys."

A wave of nausea washed over me as I looked at our children's sweet innocent faces. How could any soul be evil enough to murder children to weaken their opposition?

Bob placed a hand my arm, grounding me. "We'll figure a way out of this."

"Hell hounds never lose the scent of their prey," I said, turning toward him. "They will never stop hunting them."

Bob shook his head. "Then we'll just have to take them out."

"How do you take out a target you can't see?" I asked, blinking back tears. "Hell hounds are invisible."

James placed a gentle hand on my arm. "I do have a plan I've been contemplating."

I turned back to him, hoping with all my heart that he had a viable solution. "What is it?"

"Well, I'm something of a wizard when it comes to chemical reactions," he replied with a humble grin, pulling a small vile from the pocket of his jacket. "This should be enough to do the trick."

"What is it?" Nellie asked, leaning forward in her seat.

James held the vial out so she could get a better look. "It's called Greek fire, and there's no putting it out once the flames erupt. If we could lure all the hounds into one contained area and then let this loose, that would be the end of them."

Bob raised an eyebrow. "Then what've you been waiting for?"

My husband shrugged. "I've no way to launch it. That bit of weaponry was destroyed when the first members of our tribe tried to take the beasts out."

Nellie leaned back in her chair with a sigh. "Then what good is that fire stuff to us?"

"Children," James said, in the same gentle paternal voice that he used to read their bedtime stories in the waking world, "why don't you go and play in your room while the grown-ups talk?"

The boys nodded and smiled at me as they got up from the table and left the room.

"I've been holding out for as long as I could," James whispered. "But I suppose in the end, I've always known I would have to let the hounds inside the castle. Once my boys make a run for it, I can unleash the fire and destroy them along with myself."

I shook my head. "You can't sacrifice yourself like that. Those boys need you."

"Better me than them," James replied with a calm resolve that turned my stomach.

"Let me do it," I whispered. "We can lure the hounds inside with your scent. Then once they're all inside the castle, you can run out the back with our boys while I take them out."

"Our boys?" James muttered.

"What?"

"You said *our* boys," he replied with a pensive frown.

"Oh, I guess…I misspoke."

The sad half smile on his face suggested he wasn't convinced. "Do you really expect me to let the woman of my dreams sacrifice herself for me, just a few hours after she walked into my life?"

"Maybe we can wait a day or two," I said.

"Absolutely not," James replied, laying his hand on top of mine. "I would never allow any harm to come to you."

I thought of the two of us in my dorm room all those years ago. *I would never hurt you, Addie. Never.* "You just met me," I whispered.

Tears filled his eyes as he squeezed my hand. "And you've already captured my heart. It makes perfect sense to me now. You are the answer to my prayers. The boys seem as taken with you as I am. I know they'll be safe in your care, so I don't need to worry about them fending for themselves out in the world. You can watch over them, and I can end this knowing that they will be all right."

"Don't you dare," I muttered, pulling my hand away from his as I stood up from the table. "I just found you. I won't let you leave me."

"I'm not leaving you," he whispered, standing up beside me. "I'm entrusting you with everything that matters to me."

"I won't let you," I said, melting against him as his arms wrapped around me. "It has to be me."

"Addie," Bob whispered as he stood up behind me. "Why do you think I'm here?"

My stomach dropped as I turned to him. "No…you can't."

"It has to be me, Addie," Bob said as he touched my cheek. "I should have died decades ago when that bullet hit my brain. Why do you suppose I survived?"

A tear slid down my cheek as I whispered, "Because you weren't meant to die."

"No, Addie," he said, wiping away my tear. "I believe I stuck around so that I could save the day for you one more time, and this is it. I can feel it. This is what I was made for."

I looked at Nellie, hoping she would chime in and take my side.

"He won't be alone," Nellie said as she stood up beside her soul mate.

I swore I could feel my heart shattering into a million pieces. "There has to be another way."

Nellie shook her head. "Don't you see? This is how I redeem myself for all the wrongs I've done."

"No," I whispered. "I can't lose any of you. My heart couldn't take it."

"You've done your part to make this world a better place," Bob said, brushing another tear from my cheek with a loving smile. "You served bravely in the nomadic knighthood, protecting the Unsighted for years. Now it's time for you to get your family to safety and live the rest of your life in peace. You'll still be watching over the Unsighted. It will just be a smaller tribe. This is what I was made for, Addie. It's a noble death. Dying old and feeble—on some couch in front of a television in that other world—was never how I was meant to end. But I have to end this alone. I need you to promise you'll take Nellie with you."

"You stubborn old fool," Nellie muttered under her breath. "There's no way I'm leaving you behind."

21

BRIAN

Tristan, Zeke, and I had been walking through the forest for so long that I was pretty sure all three of us were going out of our damn minds at this point. Physical exhaustion led to mental fatigue, which made it harder to tune out the dryads' discouraging words.

You are wasting your time, soldier, they whispered in my head as we marched on in silence. *No matter how many noble deeds you perform, you will never be any better than your good-for-nothing father.*

I shook my head and tried to remind myself that their taunts were meaningless. The dryads were just trying to get under my skin—and I'd be damned if they weren't doing a fantastic job.

Your mother was right. You are just like him. That's why she gave all her love to Tristan, even though you were the son she carried in her womb. She knew how rotten you truly were, just like that selfish incubus who fathered you. You'll never be good enough, and you will never be worthy of any woman's love.

I sunk my teeth into my bottom lip, hard enough to draw blood, and focused on the pain to distract myself from their voices. A glance at the expressions on Tristan and Zeke's faces told me they were both trapped in their own private hells.

Someone in our group needed to keep a clear head, so I forced myself to think of a memory that was stronger than the dryads' power to resurrect my demons...

...If it'd been up to me, I never would've tapped into my charm because anything that came from my dad was tainted. But I'd never really been able to escape what I was.

My sergeant had hated me since the moment his commander went over his head and accepted me into the nomadic knighthood. When he was young, an incubus had wronged his family by manipulating his sister with his charm. In his mind any man with incubus blood in his veins was evil incarnate, and he spent the majority of my training telling me that and trying to break me.

Ironically enough, it was my charm that saved his life on the battlefield a few years later. We'd been embroiled in a chaotic mess of hand-to-hand combat for hours when my sergeant got knocked off his horse by a sorrow. The potbellied demon was hunched over his body with a blade at his throat when I reached them. "You know what to do," I'd murmured, blasting the sorrow with my charm till he backed away from the sergeant and sliced his own throat.

After that, the sergeant decided my charm was an invaluable asset. And despite my conviction to devote my life to a noble calling among my elven brothers, I found myself interrogating enemies with my charm. I could make them spill their guts faster than any method of torture ever could. I could even get them to finish themselves off after they outlived their usefulness. And I could take down an enemy on the battlefield by stunning him with my charm so he'd stand there—hard as a fucking rock—as he watched me walk up and run my blade through him. Sometimes the poor bastards even came before they bled out.

The ends justified the means. That's what I kept on telling myself as I hiked through the Dark Forest toward the Purists' auction site. Those sons of bitches did unspeakable things to their captives, so anything I did to them would be well deserved.

As I reached the hilltop post that Zeke had described in perfect detail, I grinned at the two trolls standing sentry over the Purists' meeting place in the valley down below. "Evening, boys," I murmured, laying the charm on nice and thick as they watched me approach with their mouths hanging open.

A lecherous grin spread across the fatter one's dirt-smudged face. "Hello, beautiful. What do you want?"

"Oh, I don't know," I said with a shrug. "I think I'd like to watch you big fellas fight to the death."

The less chubby troll scratched his head. "Why the hell would we do that?"

I flashed him a killer smile. "Because the winner gets to spend the night with me."

Without another word, the morons both turned, grabbed their swords, and stabbed each other in unison as if it'd been choreographed.

I let out a laugh as I strolled past them, both of them still eyeing my every move even as the light drained from their eyes. "Rotten luck, fellas. Guess I'll have to find someone else to warm my bed tonight."

As I approached the meeting place down in the valley, the demon standing guard outside the building narrowed his pitch-black eyes at me. According to Zeke, the dark-haired pretty boy warded their buildings with blood magic so he could detect the presence of a captive's relative. He'd also concocted some sort of spell to mute Davina's charm—which was no small trick, since Zeke's sister was a pure-blooded succubus.

I squared my shoulders as I stepped up to him, his striking good looks leading me to believe there was a touch of incubus blood in his veins.

He flashed me a wide grin, displaying a set of razor sharp teeth that knocked his sex appeal down several notches. "What brings a nice boy like you to a place like this?" he asked in a highborn demonic accent.

"What makes you think I'm a nice boy?" I said, lacing my words with a hefty dose of charm.

He let out a deep-throated chuckle as his eyes wandered over me. "Those pointed ears of yours."

"Looks can be deceiving," I replied, biting my lower lip.

His eyes dropped to my lips with a hushed groan that he probably didn't even realize he'd let slip. "All right. Same question then," he said, his accent a bit thicker than when he first spoke. "What brings a man with elven blood to our door?"

I raked my teeth over my bottom lip, drawing his attention back to my mouth. "Same thing that brings any man to your door."

The demon raised an eyebrow. "Which is?"

"You've got something that I want."

He let out another muffled groan. "Is that so?"

"Yeah, she's inside."

He scowled at me and shook his head. "It's not nice to tease a man like that."

"There you go, assuming I'm nice again."

"Actually, I am really hoping you're not," he said, licking his lips as he sized me up. "But humor me, and tell me why a member of the nomadic knighthood would be interested in our merchandise."

"Your slavers took a creature I've had my eye on for a long time. I'd been waiting years for her to reach maturity before I claimed her, and your boys came along and snatched her right out from under my nose."

"Finders keepers," he said with a shrug. "Isn't that the expression?"

"I don't give a fuck about expressions. I just want what's mine."

"If she is here, she's not yours."

"I'm willing to pay top dollar," I said, glancing at the door behind him, "but I want her untouched."

He let out a demonic chuckle. "That is not how we do things here."

I cranked the charm up a little higher. "I don't give a damn how you do things. That's what I want."

He inched close enough for me to smell the fermented blood on his breath. "Perhaps we could come up with a mutually beneficial arrangement."

I wrapped a hand around the hilt of his sword and pulled it toward me, drawing him closer without breaking eye contact. "I'm sure I could think of something that'd make it worth your while."

Aroused but still wary, he covered my hand with his to prevent me from making a move for his blade.

"Aw, come on," I murmured close to his ear. "I'll let you touch mine."

His eyelids drooped lower. "I could find a room for us now."

I drew him closer by the hilt of his blade. "No. First I want proof that the girl is untouched."

"Proof?"

"Let me inside, so I can get her alone in a room with me. Then we'll work out the details between us. Hell, maybe I'll even have her join us, but I'm not agreeing to anything till I inspect the merchandise."

"Suit yourself," he said, licking his lips, "but I expect compensation when you're done with the girl."

"You got it," I said as he opened the door and waved me in. To quell any lingering doubts he might have, I grabbed him by the collar and pulled him into a kiss as I charmed all suspicion from his mind. Then I winked at him, stepped inside, and shut the door.

As I made my way into the crowded meeting room, a gorgeous blonde shadow in a skintight gown welcomed me with a seductive smile. "Hello, handsome. What brings you to our party?"

"I'm interested in a girl who was taken from an Unsighted settlement," I said, cranking up the charm. "I was planning to take her for myself before your goons snatched her up."

"What sort of girl?" she asked in a throaty whisper. "I could be your girl. Free of charge."

I shook my head. "She's a succubus, and I'm willing to pay whatever it takes to acquire her untouched."

She let out a breathy chuckle that made me want to bash her pearly-white teeth in. "It may be too late for that."

I shoved a hand in my pocket and pulled out a handful of gemstones. "Just show her to me."

"My goodness," she said as her gaze moved from the gems to my face, and then shamelessly lower. "You certainly are an impatient fellow, with a barely concealed temper. Now I really want to play with you."

"I'm only interested in untouched merchandise, and you don't fit the bill."

"Well, I can't argue with that," she said, reaching for the stones in my hand.

I stuffed the gems back in my pocket. "Show me the girl first. I want proof that she's unspoiled."

A wicked grin spread across the shadow's face. "And what if she isn't?"

"I'd have to rethink my price," I said, suppressing the urge to strangle her.

"She's this way." Taking me by the hand, the shadow led me across the room and down a narrow hall to a closed door. "Enjoy," she whispered as she reached around me to unlock the room.

I winked at her as I slipped inside and shut the door. Then I turned around, and my heart stuttered the instant the girl's eyes met mine. A split second later, she dropped her gaze to the floor in a fearful, subservient manner that turned my stomach.

Zeke's sister was huddled in the corner across the room with her wrists and ankles bound by thick cords of rope, doing her best to hide her nakedness with her long dark hair and tethered limbs.

Tears filled my eyes as I stepped toward her, shedding my coat and shirt.

She let out a hushed whimper and shrank from me as I knelt down in front of her.

"I'm not here to hurt you," I whispered, wrapping my shirt around her. Then I took out my knife. When she responded with a strangled sob, I said, "I'm going to cut these restraints now. All right?"

She nodded but kept her eyes averted, and my heart ached at the way she trembled as I placed her bound hands in my palm to still their shaking so I could slice through the rope.

"I came to get you out of here," I said. "I was sent by your family."

A tear slid down her beautiful face as she looked up at me. "My family is dead."

"You're just gonna have to trust me," I said, lacing my words with a bit of charm to calm her, and hating myself for doing it...

...The sky was pitch-dark as we neared the edge of the forest. My eyes couldn't make out the settlement by the Water in the distance ahead, but I could smell it. The unmistakable scents of blood and death hung thick as smoke in the breezeless night air.

"Fuck," I muttered as we stepped from the trees.

A dainty porcelain-skinned demon with long black hair, full pink lips, and a gown of pink silk stepped out from behind a rotting tree and grinned at us. "You're too late, boys."

Zeke let out a growl as he stepped toward her. "What the hell are you talking about?"

Her ghostly pink eyes flickered in the dark as she shook her head. "You came to protect that Unsighted woman who raised the rightful King's son in the waking world, did you not?"

I moved past her toward the shore, confident that Tristan and Zeke had my back. Behind me, the demon giggled as I surveyed the wreckage for signs of life. Burnt remnants of the settlement were scattered all over the ground, along with a disturbing amount of blood—but not one body, living or dead.

I turned back to the demon. "Where is she?"

A grin spread across her pretty face. "Who?"

Zeke grabbed her by the collar of her dress, yanking her off the ground. "Charlie's mother, you evil little bitch."

"You know, I had no idea the soldiers I was ordered to wait for would be so"—she paused midsentence, raking her eyes over the half-giant's muscular frame—"delicious."

"I will split your fucking skull, she-devil," Zeke growled. "Start talking or—"

"Zeke," Tristan murmured, "you catch more flies with honey."

A growl rumbled in the base of Zeke's throat as he let the demon drop to her feet. "I don't wanna catch her. I wanna crush her."

A dazzling smile spread across Tristan's face as he touched the demon's arm. "We don't blame you for what happened here."

"Oh no, please do," she said, grinning at Tristan the way people always grinned at him—like they'd gladly let him do absolutely anything he pleased to them.

"What happened to Charlie's mom?" my brother asked, his voice smooth as silk. "Have the Purists taken her somewhere?"

She licked her full pink lips as she shook her head. "Oh, you sweet innocent man."

"There's nothing innocent about me," Tristan murmured, cranking the charm up higher.

Her smile widened as she took a step toward me. "You're wasting your time here, boys."

"And why's that?" I asked.

"You traveled all this way just to save that wretched woman who caused our ruler's heir so much pain during his formative years," she said as she started walking toward the Water.

"What's it to you?" Zeke growled as the three of us followed her.

The demon shrugged. "It's nothing to me. I could care less about that worthless woman, or any other Unsighted cretin who inhabits the fringe."

"You're just spouting nonsense," Tristan said, falling into step beside her.

"No," she replied, "I'm making perfect sense. You boys just aren't listening."

Zeke grabbed a fistful of the demon's hair and yanked her back toward him. "So fucking say it in plain English."

"Oh, I almost forgot," she whispered, her pink eyes twinkling with amusement. "Charlie asked me to say hello to you boys. After he assured us that he didn't care what happened to that filthy Unsighted bitch who raised him, we decided to switch things up a little."

"What does that mean?" Zeke snarled, yanking the demon's hair so hard that she lost her footing for a second. When she let out a shriek and started clawing at his hand, he let her drop on her ass. "Start talking."

"We didn't kill her here," the demon whispered, grinning up at Zeke. "We finished her off in the waking world."

Tired of this demon wasting our time, I grabbed her, dragged her the rest of the way to the shore, and sent her sprawling toward a pile of debris. "What the fuck are you talking about?"

She pushed herself back to her feet and winked at Zeke as he and Tristan caught up to us. "Charlie has joined his father, and he is quite anxious to end all this fighting so he can get on with his happily-ever-after."

Zeke took her by the chin and turned her deceptively sweet face in his direction. "What the hell are you babbling about?"

"Rose was quite helpful in guiding us toward Unsighted targets whose deaths would weaken our enemies," she said, grinning despite Zeke's grip on her jaw. "But the intel we've now received from Charlie has been invaluable. I think you boys especially will be moved by what Godric's son has set into action."

"I'm about five fucking seconds away from crushing your skull," Zeke growled, tightening his grip on her face.

"Charlie told us where to find that woman who raised him in the waking world so we could go to her there before you reached her here in Draumer," the demon said, grinning at Zeke like the cat that ate the damn canary. "Our men left that Unsighted piece of filth lying on her living room carpet, drenched in her own blood."

Zeke grabbed a fistful of her hair and gave it a violent tug as he snarled at her.

"They slit her throat," the demon continued, in a matter-of-fact tone that had me seconds away from finishing her off myself.

Having no further use for this demon, I was debating whether or not to give Zeke the signal to end her.

Before I could come to a decision, the demon sealed her own fate. "Oh, and here's something you boys might find interesting. We found it delightfully efficient to eliminate our target while her rescuers were racing through the wrong world to save her. So after we finished off Charlie's mom, he told us about that sweet little succubus you boys are so fond of. What's her name?"

"No," Zeke muttered, ripping the hair in his fist clean off her head.

"Davina," she growled without even flinching. "You boys tucked her away in the Light Realm for safe keeping, but nobody thought to concern themselves with how vulnerable the poor girl is in the waking world."

As Zeke moved to wrap his hands around her throat, she lunged forward and sunk her teeth into his forearm.

The half-giant pulled her off and tossed her to the ground. Then he stumbled back, clutching his arm in wide-eyed confusion as he collapsed.

The demon's laughter hit me like a blow to the chest as Tristan dropped to his knees beside his oldest and dearest friend. "Oh my, did I forget to mention that I'm half innocente? My saliva is poison. One bite from me, and it's game over for you."

Zeke's breathing stopped before she even finished her sentence.

I yanked her off the ground by the back of her neck, being careful to stay clear of her venomous mouth.

But she just kept laughing. "That half-giant was the only one of you who knew where to find your dear succubus in the waking world, wasn't he?"

"You're bluffing," I growled. "Charlie would never betray us like that."

A wicked grin spread across the demon's face. "Then how did I know the girl's name?"

A crunch punctuated the end of her sentence as I snapped her neck.

22

ADDISON

As James, Bob, Nellie, and I sat by the window—keeping watch for an enemy we'd never see coming—I couldn't shake the feeling that I'd been tethered to an anchor. James had cracked open a bottle of honey wine, and we were all just sitting there drinking as if this were any ordinary afternoon. With each sip I took, the anchor sunk a little lower, dragging me deeper, filling me with the urge to scream.

Shaking my head at the wrongness of it all, I set my glass down on the table. I'd tried so hard to get somebody to realize how stupid Bob's plan was—so they could help me talk him out of it—but everyone else seemed to think this was the perfect solution. Well, that's not entirely true. Judging by the paleness of James's complexion, I suspected he hated this as much as I did.

Too distraught to pretend nothing was wrong, I stood up from my chair and started pacing the floor. "I can't do this. How can you all just sit there sipping your wine and acting like this is all right?"

"It is all right," Bob said as he stood and crossed the room to me. "I am at peace with this decision, perhaps more at peace than I've ever been before."

"Then you're a cruel old man," I said in a broken whisper, "because this will break my heart. Do you honestly think I'll be able to live with myself after letting this happen?"

Bob smiled at me with a tenderness that brought tears to my eyes. "This is how it has to be, Addie. Please don't spend our last minutes together being angry with me."

"Then don't leave me," I muttered, choking back a sob. "I can't lose you. You're too important to me. I owe everything to you."

"And I you," Bob whispered, wrapping his arms around me.

Furious as I was with him, I dropped my head to his shoulder and hugged him back. "What do you mean?"

"What I am at my core, that's because of you. I'm not sure I could even consider myself a knight if it weren't for our past. I owe it all to you, my dear girl."

"If you owe me, then do what I'm asking and let me take your place."

"No one in this castle would ever let you do that, Addison," he replied softly. "You have always undervalued your own life. Do you realize how much good you've done? I know how much you had to overcome to transform yourself into the valiant warrior you are today, and I couldn't be prouder of you."

A tear slid down my cheek as I looked up at him. "This can't be how it ends for us."

A nostalgic grin spread across his face as he wiped away my tear. "I can't imagine a more perfect ending."

"How about all of us getting out of here alive?"

Across the room, James pushed his chair back from the table. Setting his glass down with a resolute sigh, he stood and marched across the room to us. "This is all my fault. I'm the one those beasts out there are after. None of you should be sacrificing your life to destroy what's meant for me."

I reached out and took his hand without leaving Bob's arms. "I can't lose you either."

"You've only just met me," James muttered, glancing down at our hands. But there was no conviction behind his words because I think deep down he sensed that there was more to us.

"I love you, James. You and I are meant for each other. I know that sounds crazy, and I can't explain it, but—"

"The only crazy part," he said, giving my hand a squeeze, "is that it doesn't sound crazy at all."

"Tell me there's another solution," I whispered, looking from James to Bob, "because I can't lose either of you."

I was too overcome with emotion to notice the barking in the distance, let alone process the fact that it'd been steadily growing louder. In fact, all three of us were so engrossed in our heartfelt exchange that none of us realized Nellie had left the room until my children came running up the stairs.

"They're back, Daddy," Danny whimpered.

The color drained from Bob's face as we dropped the hug. "Where's Nellie?"

My firstborn tugged on his namesake's sleeve. "She told us to go find the grownups and get you all to the back exit."

"For the love of God, Nellie," Bob muttered as he rushed toward the stairs.

The barking of the hell hounds seemed to grow louder—echoing inside my head, and chilling me to the bone—as the rest of us followed him.

We reached the top of the staircase to find Nellie standing at the bottom. A loving grin spread across her youthful face as she looked up at us. "All of you belong together. I feel truly blessed to have spent the end of my life with you." Before any of us could respond, Nellie pulled James's vial of Greek fire from her sleeve and uncorked it. "Thank you for everything," she said, smiling at Bob as she threw the vial at the stairs.

"What the hell are you doing, woman?" Bob hollered as the vial smashed, engulfing the staircase in flames. "The hounds aren't even inside."

Nellie's eyes glistened with tears as she met Bob's tortured gaze and backed away from the stairs. "Now there's the crusty old man who stole my heart in the waking world." With that, she opened the front door.

Lured by the scent of their targets, the hounds came spilling in despite the flames. Although we couldn't see them, a chorus of bone-chilling snarls bounced off the walls and echoed up the stairwell as the invisible beasts backed Nellie up against the wall; and it wasn't long before all the growling was coming from inside the castle.

Once she was certain all the hounds were inside, Nellie began to make her way toward the door while the invisible beasts were busy snarling at James and the boys. Heart in my throat, I watched as she inched closer to the exit.

It all happened in the blink of an eye, yet somehow in the moment it felt like an eternity.

When Nellie's fingers finally connected with the edge of the door, I let out a sob of relief—that morphed into a horrified gasp as one of the beasts we couldn't see knocked her off her feet. Determined not to let any of the hounds escape, Nellie swung her leg out and kicked the door shut, closing off her only means of escape. With her fate now sealed, she scrambled to her feet and flattened her body up against the wall as her eyes locked with mine. "Go! Get your husband and those beautiful boys of yours to safety, and take care of our knight in shining armor for me."

The flames were spreading at an alarming rate, and the smoke was so thick that I could barely see Nellie as James wrapped an arm around my waist and steered me toward our boys. "We have to get them out of here," he shouted above the howling of the hounds.

I turned to take Bob's hand.

But he was gone.

Terrified by the thought of losing him, I lunged for the staircase.

James caught me by the arm. "We can't let their sacrifice be in vain."

I couldn't do this. How could I run away and leave that heroic knight who'd saved my life behind to die? "I can't go without Bob," I muttered, pulling away from my husband.

James grabbed our son Danny and pushed him into my arms. "You have to, Addie. You need to help me get the boys to safety."

I looked down at our son's cherubic face, slick with tears. I'd never realized before how much he looked like my brother, at the age he was when we were abducted. My life didn't matter. I would give it up in a heartbeat to save Bob. But that knight in shining armor, who I looked up to more than anyone, would want me to set my own needs aside and get the children out of harm's way. *That's what he did for me all those years ago.*

"I love you, Bob," I yelled over my shoulder as James and I raced toward the door with our sons in our arms.

Minutes later, we dropped to the ground at the forest's edge, coughing and gasping for breath. Tears streamed down my cheeks as I turned to my husband. "I'm so sorry, James. I can't let it end like this." As soon as the words were out of my mouth, I pushed myself to my feet and started racing toward the castle.

I only made it a few strides before a massive explosion shook the ground beneath my feet, littering the air with a shower of sparks as the flames engulfed the entire castle by the Water's edge. The tortured wailing of the hounds filled my ears as I stood there, staring at the thick black smoke pouring from the windows of my husband's dream home.

James drew me into his arms the second he reached me, and I buried my face against his chest and broke down in tears.

We stayed there at the edge of the forest, watching in horror until all the hounds had stopped wailing and the sun had sunk below the Water. Still the fire burned on, lighting the darkness with its nightmarish glow, and I felt my heart melting along with the two precious souls inside.

If it took every last breath in my body, I intended to see to it that their deaths were not in vain. I would not rest until Godric paid for what he'd taken from me.

23

BOB

Tears stung my eyes and smoke scorched my lungs as I raced down the stairs through the flames, but I barely noticed the feel of my flesh burning. The only thing that mattered to me was the look of terror on Nellie's face as I reached the bottom of the staircase and pulled her into my arms. "Did you really think I would let you do this without me?"

"I hoped you would," she whispered, "because I don't want to watch the man I love die."

Tears streamed down my blistered cheeks as I kissed her lips. "Damn it, woman. Don't you know by now that there is no life for me without you?"

"Addison needs you," she muttered, shaking her head.

"No," I said, holding her tighter. "Addison will miss me, but she's got her husband and children. She's going to be fine. You're the one who needs me now."

"You're right. I do," she replied, clinging to me like a lifeline. "Thank you for saving me, Bob."

"I'm afraid I don't know how to save you from this," I confessed as the hounds and the flames inched closer, boxing us in.

A tear slid down her cheek as she shook her head. "You saved me the night you welcomed me to your shore, you old fool."

I smiled at her and stroked her cheek with my thumb. "Then we're even because you woke me up."

"Woke you up?"

"To everything that'd been missing from my life," I said, touching my forehead to hers. "My heart is yours, Nellie, and my place is with you till the bitter end."

"I don't think we're far from that end," Nellie sobbed as the howling of the hounds began to morph into panicked yelps.

"No, but that's all right. I can't think of a better way to end my life than with you in my arms."

She looked up at me, her porcelain cheeks slick with tears. "Do you think it will be enough?"

"What do you mean?"

"To make up for my sins."

I kissed the top of her head. "That was not your fault, Nellie. That evil son of a bitch tricked you into doing what you did to your daughter."

"Do you believe in heaven?" she asked, as if she hadn't heard me.

"I believe I found it when I first held you in my arms."

"No," Nellie muttered as the flames crept closer. "I mean, do you think she'll be there when I get there?"

"Yes," I said, hoping with all my heart that it was true.

"What if I don't end up in the same place as my Lilly, after what I've done?"

"You will," I replied with absolute confidence, "because you belong in heaven. You're an angel."

She let out a weak chuckle. "And you're an idiot."

"I'm serious," I whispered as she reached up and touched my cheek. "You are my angel, Nellie. You saved me, the day you woke me up to everything I'd been sleeping through. How could that not earn you a spot in heaven?"

"I don't know," she muttered. "Wherever we go, I just hope we're together."

"I'd refuse to go anywhere you weren't," I promised her as the flames reached our feet. "You said you didn't want to watch me die. So close your eyes. Tune out all the rest of this, and focus on what you feel for me."

She did as I said, and the wailing of the hounds filled my ears as I shut my eyes and kissed her. She kissed me back just as passionately, as if our lives depended on it.

And an overwhelming sense of peace washed over me as my life flashed before me...

...carrying Addie's broken little body in my arms, setting her in my backseat...her frightened eyes as the gunshot sounded...finding her on my shore in Draumer...teaching her to fight so that no monster could ever hurt her again...Charlie showing up on my shore, years after Addie had left...Charlie bringing Nellie and Lilly to my shore for safekeeping...Godric taking them, and me being powerless to stop him...meeting Pip in the forest...searching for the love of my life with his help...Addie coming back into my life after all those years...cradling Pip's tiny lifeless body in my

hands…Addie and Nellie loving me more than I ever deserved…

In that final breath as the flames engulfed us, I held my Nellie tight and thanked God for the man who'd brought us together. I was proud to have done my part to help Charlie fulfill his destiny and restore peace to Draumer.

24

BRIAN

My heart was pounding so hard I could hear it hammering inside my head, making it almost impossible to collect my thoughts. *How could I have been so wrong about Charlie?* I had trained the guy. I'd stood up for him when the boss was ready to send him packing. At every step of the way—whenever someone doubted him—I'd been in his corner, assuring whoever it was that Charlie belonged with us. Sickened that we'd welcomed him into our family, only to have him stab us in the back like this, I turned away from the body of the demon who'd just killed my brother's friend.

The sight of Tristan weeping over his fallen brother's body damn near incapacitated me as I started walking toward him. I stopped at Zeke's feet, but my brother didn't seem to notice me. So I cleared my throat.

"What the fuck do we do now?" Tristan asked without looking up.

"I don't know." It was my job to be my younger brother's rock, and I knew how much he was hurting; but all I could think about was Zeke's sister—out there somewhere in the waking world—completely unaware of the danger she was in.

Tristan's eyes remained fixed on Zeke as he stood up. "We can't leave his body here." When I didn't respond, he took a step back and narrowed his eyes at me. "Shit," he muttered, pulling me into a hug. "We'll get to her before they do, Brian."

Tristan's words delivered the fatal blow to the crack in my armor that'd been deepening since the moment that demon said Davina's name. Despite my determination to stay strong for my brother, I broke down in tears as I hugged him back. But it didn't take me long to regain my composure.

I couldn't afford to fall apart. There were too many souls depending on me. I was Emma's primary guard. The plan had been for me to help get Charlie's mom to safety, then go back to protecting the Queen. On top of that, Tristan had just lost his best friend, right on the heels of losing our mother. I wanted to stay strong for him, but all I could think about was my brief exchange with Davina before we left the Light Realm. *Promise me you'll come back.*

Not only had I promised Davina that I would come back, but I'd also promised her brother that she would be safe. Instead of making good on my promises, I'd let the person Davina loved most in the world die right in front of me—leaving her all alone, with no one to protect her from the monsters who were coming for her. "Davina doesn't have anyone now," I muttered.

A sorrowful smile spread across Tristan's face. "That's not true, Brian. She's got you, and her life is in danger. So you need to get over that whole I'm-not-worthy thing you've got going, and go save her."

I took a deep breath, willing my heart to stop pounding so I could hear myself think. "Well, obviously the Purists know where we are, since they fucking beat us here. So traveling through the Waters won't alert them to a damn thing they don't already know."

Tristan nodded. "So we grab Zeke's body and head back to the palace."

With nothing left to say, we hoisted the big guy up between us and carried him to the Water's edge. As the Water pulled us in, I let go of our fallen friend. It'd be less cumbersome for one of us to take him back through the Waters, and Zeke was my brother's loss to mourn.

With everything that was racing through my head, I was too distracted to even think about charming the Water creatures into speeding up my passage. So I let them carry me off as I let myself remember…

…Davina kept her eyes on her wrists, her fingertips hesitantly tracing the marks from the rope they'd bound her with, as she sat beside me on the floor. I'm not sure how long we sat there in silence—waiting for enough time to pass, so the bastards outside would think I'd done what they believed I was there to do—but after enough time passed without me laying a hand on her, Davina's curiosity seemed to surpass her fear. "Why did you come?" she asked in a timid whisper.

I looked up at her breathtakingly beautiful face, and hated myself for the way my heart skipped a beat. It wasn't right to react that way to her in the middle of all this. Realizing she was waiting for an answer, I cleared my throat. "I came to get you out of here."

She shifted toward me, searching my eyes. "But why?"

"Your brother sent me," I muttered, knowing it wouldn't make any sense to her but unable to think of anything else to say.

She dropped her eyes to the marks on her wrists. "I don't have a brother. I had a tribe mate who was like a brother to me, but they killed him after they brought us here."

"I'm sorry for your loss," I said, hating myself for not getting there soon enough to spare her that pain, "but you do have a brother by blood who you've never met. He's the one who sent me."

She studied me in silence for a few heartbeats, sizing me up with doe-eyed innocence. "If that's true, why didn't he come here himself?"

"He would have if he could, but these monsters ward their buildings with blood magic. They would've realized he was your kin and executed him before he ever got inside the building."

Tears filled her eyes as she shook her head. "I don't understand any of this. Why would anyone want to take me?"

Innocent as she was, I wasn't sure how to answer. I just thanked God I'd gotten there soon enough that she honestly might not know what they'd taken her for. They'd obviously manhandled her. Her body was covered in bruises, and her left ankle was swollen to twice the right one's size, but the scent of her virginity was still a blatant presence in the room. Nothing had ever smelled sweeter to me than the olfactory proof that I'd reached her in time.

"I'm not an idiot," she whispered.

"What?"

She glanced down at the shirt I'd taken off and wrapped around her naked body. "You were wondering how to explain what they'd want me for. I understand that. What I don't get, is why they would raid my home and kill everyone I love just to bring me here."

"These are wicked creatures. They don't give a damn about anything but themselves and their own twisted desires."

"But why would they desire me?"

Was it possible that she didn't realize how gorgeous she was? I cleared my throat. "It's about time for us to make our exit."

Fear replaced the confusion in her eyes. "How? I'm pretty sure I can't walk."

"I can carry you out of here," I said, patting my pocket as I added, "and I'm gonna offer them a heaping handful of gemstones as payment."

"Then why do you look so worried?"

"Because they're not real, and the guy who enchanted them to look like precious gems was only skilled enough to put a temporary spell on them. I don't have any idea when the magic will wear off and alert them to the fact that I'm paying for you with a bunch of river rocks."

She seemed oddly offended by that. "Then why didn't you bring real gems?"

"I would if I was wealthy enough to have them," I said, suppressing a grin, "but you don't get rich in my line of work."

She considered that for a second. "What is your line of work?"

"What do you say we get the hell out of here, and save the small talk for a less dangerous time?"

"Right," she whispered, blushing. "So what should I do?"

"*Pretend you're not happy with what happened in here, or the fact that I'm paying these assholes for ownership of you.*"

"*I'm not much of an actress.*"

"*Then just think about what'll happen if the stones in my pocket lose their magic, or what they did to you before I got here,*" I suggested. When she nodded, I whispered, "*Now or never.*" Then I scooped her slender body up in my arms and stood up from the floor. "*Just remember, you're not happy about leaving here with me.*"

"*I think I'll be plenty convincing if I look at the ones who took me.*"

The fear in her eyes turned my stomach, but it was exactly what we needed to make it out of there in one piece. So I opened the door with a regretful sigh. Then I carried her down the hall and stepped into the main room with her in my arms, clinging to me.

As the blonde shadow walked toward us with a wicked grin, Davina shuddered in my arms and buried her face against my shoulder.

I pulled the bag of stones from my pocket and held it out to her. "*Take them all. She's worth every cent.*"

The shadow's grin widened as she took the bag and dumped its contents into her palm. "*Care to stay and play with the rest of us for a while?*"

"*No,*" I said, thankful the magic was holding. "*I got what I came for.*"

"*Well, feel free to come back and visit whenever you like,*" the shadow replied as she reached out and stroked the back of Davina's head.

"*Get your fucking hands off my property,*" I growled, fighting the overwhelming urge to put Davina down and wrap my hands around this shadow's throat.

"What I wouldn't give for a few hours alone with that rage," the shadow said, retracting her hand. Leaning close to Davina's ear, she whispered, "You lucky girl."

Fury crackled through every fiber of my being. "Back the hell up, or I will bite your damn ear off."

The shadow narrowed her eyes at me, like she was debating whether or not to press her luck.

"I wouldn't push me," I snarled. "You were right. I'm not a patient man."

"Lucky, lucky girl," the shadow muttered as she backed away.

Afraid the spell on the stones might be dangerously close to expiring, I turned and started toward the exit.

We made it almost all the way to the door before the shadow's voice rose above all other noises in the room. "Stop that elf!"

"Shit," I muttered, drawing my sword. I slashed my way through the handful of startled demons between us and the door with Davina in my arms. But the rest of the partygoers weren't far behind as I yanked the door open, rushed out, and kicked it shut.

The dark-eyed demon licked his lips as I moved toward him, but I sliced the tip of my blade down the side of his face and knocked him aside.

He let out a howl and swung his sword, nicking my leg with the blade as I ran off. "I've got your blood now, elf," he shrieked. "I will get you back somehow!"

"Yeah, good luck with that," I hollered over my shoulder as we sped away. I tightened my grip on Davina as I sprinted toward the trees ahead and whispered, "We don't have far to go."

Ignoring the shouts from the mob behind us, I pushed toward the tree line, picking up speed, and I didn't slow down till we reached the massive baobab tree Zeke said I'd *find inside the forest. Praying that none of the demons chasing us knew about it, I lowered Davina to the ground and pointed toward the opening at the base of its massive trunk. "Crawl inside there."*

She looked at me like I'd lost my mind. "What?"

I gave her a gentle push as the shrieking behind us grew louder. "Hurry."

The noise propelled Davina inside, and I followed close behind her.

As she hobbled around, gawking at the spacious interior of the hollow tree trunk, I sat down at the entrance that'd been warded to look like a solid tree when there were inhabitants inside.

Eyes wide with terror, Davina sat down beside me as the shouting drew nearer.

"You're safe now," I said. "I promise you, I won't let anyone lay a hand on you."

She studied me in silence for a moment before replying, "I believe you."

I shot her what I hoped was a reassuring smile as the mob of Purists spread out to search for us, their howls echoing throughout the forest. "What's on your mind?"

"I'm not sure what to make of any of this," she whispered, "or of you, my mysterious knight in shining armor."

We were a long way from home. The woods were crawling with demons who were dying to rip out my heart and do unspeakable things to this girl, and she didn't have the slightest idea who I was, or why I'd risked my neck to rescue her.

Regardless of all the danger and uncertainty, I sat back and smiled at her, unable to look away.

25

DAVID

We were just settling into our chairs in a dank cell of the dungeon, which I'd procured for our meeting with the utmost discretion, when Benjamin and Tristan came rushing in through the Waterfall entrance across the room. Startled by the intrusion, Mia and Clay both jumped.

Having sensed my shadow's presence before either of them set foot in the cell, I dipped my head in greeting to them.

Benjamin's aura was laced with a terror-inducing mixture of fury and grief that made Mia and Clay cower in their seats.

I met my shadow's gaze with a raised eyebrow. "You've come with news?"

"Charlie's mom is dead," Tristan muttered, "and so is Zeke." His normally smooth-as-silk voice echoed—hollow and broken—against the stone walls. "The demon who killed Zeke told us they murdered Charlie's mother in the waking world."

Mia and Clay both looked to me, wordlessly questioning whether to leave or stay put.

Confident that neither of them posed a risk, I motioned for them to remain seated. Then I turned my attention back to Tristan. "Where is Brian now?"

Tristan's eyes were fixed on an indistinct point somewhere in the distance behind me. "We left the fringe together."

Unable to bear her soul mate's suffering, Mia stood from her chair and crossed the room to him.

Tristan's eyes filled with tears as he wrapped his arms around her. "That bitch who murdered Zeke said they know about Davina because Charlie told them about her after he joined their side. According to her, they plan to hunt Davina down in the waking world, and Zeke was the only one of us who knew where to find her."

"Brian can locate her," I replied, standing from my chair, "just as he did in this world when the Purists attacked Zeke's mirage and she reached out to him for help."

Tristan shook his head. "With all due respect, Sarrum, it's a pretty big fucking world, and it's not like we can just pop over to the Light Realm and ask Davina for directions to her place. She's Unsighted. She wouldn't have a clue where she is in the waking world."

I held Tristan's gaze as I moved toward the Waterfall with the rest of the room's occupants in tow. "I take it Brian drifted when the two of you entered the Waters?"

"Yeah," Tristan muttered as he followed me through the Waterfall into the great hall of the palace.

"Then we'll have to retrieve him in the waking world," I said, turning to Benjamin. "I want you to start trying to locate the girl, so that Brian will have something to go on once we've woken him."

"Will do, boss," my shadow replied, nodding as he took his leave through the nearest Waterfall.

I made my exit a moment after him.

And I opened my eyes in the waking world to find myself lying in bed with my sedated wife beside me. My eyes drifted over the medical equipment attached to her as I sat up, thanking the heavens that her body was safe under the witchdoctor's care.

I stroked a hand over her cheek as the door to our bedroom opened. "Have you alerted Doc?" I asked without taking my eyes off Emma.

"Yeah, he's waking them now."

The hesitancy in Benjamin's voice prompted me to look up. "You have something more to tell me."

"We lost Bob and Nellie," he said, his Dark voice thick with regret, "and Isa's son passed about an hour ago."

"Why did you wait until now to tell me?"

Benjamin cleared his throat. "You asked not to be disturbed while you were with Mia and Clay, and it all occurred within the past hour."

I nodded as I slipped out of bed, then crossed the room to my shadow. "Charlie has joined his father."

"He has," Benjamin replied in a venomous whisper as I followed him out into the hall.

"They most likely removed Ezekiel from the picture and threatened to go after his sister because Charlie suggested it," I said as we headed toward the stairs. "It's the surest way to remove Emma's primary guard from the equation. Charlie is well aware of how much Davina means to Brian."

A low growl rumbling in the base of Benjamin's throat was his only response.

I shook my head as we descended the staircase. "As much as I despise Mackendrick, I am thankful that he is with Emma now. The commander would sooner destroy both worlds than allow any harm to come to her."

"Never thought I'd see the day when you were thankful for Lochlan Mackendrick," Benjamin muttered as we started down the hall.

"All's fair in love and war," I said as we stopped outside the ballroom.

I nodded to my shadow as we parted ways. Then I opened the door and stepped inside the ballroom.

Tristan was already sitting up in bed chugging a bottle of orange juice, and Doc was in the process of waking Brian. A pang of sorrow gripped me as my eyes settled on Isa and Addison, conversing in hushed tones by the beds where Bob and Nellie's bodies lay with crisp white sheets over their faces.

I bowed my head as I approached the two women who'd both suffered more losses than any soul should ever have to bear.

Isa welcomed me with a sorrowful smile, and tears filled my eyes as I wrapped my arms around her. "I am so sorry for your loss, Isa. I have failed you."

"No," she whispered, hugging me back. "That was Rose's doing. She sent Godric's soldiers after my son. There was no way you could've prevented that, since none of us ever dreamed she was capable of..."

I hugged her a little tighter. "I promise you, we will get her back."

Isa wiped a tear from her cheek as I released her from the hug. "We have to."

I kissed the top of my sorceress's head, then turned my attention to Addison. "We must get your family to safety in this world immediately."

She blinked the tears from her eyes as she smiled at me. "Already taken care of, boss. My sergeant is Sighted. I called him the instant I got back to the waking world. He's moving them to a safe house as we speak."

"Good," I said, taking her hand in mine as I lowered my gaze to the two bodies beneath those crisp white sheets. "I am sorry for your loss."

"Thank you, sir. They died with honor saving me and my family. I'll mourn them later. Right now, I just want to aid this fight in whatever way you need me to."

I gave her hand a squeeze. "I appreciate that."

A ragged gasp across the room put an abrupt end to our conversation.

Brian was already on his feet, yanking the tubing from his arm an instant after Doc had woken him. "I don't have time for this shit," he growled as Doc moved to stop him. "I've gotta get to Zeke's sister. You can poke and prod me all you want after Davina is safe."

Doc scowled at Brian as he turned off the equipment he'd so crudely detached himself from. "I must insist that—"

"A young woman's life is at stake, Doctor," I said, without waiting for him to finish his sentence. "Send Brian on his way with something to eat if you'd like, but he hasn't got time to waste on standard medical procedures."

Doc nodded as he narrowed his eyes at me. "As you wish, Sarrum. Who am I to dispute the King?"

I fixed him in a stern glare for a moment, then made my way to the door.

Brian was already rushing down the hall with a wad of clothing bundled in his arms.

I sped up to him. "Benjamin is in my office."

"Yeah?"

"He's been searching for Davina's address."

We both picked up our pace and entered my office a few seconds later to find Benjamin seated at my desk with a laptop in front of him.

He looked up at Brian as we walked toward him. "You're in luck. Tristan told me that Zeke always said his little sister was instinctively drawn to you in this world. Ezekiel lived clear across the country from here, but Davina only lives a few hours away."

He held out a paper with an address scrawled on it, and Brian snatched it from his hand. "Thanks," he muttered as he stripped out of his hospital gown and started putting on his clothes. "Boss, I…"

I shook my head. "It's all right. Emma is in good hands."

"Thank you, to both of you." With that, Brian stuffed the address Benjamin had given him into his pocket and raced out of the room.

"Godspeed," I replied, staring at the doorway as he disappeared from view.

26

EMMA

Something wasn't right. I hadn't seen my husband since the day of Mrs. Mason's funeral, but I often felt his presence. An overwhelming sense of bliss would wash over me, and the pendant around my neck would grow warm to the touch whenever he was near. It was a tremendous comfort, knowing David's body was beside mine in the waking world while our souls were apart in Draumer.

Loch cleared his throat and grinned at me when I looked up from my supper. "You've got that glow about you again. Your husband is nearby in the waking world?"

"He was," I said, "but something's wrong. I can feel how troubled he is."

Chuckling softly, he set his fork down on his plate. "Well, I have always thought the man was rather troubled. Perhaps all this absence is simply bringing his true nature to your attention."

I tossed my napkin on the table, pushed my chair back, and stood up. "That's not funny."

"I am sorry, my dear," the commander called after me as I started to walk away.

But I didn't stop when I heard the screech of his chair as he pushed back from the table or slow down at the sound of his hurried footfalls on the stone path behind me.

He grinned at me as he fell into step beside me. "I didn't mean to offend you."

I stopped walking and turned to look him straight in the eye. "Are you sure about that?"

A remorseful frown replaced his grin. "Perhaps I have been a wee bit insensitive of your situation. Forgive me. It's just been such a pleasure, having you all to myself."

"Why does my husband hate you so much?" I asked, sitting down on the nearest bench.

Lochlan shook his head as he sat down next to me. "It's not—"

"Don't you dare say it's not your place to tell me the story. I swear to God, I will kick you out of this kingdom and take my chances here without you."

I'd intended for the threat to make him take my question more seriously. Instead, a wistful grin spread across his handsome face. "You remind me so much of my Violet when you're angry."

My scowl softened because he rarely mentioned my grandmother, and that charming Scottish brogue of his made it really hard for me to stay mad at him. "What was she like?"

His smile widened as his focus shifted to the past. "Stubborn, headstrong, and more beautiful than any creature I'd ever set eyes on in all my years. We bickered all the time when we first met. She said I was arrogant and obnoxious."

"That's not much of a stretch to imagine."

His wistful grin widened at that. "Well, thank you very much, young lady. Take as many jabs at me as you'd like. I welcome the conflict because it takes me back to my days with her."

"What did you two bicker about?"

"Policy," he said, dropping the grin. "The current Sarrum had ordered the Light Kingdom to form an army because attacks by Dark creatures were becoming a serious threat to this realm."

"And?"

"And I was dispatched to head up the formation of that army, but your grandmother saw no need for it."

"But she appointed you commander of the Light regiment."

Lochlan nodded. "Aye, but that was sometime later on. When I first arrived here, your grandmother was still a princess. It was almost a year before Violet took the throne."

"And?"

"When negotiations began—in regards to the formation of the Light Kingdom's forces—your grandmother argued that there was no need for an army, and certainly not one manned by Dark soldiers like me."

"When did she change her mind?"

The commander's expression grew somber as he met my gaze. "After I stepped in when two Dark creatures tried to attack her," he replied, lost somewhere in the details he didn't seem inclined to share.

"Okay. Now tell me why you and David despise each other."

"Just as stubborn and tenacious as your grandmother," he muttered. "Why are you so curious about my history with your husband?"

"Because you are the dragon guarding me, and the dragon I'm married to hates you; and yet, he feels comfortable leaving me under your protection."

"Fair enough. I was meant to raise you, Emma."

"What?"

"It was your grandmother's dying wish that I be your guardian and protector until you grew old enough to take the throne."

"But David stole me from you," I said.

Lochlan nodded. "He had his shadow snatch you up the instant your newborn soul first emerged from the Waters. I went to his palace and tried to reason with him, but he already treasured you with a vengeance. He threatened to start a war between kingdoms if I attempted to take you, and I have no doubt that he would've made good on it. You became his treasured obsession, immediately and immeasurably, the day you were born."

I found myself wondering what my life would've been like if Lochlan had raised me in the Light. "I'm not sure how to respond to that."

"But you do not regret that things happened as they did."

I smiled at him as I shook my head. "No, I can't imagine my life without David in it."

"And that is his fault," the commander replied. "He was a selfish bastard to steal a Princess of Light from her home. When I first went to him, he promised to return you to us when you came of age, but we both know how that turned out."

"You can't blame him for that. He tried to send me away. In fact, he spent a year confining me to the shore and going nowhere near me, so I'd have no choice but to go to the Light Realm."

A knowing grin spread across the commander's face. "But you didn't go."

"No," I whispered with a nostalgic smile. "I couldn't leave him. However obsessed you believe David is with me, I assure you I treasure him just as desperately. I always have."

"I am aware," he said, smiling to himself. "I do not doubt your happiness, nor dispute the way that David raised you. You are perfect, and I realize he had a hand in that."

"Then why do you hate him so much?"

"Because I knew," the commander replied. "I told him back then that he'd never be able to let you go, and I knew he'd fall madly in love with you when you grew up."

"How could you know that?"

Lochlan's smile widened. "Because that's what happened with me and your grandmother, and it's what David insisted would happen between us if I raised you here. How ironic is that? He took you to save you from a fate that he then condemned you to, by doing exactly what he predicted I would do."

"I'm not sure what to say...or feel about that."

Lochlan shifted toward me and brushed the backs of his fingers against my cheek. "He was right. I would have loved you as wholeheartedly as he does. In fact, I'm not sure that isn't still the case."

"I love my husband with all my heart," I said, feeling curiously apologetic about it.

"And I loved your grandmother with all of mine, but you and I were meant to rule this kingdom together."

"And David knows how you feel; yet, he trusts you to guard me."

"Aye, because he knows I would tear any creature who meant to harm you limb from limb. There is no safer place for you during this war than with me, Emma."

"But David isn't worried I'll decide to stay here with you."

"He knows how deeply you love him."

"My grandmother was a lucky woman," I said, placing my hand on top of his. "I imagine I would've fallen head over heels for you, if I had grown up here."

"Dear God, woman," he muttered, drawing me into a hug, "you cannot say such things to an old man like me. I'm not sure my heart can take it."

I let out a hushed chuckle as I hugged him back. "You are strong enough to survive anything. Don't think for a second that I don't know that."

"No creature is strong enough to survive anything, my dear," he replied, hugging me a bit tighter. "It is simply a matter of what you are willing to lay down your life for, and I would lay down my life for you without question. That is why David trusts that you are safe here with me. His fear has never been that I would not protect you. It was that you might grow overly fond of me and choose to remain here in the Light."

27

LOCHLAN

After I'd answered all her questions about the animosity between me and her husband, Emma excused herself to pay a visit to Davina and the other Unsighted souls Ezekiel had left under our protection. Feeling far too agitated to retire for the evening, I decided to go check in with the soldiers on border patrol.

I took my leave from the palace courtyard beneath the fairytale splendor of a lavender sky, shaking my head at the exchange we'd just had as I latched the gate behind me. Then I made my way toward the border with the soft glow of a silver crescent moon illuminating the path before me.

Emma had no memory of me, but this came as no surprise. I'd realized that the day she showed up unannounced on my doorstep, accompanied by her bodyguard and the Sarrum's shadow. I had opened the door, overjoyed to see her again, thinking she'd finally come to her senses and left that selfish bastard to take her rightful place in the Light. However, it only took a moment to realize there was no recognition in her eyes. It was no matter; at least that's what I kept on telling myself. Emma was happy and whole again—which was no minor miracle, considering all that she'd been through—and whatever the reason, she'd come home to us at last. If I had detected even the slightest hint that Emma was not content with her husband, I might've attempted to jog her memory. But there was no denying how blissfully happy she was. If I robbed her of that, I'd be no better than the dragon who had taken her from me.

What I wouldn't give to see my Violet again and ask her what I ought to do. I looked up at the luminous sliver of moon lighting my way, foolishly hoping for a sign from above. There'd been so many times I had wished my old heart would just give out, so I could move on to the great beyond and join my soul mate in the afterlife. Of course, now that Emma had come home to us, my place was in the Light Kingdom with her. Even her selfish husband couldn't deny that.

Feeling rather nostalgic after my conversation with Emma, I decided to take the long way through the woods to the shore. Lost in my thoughts, I soon found myself in the stretch of woods by the Water where things had first begun to change between Violet and me...

...It'd been a brutal morning of negotiations, feeling caged within the gleaming white walls of the grandiose reception room in the Light King's palace. Desperate for a break, I decided to spend my lunch hour in the Waters till it was time to return to the room that felt far too small to contain me.

As usual, I didn't intend to venture too far from the shore because I knew the King's daughter would be spending her downtime in the woods her father had forbidden her from entering. There was no stopping Violet from doing anything she had half a mind to do, and she loved the solitude of those woods.

That was where I'd first set eyes on her, when I arrived in the Light Kingdom on my way to meet with the King. Having no idea who I was, she'd threatened to have me banned from the kingdom when I happened upon her alone in the woods reading. I introduced myself as the soldier who'd been tasked with forming the Light Kingdom's army. Then she gave me an earful, telling me exactly what she thought of the Sarrum's order to create an army in her realm.

I was captivated by her right from the start. She was the most beautiful creature I'd ever encountered, and the way her eyes sparkled when she spoke her mind made her all the more so. The fact that she made a point of attending that first meeting with the express purpose of convincing her father to send me packing didn't put me off in the slightest.

It hadn't taken me long to realize the Princess spent a great deal of time in the woods her father had forbidden her from entering, but I wasn't there to tattle. My job was to start up the regiment I'd been sent to create and get it running smoothly enough to hand over to a creature of Light's command. Whilst I was there, it only seemed prudent to watch out for the realm's future monarch, since she was too stubborn to avoid potential dangers. Of course, I wasn't about to tell her what I was up to because she would've told me to bugger off. Fortunately, it wasn't difficult to stay close without her knowing, since she had no knowledge of my true form. I'd seen no reason to unmask in the presence of any of the Light creatures. They all simply sensed there was a Darkness about me and assumed I was some sort of garden-variety demon, which suited my purpose just fine. So I kept to the Waters whilst the Princess snuck off to the woods, but I stayed alert in case of trouble.

I'm ashamed to admit that after weeks of negotiations had passed with no sign of danger to the Princess, I'd become somewhat lax in my vigilance. I was quite far from land when I heard her cry out. Propelled by the fear in her voice, it didn't take me long to reach the shore. And keen as my hearing was, I caught a fair bit of their exchange before I got there. There were two Dark beasts who'd happened upon the Princess whilst she was eating her lunch in the woods. She told them off, just as she'd done when she first met me. But these were beasts without honor, and her threats merely amused them. When she informed them that she was the Light King's daughter, it only served to push them toward far less honorable intents.

As I neared the shore, the troll and sorrow were dragging her toward the Water. I wasn't certain why they would take her away from the seclusion of the woods, but my best guess was that they meant to dispose of her in the Waters after they had their fun with her.

When I emerged from the Water, the troll had her pinned to the ground. The way she was snarling threats at him, I'd have guessed she were part dragon if I didn't know better. Of course, I could only admire her grit in retrospect. At the time, I was too consumed by fury to appreciate much of anything.

The sorrow was standing a few feet away, watching the Princess struggle to get free with sadistic amusement. He was the first to catch sight of me rising up out of the Water in my dragon form, and he pissed himself and took off running the instant he spotted me.

A heartbeat later, I was towering above the troll who still had his filthy hands on Violet, since he'd been too distracted to notice my arrival. A droplet of water dripped from my chin to the troll's head, prompting him to look up, and an angry plume of smoke rose from my flared nostrils. "Step away from her, you vile creature."

The troll shrieked and fell back. "Take her. You can have her."

"Have her?" I snarled, noting the terror in Violet's eyes as she looked up at me towering above her. "She is not property to be had, you filthy mongrel."

"I don't know what the hell you're saying," the dimwitted creature muttered, backing away on all fours, "but I'm just gonna go."

"No, I don't believe you will." I snatched the beast up with my teeth. Having no taste for such filthy prey, I tore him in two with my claws and tossed both lifeless halves aside. I paused a moment, hating the fear in Violet's eyes as she stared at me, still lying motionless on her back. I wanted to go to her, but I could not allow the other Dark creature who'd come after her to go free.

I tracked the sorrow's scent and reached him a few heartbeats later, racing through the woods in a futile attempt to escape his fate. "Please," he whimpered, "I don't want any trouble."

"Then you should never have set foot in the Light," I growled, pinning him beneath my claw.

The scent of urine soured the air. "I won't come back ever again."

"Oh, I am certain you are right about that," I replied, releasing him from my claw. Then I plunged it into his chest, and tore out his beating heart.

I raced back to the shore to find the Princess still lying on her back. Too terrified to move, she squeezed her lovely eyes shut and whispered, "Please don't hurt me." She was trembling so hard, she was practically convulsing.

I glanced down at my monstrous blood-soaked claws and felt wretched for having terrified her more than the two beasts I'd saved her from. "Princess," I said, masking myself in human form and kneeling beside her, "you are safe now. I would never harm you."

Her eyes popped open at the sound of my voice, and she gawked at me in wide-eyed disbelief. "You..."

Since she'd still made no move to get up, I smiled at her and lay down on the grass beside her. "Ah, did I forget to mention that I was a Water dragon?"

I expected her to laugh, or respond with some clever remark like she normally did. Instead, her eyes filled with tears as she threw her arms around my neck. "Thank you," she whispered.

"You're quite welcome," I said as I hugged her back, pained by the tears she was trying so hard not to shed. "It's all right. You are safe now, Princess. I'll not let any beast lay a hand on you."

She pulled her head back to look at me. "I treated you horribly."

"You stand up for what you believe in. I admire that."

"I owe you my life," she whispered.

"No, you don't," I replied with a grin, "but perhaps you might do me the honor of dining with me?"

She bit her lip as she searched my eyes, trying to reconcile the Water dragon who'd just saved her with the man she'd been bickering with for weeks. And tears streamed down her cheeks as she let out a laugh. "I suppose I would, if you're buying."

28

BRIAN

I reached over to the passenger seat and stuffed my hand in the bag Doc had thrust into my arms as I was rushing out the door of the boss's house. After fishing around for a few seconds without taking my eyes off the road, I pulled out something that felt like a power bar. Glancing at the GPS as I tore off the wrapper, I scarfed it down and growled at the ETA. Two more hours was too fucking long. God only knew how close the Purists were to finding Davina. Hell, for all I knew it might already be too late, but I couldn't afford to think like that. I had to keep positive and keep going, for her.

At least my ride was fast. The second I raced into the garage, I'd headed straight to the Bugatti. I was the one who'd flown to Amsterdam to test drive and purchase it for the boss. So I was well aware the Bugatti Chiron was the fastest car in his collection, and any time I could shave off the drive could mean the difference between finding Davina before the Purists got to her—and finding her dead.

As I drove, my mind kept going back to Tristan's comment about getting over my I'm-not-worthy complex, and what Benjamin had said about Davina being instinctively drawn to me. That was a load of bullshit; and even if it wasn't, Zeke's sister could do a hell of a lot better than me. I had no intention of fucking up Davina's life, but I sure as hell planned on saving it.

As I sped toward the address that I hoped to God was current, my thoughts drifted to the past...

...Once the woods were no longer crawling with Purists, it didn't take Davina long to fall asleep. Figuring she probably hadn't slept much since those bastards abducted her, I took off my jacket and draped it over her to keep her warm. Then I parked myself at the entrance to the hollow tree to keep watch. I wasn't about to let my guard down for a second while we were still this close to the Purists' meeting place.

I think I spent as much time watching Zeke's sister sleep as I did scanning the woods for signs of danger, and I felt like a first-rate creep for it. But my eyes just kept drifting back to her. Davina was the most breathtakingly beautiful creature I'd ever set eyes on, and the fact that I was hyper-aware of that made me feel like an even bigger degenerate. I was supposed to protect her and get her back to her brother, not drool over her.

Under normal circumstances, time always seemed to drag while I kept watch, but I could've watched over this girl forever. Before I knew it, she was sitting up and rubbing the sleep from her eyes. "Good morning," she said, flashing me a tentative smile.

Hoping to make her feel as safe and comfortable as possible after all that she'd been through, I answered her hesitance with a confident grin. "Morning."

She stood up and hobbled across the distance between us, relying heavily on her uninjured leg. Then she sat down and held my jacket out to me. "Did you stay awake all night?"

"Yeah," I said, shaking my head at the jacket. "Keep it. You looked cold last night, and it's not much warmer this morning."

She dropped her eyes to my sleeveless shirt—the only layer I hadn't shed and given to her—with an apologetic frown. "You must be freezing."

"Nah, I'm fine," I muttered, taking the jacket from her and wrapping it around her shoulders. "I'm naturally hot-blooded."

She hugged the jacket close to her body, her quivering chin making it obvious that she was struggling to keep her teeth from chattering. "You're just saying that so I won't feel bad."

I motioned for her to move closer to me. "Come on."

She hesitated, lowering her gaze to the ground.

The fear in her eyes damn near broke my heart. "You don't have to be afraid of me. I'd never hurt you."

Tears glistened in her gorgeous eyes as she looked up at me. "I believe you."

I slid closer to her, slowly and deliberately, giving her plenty of time to ask me to stop. Then I flashed her a reassuring smile as I sandwiched her hands between mine.

Visibly torn between pulling away and moving closer, she responded with a tentative grin. "You really are warm."

"Told you so. You can trust me, Davina."

She glanced down at our hands. "You know my name?"

I outstretched my arms and wordlessly beckoned her closer so I could warm her up. "Of course I do. I told you, your brother sent me."

"I don't have a brother," she muttered, sliding closer despite her doubts.

"I know it doesn't make sense to you," I said, wrapping my arms around her shivering body, "but I swear it's the truth."

A sigh of relief escaped her full lips as her body relaxed against mine, absorbing my warmth. "Why do I trust you so much, when you keep saying things that don't make sense?"

"Maybe because a part of you knows it's the truth."

She nodded and let her head settle against my shoulder. "So what do we do now?"

Blindsided by the realization that nothing had ever felt more right than the feel of her in my arms, it took me a few seconds to answer. "For now, we wait here. We need to make sure the coast is clear before we break cover."

"How long will that be?"

"I'm not sure," I said, intoxicated by her scent and the feel of her body nestled against mine, "but I can think of worse places to be stuck."

She turned her head toward the building I'd rescued her from the night before. "Me too."

I tightened my hold on her just a little. "I promise nobody's gonna hurt you on my watch, Davina."

She tilted her head to look up at me. "You know my name, but I still don't know yours."

"It's Brian."

"Brian," she murmured, sending a jolt of electricity surging through me at the sound of my name on her lips, "will you tell me about this brother I've never met?"

I let my chin rest against the top of her head. "I can tell you he'd do anything to keep you safe."

"Tell me more," she said as she drew her legs closer to her body and wrapped my jacket around them...

...I glanced at the GPS and let out a groan. Still over an hour left to go.

Feeling guilty as hell for reminiscing about the day I told Davina about her brother—*who I'd just let die*—I tightened my grip on the wheel.

I'm not sure how long I stared at the road in a self-loathing daze before my phone started ringing, startling the ever-loving shit out of me. I fished it out of my pocket and glanced at the screen as I answered the call. "What, Tristan?"

"Love you too, brother," Tristan muttered, his voice uncharacteristically rough.

I let out a sigh. "Sorry. I'm going outta my damn mind here. This drive is taking too fucking long."

"No worries. I get it. Just called to help narrow your search when you get to her town."

"What've you got for me?"

"Davina Gaumond is a romance novelist who owns a coffee house near the beach called Sinful Pleasures Coffee & Books. The bio on her website says you can usually find her tucked away in a cozy corner of her shop, reading or writing with a cup of coffee in hand."

"Huh," I muttered. "Romance novelist?"

"Makes sense if you think about it," Tristan said, reverting to his usual smooth-as-silk tone. "I'm guessing a succubus can write some pretty scorching hot sex scenes. In fact, I know she can, because I just read an excerpt on her website and it—"

"Great," I said, cutting him off. "Thanks for taking your sweet time letting me know what you dug up."

"You're on the road. So I figured I didn't need to rush, and you can never be too thorough when it comes to research. I've got you covered, brother. By the time you get there, I can probably give you some tips on what gets her—"

"I'm going there to protect her, not seduce her," I growled, in no mood for Tristan's playfulness. "Besides, even if that were my intention, I'm pretty sure I could get by without your tips, baby brother."

"*Her* tips, not mine," he said, unfazed by my temper. "I'm just trying to help."

"Uh-huh. What makes you think I need your help in that department?"

"Nothing," Tristan admitted, "except the fact that I know this woman means more to you than anyone else ever has."

"Doesn't matter. She doesn't even know I exist in this world."

"I've seen the way she looks at you in Draumer, Brian. Something tells me she'll be into you in this world too."

"Whatever," I muttered, tired of debating something so pointless. "All I'm concerned with is keeping her safe."

"You know," Tristan replied in a softer tone, "Zeke always said he couldn't have handpicked a better man for his baby sister. Keep that in mind, okay?"

"Just text me her shop's address."

I ended the call and tossed my cell to the passenger seat as my thoughts returned to her.

29

GODRIC

I sat my cup down on the table and smiled at Louise as she stepped into the dining room. "Hello, Louise. Thank you for joining me."

Azure sparks glinted in her eyes as she took the seat across the table from me. "Tell me how you're doing it."

I slid a cup toward her and picked up the pot of tea on the table between us. "I'm sure I haven't the faintest idea what you are talking about."

Nodding for me to pour her some tea, she snarled, "Don't insult my intelligence."

I raised an eyebrow as I filled her cup. "What exactly are you referring to?"

A whisper of powder-blue smoke escaped her flared nostrils. "I am referring to the way that your son has recently become such a compliant member of Team Godric. Charlie is a remarkably powerful dragon, and he has always stood in opposition to you. So what hold do you suddenly have over him?"

My eyes drifted to the windowpanes in the doors behind Louise and a smile spread across my face as Charlie and Rose strolled into view. "I have no more hold over Charlie than I ever did."

"Then how do you explain all that invaluable information he so eagerly shared with us?"

Ignoring her question, I watched Charlie open the French doors and motion for Rose to go in ahead of him. Following her inside, he took her hand in his, and they approached the table. "Son," I said, greeting him with a nod and gesturing for them to join us. Whilst they settled into the seats to Louise's left, I turned my attention to Rose. "I hear you finally grew tired of toying with that Unsighted half-brother of yours and finished him off."

A faint smile curved her sweet lips. "With a little help from Charlie."

I slid my chair back from the table with a nod. "I'm sure you are all wondering why I asked you to join me here this morning."

Charlie slid his chair back, mirroring my movement. "As a matter of fact, we are."

Grinning at my son, I stood up and summoned the Waters, and a portal immediately formed beside the table. "What's the expression? A picture is worth a thousand words. Would you three care to join me for a firsthand glimpse of our latest accomplishment?"

Too intrigued to bother asking questions, Charlie, Rose, and Louise all stood from their chairs. As they rounded the table, I stepped into the portal and motioned for them to join me.

Once we were all inside, I sealed the opening shut.

Louise raised an eyebrow as I opened the other end of the tunnel with a subtle flick of my wrist. I grinned at her and started toward the exit, and they all fell into step behind me.

Rose let out a gasp as we stepped out into a secluded cove along the fringe.

"Where are we?" Charlie muttered.

I smiled at my son, but he didn't notice. His eyes were fixed on the flames barreling from the quaint little castle near the Water's edge. "I'm afraid your friend Addison managed to save her Unsighted husband and children before the Gabriel hounds could dispose of them, but it wasn't a total loss. Nellie and that Unsighted knight of hers perished in their efforts to assist her."

Charlie responded with a stoic nod, but I saw the grief-stricken fury erupt in his eyes in a burst of orange flames. An instant later, it was gone. "And how did things go with the demon you sent to intercept Brian, Tristan, and Zeke at my Unsighted adoptive mother's encampment?"

I couldn't stop myself from grinning at the shocked expression on Louise's face. "It went quite well actually. She killed that giant-incubus mutt, and your friend Brian left Draumer to race to the rescue of that succubus you told us about, just as you predicted he would."

Charlie's gaze drifted back to the castle engulfed in flames where his friends had perished, thanks to his intel. "Good."

"But I sense you have more information to share," I said, drawing his attention away from the flames. "When I die, the throne of Draumer shall pass to you.

So I want you to have a heavy hand in reclaiming it. What do you suggest we do next?"

"Well, you've either weakened or eliminated most of the members of David Talbot's inner circle," Charlie replied, his gaze shifting to Rose. "And I think this war has dragged on long enough, so I suggest we end it."

Hearing those words from my son's lips made me feel like a giddy child on Christmas morning, but I refrained from grinning like one. "And how do you suggest we accomplish that?"

Charlie shrugged. "We do what you've been trying to do for years. Now that we've broken most of David's crew, it's time for us to cripple him."

Mesmerized by the reflection of the burning castle blazing in my son's eyes, I asked, "Cripple him how exactly?"

Charlie let out a laugh, as if the question were absurd. "You know how. We kill his beloved treasure— and in doing so, we crush his heart."

I grinned at Louise's gaping mouth. "And how do we do that?"

Charlie raked a hand through his hair, but he only hesitated for a few seconds. "Emma Talbot has taken her rightful place as Queen of the Light Kingdom. David is no longer with her. The Darkness is undoubtedly at the Sarrum's palace with his grieving soul mate, who just lost her son, thanks to me and Rose. And according to you, Emma's primary guard has rushed off to the waking world to save the succubus of his dreams. The Light Realm's army was disbanded years ago and although they've resurrected it, most of their soldiers are just newbies in training. So David's wife is ripe for the taking right now. If we attack the

Light Realm's border with enough force, it shouldn't be too difficult to get to the Queen."

Tears filled my eyes as I stepped closer and kissed the top of my son's head. "I shall be the one to finish her."

"And that should pretty much do it," Charlie said. "Once Emma is dead, the rest of this war will practically finish itself."

A smile spread across Louise's face, the light of the burning castle giving it a youthful glow. "It sounds as though we ought to rest up for our final battle."

"It may not be the final battle," I said, stepping back into the Water portal and motioning for them to join me, "but it will undoubtedly be the pivotal fight. After I kill his precious Queen, David will crumble and the throne will be mine."

30

BRIAN

The sun was starting to set by the time I pulled into the parking lot of Sinful Pleasures Coffee & Books. A glance at the sign in the window told me they'd already closed up shop for the night, but I'd be damned if she wasn't still in there. I could feel how close she was.

A nauseating mix of nerves and adrenaline had my heart pounding as I hopped out of the car and walked to the front door. I turned the doorknob and stepped inside, thankful as hell it wasn't locked. That meant she was still there. *Unless Godric's goons had already gotten to her.*

I didn't need to search the front of the shop to know she wasn't there. Close as I was to her now, I was a divining rod and Davina was the water. I headed down the hall toward the back of the shop, her pull on me growing stronger with every step.

An image popped into my head—*Davina locking eyes with me before we set off on our mission, tracing a hand over the bracelet I'd given her all those years ago*—and my thoughts drifted as I moved closer…

…After trekking through the forest for weeks, we'd finally made it to the cottage—deep in troll territory—that belonged to Tristan's friend Aubrey. We'd filled our stomachs with the food Aubrey left for us and spent most of the day sitting on a troll-sized couch, talking in front of a roaring fire. I could tell Davina was tired because her eyelids kept drooping; but each time I mentioned it, she said she wasn't ready to turn in yet.

I grinned at her as she let out a yawn. "I think it's past your bedtime. It's been a hell of a long trip. We should both grab a bedroom and get some sleep."

She dropped her eyes to the frayed rug on the floor in front of us. "I know it's stupid, but I can't sleep in those rooms."

The timid way she'd lowered her gaze turned my stomach. "Why's that?"

Tears glistened in her eyes as she looked up at me. "Those bedrooms remind me too much of the last bedroom I was in."

"There's nothing stupid about that," I said, taking her hand in mine.

"Everywhere else that we've stopped to rest, you were right there next to me," she whispered as her eyes drifted to the fireplace. "When I had a nightmare, you were the first thing I saw when I opened my eyes. Seeing you reminded me that I was safe."

I followed her gaze to the roughly hewn stones of the fireplace. We must've been talking a lot longer than I thought because the fire was nothing but a heap of glowing embers. "You're still safe, and you should take advantage of one of those nice warm beds."

She shook her head as I met her eyes. "Could I sleep on the floor in your room instead?"

I smiled at her and gave her hand a squeeze. "There's no way I'd take the bed and make you sleep on the floor, but I'll sit in your room and keep an eye on the door while you get some sleep if it'd make you feel better."

She shivered and wrapped the shawl she'd found in Aubrey's closet tighter around her. "You've barely slept at all since you took me away from those monsters, Brian. I know you need the rest."

I shrugged, debating whether to throw another log on the fire. The room felt plenty warm to me, and there was a good chance her goose bumps had nothing to do with the temperature. "I can rest later."

She looked down at my hand, holding onto hers. "Or we could share a bed."

"I don't think that's a good idea," I said, hopping up to grab the poker from its stand on the hearth. "I toss around too much in my sleep."

"I'm serious," she whispered behind me.

"So am I," I muttered as I stoked the fire. "What would your brother think if he showed up and found us in the same bed?"

She shook her head as I sat back down beside her. "I don't care what he thinks. I don't even know him." A tear slid down her cheek, and I brushed it away with my thumb. "I'd feel a lot safer sticking with you, rather than taking off with some guy who claims to be my brother. Are you sure he's even telling the truth?"

"Yeah, I'm sure."

"He sounds terrifying," she said, suppressing another shiver. "How am I supposed to feel safe taking off with some half-giant stranger who says he's my relative?"

"I wouldn't let you leave with him, if I didn't know for a fact it was true. I haven't steered you wrong yet, have I?"

"No," she said, her voice soft and uncertain, "that's why I'd rather stay with you."

"Davina," I whispered.

"Would that be so horrible?" she asked, pausing a moment to search my eyes. "Why are you so eager to get rid of me?"

"I'm not," I admitted. "If it were my call, I'd stick with you for as long as you liked."

Another tear slid down her cheek. "I don't understand any of this. Why isn't it your call?"

I responded with a somber smile, the most reassuring expression I could manage while staring into her tear-filled eyes. "I can't leave the knighthood. I took a vow to protect the inhabitants of the fringe. How could you trust a man who didn't keep his promises?"

"Is it selfish to say, I don't care about your promises to anyone else?" she asked in a broken whisper. "I just want you to stay with me."

"I wish I could," I said, hating that my words were the cause of her tears.

"Then say yes," she whispered, wiping away another tear.

Struggling like hell to keep my own eyes from tearing, I cleared my throat. "You deserve a better man than me, Davina."

She let out a humorless chuckle. "I've spent enough time with you to know there is no one better than you."

"You're sweet," I muttered, "but you're wrong."

"Just stay with me tonight," she said, melting my heart with her doe-eyed innocence. "We can debate the rest later."

I exhaled an unsteady breath and forced myself to look away, hoping to break the spell her hypnotic eyes were casting over me. "I can't."

She put her hand on my cheek and turned my head so I'd look at her. "Just sleep next to me, Brian. That's all I'm asking for."

I took her hand from my cheek, kissed it, and pretended not to notice the way she trembled at the feel of my lips against her flesh. "No, you're asking me to spend a night lying in bed beside you, and still be able to walk away when this is over."

"I'm not asking you to walk away."

"I'll take the chair in your room," I said…

…Davina's pull on me was stronger at the back of the shop, but she wasn't there either.

As I stepped out the back exit that led down the hill to the beach, my thoughts returned to our past…

…I'd been sitting in a chair in the corner of the bedroom watching over Davina while she slept for hours; and with each hour that passed, it pained me a little more to think of us parting ways. Would it really be so wrong to leave the knighthood for her?

Yes, I reminded myself, it'd be unforgivable as hell because Davina was Unsighted. If I stayed with her, I'd be no different than my father. He'd trapped my Unsighted mother in a life of misery that she never deserved. I'd be damned if I would do that to this sweet innocent girl, so I kept reminding myself that she was better off without me until my eyelids started to droop.

A muffled cry jolted me awake to find Davina tossing and turning, in the throes of a nightmare.

I hopped out of the chair and sat down on the bed. "It's all right, Davina," I said, close to her ear. "You're safe. I'm right here with you."

The instant her eyes popped open, she bolted upright and threw her arms around my neck.

I wrapped my arms around her, hating the way she was trembling, and hating myself for not lying down next to her like she'd asked me to. "You're okay. It was just a bad dream."

"I dreamed that you left me," she said, clinging to me like her life depended on it, "and those monsters came back and took me again."

"That's never gonna happen," I whispered, cradling her head in my palm as I tightened my hold on her.

"You can't promise that."

"Yeah, I can," I said, stroking a hand over her hair. "I'd never leave if I thought there was any chance of that happening."

"What about later? Anything could happen to me down the road."

I shook my head and started to pull back from her. "You should lie down and get some more sleep."

"Lie down with me?" she whispered, gripping my arm. "Please."

"Okay," I muttered, lying down on top of the blanket she was under and slipping an arm under her head as she nestled against me. "Would it make you feel better if you had a way to call me back, if you ever needed my help?"

There was a beat of silence before she replied, "Yes."

I took off the leather band around my wrist and pressed it to my lips. Then I slid it onto her slender wrist and tightened it. "As long as you wear this, you can call me back by stroking a finger over it and wishing for me to come to you."

She narrowed her eyes at the unremarkable strap of leather. "How gullible do you think I am?"

I kissed the top of her head as she tucked it under my chin. "It's the truth. I swear. As long as you keep that on, I'll always be able to find you."

She drifted off to sleep soon after, safe in the knowledge that I was beside her...

...The beach was pretty empty. There were a few teenagers messing around with boogie boards in the water, a handful of joggers and dog walkers, and a few people sitting on beach chairs and blankets.

The second I set eyes on Davina, my heart skipped a beat. All I could see was the back of her head, bowed over the paperback in her hands, but there wasn't a doubt in my mind that it was her. I could *feel* her with every fiber of my being.

Eyes glued to her, I stopped moving and took a deep breath. *She had no idea who I was in this world.* Relieved as I was to have reached her in time, how the hell was I supposed to convince her to hop in a car and take off with a total stranger?

Despicable as it made me feel, the only solution I could think of was to charm her into leaving with me. *Damn it. Maybe I should've listened to Tristan's tips on how to get her to fall for me.* I started walking toward her at a sluggish pace, racking my brain for something to say that might earn her trust.

I was still a fair distance away when the jogger to her left and the dog walker on her right converged in front of her. A heartbeat later, the dog was bounding toward the surf and the two men were yanking Davina out of her beach chair and dragging her off, kicking and screaming.

I sprinted toward them, mentally noting that the other beachgoers must be Purists because no one had even looked in their direction when she cried out for help.

I reached in my jacket and pulled my pistol from the holster, keeping it concealed in my sleeve as I raced after them. They disappeared around the corner of the public restrooms, and I pushed harder, desperate to catch up.

By the time I reached them, they had her pinned up against the wall in the narrow walkway between the men and women's rooms. Both of them were trolls, and I was thankful for that. It meant they were too stupid to kill her and get out of there fast, and too depraved to execute their orders without having some fun with her first. The taller one had a hand over her mouth to muffle her screams, and the shorter one's grubby hands were all over her. Both of them were too preoccupied—and too dimwitted—to keep an eye out for trouble, which made it easy to sneak up without drawing their attention.

The bastards were too damn close to Davina for me to shoot them, so I hit the one that was groping her on the side of the head with the butt of my gun. He stumbled sideways, and I punched the one with his hand over her mouth square in the nose. As he yelped and raised both hands to his face, I grabbed Davina, tugged her toward me, and fired a shot to each of their heads before either of them could process what was happening.

Davina doubled over, gasping for breath as she eyed the blood pooling around their heads.

"We've gotta get out of here before more of them come for you," I said.

Startled by my voice, she spun around to face this third stranger who'd snuck up on her. But the instant our eyes met, she froze. "You…"

"We've gotta go now," I said, ignoring the jolt of electricity that surged through me at the look of recognition in her eyes.

"Okay," she muttered, her pupils dilated and her eyes fixed on me.

Not sure what to make of her reaction, I holstered my pistol and wrapped an arm around her waist. She was clearly in shock, and she kept a wary eye on me as I guided her up the hill, but she moved as fast as I needed her to.

When we reached the back parking lot, I glanced over my shoulder at the beach. There were five more beachgoers heading toward us. "Look, I know you don't know me," I said, picking up the pace as I whisked her around the side of the building to the front lot. "But I need you to trust me and get in my car because there are more people coming after you."

She peered over her shoulder and nodded.

A few seconds later, I was unlocking the car and opening the passenger side door for her. She only hesitated a second before getting in and letting me shut the door. I raced around the car and hopped in the driver's seat just as the first of Godric's goons reached the front lot. A heartbeat later, we were pulling out onto the road.

I glanced over at Davina, wondering what to say to her. *How the hell was I supposed to explain all this?* She was still staring at me, eyes wide with shock. "I'm one of the good guys," I said. "I promise."

"I must be dreaming," she muttered. "This is…"

I smiled at her, hoping to somehow gain her trust without using my charm. "No, I'm afraid not. This is real."

"But…" She shook her head as her voice trailed off. "You're him."

Unsure what to make of that, I raised an eyebrow.

She held up the paperback she'd somehow managed to hold onto during that whole struggle and escape. "You're…" She frowned at the book, then looked up at me. "You're the man in every one of my stories."

"What are you talking about?"

"I dreamed about a man who looked just like you when I was a teenager," she muttered, narrowing her eyes at me. "I've never dreamed of any other person that I could remember so clearly when I woke up, and my mental picture of my dream man never faded."

I nodded and forced myself to suppress the grin tugging at the corners of my mouth.

"In every single one of my romance novels," she muttered, dropping her eyes to the book in her hands, "you were the love interest I was picturing when I wrote the story. I varied the character's description so my readers wouldn't get bored, but it was always you I envisioned doing…the…things…in my books."

Unable to hold it back after hearing that, a dopey grin spread across my face. "Well, thanks. That's a pretty incredible compliment."

"How the hell is this possible?" she asked. "How am I riding in this insanely expensive sports car with *you?*"

How was I supposed to respond to that? Out of every possible scenario that'd come to mind while I was racing to get to her, I never imagined it playing out anything like this. "It's kind of a long story, Davina."

"You know my name?" she muttered, tightening her grip on the book. "Of course, you do. Maybe I'm having a stroke."

"Listen, why don't I start by introducing myself? My name's—"

"Brian," she said, cutting me off. "Your name is Brian, and I'm pretty sure I've lost my mind."

31

DAVINA

Despite all the reasons to stay alert, not to mention all the reasons not to have hopped in a car with this impossible manifestation of my dream man, I found myself dozing off as Brian sped toward wherever the hell he was taking me. As I drifted between wakefulness and sleep, I dreamt—only, it felt more like a memory than a dream...

...When I woke up, sunlight was streaming in through the bedroom windows and Brian was sound asleep on the bed beside me. I didn't want to wake him because he needed the rest, and there was nowhere I would rather be than lying next to him.

He was so beautiful, inside and out. He was brave, and kind, and selfless, but he said I deserved someone better than him. Why couldn't he see how perfect he was?

My eyes drifted to the leather band Brian had slipped onto my wrist after joining me on the bed. He must've thought I was an idiot to believe that little strip of leather possessed the magical power to connect me to him. I traced a fingertip along the bracelet's edge—imagining how it'd feel to trace the contours of his muscles—wishing with all my heart that he'd change his mind and stay with me.

The instant the wish finished forming in my head, Brian's eyes popped open.

Startled by the timing, I muttered, "Good morning."

He smiled and nodded at the band around my wrist. "That's not a toy."

"What?"

"You were testing it out to see if I'd feel it," he said, tracing the band with his index finger. "Well, I did."

I lifted my wrist and considered the bracelet with renewed interest. "Do I have to be in danger to use it?"

"That's the idea."

"But what if I just miss you?"

I never got to hear his answer because a knock on the front door of the cottage interrupted us. A second later, the sound of the front door opening had us both scrambling out of bed.

"Stay here," Brian whispered, grabbing the sword he'd propped against the chair in the corner. "I want to make sure that is who we think it is."

The only response I could manage was a nod because the notion that it could be someone who meant to harm us scared me speechless.

Brian flashed me a reassuring smile as he slipped out the door and shut it behind him.

I listened at the door, feeling comforted by the sound of Brian's voice, even though it was too muffled to make out his words.

But the deep booming voice that answered him made my stomach drop.

I stood there, frozen, listening to the back and forth of their conversation. It didn't sound like a hostile exchange. Neither of them raised their voice. But every time that deep rumbling voice answered Brian's, my throat tightened and it took a little more effort to draw my next breath. How was I supposed to feel safe taking off with the stranger who belonged to that voice?

"Davina," Brian called out, his voice closer to the door, "you can come out now."

I didn't want to go out there, but there weren't really any other options. My only hope was that Brian might change his mind and let me stick with him, after he saw how terrified I was of this stranger. Drawing an unsteady breath, I opened the door and stepped out into the main room.

Brian grinned at me and nodded toward the front door of the cottage.

The man standing in front of the door was humongous, and he had this overwhelming aura of cruelty and menace about him that made the hairs on the back of my neck stand up. His bulging muscles were decorated with tribal tattoos. His long dark hair was tied back from his bearded face; and although he was strikingly handsome, there was an unsettling severity to his strong masculine features that made my heartbeat quicken. His flared nostrils, sharply arched eyebrows, and fierce Dark eyes stopped me dead in my tracks.

I was about two seconds away from turning around and running back into the bedroom when the man dropped to both knees with a resounding thud. Tears filled the half-giant's eyes as they locked with mine, his harsh features softened, and suddenly he didn't seem quite so terrifying. "Oh thank God, baby girl," he said. "It's so good to see your face."

I took a tentative step closer and glanced back at Brian. When he nodded, I took another step toward the kneeling giant.

As Zeke watched the hesitant way I moved toward him, he bowed his head. It was an unmistakably subservient gesture, clearly meant to put me at ease. "I realize you don't know me in this world, Davina," he said, tilting his head sideways to look up at me. "But in an alternate world, you and I are thick as thieves. It broke my heart when I learned you'd been taken. If I could've come for you myself, I would have."

I took another step, narrowing my eyes at him.

"I swear to you, baby sister," Zeke went on, "I would cut off my own arm before I'd ever hurt you or let anybody else lay a finger on you. Just tell me what I need to do to prove that to you, and I'll do it. Anything."

"I believe you," I said, shocking myself with my words and the sincerity behind them...

...The car hit a bump, and I woke with a start.

Brian was still in the driver's seat, the literal man of my dreams, driving me off to God only knew where. *Was this all just a remarkably vivid dream?* Maybe I'd dozed off in my beach chair while proofreading the sample copy of my latest novel, and this was nothing but the wildly imaginative fantasy of an over-caffeinated author's mind. That's what I got for drinking coffee so late in the evening.

"I just had the strangest dream," I said as Brian welcomed me back to wakefulness with the warmth of his smile. "You were in it, and so was my brother."

The smile slipped from Brian's face as his grip on the steering wheel tightened. The tension in his jaw muscles and the telltale bulging of the veins in his hands and forearms probably should've frightened me. Instead, a thrill coursed through me. "There's something I need to tell you about your brother," Brian said in a gruff whisper that I *felt* deep inside me.

Then his words sunk in. "You know Zeke?"

"Yeah," he muttered, "I did."

The sorrow in his voice made my heart hurt. "Why do you look so sad?"

Brian's grip on the wheel tightened again as he cleared his throat. "Because Zeke was murdered in front of me yesterday."

"No," I whispered. "This is insane. Stop the car, and let me out."

The tension in his body dissipated as he glanced over at me with an apologetic frown. "Where is he, Davina?"

"I'm serious," I said. "Stop the car. Now."

Tears shimmered in his eyes as he shook his head. "Do you know where your brother is right now?"

"He's back home...alive," I muttered, gripping the seatbelt that suddenly felt too constrictive for me to draw enough air into my lungs. "Why are you saying these things?"

"Believe me, I'd give anything to go back and undo what happened to him."

"None of this makes any sense," I muttered, but— crazy as all of this was—a feeling in my gut told me he was telling the truth.

"I know," Brian said as he reached over and gave my hand a squeeze.

The familiarity of the gesture struck me like a lightning bolt. "We've done this before," I whispered, staring at our joined hands. I wanted to pull away from him, but I also wanted to lose myself entirely beneath the heat of his touch. This wasn't just déjà vu. We'd been here before—Brian saving me from danger, then comforting me after the terrifying ordeal was over.

"You're right," he said as he pulled off the highway into the vacant parking lot of a closed convenience store. "We have done this before."

I stared at him as he parked the car and felt inexplicably placated by the warmth of his hand, still holding onto mine. "What the hell is happening? None of this makes any sense, but somehow I know without a doubt that I can trust you with my life. I can feel it in my bones."

Brian looked down at our hands and brushed his thumb across the back of mine. "Soul mates."

For a moment I was stunned speechless, mesmerized by the feel of the connection between us—so slight, and yet so overwhelmingly erotic. "What?" I finally managed to whisper.

"I've been denying the truth since the day I first set eyes on you," he said, "but if I'm honest, I always felt it. You and I are soul mates, Davina, made for each other in both worlds."

"Both worlds?" I whispered, both terrified and elated by his nonsensical statement. "We've never met before today...but I've been dreaming about you for years."

Brian shook his head. "We have met before. All those vivid memories of the dreams you've had of me? That's our history in the other world, where we've known each other for years."

"You're scaring me."

He shifted in his seat to face me, bathing his beautiful features in the harsh glow of the parking lot's overhead lights. "You don't ever need to be scared of me, Davina."

"I know," I said in a rough whisper. "That's what scares me the most..." If I believed him—*and I was pretty sure I did*—my brother was dead.

"Damn it," Brian muttered as he leaned closer and wrapped his arms around me, enveloping me in his warmth. "I'm so sorry."

"For what?"

"I don't know," he said. "For startling the hell out of you by showing up the way I did today. For not finding you years ago."

Too confused to have any idea how to respond, I shut my eyes and focused on the feel of his strong arms around me and the warmth of his cheek pressed against mine.

"I swear I'll explain it all to you," he said, the rough edge to his voice and the heat of his breath electrically charging every molecule of my being. "But right now, I need to get you somewhere safe."

"I want to jump out of this car, or wake up and find out this was all just a really vivid dream," I whispered. "But I also want to do everything my characters have done with the mental image of you that I've been clinging to since I was a teenager. Every sex scene I've ever written, every man who's ever touched me, it was always you I was thinking of." Mortified that I'd blurted all that out loud, I jerked myself free from his arms. But I couldn't bring myself to look away. "I'm sorry..."

"Don't be," he said in a harsh rasp. "I want that too, Davina. Damn it, I've wanted it since the first second I laid eyes on you—which makes me a horrible person, considering the way I found you."

A rush of heat pooled between my legs at the gravel in his voice. "How did you find me?"

"Naked," he whispered, squeezing his eyes shut, "and bound."

That probably should've terrified me. Instead, a hushed whimper escaped my throat. "That doesn't make you a horrible person…or if it does, I'm horrible too. I've been writing about the two of us coming together for years, and I'm not some sappy PG-rated love-story author. If you had any idea what I've imagined you doing to me, you'd know there's no reason to feel guilty."

A low groan rumbled in his throat. "This is why it's dangerous to leave an incubus and a succubus alone together."

Maybe his strange remark should've been off-putting, but I was too busy—noticing how each syllable sounded more like a feral growl than a spoken word—to be bothered by the fact that what he was saying made no sense.

"The honorable half of me knows I need to get back on the road and drive you to safety, but the other half is fighting pretty damn hard to take control right now. I'd love to play out every one of those scenarios in your books, but there are things we need to take care of first."

I was about to protest when he lunged toward me, his long fingers fisting in my hair as he gripped my head with every ounce of the alpha-male dominance he always exuded in my stories. He angled my mouth toward his and crushed his lips against mine, devouring all of my worries as he drew me into an earth-shatteringly passionate kiss.

That's when it hit me. *This was a dream.*

There was no possible way this could actually be happening; and if this was a dream, there was no time to waste acting proper or shy. My alarm clock could wake me up at any moment, denying me the single most erotic experience of my life. I'd been waiting my entire adult life for this—for *him.*

Desperate for more of him, I maneuvered my way over to his seat—wedging myself between him and the steering wheel—and straddled his legs without breaking the connection between our mouths. He repositioned his seat, sliding it back to give me more room. Then he pulled me tighter against him, aligning our bodies so there was no doubt that he wanted this as much as I did.

Everything beyond the two of us melted away as I slid my hands under his shirt and traced the contours of his muscular frame with my fingertips, the way I'd always longed to. His hands slipped beneath my shirt and unclasped my bra with dominant precision, and he hungrily swallowed the moan he drew from me as the heat of his touch set my insides ablaze.

He groaned against my mouth, summoning another gush of heat between my legs. Then he broke the kiss and muttered, "We should get out of here before they catch up to us." But the warmth of his hand—sliding down my belly, stopping to unbutton and unzip my jeans, then plunging lower—sent an entirely different message.

"I don't care if they catch us," I whimpered as his fingertips brushed over my flesh.

His strong fingers sunk inside me, erasing all good sense from us both; and the feel of his fingers and the heat of him throbbing beneath me nearly made me come undone. Afraid he might change his mind and insist that we get back on the road, I slid back on his lap just far enough to unbutton his jeans and drag down the zipper.

The groan that barreled up his throat as my hand slipped inside his boxers assured me that he was too far gone to be rational. Determined to milk this dream for all its worth before my alarm clock wrenched me away from him, I broke our kiss with a devious grin, coiled my fingers around him and stroked. "I'm not going anywhere with you until you satisfy me."

A wicked grin spread across his face as he tipped me sideways, catching me with one strong hand while the other peeled off my jeans and panties, and hastily tugged his jeans and boxers down out of the way. I'm not sure whether the sound of the car doors locking was meant to make me feel safe or caged, but a thrill coursed through me as he growled, "Satisfy you? Sweetheart, I'm gonna make you scream."

With that, he tugged me upright, gripped my hips and pulled me down hard—burying the entire length of himself inside me—in one powerful thrust that made us both cry out.

Every molecule of my being hummed with bliss at the feel of this man. Our bodies fit together so perfectly that it felt as if I'd found the lost half of myself—a half I'd never even realized was missing. No man had ever made me feel anything close to this. It was primal and magical, and he made good on his promise. I didn't intend to scream because I didn't want to give him the satisfaction. But I lost myself with our bodies melded together, and screams escaped my parted lips without any conscious decision on my part.

Exhausted, I collapsed against his chest and let out a sated sigh as the warmth of his arms enveloped me. *Was I really sure this was all just a dream?* The intensity of it made me wonder. *Because that sure as hell felt real.*

"So, did I satisfy you enough for you to let me get back on the road?" he asked, the heat of his breath against my ear prompting another involuntary spasm. Still inside me, he twitched and let out a deep-throated groan.

"I'll go anywhere you want to take me," I said as my eyes locked with his.

We'd barely finished, but there was so much heat in his gaze that I half expected him to start all over again. Although, there was something else in his eyes that I didn't want to acknowledge. *Regret.*

I couldn't decide what to fear at this point.

If this was a dream, I was terrified of waking up to find that he wasn't real; and if—against all logic—I was awake, the thought of being without him ever again after this was unbearable. In my exhausted state of bliss, my mind refused to even acknowledge the most terrifying part about this being real: *if Brian's words were true, my brother was dead.* I wanted no part of a reality that no longer included my brother.

Dream or not, there was one thing I knew for certain.

I needed this man like I needed air.

32

GODRIC

I stepped out the door to find Louise waiting for me in the corridor. "Hello, Louise. You seem to be making quite a habit of stalking me lately."

She inched closer to me, craning her neck to get a glimpse inside the room as I pulled the door shut. "That's because I don't trust you any farther than I can throw you."

I grinned and placed a hand on the small of her back, ushering her away from the door as I started down the hall. "Absolute trust is such a dull concept. Personally, I've always found that a bit of uncertainty makes life far more interesting."

Louise narrowed her eyes at me but allowed herself to be swept down the corridor at my side. "Would you mind telling me what that meeting was about?"

"You needn't concern yourself with every infinitesimal aspect of our plans, my future Queen."

She stopped short and gripped my arm to stop me as well. "What were you and the doctor discussing in there?"

"Our plans for his patients. He was rather displeased that I allowed Rose to terminate her half-brother whilst the man was under his care."

Louise turned up her nose at that. "What does it matter to him? The man was Unsighted, and not very bright at that. He was an utterly useless human."

I crossed my arms and leaned back against the wall. "The doctor took offense because we didn't make our intentions known from the start, so I sat down with him to discuss our plans for the future."

"And is he satisfied now?"

"Quite. He is delighted with the part he's to play in the rest of this."

A howl sounded from the other end of the corridor, and Louise turned toward the door that stood between us and the creature who'd cried out. "Who cares what the doctor thinks of any of our plans?"

"He does, of course," I replied, frowning at the way her eyes remained fixed on the door, "and I have found that it is best to keep one's allies satisfied."

She turned and narrowed her eyes at me. "Then why won't you satisfy me with a straight answer?"

"To what question?"

"What do you mean, *what question*? The same bloody question I have asked you a hundred times. How are you controlling Charlie's actions?"

I started toward the door that'd captured Louise's attention and held her gaze as she fell into step with me. "I told you. I am not controlling my son's actions." When she snarled at my response, I said, "Well, I am not directly controlling him."

Her eyes drifted to the door as we stopped in front of it. "How then?"

"We have your adopted daughter to thank for my son's cooperation, Louise. Charlie treasures Rose above everything else, and his desire to please her grows stronger with every second he spends in her presence."

"But you are controlling Rose with your blood magic," Louise whispered, as if she feared someone might be listening. "In her heart, Rose's loyalty does not lie with us. Charlie is far too strong to be brainwashed by magic tricks, even yours. So why can't he sense Rose's true desires?"

I unlocked the door and gestured for her to follow me inside. "My control over Rose is absolute. Thanks to my blood, even her desires are mine to dictate so entirely that Charlie perceives them to be genuine."

Louise's eyes widened as she looked over the assortment of ravenous demons chained within the confines of the stone cell. "That still seems implausible."

I stepped toward a malnourished sack of flesh and bones with sunken yellow eyes. "Whose side are you on, Louise?"

"Yours," she said, grimacing as the demon's lifeless eyes fixed on her, "but Charlie is much too powerful to be fooled by your blood's control over Rose."

"Yes, he is," I replied as I unchained the skeletal creature who'd stolen Louise's attention away from me with his howl. Summoning a Water portal, I added, "However, it is not my blood that is controlling Charlie."

Louise took a step toward the portal. "What do you mean?"

"Under normal circumstances, Charlie would certainly see through the deception; but it is Rose's blood that I am using to control his actions."

Louise bit her lip as she considered this new piece of information. "And how exactly did you manage to get her blood into Charlie?"

I shook my head. "Come now, Louise. You don't expect me to divulge all my secrets at once, do you? What fun would that be? Show me a little trust. You have my word that Rose's blood has indeed found its way into Charlie's system, and blood magic that is created with the blood of a dragon's dearest treasure is an insurmountable force. So as long as I am in control of Rose, Charlie's will is mine to dictate."

Louise smiled as her eyes dropped to the skeletal creature cowering before me, too leery of the consequences to chance the freedom that fleeing into the portal might offer him. "You are a cunning old dragon, Godric. I will give you that."

I winked at her, then looked to the beast at my feet. "Your freedom is granted," I said in his demonic tongue. "All I ask in return is that you scout out the border region and report back to me with your findings. Any creatures you happen upon along the way are yours to do with as you wish."

"Thank you, my King," the demon replied as he rose to his feet and entered the portal.

I grinned at Louise as I snapped my fingers, sealing the portal shut. "It won't be long till you and I are sitting on *his* and *hers* thrones in the Sarrum's palace."

A deep worry line creased Louise's forehead, aging her decades in a matter of seconds. "You had better keep your word on that."

"I always keep my word," I said, "and I promise you, my son will continue to do exactly what I want him to. This war is all but won, Louise."

She grinned at me as we made our exit, much to the chagrin of the remaining souls chained up in the room. "Then what are we waiting around here for?"

"We shall head out as soon as my son informs me that he is ready."

33

LOCHLAN

The day started off like every other perfect day in the Light Realm. The sky was a brilliant cloudless blue. Songbirds were cheerily worshipping the rising sun, and Emma and I were seated on a bench in the palace courtyard—flanked by a row of cherry blossom trees in full bloom—with our morning coffees in hand.

I frowned as she set her untouched coffee down on the bench beside her. "Something on your mind, lass?"

She met my gaze with a pensive grin, the rosiness of her cheeks accentuated by the petals falling from the trees around us like fragrant bursts of pink snow. "Always. Why do you ask?"

"Well, you are too preoccupied to drink your coffee, which leads me to believe that whatever is troubling you must be of great importance."

The smile slipped from her face as she nodded. "From what Benjamin said, things didn't exactly go as planned on the retrieval mission."

I set my half-finished coffee aside. "And you are worried about your friend Charlie?"

"I'm worried about all of them," Emma replied, her voice little more than a whisper. She turned her head as Benjamin and Isa entered the courtyard, and a welcoming smile spread across her face. "I'm glad you two decided to join us."

Isa forced a smile as they approached. "So am I."

Eyes glistening with tears, Emma stood and wrapped her arms around the sorceress. "I'm so sorry for your loss, Isa."

"Thank you," Isa whispered, hugging her back.

"We will bring Rose home," Emma said as they dropped the hug. "I promise."

A mournful smile spread across Isa's face as her gaze shifted to Benjamin. "I hope you're right."

The Darkness dipped his head, wordlessly echoing the Queen's promise. Then he kissed Emma on the forehead, and his pitch-black eyes fixed on me. "Brian and Tristan should be arriving soon."

Emma picked up her coffee and took a sip. "How's Brian doing?"

Benjamin shook his head. "He blames himself for Zeke's death."

An explosion in the distance brought our conversation to a swift end; and all of us turned, watching in horror as a burst of orange flames—shadowed by a Dark cloud of malignant smoke—defiled the pristine blue of the morning sky.

The cup slipped from Emma's hand and shattered on the ground, and her eyes dropped to the broken pieces for a moment before she turned to me. "What was that?"

I stood from the bench and studied the darkening sky through flame-filled eyes. "I believe that is your pal Charlie. He must've given you up. That is the only thing that would draw the fight to the Light Kingdom's border."

Emma's eyes welled with tears as she watched the ominous cloud of Dark smoke spread across the sky like a cancerous growth, while a bone-chilling chorus of monstrous shrieks, feral howls, and demonic battle cries rose from the border.

Benjamin nodded. "Yeah, that's definitely Charlie's doing."

I took Emma's hand in mine, pulling her attention away from the sky. "You must go inside now. It's not safe for you to be out in the open."

Emma bit her lip whilst her gorgeous green eyes drifted skyward. "Not yet. I want to observe things from here for a while."

The Darkness scowled at her. "I don't think that's wise."

Emma squared her shoulders as her eyes locked with his. "I didn't ask what you thought, Benjamin."

"You've always been such a stubborn thing," Benjamin muttered. "The Sarrum would have my fucking head if I let you stay out here in the open, and I wouldn't blame him for it." With that the Darkness enveloped himself in shadow, and he drew the Queen in with him.

With no time to waste, I rushed toward the training facility—the agreed-upon meeting place for our troops in the event of an attack—while the commotion at the border grew louder, and my thoughts were inevitably drawn to the past...

...Alexander Talbot emerged from the portal and entered the meadow just inside the border, and I greeted him with a respectful nod. "Welcome to the Light Kingdom, Sarrum."

"Hello, Commander," he replied, shielding his eyes from the realm's blinding light. "Thank you for taking the time to meet with me."

"Thank the Queen," I said, gesturing for him to follow me to the path through the forest that led to the palace.

"Indeed, I will," he replied, following my lead, "although we could have made this much simpler by meeting in the waking world."

I stopped short and turned to look him in the eye. "Simpler for whom?"

"For me, and for your Queen," he replied with a shrug.

I narrowed my eyes at him. "I would have had to make a far more arduous journey."

"And why should that concern me?" he asked in an infuriatingly condescending tone. "Sharing the Queen's bed does not make you King."

Although I wanted to smack that patronizing grin off his face, I restrained the impulse for Violet's sake. "That's an interesting statement, coming from the dragon who sits on a throne that was never meant to be his."

His smile faltered for a moment, but he was quick to paste it back in place. "That is not really any concern of yours though, is it? You are not even of this world, Water dragon. However, I am well aware that you hold the Light Queen's ear, so I will be frank with you. The Henry Godric you met at the delegations was without a doubt more qualified to be Sarrum than I am; but that version of Henry no longer exists."

Shaking my head, I started down the path again. "What does that mean?"

"No one is coming out and saying it, including me—because I want to keep my Queen happy, and she treasures that brother of hers more than anything—but Henry Godric murdered his father in cold blood. It was a justifiable act, committed to protect his sister, but he made the mistake of draining every trace of magic from the old man while the light left his eyes. Lilly and Henry's father was a wicked soul, and devouring that much of his essence polluted Henry's mind. The Henry Godric who exists now is a bitter, dangerous, and downright evil dragon. If you don't want to take my word for it, you can judge for yourself when you meet with him."

We walked the rest of the way in silence, since I saw no point in engaging further with this King who was never meant to rule. The crown didn't sit well on him. Henry Godric had been groomed for the position since the day of his birth. Alexander, on the other hand, had been slated to live a carefree life of luxury whilst his sister Louise fulfilled the family's royal obligation. Alexander Talbot was ill prepared to take the throne, and it showed.

Violet greeted us with a smile as I escorted the substitute monarch into her courtyard. I'd urged her countless times to conduct business in a more secure setting within the palace, but she did as she pleased, and she said she loved the outdoors too much to spend her days in some stuffy conference room. Looking back on it, I suspect she'd used that as an excuse to make me more comfortable since she knew how much I loathed the confines of small spaces.

I winked at the Queen, breaking formality since the King standing behind me would be none the wiser for it. "Hello, my Queen," I said, grinning at the way her cheeks flushed with color as she stood from her chair. "May I present Alexander Talbot, Sarrum of Draumer?"

Watching me pull the chair next to hers back from the table, she replied, "Thank you, Commander." Then she turned to the Sarrum and gestured for him to take the seat across from us. "Welcome to the Light Kingdom, Sarrum."

Alexander smiled at her. Then he sat down and leaned back in his chair. "Thank you, Violet. It's lovely to be here."

She nodded and signaled for her attendant to come forward as the two of us took our seats. "To what do we owe the pleasure of your company this morning, Sarrum?"

Alexander's gaze momentarily shifted to the Queen's attendant approaching the table with a silver-trimmed floral tea set. "I have a proposition for you."

Violet raised an eyebrow. "What sort of proposition?"

Alexander nodded absently to the attendant as she stepped up to him and raised the teapot. "I think that you and I could be quite useful to each other."

"What makes you think that?" I asked, shaking my head as the attendant stopped beside me.

"I believe we have the means to help each other out with the dilemmas we are both facing," Alexander said, picking up his cup.

Violet's expression remained impassive as the Sarrum sipped from his cup and grimaced, although she knew bloody well the Dark creature would detest nectar—the Light creatures' sugary beverage of choice—as much as I did. "What dilemmas are we facing exactly?" she asked with a polite smile.

The Sarrum cleared his throat, then set his cup down on the table and pushed it away. "I am told that your one-year-old son is Unsighted, and since your Unsighted husband is now deceased," he said, casting an accusatory glance toward me, "you need your son to marry a female of pure fairy blood, so that they might provide you with a Sighted heir to the Light Kingdom's throne."

Violet fixed the Sarrum in a death glare since she did not take kindly to accusations that her husband's death was no accident. "What concern is that of yours?"

"None really," Alexander admitted, "but my current dilemma is of great concern to me."

"And what dilemma is that?" I asked in a menacing tone that wiped the smug grin off his face.

"My wife will be giving birth to my heir to the throne soon," Alexander replied.

My Queen set her cup down on the table. "And?"

Genuine grief flickered in Alexander's eyes. "As you well know, there is little chance that she will survive the birth; and it would be best if her brother were not there to witness her death."

Violet took a sip from her cup before asking, "What are you proposing I do about that?"

Alexander dropped his eyes to his cup and pushed it a bit farther away. "Reach out to Henry Godric. Tell him you wish to form an alliance in hopes of overthrowing my rule, and invite him to meet with you in the waking world at your office in America."

I leaned forward in my chair. "Why in God's name would they meet there?"

"Because Lilly will be induced to give birth to my son in the waking world whilst Henry is far away from England," Alexander replied without the slightest trace of remorse in his tone. "If you would prefer to move the meeting to Draumer the instant he sits down in your office, by all means do so. That way you can be present for the meeting, Commander, and Henry will still be kept out of our way."

Violet stared at the Sarrum for a moment, taking another unhurried sip of her tea. "Why should I even consider deceiving the man who by all rights should be sitting on the throne you now occupy? How could you possibly reciprocate and help me with my dilemma?"

A cavalier grin spread across Alexander's face as he leaned forward, resting his arms on the table. "Our sons will be very close in age. Help me keep Henry away now, and I vow to send my son to the same university as your Unsighted son. I will also see to it that your son's intended fairy bride attends that university. Whilst there, my son will befriend your boy and ensure that he and the Unsighted female fairy meet and fall in love."

Violet sat her cup down on the table with a skeptical frown. "How can you possibly guarantee all of that?"

"With enough connections and monetary resources, you can accomplish just about anything," Alexander replied. "I will make donations to the school they're to attend—the school of your choosing—and I will see to it that Albert and his future bride are offered scholarships that are simply too generous to turn down. Then I will instruct my son to employ any Sighted creatures necessary to bring the two of them together whilst they are there. My son will even remain a part of their lives after university, so that he may oversee their union and protect your investment in the future of your kingdom."

I narrowed my eyes at the Sarrum. "That's an awful lot to promise in exchange for occupying a bit of your brother-in-law's time."

The Sarrum shrugged. "It's well worth it to me to ensure that my son is brought safely into the world."

I shook my head at his cowardice. "Why not be at your wife's side yourself, and personally see to it that she and your infant are protected?"

Alexander let out a bitter chuckle. "My wife would never willingly be parted from her brother to have me beside her in his stead."

"It's wicked," Violet whispered, as if she dared not speak of it any louder. "What you are proposing we do, it is deplorable. How can you dismiss your wife's connection to the brother whom she treasures so dearly? How can you deny her the opportunity to spend her last moments in his company so that he might bring her some comfort?"

A gust of ice-blue smoke escaped Alexander's flared nostrils as his eyes filled with flames. "I have stepped aside and spent most of her pregnancy away on business, allowing her to be with him. But if Henry witnesses her death, caused by my son's birth, he will lose his last shred of compassion and take his rage out on my newborn heir. I cannot risk that happening. The only solution is to remove him from that equation and banish him from our lives as soon as he returns from your meeting."

"So you want me to make an enemy of the powerful dragon you're plotting to grievously wrong?" the Queen replied. "Why would I do such a horrific thing?"

Alexander let out a chuckle that left me itching to forcibly remove him from our realm. "Do you have a better plan to ensure that your son weds his intended fairy bride and produces a Sighted heir to your throne?"

"No, I don't," Violet admitted as her gaze shifted to me. "God help both our kingdoms when the rightful Sarrum seeks his revenge."

I urged Violet to reconsider, both in Alexander's presence and in the days leading up to her meeting with Henry Godric, but I had no better solution to her dilemma...

...I stepped inside the training facility, shaking my head. "We could have avoided all of this, Violet," I muttered under my breath. "That meeting damned both kingdoms to this fate."

I could only be grateful that Violet hadn't been around to witness the way David Talbot broke his father's promise to her.

Of course, David did facilitate the relationship between Violet's son and the Unsighted fairy he wedded—just as promised—and he went into business with Albert after they graduated from university, so he could remain close to the couple. However, when it came time for me to bring Violet's granddaughter to the palace, to raise her and oversee her rule of the Light Kingdom, David Talbot behaved more like a spoiled child than the ruler of an entire world.

34

ADDISON

I wasn't sure what to think as we all filed into the training facility to meet up with our units before heading off to join the fight at the Light Realm's border. The screeches, howls, and bone-rattling explosions echoing from the battlefield were making it difficult to concentrate. On top of that, my heart was aching over the loss of my loved ones who'd sacrificed their lives to save my family. Bob was supposed to be leading our unit with me, but I couldn't afford to think about that right now. If I did, I'd be useless in battle, and I wasn't about to let the Purists take anyone else from us.

I nodded to the soldiers in my unit, hoping to convey a sense of confidence that I sure as hell wasn't feeling—although, my inner turmoil had nothing to do with my fighting skills. Thanks to Bob, I could hold my own in battle against the best of them, but I wasn't a loner in this world anymore. Instead of focusing solely on this fight, I couldn't help worrying about how

James and our boys were holding up. I tried to placate myself with a reminder that my family was safe and sound back at the Sarrum's palace as I watched the soldiers pour into the facility, keeping an eye out for the rest of my unit.

When I caught sight of my Unsighted husband walking in with Davina and the other refugees who'd come to the Light Realm after Zeke's mirage was destroyed, my stomach dropped.

I shook my head as he walked up to me. "What are you doing here?"

James smiled at me with that same endearing mix of kindness, awkwardness, and quiet strength that'd captured my heart in the waking world. "Every able-bodied creature has an obligation to join this fight, Addison."

"This isn't your battle to fight," I muttered. "You should be back at the palace with our children."

"*Our* children," James replied with a knowing grin. "You said it again. The children are safe at the Sarrum's palace. I don't really understand any of this, but I know my place is beside you now. If you are going into battle, then I'm going with you. No matter what happens out there, you and I will be together till the end."

I pictured that burning castle where my knight in shining armor sacrificed his life to be with his soul mate until her last breath, and a lump formed in my throat. "Together till the end."

I smiled at Davina as she approached us, along with the rest of the souls her brother had rescued from the Purists. "Shouldn't you all be taking shelter inside the Queen's palace?"

Davina's gaze seemed instinctively drawn to the entrance the moment Brian stepped into the training facility along with Tristan. "We won't sit this fight out either," she said as the brothers joined us. "Together till the end, right?"

Entwining his fingers with hers, Brian nodded. "Right. We're all in this together now. Zeke trained Davina and the rest of this group to fight like warriors. He may not have wanted them to join this fight, but they've got just as much to lose as everyone else."

I nodded and tried to focus on not tearing up. "A few of our units have lost their leaders, Sir. How would you like us to proceed?"

"Together," Brian replied, smiling at Zeke's sister.

"Till the end," Isa chimed in as she slipped out of the incoming crowd.

The steady hum of an army of voices died off the instant Commander Mackendrick entered the facility with his unit of seasoned warriors in tight formation behind him. "We have trained for this," he said, his commanding presence capturing every soul's attention as his deep booming voice bounced off the walls of the cavernous room. "We had hoped to keep the fight away from our border, but now that it's here we shall not shy away from it. The Light Realm will not cower before the Purist army, and we shall never bow to Henry Godric."

A chorus of cheers rose up from the troops.

As Mackendrick began directing the units to their posts on the battlefield, I motioned for my soldiers to fall into step behind me, and we headed for the door.

"Just so you know," James said, his voice low as he came marching up to my side. "I have no intention of following you into battle. I plan to fight alongside you."

I blinked back the tears in my eyes and shook my head. "How can I fight if I'm worrying about you surviving this, James?"

"How could I fall behind and leave you to fight at the front alone?" he replied with a lopsided grin. "Your friends gave their lives to save us, Addie. I wouldn't dream of leaving you to face this battle alone."

I couldn't have answered him even if I had known what to say. Conversation ceased to be an option the instant we stepped outside. The roar of the battle at the border up ahead was deafening. James took my hand in his, and I offered up a silent prayer that somehow we would survive this.

The Light Kingdom's sky was no longer the serene blue of a lovely summer day. Thick black storm clouds were choking the light from the sky, darkening the realm to a dimness better suited to the Dark creatures advancing on its border. Fires raged all along the border in a blinding array of hues; their multicolored smoke spiraled toward the heavens, further muddying the sky. There were more dragons on the Purists' side than I'd ever set eyes on; and those monstrous beasts were backed by an unending stream of giants, and trolls, and all manner of demons. Thankfully the warding along the Light Kingdom's border would prevent the dragons from taking flight and setting the realm ablaze from above, but the warding couldn't hold out forever.

My unit and I were near the middle of the pack on our side of the border, but there was enough of a crack in the ranks ahead for me to keep an eye on the frontline. The dragons on the attacking side were still arriving in droves, populating every inch of the border.

Adrenaline coursed through my veins as an outpouring of dragons broke through from behind us to take the lead on our side. I wasn't sure where they'd come from, but as my heart hammered in my chest, I thanked the heavens that they'd arrived.

A few pounding heartbeats later, every creature on both sides stilled as a massive ball of orange flames exploded at the frontline—barreling skyward like the blast from a hydrogen bomb—while a monstrous copper-scaled dragon advanced to the front of the enemy ranks.

I knew that dragon. He'd saved us from certain death on our mission to locate the Purists' meeting place.

"Surrender, and we will leave you unharmed," Charlie roared, the magnitude of his booming voice drowning out all other sounds. "We do not wish to conquer the Light Kingdom. All we ask is that you hand over the fairy Queen who recently decided to rule your realm after leaving you to fend for yourselves for decades. Your kingdom did just fine without her all those years. So why should you risk your lives to protect her now?"

A thunderous roar—louder than anything I'd ever heard—drowned out the remainder of Charlie's speech, and the ground shook as a jaw-droppingly massive Water dragon stomped toward the front on our side of the border. This magnificent beast towered above all the other dragons, his aquamarine scales shimmering like ocean waves bathed in sunlight.

"You traitorous fool," Mackendrick growled in a voice so deafening that most of us had to cover our ears to withstand it. "How will you ever look yourself in the eye again? Win or lose, this battle will cost you your soul. Even now, Emma is worrying about the welfare of her dear friend who always had her back at the mental institution. You have betrayed her in the most deplorable way, and still she worries about what will become of you."

The massive copper-scaled dragon stilled at the commander's words, and the orange flames blazing in his eyes diminished until they were little more than flickering embers. Plumes of reddish-orange smoke streamed from his flared nostrils, unfurling in the air like fiery ribbons while his muscular chest rose and fell.

And time seemed to stop as the entire battle stilled with him.

35

CHARLIE

Even now, Emma is worrying about the welfare of her dear friend who always had her back at the mental institution. You have betrayed her in the most deplorable way, and still she worries about what will become of you. As Commander Mackendrick's words reverberated inside my head, my muscles locked in place, the world around me stilled, and my heart began to crumble.

What the fuck was I doing? Godric was controlling me somehow. That much was obvious—and whatever he was doing to me, it was working brilliantly.

Benjamin and Isa had trusted me to rescue Rose and bring her home to them. The plan had been for me to infiltrate the Purists, ask them to take me to Godric, then figure out a way to get my girlfriend the hell out of there. Instead, I'd led Rose into this bloody battle with both of us fighting on the enemy's side. I wanted to fix this, but I wasn't powerful enough to fight whatever hold Godric had over me. Ever since I joined up with the Purists, I'd found myself saying and doing horrific things.

I gave the order to kill the only mother I'd ever known. There was no denying that the Unsighted woman who raised me as her son made my life miserable. But she took me in and raised me as her own because the man she loved had begged her to, and she continued to raise me the best she could even after his death. She had plenty of shortcomings, but she didn't deserve to die for them. Yet, the Purists slit her throat in the waking world and left her to bleed out on her living room floor, and they did it because I commanded them to.

I also told Godric about Zeke's Unsighted sister, Davina. And the Purists poisoned Zeke—leaving his younger sister vulnerable in the waking world—since he was the only soul who'd known where to find her. That half-giant incubus was Tristan's dearest friend. The two of them were like brothers, and Tristan's friend was dead now because of me. Davina was almost certainly dead at this point too.

I didn't know her well, but Davina seemed like a beautiful person inside and out. According to Tristan, she was also the love of Brian's life. Brian was my first guide, and he'd been one of my biggest supporters right from the start. And how did I repay him for everything he'd done for me? I orchestrated the murder of his brother's best friend and sentenced his soul mate to death.

Then there was the Sarrum. David Talbot changed the entire course of my life after meeting me at the mental facility. Despite my smartass attitude, he took me in and trained me to be the dragon I was always meant to be. The man welcomed me into his family of Sighted souls. When he was confident that I was ready, he sent me to infiltrate the Purists—trusting me to save his shadow's daughter—and he named me as successor to his throne. And what did I do in return? I betrayed his confidence and gave his worst enemy the means to destroy him.

Emma Talbot had been the first person to look at me like I wasn't crazy in a really long time. She was my dearest friend. She'd loved me, and trusted me. On top of that, Emma was my mentor's soul mate. *And I gave her up to Godric.* The Sarrum had trusted me to protect the secret of his wife's whereabouts. Instead, I served Emma up on a silver platter to the monster who fathered me because I was too weak to stop myself. *Some King I would've been.*

If I had the strength to do it, I would've ended my own life before letting it come to this. But even that was beyond my control. I'd tried fighting against Godric's hold on me with the buried part of my mind that'd been crying out in horror at every wicked deed I'd been coerced into doing. Even now, as I stood against the soldiers who were fighting to protect my dear friend, I desperately wanted to stop. I wanted to surrender. Hell, I wanted to turn around and join the side that I should be fighting for, but I wasn't strong enough.

I'd failed all of them. Emma should never have gotten close to me back at the facility. David never should've invited me to join his family and taken me under his wing. And Rose should never have opened her heart to me.

While Mackendrick and I were spewing threats and sparks across the border at each other with our armies at the ready behind us, I had caught sight of Rose manning her post at the border. There wasn't a doubt in my mind that Benjamin was somewhere on the other side of that border, and I was pretty sure Isa was too. I'd be damned if I would condemn their daughter to a lifetime of misery because I was too weak to rescue her like they'd trusted me to.

Brainwashed as Rose was by Godric's blood, there was no way she would willingly walk away from us to go back to her parents. But there was one thing that just might work. Rose had always been jealous of my connection with Emma. I'd assured her a hundred times that Emma and I were just friends, but Rose was my dearest treasure. I could *feel* what she felt and sense what she needed, so I knew for a fact that she still felt inferior to Emma. Rose desperately needed to know that my whole heart belonged to her. My only hope of getting her back to her family where she belonged was to exploit that weakness. If I could make Rose believe Emma was the woman I truly treasured, I just might be able to push her away. It would break her heart—and destroy mine in the process—but if it saved her, it'd be worth it.

Godric's hold over me was too absolute for me to act against his wishes. Although, if my words seemed geared toward infuriating Mackendrick, maybe I could get away with saying just enough to break the spell that Rose was under.

All these thoughts raced through my mind in a matter of seconds—my heart pounding, and adrenaline coursing through my veins—as both sides of the battle stood motionless, awaiting my response. I shook my head and mentally replayed Mackendrick's words to me: *You have betrayed her in the most deplorable way, and still she worries about what will become of you.* Then I took a step closer to him and snarled, "I don't believe that's any of your concern, Commander."

The Water dragon's laughter was every bit as thunderous and fearsome as his roar. "The safety of the Light Queen and her kingdom are my only concerns, but I don't imagine a spineless turncoat like yourself can wrap his mind around the concept of absolute loyalty."

"Loyalty?" I roared, matching the commander's laughter in decibel and ferocity. "Who do you think you're kidding, Mackendrick? You are not loyal to a kingdom. You're loyal to the fairy you desperately want to love you, but I've got news for you: she won't. Trust me, I speak from experience. Emma may look at you like her whole world revolves around you. She'll say things that make your heart sing, and make you feel more alive than you ever thought possible, but it's all a lie. Emma Talbot is a whore who toys with the hearts of dragons she finds useful. There is only one dragon your precious Queen has ever had any intention of loving. Although, if it suits her purpose, she'll bat those lovely lashes, and mesmerize you with the sparkle in her emerald eyes, and make you salivate at the sight and the scent of her every time she enters a room."

Plumes of greenish-blue smoke spewed from the commander's flared nostrils, scenting the air with the same fragrant blend of notes that'd wafted inside the pub in Glasgow each time he stepped inside. His ancient sea-blue eyes filled with flames as his massive chest rose and fell, but he let me go on without interruption.

"But there is only one dragon Emma Talbot has ever had any intention of fucking," I snarled, spewing orange sparks across the distance between me and Mackendrick. I chanced a sideways glance at Rose. The hurt in her eyes nearly incapacitated me, and I had to remind myself that breaking her heart was my only shot at saving her. "It was never me that Emma intended to spread those shapely legs for, and it will never be you either, Commander. That bitch will use you and toy with your heart as she pleases, but David Talbot is the only dragon who will ever get inside her—well, with her consent at least."

I *felt* Rose's anguish. It was a searing ache in my chest. Hating myself for what I was doing to her, I let out a thunderous bellow that shook the ground beneath us as a burst of orange flames barreled from my mouth toward the troops across the border.

Mackendrick calmly raised a clawed hand, summoning a wall of Water that rose up like a tsunami from the sea that bordered the western side of the kingdom. It towered above all of us, ascending to impossible heights as it rushed through the space between our two sides, extinguishing my flames with such precision that there wasn't a single casualty.

Taking that as their cue to advance, the other dragons on Mackendrick's side charged toward us, spitting fire and shaking the ground with the weight of their monstrous limbs and the deafening sound of their roars. And the dragons on our side charged toward them, decimating the invisible barrier of warding between our two sides as they collided in an explosion of multicolored flames.

36

ROSE

Tears filled my eyes as the battle raged on—dragon against dragon, Dark creature against Light—until it was almost impossible to sort out who belonged to which side. I did my part and fought beside the others because my will was no longer my own. Try as I might, I couldn't break free from Godric's control.

I could forgive all of Charlie's behavior since he'd joined the Purists because I was certain Godric was controlling him, although I didn't understand how. But as I listened to Charlie snarl at that Water dragon who fought for the Light Realm something inside me shattered. *Still, after all this time.* Isa had severed the hold Emma's charm had over Charlie. I had given my heart and soul to him—and yet, it was still *her* that he truly desired. His words were cruel and callous, and he said horrible hateful things about Emma, but there was no denying the passion fueling his rage. Charlie still wanted her, and all of his fury stemmed from the fact that he couldn't have her.

And just like that, my worth was diminished.

Our entire relationship had been a lie. Charlie never really treasured me. He took my heart as a consolation prize, but I wasn't the trophy he truly desired. That distinction would always belong to Emma Talbot, despite the fact that she had no interest in it.

I hated the Light Queen with a ferocity that combusted in the pit of my stomach, darkening my vision in a haze of violet flames. Godric had made it clear that Emma was his to finish off. But if I made it to her first, I wasn't sure I'd be able to stop myself from ripping that vile fairy heart of hers out of her chest. Emma Talbot was weak and broken. I could snap her in half without breaking a sweat. What did all these powerful males see in her?

Feral rage propelled me forward, trampling lesser creatures beneath my clawed limbs, bathing them in fire, and grinning as they screamed and flailed while the flames melted the flesh from their bones. I'm not sure how long I carried on like that. It felt like such a brief release from my heartache, but I suspect it may actually have been much longer.

The sky of the Light Realm continued to darken as more and more smoke filled the air while our flames spread across the ground, burning everything in their path.

I didn't even stop to catch my breath until Charlie took flight. As I watched him rise from the flames, I couldn't help marveling at the magnificence of this royal dragon who'd finally come into his full power.

I'm ashamed to admit that despite everything, when his fiery gaze locked on me, my body felt as if it would burst into flames.

Charlie nodded to his troops on the ground, signaling to all of us that the fight had progressed far enough. The Light creatures were holding their own with the aid of the Sarrum's finest warriors, not to mention the Water dragon hell-bent on crushing us, and an army of royal dragons. Now it was time for us to turn the tide.

"Penny for your thoughts," Charlie's deep booming voice roared, both aloud and inside the heads of every creature in the realm.

For a moment the battle stilled—both sides immobilized by the mental intrusion—but as we all regained our bearings, a great majority of the royal dragons fighting with the Light Realm's army turned on those weaker creatures they'd come to protect. As they barreled forward, mindlessly attacking their own allies, that ancient Water dragon took flight.

In the utter chaos that ensued, the Water dragon collided with Charlie in the airspace above us. Many of the creatures on both sides froze, utterly in awe of the two massive beasts brawling in midair. They tumbled through the air above us—weaving in and out of thick clouds of smoke, tearing at each other's flesh, raining a shower of fire and water down on us—as they spilled each other's precious blood.

As I watched them battle, I realized all of this was still about *her*. Both dragons in the air above us wanted Emma Talbot. Neither of them possessed her, but they would still fight each other to the death for nothing more than an improbable chance to claim her.

As their shower of sparks rained down on us, I shook my head and continued to fight. *But who was I fighting for at this point?* Charlie obviously didn't love me, and my mother and Benjamin probably wanted me dead because I'd murdered my half-brother.

My stomach roiled as I surged through the enemy forces, destroying Light creatures right and left alongside all the other dragons who'd turned and joined the Purists' side. *I had no side.* No one truly cared about me. I'd been a fool to believe my relationship with Charlie was anything more than a means to satisfy the urges he couldn't satisfy with the woman he truly desired.

The sky continued to darken as the battle raged on. I lost count of how many lives I'd taken, or how far I had trampled into enemy territory, or where Charlie and that Water dragon were.

I sunk my teeth into a pointy-eared Light creature wielding an elven blade, and froze with her clamped between my teeth as a cry of alarm sounded behind me. *My mother's cry.* Isa sounded no less shocked than she'd sounded the day she arrived at the battle in Zeke's mirage to find me locked in a fight to the death with Charlie. I let the Light creature drop from my mouth as I turned toward my mother.

Isa's eyes filled with tears as she knelt down on the scorched ground before me. "Come home to us, Rose. I don't blame you for anything you've done. None of it was your fault."

My initial instinct was to devour her—because she was an important member of the Sarrum's inner circle—but I froze, unable to harm the woman who'd given birth to me. Isa had endured a dangerous pregnancy and risked her own life to bring me, the child of the Purist who'd attacked her, into the world.

As I opened my mouth to speak to her, the world around us darkened until the Darkness enveloped me, and everything else ceased to be.

I made a promise to your mother, a Dark voice whispered in my head. *We will not lose you, Rose. Your place is with us.*

I knew this voice, although I couldn't seem to place it. *I have done terrible things.*

We all have, the Dark voice assured me as I sunk farther into its depths, losing all sense of direction. *But your actions were beyond your control.*

If that's true, who was controlling me?

No answer came.

The thoughts in my head began to evaporate, one by one, erasing all sense of self until I had no idea where...or who...or what I was. Only one dreadful thought remained: *No one has ever really loved me.*

That is not true, the voice said, somehow comforting me in the same breath that it filled me with terror— that is, if there even was a *me* left to terrify. Whatever remained of the *me* that'd existed before had no shape, or form, or substance. I was nothing but a collection of disjointed thoughts, and those were rapidly evaporating. Soon there would be nothing left of me.

We love you, Rose, the Dark voice assured me. *I love you, and so does your mother. She is counting on me to bring you back, and I do not intend to fail her.*

I wasn't sure who this voice belonged to, or why I felt such a connection to it, but a response came from whatever small scrap of me remained. *You just want to please the woman you love. You don't actually care about me.*

I'm nothing more than the catastrophe that brought your soul mate into your life.

You are wrong, daughter. I do love you. What brought you into our lives is not relevant to either of us. An act of violence brought you into being, and I destroyed the perpetrator of that act. But you had no part in that. You are the child of my soul mate, her only Sighted child. I have always considered you my daughter, and I will not let that son of a bitch corrupt your kind and noble heart. Do you hear me? You do not belong to Godric. You don't belong with the Purists. You belong with us, Rose, and it's time for you to come home.

I wanted to answer, but the Darkness intensified until it was so absolute that it swallowed up every last trace of me.

37

GODRIC

As the battle at the border raged on, I managed to slip inside the Light Queen's palace undetected. That old Water dragon who defended the Light Realm was far too preoccupied with the fight to notice the intrusion. The clashing of dragons, and giants, and all manner of creatures—Dark and Light—shook the gleaming marble walls as I made my way down the palace corridors, guided by the faint fluttering beat of the fairy Queen's heart. This was almost too perfect to be true.

I'd been intent on destroying David Talbot since the day he took my sister's life all those years ago. After finding Lilly's lifeless body on that bed in the guesthouse, I had torn my way through the Talbot household, destroying every creature that stood between me and their precious heir to the throne who'd savagely torn his way out of my sister's body. I made it all the way to his nursery, venom and blood dripping from my lips, salivating at the thought of sinking my teeth into that little monstrosity. It was not right that my sister's killer should live, and thrive, and ascend to the place of honor that was mine by birthright. Distracted by fury and bloodlust as I'd been, I didn't detect the presence of Alexander Talbot's shadow in the nursery until I lunged toward that murderous infant's crib. The shadow enveloped me in Darkness before I could lay a hand on the child, and I didn't regain consciousness until he tossed me into the abyss—the forsaken territory of No Man's Land—banishing me from the very kingdom I was meant to rule.

As I drew nearer, the beating of Emma Talbot's heart grew louder and I began to salivate. This was a far more satisfying revenge than killing my sister's defenseless infant would've been. David Talbot was an adult now, fully cognizant of the fact that he'd killed the woman I treasured above all else. Now it was my turn to destroy his dearest treasure and take back the throne that was rightfully mine, leaving him to wallow in grief for the remainder of his miserable existence.

Hardly able to believe I'd made it this far, my fingers trembled with anticipation as I gripped the knob of the door the fairy Queen's heartbeat had led me to. Drawing a deep breath, I turned the knob and opened the door that stood between me and David Talbot's dearest treasure. Then I stepped inside her blindingly bright bedchamber.

Squinting, I walked toward the Queen of Light. She was seated in an armchair beside a stained-glass window—depicting a lush fairy-garden scene—with her nose in a book, utterly indifferent to the carnage that was littering her kingdom's border.

A pang of guilt struck me as Emma Talbot shut her book and looked up, meeting my gaze with wide-eyed dismay. This poor helpless creature had never been David Talbot's to claim in the first place. In one way or another, every bit of the destruction that would occur this day was the result of her vile husband's mindless greed.

A wicked grin spread across my face as I stepped toward my enemy's fairy bride. "Hello, Princess—or, I suppose I ought to call you Queen now. Congratulations on breaking free from my nephew's iron grip and finally taking your rightful place as ruler of the Light Kingdom. As much as I admire you for that, I'm afraid I have no choice but to slaughter you after violating you in every imaginable way."

"What have they done to you, Henry?" a voice behind me asked, its sweet feminine familiarity gutting me like a knife.

A lump formed in my throat as I turned toward that voice. I blinked, willing my Dark eyes to adjust to the light. As the young woman before me came into focus, my heart stuttered and I sunk to my knees on the floor. "Lilly?"

My sister smiled at me, infusing new life into my long dormant heart as she took a tentative step toward me. "Hello, Henry."

My heart hammered in my chest as I watched her move closer, too afraid of losing this specter before me to blink. "No…this isn't possible." Senseless as I knew it was, a tear slid down my cheek.

She touched her small hand to my face, brushing away the tear; and I raised my hand to hers and pressed it to my cheek, marveling at its solidity and warmth.

"It's all right, Henry," she whispered, kneeling on the floor in front of me. "I'm here now. You are not to blame for any of this. I forgive you for all of it."

I blinked back the tears threatening to obscure this miraculous vision before me. "What?"

"This war, and all the destruction and hurt that you've caused," she said, "none of it was your fault. Father poisoned your mind with his malevolence the day you absorbed his magic. I knew it the moment you came back to your bedroom to tell me you'd fixed things so I wouldn't have to leave home. I could feel the coldness that'd always been a part of Father coursing through your veins, but you weren't to blame for that. You never would've killed him if he hadn't been planning to send me away."

"That's not true," I whispered. "I always intended to kill him for treating you with such cruelty."

"You were the one he hurt. Father never once laid a hand on me because you were always there to stop him."

"But I failed to protect you in the end," I said, searching her eyes. *This couldn't possibly be real.* It was obviously a deception of some sort. Yet, she was such a welcome sight that I didn't care. "What is happening? This cannot be real."

"No, it isn't," David Talbot said as he emerged from the shadows in the corner of the room, "but the memory of her is true nonetheless."

An apologetic smile tugged at the corners of Lilly's mouth as she stood up and stepped back whilst David approached. I remained still and speechless on my knees, unable to take my eyes off her, no matter how false the image was. "What are you talking about?"

"The message was meant for you," David said, offering a hand and tugging me to my feet when I reluctantly accepted it. "She entrusted it to me with her final breaths."

My heart stilled at his words. "What?"

"My mother wanted you to be there beside her," David replied. "She loved you till her last breath, and she never stopped hoping you'd burst through the door to be there with her at the end."

I opened my mouth to speak, but the air in my lungs escaped me in a strangled sob. *I had no words to respond to that.*

"She fed me more memories than I imagine most newborn dragons would be capable of absorbing in their first moments of life," David said. "Everything she needed to say to you, she said to me whilst I drained the life from her. If I could undo that, I would. You have no idea how many hours I've spent hating myself for killing the woman who gave me life. That act of savagery was an unforgivable sin, defining my existence in my first hour of life as I condemned both men who loved her to a lifetime of misery."

David's words seemed to echo from a great distance as the flesh-and-blood vision of my Lilly stepped closer to us. I could have asked who or what she was. I'm almost certain I heard David call her Mia as his voice echoed from afar, but I didn't want the truth to dissolve this miraculous glimpse of the woman I'd been mourning for most of my life.

"Tell me what she said," I whispered as the specter of my sister took my hand in hers.

"I could, but I would prefer to show you," David said as another man stepped out of the shadows.

I knew this man. He was the satori who'd helped Charlie's mother evade my men with my heir in her belly.

"Would you like to see your sister's final moments?" David's voice asked from afar.

I turned my attention back to the ghost holding onto my hand. "Who are you?"

She smiled at me. "Does it matter, Henry?"

"No, I need to see how…" My words trailed off as the satori stepped closer, placing one hand on David's arm and the other on mine.

The instant he touched me, I was swallowed up in a vortex while still desperately trying to cling to the feel of my sister's hand…

…The next thing I knew, I was staring up at my sister's face from the disorienting vantage point of the newborn son cradled in her arms.

I studied Lilly's delicate facial features, mesmerized by the brilliant blue of her eyes. She looked so pale and fragile. Her cheeks were sunken, and broken blood vessels streaked the whites of her eyes. This was exactly how she'd looked when I found her, and this was the room in the guesthouse where they had left her lifeless body. There was no way anyone could craft a false version of her final moments with such accurate details, which only left one explanation: *This was real.*

Heartache gripped me as she smiled at me. I had failed her. I should've been there to hold her hand and comfort her until the end.

"This wasn't your fault, Henry," Lilly murmured, piercing my heart with her words, spoken to me across a vast expanse of time and place. "None of it was your fault. You did everything in your power to protect me all my life. However, I know you too well. You're going to blame yourself for not being here for me now, but you shouldn't. I'm the luckiest dragon in the world," she sobbed as her bloodshot eyes welled with tears. "How many creatures can say with absolute certainty that they were the center of someone else's universe? I know without a doubt that you loved me and treasured me more than anything, Henry. Your actions made that abundantly clear to me every moment of my life."

A tear dripped from Lilly's cheek to my forehead, and I relished the contact with anything that'd come from her. Warmth flooded my insides as she smiled at me and wiped her teardrop from my face with a loving caress of her fingertips.

"I'm so sorry they robbed these final moments from us," Lilly whispered. "I want you to know that I tried to fight it—getting induced while you were away, losing my life to this birth—but I wasn't strong enough, Henry. I'm so sorry to leave you like this without saying goodbye. I hope you can find it in your heart to forgive me."

She hugged me close to her chest, and my heart ached with a ferocity that I would never have believed possible after all these dispassionate decades.

"I need you to promise me something, Henry," she whispered. "Promise me that you will love my son. The Talbots are so cold and cruel. I know in my heart that Alexander will never love our son like I would have, so I need you to love my baby boy for me. Nurture him with every bit of the love that you have for me, and a piece of me will always remain with you."

Another tear slipped from her cheek, landing on the arm of her newborn child who did not yet possess the dexterity to wipe it away. "Hello, my sweet boy," she whispered, smiling down at him. "I am so sorry I can't stay to raise you, but don't worry. I'm not leaving you alone. Your uncle can safeguard you from the coldness of the Talbot family, but I need you to do something for me. Your uncle is my dearest treasure, and I am his. I'm not sure how he will do without me. So please look after my dear Henry for me, and remind him how loved he is."

I wanted to weep for my dying sister. I wanted to cry out to her and beg her forgiveness for breaking all the promises I never knew she'd asked me to keep, but the room blurred and everything in it dissipated, including my dear Lilly…

…I stumbled backward as the Light Queen's bedchamber reformed around me. David reached out and steadied me, guiding me to a chair someone had placed nearby.

My eyes locked with the eyes of the flesh-and-blood specter of my sister as I dropped into the chair. It didn't matter who or what she actually was. The memory I'd just witnessed was real, and I had spent every moment since my sister's death hell-bent on destroying the son she had asked me to watch over. "I failed you," I muttered.

"She meant for me to bring you comfort," David said as he crouched down next to my chair, "so I suppose we both failed her."

"You were just an infant," I muttered, shaking my head as my gaze drifted to my nephew. "You are my sister's child, and I've spent every moment since your birth trying to destroy you."

"That wasn't your fault," David replied. "I've always known that. My mother made certain of that before she left us."

"I need to go to her and beg her forgiveness," I whispered. "My sweet Lilly has been alone in the afterlife for far too long. Please, David. I know I've done nothing to deserve your mercy, but I need you to end my suffering and send me to her now. If not for me, then do it for her."

A sorrowful smile spread across David's face. "She would not have wanted that."

"How can you be so certain?" I muttered. "I knew her better than anyone. Don't you see? This is how it has to be. You were always meant to end my suffering."

David shook his head. "You are not making an informed request. You should know that I have named Charlie as my successor to the throne. I think you ought to stick around for your son's coronation, so that you may see the wrongs that my family did to you and my mother righted."

My gaze drifted to the stained-glass window, although it offered no view of the outside world. "Charlie is out there attacking your allies as we speak."

"Yes, just as we expected him to," David replied. "When we sent Charlie to gain your trust and infiltrate your ranks, we knew he'd be unable to resist falling under your control. I have been certain of that since the day you coerced Rose into joining your side. That is why we made certain Charlie knew Emma had taken her place in the Light, so he would inform you that she was here. It was the surest way to draw you out, and a changeling in your sister's form was the only way to immobilize you and get you to listen to the message I've been incapable of delivering my entire life."

"I don't know what to say," I whispered.

"Say that you'll be there to watch your son take the throne," David replied with a shrug. "That's the surest way to end this war and restore peace to Draumer. Both sides will follow the dragon who shares our blood."

"But Charlie has done terrible things to your side."

"Nothing that cannot be forgiven," David said. "Rose was controlling his actions whilst you were controlling her with your blood. It is common knowledge that a dragon can be driven to madness in matters concerning his treasure."

My gaze drifted back to the vision of my sweet Lilly as I sat there—stunned and speechless, hating myself for failing her—until Emma Talbot stood from her chair in the corner to join her husband in this monumental moment.

As I watched my sister's son smile at his fairy wife and take her hand in his, an ache flared in my chest. "I have failed you, David."

"That's all behind us now," David replied. "You and I will end this war together. Then we can all move forward and atone for our mistakes."

"No," I muttered, too overcome with self-loathing and regret to spit the words out fast enough. "You don't understand. I am so sorry…"

The rest of my apology died on my tongue as Emma Talbot stumbled backward, clutching her throat as she gasped for air.

David caught her before she hit the floor, but it didn't matter.

An instant later, the Queen of the Light Realm was gone.

38

EMMA

Panic gripped me as the Water dragged me down into its depths. *How did I end up in the Water?* My lungs were burning, begging me to breathe, and it was so cold. Somewhere deep inside, I'd always known this was how my story would end. Frozen and alone. Terrified and forgotten. Unable to resist the urge, I sucked in a desperate attempt at a breath, filling my lungs with ice water. I wanted to cry out for help, but I couldn't. There was nothing I could do to stop this.

I was meant to die in these Waters. I'd felt it every time I passed between worlds. The Water creatures had been desperate to claim me, ever since that day my Unsighted father showed up in the heart of the Dark Forest outside our clearing. The Waters erased so much of me after the doctor poured that potion down my throat. I lost my Sight because of it. I'd stumbled around, blind in both worlds—unable to recall whichever world I wasn't in—existing in only half-truths for months; and when I finally regained my Sight, the Water creatures were furious.

As I sunk deeper, the events of that nightmarish day that'd started it all came rushing back to me…

…Isa and I were in the clearing, busying ourselves with our favorite pastimes. The Purists had been raiding the fringe for days now, and the Sarrum and the Darkness were off leading the counterattack to send a clear message. Harming the inhabitants of the fringe was forbidden, and those who broke the law would be swiftly put to death.

Forcing myself to focus on the landscape I was painting, I scooped a glob of white into an inkwell and dipped my brush in the red. But before I could blend them into the perfect shade of cotton-candy pink for the clouds, an agonized shriek echoed from the Waters.

I dropped my paintbrush, stood up, and stepped toward the Waterfall at the edge of the lake.

And it sounded again, a shriek of desperation from beyond the mirage. "Emma! Please! Help me!"

I stuck my hand into the Waterfall with detached curiosity.

"Emma! Please! Come help your father!"

The urgency in his tone drove me to act before I could really process what I was doing. Heart racing, I stepped through the Waterfall.

I hadn't seen my father since the night he caught me in bed with David when I was eighteen.

…My parents had gone out of town for the weekend, but they ended their trip early and got back in the middle of the night. When my father came into my room to let me know they were home, he found me lying naked in his best friend's arms.

He yanked me out of bed by my hair, and I woke up disoriented and terrified with my father's hands around my throat. At first, I feared the consequences of getting caught but as his grip tightened, I started to fear for my life. A thick blue vein bulged on his forehead as he hollered, "You filthy little whore! What the hell did you do?"

I could feel myself fading, and I didn't want to die naked. Desperate to cover myself, I made a weak attempt to grab the sheet off my bed.

"What the fuck are you doing?" my father shrieked, spit flying from his lips. "I MADE YOU! But you cover yourself from me and spread your legs for my partner? You fucking whore!"

It was only a matter of seconds, but—naked, and humiliated, and terrified that I was about to die—they were the longest seconds of my life.

Everything beyond my father's face was a blur. I didn't see David get off the bed, but I heard his fist slam into my father's face, followed by the crunch of breaking bone. As my father lost his grip on me, David caught me in his arms. He sat me down on the bed, grabbed his shirt, and wrapped it around me. Then he slipped his pants on while my father lay curled on the floor, clutching his broken nose.

David stepped toward my father and gave him a swift kick to the ribs. "Lay a finger on her ever again, and I'll kill you."

My father didn't say anything. He just stared at David in wide-eyed disbelief as blood seeped through his fingers.

When his gaze shifted to me, David kicked him again and snarled, "No! You are not to look at her ever again. I'm taking her with me. You don't deserve her, you sick fuck. You never did." Then David scooped me into his arms, and we left my father bleeding on the floor...

I hadn't seen my father's face since that night. Yet there he was, my Unsighted fairy father standing in the heart of the Dark Forest.

Isa raced from the Waterfall to come to my aid, but two Dark creatures grabbed her before she reached me.

My father's gaunt face looked so much older than I remembered. "I've missed you, Emma." When I didn't respond, he took a step closer.

"How are you here?" I whispered. "And how do you know who I am?"

He let out a bitter laugh. "How could I not after all the years your precious King kept me chained up in a damp cell?"

My stomach turned at his words. "What? Since the night you choked me?"

"No." He stepped closer, and the stench of fermented cider on his breath nearly made me vomit. "Since the day you were born, you filthy whore."

It felt as if the ground were crumbling out from under me. "What?"

"Every day of your precious little life, he'd torture me and remind me that fathers don't touch their little girls. He said it was necessary to cause me enough pain that my Unsighted mind would still fear the consequences of touching you when I woke. And the whole time, your self-righteous King was just keeping you for himself. He raised you like he was your daddy, and he fucked you like you were his whore. He's a daughter-fucking hypocrite! You were supposed to be mine!"

I was too stunned to react when he grabbed me by the shoulders and pushed me to the ground.

Isa's distant screams echoed in my ears as my father crouched over me. "Don't touch her, you son of a bitch! Get your hands off her!"

"You were always supposed to be mine, Emma." An ugly smile spread across his face as he whispered, "And I have a lot of lost time to make up for."

His voice grew distant, until the only sound I could process was the pounding of my own heart. I was too numb to fight as he pinned me beneath him. Immobilized by shock and fear, all I could do was squeeze my eyes shut as he tugged up the hem of my dress.

"I TOLD YOU I'D KILL YOU IF YOU EVER TOUCHED HER AGAIN!"

My eyes flew open at the sound of my husband's voice, and I watched him unmask as he towered above my father. He plunged a massive claw into my father's back and pushed it out the front of his chest. Blood trickled from my father's lips as he stared at his own beating heart in the Sarrum's clawed hand. The King squeezed, dousing us both in my father's blood, and his lifeless body fell to the ground beside me.

His blood was everywhere. It soaked the front of my dress. It was in my hair and on my skin. It was even in my mouth. I barely managed to roll to my side before vomiting.

Masking himself in human form, David picked me up and started rushing toward the cave. I heard him tell Benji to fetch the doctor, but everything felt distant and out of focus. It was all just too wrong to process.

The doctor told David that I was in shock, and he poured something sweet down my throat that he said would help—only, it didn't.

I found myself in the Waters, and everything started slipping away. Every painful memory that I was desperate to be rid of was mercifully washed from my mind.

The next thing I knew, the Water creatures' king had me. Eyes full of hatred, he informed me that he was claiming me for himself as he carried me off to his home.

But my husband came for me. David set fire to the Waters, and he killed every creature who got in his way…

…I'd been in a state of shock while all of that was happening, and I was desperate to forget. I wanted to forget David—forget what I'd watched him do to my father, forget what he'd stopped my father from doing to me—but now, I didn't want to forget.

I refused to let go of my memories. They were far too precious to me. The Waters could fill my lungs and stop my heart; there was nothing I could do to prevent that, but I intended to die with a smile on my face, remembering the man who meant the world to me. David Talbot had always been my everything. It didn't matter if anyone else had ever understood our relationship. David was the only thing that mattered to me. He was all that'd ever mattered.

As I sunk lower, the Water creature's pull on my mind grew stronger, determined to make me forget my husband.

Kill me, I thought, communicating with those unseen creatures the only way I could. *What are you waiting for? Go ahead and drown me now because I will never forget him! I refuse to let you take my husband from me. You can steal the air from my lungs and stop my heart, but I will die clinging to my memories of David Talbot.*

When conscious thought became too difficult, I focused on the memory of David's face. I pictured those brilliant blue eyes filled with flames, and I remembered the way it'd set my blood on fire when those eyes fixed on me.

Out of nowhere, a forgotten memory flickered in the back of my mind. *The monstrous Water dragon's sea-blue eyes were full of rage as he snarled at the Water creatures' king, furious with him for daring to try and claim me.*

That day when Benji, Brian, and I had first visited Lochlan Mackendrick's cottage overlooking the sea at the edge of the Light Kingdom, the commander's reaction had prickled something in the back of my mind. Although, at the time, I didn't understand the reason for it. When Lochlan opened the door and found me on his doorstep, he smiled at me as if we were old friends.

Now I understood why. *We had met before.* Lochlan was there in the Waters that day.

My father attacked me outside the mirage that concealed our clearing. David killed my father for it. Then he rushed me to the doctor, who gave me something that he said would help calm me. But Godric's men were controlling the doctor. Whatever he poured down my throat had come from the Purists, and it was meant to kill me. The Waters swallowed me up, and I would've died there as the Water king's property, having no memory of who I really was. But Lochlan Mackendrick found me.

When Isa and Doc's memory potion finally restored my Sight and my memories came back to me, a portion of what'd happened that day was still missing. David had searched the Waters for me. He'd set fire to the Waters, and he'd killed every Water creature who got in his way. So I'd assumed it was David who killed the Water creatures' king to save me, *but it wasn't.*

The ancient Water dragon who protected the Light Realm rescued me from a watery grave that day.

I should've recognized those oceanic-blue eyes the moment Lochlan Mackendrick opened the door of his cottage. They were the eyes of the dragon who'd saved my life. The commander of the Light Kingdom's army—my grandmother's soul mate—was the one who killed the Water creatures' king for running off with me.

As my body sunk lower, the forgotten part of that nightmarish day when I lost my Sight came back to me...

...Confused and disoriented, I sunk into the arms of the Water dragon who'd just killed the creature that meant to claim me. I looked up at his kind smile and his lovely eyes, the same brilliant blue as the Waters. Who are you?

Although I could only communicate in thought, the Water dragon answered with spoken words. "It's all right," his deep voice assured me in a charming Scottish brogue. "You are safe with me, Princess."

My head throbbed as I tried to think of a response. Something awful had just happened to me, and I was desperate to forget it. But there was a beautiful dragon attached to the memory, with scales black as night and wings that sparkled with the brilliance of thousands of stars. That dragon had done something that terrified me, and so had the man he'd found me with. I wanted to forget about all of that, but I needed to remember that dragon. Panicked, I blinked up at the Water dragon. Where am I?

He smiled at me and brushed the wet strands of hair from my face with the tip of a massive claw. "You are in my territory, lass."

My mental image of that dragon I was desperate to remember was fading fast. I could feel it slipping away. Terrified of losing him, I shook my head. But where is he?

"Who, my dear?" the Water dragon replied with a grin that assured me I could trust him with anything. "Who are you looking for?"

An ache throbbed in my head. *I can't remember, but I know I belong with him.*

The Water dragon frowned at that. "You belong with me, dear girl. I would never have allowed such harm to come to you."

No. That's not right. I can't recall his face, but I know it's not yours. Please. I am nothing without him.

Sorrow swam in the Water dragon's sea-blue eyes. "That's not true, my sweet girl. You are far more than that dragon's prized possession. If you ever doubt that, I want you to come back to me. Promise me that you will?"

I didn't know who this creature who'd saved me was, or how I was supposed to find him if I ever wanted to. But it didn't matter. *Yes, all right. Now can you please help me find him?*

"Aye, lass, I'll find your husband for you," the dragon replied with a sorrowful smile. "Just try to remember that there is another man who loves you. If you ever tire of that selfish dragon's foolishness, come home to me. I will help you lead the kingdom you were always meant to rule."

With that, he started moving through the Water at a dizzying speed, and he didn't stop or slow his pace until he located the dragon I was so desperate to find.

When we reached him, the Waters around him were ablaze with blue flames and the carnage surrounding him was horrifying. The severed limbs and dismembered parts of countless Water creatures were scattered throughout the Water all around him. The instant he sensed my presence, the dragon I loved with all my heart turned toward us.

The Water dragon who'd rescued me glared at my husband as he placed me in his arms. Then he gave us a gentle shove toward the surface.

As we rose through the Waters, I studied the handsome, aristocratic features of my husband's face and an overwhelming sense of relief washed over me.

And I forgot all about that selfless Water dragon…

…I blinked my eyes, ashamed that I'd forgotten the dragon who saved me that day.

The commander must've been watching out for me from afar all my life. *Lochlan had always been there for me,* waiting at the ready in case I ever needed him. How else could he have happened upon me in my hour of need like that? He saved me from death that day and placed me back in the arms of the man who'd stolen me from him *because I asked him to.* And when I finally took my place as Queen of the Light Kingdom and went to Lochlan like he'd asked me to, I didn't even remember him. I could only imagine how much that must've hurt him. Now I had no way to apologize, no way to ever make it right.

A vision of the commander's kind oceanic-blue eyes flashed before me clear as day.

I remember you, Lochlan.

That was the final thought to cross my mind before my heart gave out and the Waters claimed me for good. I had meant for my last thought to be of David, but the Waters robbed me of that.

I had always been destined to die in the Waters.

I belonged to them now, and my memories of the dragon I had loved all my life were no longer mine to keep.

39

DAVID

One moment Emma was gasping for breath in my arms, an instant later she was gone. A debilitating burst of pain detonated in my chest as she vanished, leaving an unbearable emptiness in its wake.

A blaze of sapphire flames filled my visual field as I yanked Godric out of the chair. "What have you done?"

The color drained from his face as our eyes locked. "I'm afraid...I have failed you one last time."

My fingers tensed—desperate to choke the life from him—but I resisted the impulse. I needed him to tell me what he'd done to my wife first. "How?" I demanded, tightening my grip on him. "How did you fail me?"

"She is gone, David," he said, lowering his gaze to the floor. "My side has won."

I gave him a violent shake, splintering several of his bones. "Talk, you miserable old fool. What have you done to my wife?"

"Your old friend Jeremy Price…the doctor you've trusted with your life and the lives of all your closest allies, including your precious bride…your witch-doctor stands with us," Godric croaked as he looked up at me. "He has injected poison into your unconscious wife's vein back in the waking world. It was to be done at a prearranged time after the attack on the border began, in the event that I failed to kill her myself."

Mindless rage erupted within me—gushing from the wellspring of molten fury that I'd kept caged and suppressed for decades—like a long-dormant volcano awakening. As madness decimated reason, my hands moved to his throat.

Do it, David. I deserve to die for what I've done.

I should have had more self-restraint. Providing a swift end to his suffering was far too merciful a death for this despicable creature who'd so coldly orchestrated my wife's demise, but rational thought escaped me the instant I stopped feeling any connection to her. *Emma was gone.* Blind fury was the only thing guiding my actions as I tore into him, lashing out with every ounce of the rage bubbling up from deep within me, until the room and everyone in it was drenched in Henry Godric's blood.

When I regained enough composure to step back from what little remained of my mother's sibling, the horrified looks on Mia and Clay's blood-spattered faces should have brought me to my senses. But my stubborn mind refused to accept the truth. *Perhaps I could still save her if I hurried.* Desperate to find her, I summoned the Waters and dove in the instant they came spilling into the room.

But as I sunk through the Waters' frigid depths, it became far more difficult to deny the truth. I didn't have the slightest inkling where to search for her. I could barely see through the flames in my eyes, and I felt no trace of the woman whom I treasured more than life itself. I sensed no heartbeat...no panicked need to draw a breath...no hint of fear. There was nothing at all to suggest that my wife was still alive, but I could not accept her death.

What the fuck had I been thinking, going along with that preposterous plan of hers? I'd been opposed to the whole bloody scheme since the moment Emma first suggested it, and yet I indulged her. Now here I was, frantically trying to undo the catastrophic results.

Desperate to find her, I pushed onward with our initial conversation replaying in my mind...

...Emma's silence had been a rather troublesome distraction—making it impossible for me to focus on anything else—since we'd returned from our trip to the Light Kingdom to rally support. I'd respectfully kept my distance for several hours after she left to take a stroll through our clearing because she said she needed time to clear her head. But the longer she took, the more I feared that glimpsing the path she was meant to take might've made her resent the course her life had actually taken.

When she didn't return to the waking world to join me for dinner, I summoned the Waters and went back to Draumer to look for her.

It didn't take long to find her sitting by the lake at the edge of our clearing, gazing up at the stars. An affectionate grin spread across my face as I sat down beside her. "Would you care for some company?"

"For your company?" she replied, momentarily making me regret having asked. "Always."

I expelled a sigh of relief. "I was afraid you might not be speaking to me after our visit to the Light."

Her brow furrowed at my words. "Why?"

"Well, you seemed rather displeased with the fairy who laid claim to your throne."

"I am displeased. That greedy self-indulgent woman has no business ruling over a kingdom. Don't tell me you're pleased with the job she's been doing?"

"Of course, I'm not," I said, taking her hand in mine, "but I am quite pleased to have you here with me whilst she sits on that throne in your stead."

Tears glistened in my fairy bride's emerald eyes as she smiled at me. "Me too, but it's selfish of us to sacrifice the fate of an entire realm for our own happiness."

"I have always been selfish where you are concerned. I make no apologies for that."

Her gaze shifted to the glass-like surface of the lake, giving me the distinct impression that she was too dissatisfied with my response to look at me. "It's wrong, David. The Light Kingdom needs a capable ruler during this war. They stand no chance of surviving an attack with that imposter queen at the helm."

She started to shiver; and I slid closer, wrapping an arm around her. "So what would you suggest we do about that?"

Her eyes remained fixed on the reflection of the waxing moon shimmering on the surface of the lake. "You know exactly what we ought to do."

An ache flared in my heart at the thought of losing her to the Light. "I'd let their realm fall before I would ever put your life at risk."

"I've been thinking it over since we got back from our visit," Emma continued, *as if she hadn't heard me. "We could end this entire war by luring Godric to the Light."*

"Whatever you are proposing, I vehemently object to it."

Emma shifted in my arms to look me in the eye. *"If Godric were to learn that I'd taken my place as Queen of the Light Kingdom, he would do everything in his power to get to me."*

Ribbons of blue smoke wafted from my nostrils, lazily unfurling in the night air as they drifted toward the stars. "Which is exactly why you must stay here, where I can protect you."

Emma's pupils dilated in response to my scent, but she clearly had no intention of letting this drop. "What if you were there in the Light when Godric came for me?"

"What are you proposing?"

"You've been lamenting the fact that you couldn't deliver your mother's dying message to your uncle all your life. What if you were there to greet Godric when he came to kill me?"

"Do you expect him to just sit down for tea and listen to what I have to say?"

"No," Emma replied, *ignoring my sarcasm, "but I suspect he would stop dead in his tracks to listen to your mother."*

"What are you talking about?"

"Clay could share your memories of your mother's final moments with Mia, and Mia could morph into her form. I believe your uncle would freeze at the sight of his beloved sister, especially if she said things that only Lilly Godric would know. Then after Mia got his attention, I'm betting he would let Clay share your mother's dying message with him."

"That is a brilliant plan, but I will not risk your life for it."

A sorrowful smile spread across my wife's face. "I don't need your permission, David, but I would like your support. I've already made my decision. I'm going to take back my throne, and I've spoken to Mia and Clay. They've both agreed to what I'm proposing. It's up to you whether you choose to help me put my plan into action, or just stand back and let the chips fall where they may."

"You are far too stubborn for your own good."

There was a hint of mischief in her eyes as she stilled my heart with a dazzling smile. "I prefer to think of myself as determined, and the Light creatures need a determined ruler who will put their needs ahead of her own."

"And what of my needs?" I asked in a gruff whisper.

"I don't intend to leave here for good." She paused a moment to kiss my cheek, a move that felt far too much like a parting gesture. "The sooner you agree to help me put my plan into action, the sooner we can end this war and I can come home to you. Then I'll be more than happy to attend to all of your needs."

Too distraught to react to her amorous tone, I shook my head. "How can you possibly expect me to be on board with a plan that involves putting your life in danger?"

She lifted a hand to my cheek and planted a tender kiss on my lips. "What's to worry about? You'll be there to keep me safe."

"You will be the death of me," I whispered, stroking my thumb across her lower lip.

She slid onto my lap and wrapped her arms around my neck, overwhelming my senses with her delectable scent. "Maybe, but you'll die with a smile on your face."

I could have been angry with her for charming me into acquiescence, were it not for the fact that she'd learned that trick from me...

...No matter how much I despised Emma's plan, I could deny her nothing. I was genetically hardwired to please my dearest treasure by satisfying her every desire. Emma knew damn well that I'd have no choice but to go along with it in the end.

I should have fought harder. Hell, I should've locked her up to keep her safe from the consequences of that ridiculous scheme of hers. *I refused to let her life end like this.*

I could sense the Water creatures lurking nearby, hiding from me. ***Where is she?*** I demanded, setting fire to the Water as my voice thundered in their heads.

I felt them cower at my words, but none of them came forward.

Find my Queen and bring her to me, or I shall destroy every last one of you!

Their fear bled through the Waters, thick enough for me to taste it. Yet, despite the magnitude of their terror, none of them answered. Enraged, I tore through the Waters—decimating everything in my path in a blaze of blue flames as I pushed onward—desperate to find her.

Ever since the day she'd been poisoned and forced into the Waters, in shock—desperate to forget that she'd watched me rip her father's beating heart from his chest, needing to forget what her father had tried to do to her—the Water creatures had felt entitled to claim her.

Visions of the destruction I'd caused that day flashed through my mind as I raced through the

Waters in search of her now. I tore through everything in my path, just as I'd done that day. I had set fire to their homes. I had murdered any of them who dared get in my way, and all the while I'd felt Emma's mental clarity slipping—shedding all those painful memories she was desperate to be rid of.

This was the Water creatures' opportunity for revenge for what I'd done to their kin that day. My Queen and I were both going to perish in these Waters, and there was nothing I could do to stop it. On dry land, I could decimate both worlds to save her; but in the Waters, I was a far less powerful protector than the Water dragon who was meant to raise her.

If I had known it would end this way, would I have done things differently?

Snapshot memories of our time together flashed through my mind, one after another as I sunk through the Water, dragged deeper and deeper by the creatures I'd threatened and tortured to retrieve the fairy I'd never had any right to take.

If I had known it would end this way, would I have handed Emma over to the Water dragon her grandmother had appointed as her guardian? It was impossible to say for certain, but an ache in my chest told me I would not have changed a thing. If I had it to do over again and again, I'd choose to keep her with me every single time.

And Emma wouldn't have wanted it any other way.

My thoughts began to slip as I sunk lower, my memories dissolving one by one as the Water creatures dragged me deeper, erasing everything but Emma and my time with her...

….I remembered the warmth that spread through me as those tiny emerald eyes looked up at me and shined for the very first time…teaching her how to skip stones when she was a child…watching her drop the pendant I'd given her to the ground and let her nightgown slip down each exquisite curve as she bound herself to the Dark because she refused to leave me…an onslaught of memories of the nights we'd spent with our limbs entangled beneath the stars in our clearing…and on the beach in the waking world…our bodies and souls entwined till the end…

That's when I finally caught sight of my wife—lifeless and limp—sinking through the Waters below me. Hell-bent on saving her, I fought my way toward her with every ounce of strength left in me.

But something struck the back of my head, and everything went dark as Emma slipped away from me forever.

40

CHARLIE

I couldn't even begin to estimate how long Mackendrick and I had been locked in this bloody fight to the death. A primal part of me felt as if there had never been anything before this battle and nothing else would ever come after it. *This was what I was made for.* It was my time to rule, and no one was going to stop me from taking what was rightfully mine. Every spilled drop of blood, both mine and Mackendrick's, added more fuel to the fire raging inside me.

Despite my betrayal of her now, my friendship with Emma was one of the first things in my life that I'd ever truly treasured. The commander also treasured Emma, with every bit of the love he had for her grandmother. So when the beating of Emma Talbot's heart came to a screeching halt, Mackendrick and I both felt it. We froze—midtumble in the air—as its sudden stillness struck us like a lightning bolt, knocking us out of the sky. We plummeted to the ground and landed in a bloody heap, although neither of us understood what'd caused our fall.

As we got to our feet, I turned to Mackendrick and muttered, "What the fuck just happened?" as if we hadn't been locked in a battle to the death a few seconds ago.

The Water dragon shook his head, but I'm not sure whether he answered because something inside me *snapped* as my birth father took his last breath.

It felt as if I were waking up from a horrific nightmare—only, every unforgivable thing that I had done was real. I couldn't be certain Godric was dead. All I knew for sure was that some sort of cosmic shift had taken place.

Every Dark and Light creature that'd been locked in battle clearly felt it too because they all dropped their weapons to the ground and looked toward the two of us. The ground fires died down, and the smoke in the air dissipated until the crystal blue of the Light Realm's sky was visible once again.

My heart hammered in my chest as I surveyed the gruesome destruction that surrounded us. *I had led the Purist army into this battle.* Every single one of these deaths—Light and Dark—was my fault. Remorse constricted my throat as I met the commander's stare, and I couldn't bring myself to voice the question on my tongue.

He answered my silence with a somber nod. "It is done, lad."

I drew a deep breath as my eyes wandered over the hordes of creatures who were all waiting for me to comment on the palpable shift in energy. **"Godric has fallen,"** I roared, loud enough for even the farthest creatures to hear. **"My father is no more."** There wasn't so much as a labored breath to diminish the silence as every set of eyes remained laser-fixed on me. **"I am what remains of Godric's blood now. Who among the Purists will pledge their loyalty to me?"**

A chorus of howls and snarls of allegiance rose up from the Purists.

"Then kneel before me," I commanded, watching in amazement as every Dark soul dropped to their knees on the scorched ground of the battlefield. I looked to Mackendrick, and he gave me a subtle nod. **"It is time for us to end this war. We will not shed another drop of blood here today."**

"Aye," the commander roared as the Purist forces began retreating toward the border. **"It is time for all of us to stand down."**

At that, the Light forces stepped aside and allowed their enemies to pass without further incident. I shook my head as I watched them. "I didn't expect it to be this easy."

"Easy?" the commander replied. "Look around you, lad. Every death that occurred here today was a tragic waste, but it is time for us to move forward and heal from our collective wounds now."

As we masked ourselves in human form, a thought that'd been obscured—by the haze of whatever control I'd been under—sprang to mind, and my stomach dropped. I grabbed the commander's arm. "Emma..."

Mackendrick's eyes darkened at the desperation in my tone. "What about her?"

"Doc...the Sarrum's doctor is one of Godric's spies. He was ordered to poison the Queen in the waking world at a prearranged point after the battle began, if her heart was still beating."

Flames erupted in the commander's eyes. "Then you must stop him."

"I can't," I muttered. "I'm sedated and under the doctor's care in the waking world, just like everyone else."

"But you are not like everyone else," Mackendrick growled. "You wish to atone for the carnage that occurred here today under your command? Then go back to the waking world and protect the Queen."

"That's impossible. I'm in a medically induced coma in the waking world."

"Then you must either fight your way out of it or die trying," the commander replied. Without waiting for a response, he flicked his wrist and summoned a massive wave of Water that came barreling out of nowhere.

Before I could even think about reacting, the wave engulfed me.

As the Water dragged me down through its depths, a vision sprang to mind: I could see Emma clear as day, walking through that door in the middle of our group therapy session. Every moment we'd spent together at the facility flashed before my mind's eye, right up to the moment when the dragon—that'd always shadowed Emma—materialized right in front of me, as David Talbot wrapped his arms around her during visiting hours.

How the fuck did I let Godric get the better of me? That'd never been part of the plan. I was supposed to infiltrate the Purists and endear myself to my birth father, so I could get to Rose and get her the hell out of there. Now that Godric was dead, I no longer felt the merciful absence of conscience that I'd experienced while under his control. My will was my own again, and my heart was burdened with enough guilt to cripple me. *I led Godric right to Emma and distracted the creatures who were supposed to protect her, so that he could kill her.*

I shook my head. The Water creatures were trying to distract me with these thoughts of self-loathing. They were toying with me to make me forget where I needed to go, but I'd be damned if I would let that happen. The war was over. I was a free man now, and nobody was going to seize control of my mind ever again. Yes, Emma's life was in grave danger, but I couldn't have prevented that. I had no idea Doc was with the Purists until after I joined up with them, and there'd been no way to get a message back to the Sarrum at that point. Besides, my actions had been under Godric's control at the time. Despite those perfectly valid reasons not to blame myself, I knew I'd never forgive myself if Emma didn't survive this. I owed everything that I'd become to Emma Talbot. If the two of us had never met, I would've spent the rest of my life in mental institutions doubting my sanity and my worth.

Shit. The Waters were still distracting me. I'd stopped paying attention to where I was, and now I had no idea how far I'd sunk through the Waters' depths. But I wasn't about to let that stop me. This wasn't the waking world. You didn't necessarily need to move in a straight line to get from Point A to Point B, and I wasn't just any random Sighted schmuck. I was the heir to the Dragon King's throne.

Release me. As my telepathic demand rang out through the Waters, I could feel the Water creatures dismissing it. *I do not bow to you, Water creatures. Release me now, or all of you will suffer the consequences.*

I lurched forward, pushed by the creatures my eyes couldn't detect as a slideshow of mental snapshots flashed through my mind's eye: *Rose snapping Pip's neck after Godric's blood had seized control of her...the look of anguish on Bob's face as he cradled our tiny friend's body in his hands...the hurt in Rose's eyes as I fled the Purists' meeting place, leaving her behind because of what she'd been forced into doing...the look of devastation on Rose's face when I said all those awful things during the battle to convince her that Emma was the woman I truly desired.*

I would spend the rest of my days apologizing to Rose for hurting her like that, but I didn't regret the things I'd said. Breaking Rose's heart had been my only shot at getting her back to Benjamin and Isa, and by some small miracle that'd actually worked. From my aerial vantage point, I'd seen Rose freeze when Isa dropped to her knees in front of her, and I'd watched the Darkness swallow her up. I just hoped Rose could eventually forgive me for saying all those hurtful things after I explained why I'd done it.

Thinking about all the pain I'd caused Rose finally pushed me to the breaking point. As I pictured the tears in my soul mate's eyes, I let out a roar that rippled through the Water like a shock wave. *Release me now!*

With that, I rocketed to the Waters' surface—only to discover that I wasn't any closer to stopping Doc from poisoning Emma. I could see the surface of the Water right above me, but it looked like a lake frozen over in the dead of winter. There was no way I could penetrate the thick sheet of ice above my head to breach the surface and enter the waking world.

Desperate to break through, I pounded on the ice as hard as I could and rammed into it with the full force of my dragon weight. It shook with the blows, but it didn't break.

Well, duh. Of course it didn't. I was in a medically induced coma.

The drugs pumping through my veins wouldn't allow me to pass through the Waters and enter the waking world. That was the whole point of the medically induced coma; no matter what happened to me, my body would remain asleep in the waking world so my soul could stay in Draumer and do what I'd been anchored there to do. We were all suspended in medically induced comas at the Talbots' house in the waking world, and Doc had total control over all our unconscious bodies. How long would it be till he realized the war was over? And if he learned that Godric was dead, would he answer to me? Doc was never forcibly placed under Godric's control. He'd willingly chosen to side with him.

Furious with myself for being weak enough to fall under Godric's control, and terrified for my family members—unconscious and vulnerable in the waking world—I hammered on the solid sheet of ice above me with every bit of strength I possessed. But no matter how hard I hit it, it wouldn't break.

I squeezed my eyes shut and took a moment to collect my thoughts. There were so many skills it'd taken me way too long to master, as an adult who'd never been taught any of the stuff the Sighted normally learned as kids. Whatever the lesson was, my reason for sucking was always the same: I lacked the confidence required to master the skill. But Emma's life was in grave danger now. I didn't have time to take forever figuring this out.

My stomach turned as another disheartening thought occurred to me. When David Talbot took off to search for Emma after Godric kidnapped her, he had Doc sedate him so he could remain in Draumer till he found her. If *he* wasn't capable of escaping the Waters and returning to the waking world from a drug-induced coma, *was it even possible?* It didn't matter. I had no other options. If I couldn't break through that ice and get to her in time, Emma was going to die. I'd already endangered her life once with my stupidity, when Godric abducted her from her clearing with my clueless assistance. I'd be damned if I was going to fail her again.

The whole time I was thinking this over with my eyes squeezed shut, I kept ramming into the ice with every ounce of strength in me. It was pretty obvious at this point that brute force wasn't going to cut it. So what else was there?

Channel your rage, an echo of the Sarrum's voice replied in my head. That was his advice to me during my final flying lesson. *Use it to power your actions during flight, interrogation, combat.* I wasn't sure if this situation fit into any of those categories. All I knew was that Emma's life depended on me busting through that ice above my head.

But what rage was I supposed to draw on? As I opened my eyes, a lifetime of hurt cried out from where I'd buried it deep inside me. I didn't have time to waste, suppressing what I needed to utilize like I normally did, so I released it.

I pictured my mother dropping me off at all those mental institutions, time and time again, assuring me that it was for the best. She wasn't my biological mother. But she was still the woman who'd raised me, and she led me to believe that I was fundamentally worthless and broken. She'd discarded me like a piece of trash and carried on with her life. *And I fucking hated her for it.*

I pictured all the mental patients and doctors who'd morphed into monsters in all those places my mother had dumped me off in. They'd threatened, and bullied, and terrorized me when I was still just a kid. They made my life a living hell. Every single one of their faces sprang to mind. *And my rage began to emerge from the Dark place where I'd been keeping it locked away all these years.*

I thought of the way Dr. Spenser tortured Emma back at the facility by cultivating her misery so he could feed on it; and I pictured the pain and confusion in Emma's eyes when she was blind in the waking world while Godric was keeping her prisoner in Draumer. *And my rage intensified as it spilled forth from that Dark place deep inside me.*

I recalled the memories Clay shared with me, and all of the suffering Godric had caused my mother—*my real mother.* If I could, I'd bring that bastard back to life so I could make him suffer for what he'd done to her.

I thought of what Godric did to Nellie, and of the sister I would've had if he hadn't manipulated Nellie into murdering her own child. I pictured the horrified look on Nellie's face when I placed the lifeless body of her enchantment—that echo of her child she'd been clinging to all those years—on the couch between her and Bob. *And a blaze of orange flames filled my eyes.*

I pictured the look on Mia's face when Tristan carried her battered body, still cloaked in Emma's likeness, out of the Purists' cabin in the woods. Those monsters had forced her to take Emma's form, then abused and tortured her in unspeakable ways just so they could lure the Sarrum there. *My rage burned hotter, and hotter, until the Water around me took on a fiery glow.*

I pictured the fear in Rose's eyes when she first came to stay with us at the house on Sycamore. She'd been raised by the Sarrum's bitch-aunt Louise to believe she wasn't good for anything except bringing a new dragon into the world. *More rage bubbled up like molten lava from deep within me.*

I thought of the hurt in Rose's eyes at the Purists' meeting place on our last mission, after that demon had whispered the trigger phrase that brainwashed her into snapping Pip's neck. She'd pleaded with me to join her. She said she needed me, but I fled that awful place with the rest of our team and left the love of my life behind with the Purists. *An anguished howl worked its way up my throat as a geyser of molten lava started spewing from my mouth.*

As the heat of my fury spread through the Waters, I thought of that impromptu memorial service we had for Pip after we buried him in Zeke's mirage, and the sorrow on my friends' faces. *The Waters began to boil as I continued to spew forth the lava born of all the rage I'd suppressed and kept buried deep inside for so long.*

The ice above my head was starting to weaken and fracture because of the heat and pressure of the Water roiling beneath it. Desperate to reach Doc before he could poison Emma, I let out a rage-fueled bellow; flames barreled from my mouth, pummeling the massive sheet of ice fracturing above my head. With one tremendous deafening crack the ice split, sending its monstrous pieces toppling into the boiling Waters.

I sprang up to a seated position on the hospital bed, gasping for air as I surveyed the room through flame-filled eyes. My friends all seemed to be safely sedated. There were a few empty beds here and there, but I didn't have time to worry about who'd been in them. Emma might only have seconds before Doc poisoned her.

I yanked out all the tubes and wires attached to me and sprang to my feet, without a fleeting thought to the fact that my ass was hanging out of a flimsy hospital gown. The world tilted with my sudden movement and I doubled over, bracing my body against the bed as my vision blurred. The drug-induced slumber I'd just busted my way out of was obviously still affecting me. Those sedatives were still in my system, but I didn't have time to wait this out.

I pushed myself up and ignored the way the world slipped even further out of focus. There were no conscious people in the ballroom, which seemed like an ominous sign. I figured it meant that Doc was already in Emma and David's bedroom, where she lay defenselessly sedated.

Heart pounding, I raced out of the ballroom and rushed toward the stairs as fast as my altered body could manage. As I reached the bottom of the staircase, a wave of nausea washed over me and I broke out in a cold sweat. But I gripped the railing and hauled myself up the steps, taking as many at a time as I could.

Choking back the need to vomit, I reached the top of the staircase and found the door to Emma and the boss's bedroom closed. Rage coursed through me as I rushed toward that door; but when I turned the knob, it was locked.

I let out a growl that didn't sound remotely human as I barreled toward the door with every ounce of fury in me, throwing my full weight against it.

The door burst open, splintering into pieces as it swung into the room; and the witchdoctor's head snapped in my direction. His eyes widened at the sight of me—dressed in that ridiculous hospital gown, hair sticking out all over the place, eyes full of flames.

Plumes of orange smoke wafted from my flared nostrils as I stormed toward the traitorous bastard, but the satisfied grin on his bony face as he unmasked told me everything I needed to know.

I was already too late.

41

ISA

When Benji drew our daughter into the shadows, I stayed behind on the battlefield at the Light Kingdom's border. I knew I wouldn't be able to get through to Rose until Godric's hold over her was broken, and my soul mate certainly didn't need my help subduing her. That was Benjamin's area of expertise, and I trusted him without question. If he said he could bring Rose back to us, I had no doubts that he could. Besides, I had another matter to attend to.

The instant Godric's hold over his followers was broken, the change that came over every soul on either side of the battle was remarkable. Those who hadn't been following the would-be-king of their own accord were mortified by the things he'd forced them into doing. Those who had chosen to follow Godric of their own free will had already vowed to follow his heir without question in the event of his death. And those who fought for the Sarrum and the Light Realm were just relieved to see an end to this ugly war that had plagued Draumer for far too long.

The sky above us gradually cleared as the fires along the border burned out and their monstrous plumes of smoke dissipated. The enemy forces began to retreat under Charlie's orders, and our side parted to let them pass after Commander Mackendrick echoed Charlie's cease-fire.

Relieved as I was to witness the end of this fight, there was something I needed to do before laying down my weapon and embracing peace. Heart in my throat, I fell into step with the retreating troops as my eyes searched their ranks. With each unfamiliar face, my confidence wilted a bit more. It had been decades since I'd set eyes on her. What if identifying her after all these years wasn't the sure thing I'd expected it to be?

The instant I spotted Louise Talbot up ahead, doing her best to blend in with the retreating troops, a jolt of electricity surged through me. A vindictive grin spread across my face as I raised a hand overhead and focused all the magical energy I possessed on immobilizing that bitch who'd caused my daughter so much pain.

Louise let out a yelp as her muscles locked in place, but the soldiers around her kept on marching as if they didn't notice. Not one of them moved a muscle to come to her aid or even glance in her direction.

I rotated my raised hand, spinning her around to face me as I stepped up to her. "Hello, Louise. It's been a while, and the years have clearly not been kind to you. I almost didn't recognize you."

"Isabella," she muttered through gritted teeth, her jaw muscles locked in place by my magic, "you heard Charlie. Enough blood has been shed here today."

I let out a merciless laugh. "I have no intention of spilling your blood here. Why would I grant you a quick death after everything you've done, you miserable traitorous bitch?"

"Traitorous?" Louise croaked. "The Talbot family treated me like rubbish, casting me aside when the destiny they'd promised me no longer suited their plans. They robbed me of my rightful role as Queen of Draumer, and sterilized me to bring truth to their lie—that I'd fallen ill and become infertile. Then, as if all that wasn't cruel enough, they demoted me to the task of raising their demonic spawn after destroying my chance to ever mother a child of my own."

"I trusted you to raise my daughter. You were supposed to be a mother to Rose."

"I was," Louise replied with as much of a sneer as she could manage. "I raised Rose the way female dragons have always been raised: to believe that their only purpose is to satisfy the desires of males and birth more dragons for the Talbots to use however they please."

"If you were so grievously wronged," I said, my blood boiling with fury, "why didn't you warn me to raise Rose myself?"

A huff of indignation escaped her clenched teeth. "Why would I do that, when I could raise her to serve the dragon I was meant to wed? The Talbots robbed both me and Godric of the destinies we were owed. So why would I follow an order from David Talbot—the son of the dragons who stole our thrones—to raise your baseborn child as my own?"

I tightened my spell's grip on her till every nerve in her body was firing at maximum capacity. "We're done talking."

"What now?" she whimpered through clenched teeth.

"What now?" I replied with mock pleasantry. "I'm going to return to the Sarrum's palace, and you are coming with me."

A muscle in her jaw twitched. "Why?"

"We've reserved a special place in the dungeon just for you," I replied, tweaking her nerves a bit more till she cried out in pain, "and my husband made me promise not to have all the fun without him."

"No," she whispered as her eyes filled with tears, "please."

A grin spread across my face. "I take it you remember Benjamin?"

"No one forgets the Darkness."

"Well, then you ought to feel quite special because the Darkness hasn't forgotten you either."

Tears streamed down her cheeks as she whimpered, "Please. Show me mercy."

"If you had mistreated me, I might've considered showing you mercy. But you wronged my daughter, and I have no forgiveness for that."

42

BENJAMIN

Isa and I stopped in front of the Waterfall at the end of the dungeon's corridor, and I flashed her a smile. Then I took her by the waist and kissed her. It was just a quick brush of my lips against hers, but it hummed with electricity and the promise of much more once we were alone together.

Tears filled her eyes as we broke the kiss. "I love you."

"Right back at ya, gorgeous," I said, pulling her into a hug.

A grin spread across Charlie's face as he and Rose caught up to us. "Should we give you two some alone time, and come back a little later?"

I dipped my head in a show of respect to the soon-to-be Sarrum while simultaneously cranking up the fear I was projecting his way. "No, let's get on with it. We've been waiting too fucking long for all this to end."

"Amen to that," Charlie said, taking Rose's hand in his.

Isa smiled at the gesture of affection. "It's good to see the two of you together again."

With all eyes on her, Rose's cheeks flushed with color. "We sat down and talked things out like you encouraged us to. Charlie explained that he said all those hurtful things on the battlefield to push me away, hoping you two would be able to bring me back. I know better than anyone how hard Charlie had to fight to do that while Godric was controlling him, and I'll never be able to thank the three of you enough for breaking Godric's hold over me."

I bent and kissed the top of her head. "We're just glad to have you back, Rose."

Charlie watched with a pensive grin while Isa nodded and wrapped her arms around our daughter; a moment later, he dropped the smile and cleared his throat. "We should probably get on with this."

"You got it, boss," I said, stepping into the Waterfall and grinning to myself because I could feel the kid beaming at the term of respect.

As I stepped out into the dank cell, my grin morphed from proud papa to specter of death. The sight of the two souls chained against the far wall with their hands stretched just a bit beyond their natural reach was perversely satisfying.

The rest of our crew followed on my heels, and Louise let out a whimper, but Doc held his tongue. The only sign that the bastard was terrified was the pounding of his traitorous heart.

I stepped closer and cranked up the fear I was projecting toward them. "I am sorry we've been such neglectful hosts to you both. I assure you, we intend to make up for that today."

"Please," Louise muttered, tears streaming down her cheeks. "You have to understand. We were Godric's victims too."

I stopped at her feet, bent down, and took hold of her chin. "You *chose* to align yourself with that psychopath," I snarled, cranking the fear I was projecting up till a thin stream of blood began trickling from her nose. "If I hear you refer to yourself as a victim again, I will personally see to it that you understand exactly what it means to be a fucking victim."

Louise let out a sob—somewhat muffled by my grip—as the smell of fresh piss permeated the stagnant air in the cell. Releasing her chin, I cranked the terror factor up another notch. She whimpered as her muscles twitched from the pain, while I moved on to the witchdoctor.

Dr. Jeremy Price had been a member of the Sarrum's inner circle ever since the two of them had come to America to attend college together. I never particularly liked the bony-faced bastard, but I'd always trusted that he had our backs. I had promised Isa that Louise was hers to punish—with a little help from a colossal dose of fear provided by me—but Doc was all mine.

The witchdoctor shrunk from me as much as he could with his wrists shackled to the wall. "Please, my old friend," he pleaded in a trembling whisper, "show me mercy…for old time's sake."

I took hold of his bony chin with a much rougher grip than I'd used on Louise, and stuck my face so close to his that our noses almost touched. "Shut your fucking mouth. I don't want to hear so much as a whimper from you unless I ask for it. Do I make myself clear?"

He tried to nod, but couldn't with his chin in my grip.

I yanked his face forward then smacked the back of his head against the stone wall behind him. "I asked you a fucking question, you traitorous piece of filth. When I do that, I expect an answer from you. Do you get that?"

His bony chin trembled in my hand. "Yes."

"Why the fuck did you betray us, you son of a bitch?"

"What?"

I slammed the back of his head against the wall again, and the spineless bastard soiled himself. "That's not an answer. It's a question. So I'll ask again. Why the fuck did you betray us?"

"You betrayed me first."

I tightened my grip on his chin. "What the hell's that supposed to mean?"

"When David and I came to America to attend college together—"

"Show some respect when you speak of the Sarrum of Draumer, you whiny pathetic piece of shit," I growled. "Refer to our late monarch as *David* again, and I will split your worthless skull."

"I'm sorry," he croaked, wincing at the threat. When I narrowed my eyes at him, he said, "As I was saying, the Sarrum and I traveled to America to attend college together. After graduation, we were supposed to return to England and assume our intended positions: as the next Sarrum, and the Talbots' personal physician. Instead, our old chum chose to ditch me and remain in America. Whilst the two of you happily set up shop in the States, I had to go back home and fulfill my obligation to the Talbot family. Then to add insult to injury, he appointed some random Yank as his royal healer when he took the throne a few years later; and I didn't hear a word from either of you until the Sarrum decided he needed me to heal his fairy wife. Is it any wonder that I jumped at Louise's offer—to be royal healer to the new regime when Godric took back the throne—after the way your precious Sarrum discarded me?"

I engulfed the witchdoctor in my shadow and projected more fear toward him than I'd ever blasted anyone with. "Did it ever occur to you to just straight up *ask* if you could stay and serve the Sarrum in America?"

Blood trickled from the corner of the witchdoctor's mouth as he whimpered, "Well, no."

"Then that's on you, isn't it? You brainless asshole, how the hell was he supposed to know you'd rather not go back to the job you'd been training for your whole miserable fucking life?"

"I…" The witchdoctor's eyes widened as they filled with tears, as if that simple thought had never crossed his mind. But despite all his faults, Doc wasn't an idiot; and I sure as fuck wasn't born yesterday. He'd made his choices—whatever his fucked up reasons actually were—and he deserved what was coming to him now. "If I could take back what I did," he muttered, "I swear to you… I would."

"Well, you can't," I snarled, tightening my grip on his chin till his jawbone snapped.

He let out a howl and pissed himself.

"If the Sarrum were still with us," I snarled, "he would torture you to the brink of death for what you did to the Queen, and he'd heal you at the end of each day so he could start all over again in the morning."

A whimper squeaked from the witchdoctor's broken jaw.

"But I don't have the patience for that sort of thing," I growled, "never have."

His heart was beating so fucking hard I was afraid it might explode before I was done with him, so I eased back on the fear I was projecting just a touch.

"It might interest you to know that the next monarch has appointed a new royal healer," I said. "That could've been you if you weren't such a filthy piece of shit. Now, the job is going to Clay Barker. The man is a fucking wizard when it comes to chemicals and potions, and he informed us that the strychnine you poisoned the Queen with causes an extremely slow and painful death. I don't know if Emma felt that, since she was in a medically induced coma when you injected her with it, and she was sucked straight into the Waters from Draumer, but I'm gonna assume she felt every fucking spasm of her muscles. Now I've got just one last question for you before I kill you nice and slow, inflicting as much agonizing pain as you deserve. How did Godric manage to get his blood into all those royal dragons while he was banished?"

"He gave his blood to Louise months before Alexander Talbot banished him," Doc muttered through his fractured jaw. "They started plotting their revenge on the Talbot family long before David Talbot was even born. Louise brought the dragons to me when they were children—which raised no suspicions, since she was their nanny and I was the family doctor—and I administered a drop of Godric's blood to them as if it were a routine vaccination. The intent of the blood was simple: it was meant to control the recipients' minds when the rightful King called them to action. They were programmed to follow him and his heir without question."

"Well, that explains how he was able to control Rose since you assholes raised her," I snarled, fighting the urge to bash his bony skull in and be done with it. "But how did Godric manage to gain such absolute control of Charlie?"

Doc's eyes lit up, giving me the distinct impression that he would've smiled if he were still able to. "I watched over all of them whilst they were sedated and under my care in the Talbots' ballroom. Taking a bit of blood from Rose and injecting it into Charlie's vein was child's play after everything else I'd accomplished."

"You know, I never liked you." I spit in his face, then stepped back to watch my venom sizzle, and cripple, and paralyze while he cried out, begging me to kill him and put an end to his misery. I sat down, leaning back against the far wall with my arms crossed, and watched the show for the entire four hours it took for my venom to stop his traitorous heart; and I savored every fucking second of his torment.

After another hour, spent staring at his corpse—mangled from the convulsions that'd ripped his muscles clean off the bone—I stood up. "I made him pay, boss," I muttered as I stepped out of the shadows, releasing Doc's body along with me.

Charlie and Rose were gone, but Isa was still in the cell. She was sitting on the stone floor, still as a statue with her eyes glued to Louise Talbot's corpse.

I sat down next to her. "Feel better?"

"Not really," she whispered, dropping her head to my shoulder as I wrapped an arm around her. "I will never forgive myself for leaving my daughter to be raised by that wicked woman. You and the Sarrum both urged me not to, but I listened to my grandmother instead of heeding your warnings. If I could go back in time and do things differently…"

"Rose is here with us now. We can't change the past, but we sure as hell can learn from it and create a better future." I kissed the top of her head, then stood up and held a hand out to her, tugging her to her feet when she accepted it. "What do you say we leave these traitors behind us for good and move on to more pleasant business?"

Isa took one last look at the two lifeless bodies across the room. Then she nodded, and we entered the Waterfall side by side.

When we stepped out into the corridor, Charlie and Rose were there waiting for us. "You said you had something to discuss with me?" Charlie asked.

"Yeah." I stepped back into the Waterfall, confident that they would follow, and I stepped out into an opulently furnished dining hall.

They stepped out after me and followed me to the table with a feast fit for a king already spread out on it.

I locked eyes with Charlie as we all settled into the black-velvet-cushioned chairs. "There was a conversation the boss intended to have with you after the war was over."

Charlie's face fell as he slid his chair closer to the table. "Well, I doubt he would've felt much like chatting with me after I led Godric to the love of his life and helped distract her guards while my birth dad had her murdered. Of course, he doesn't get a say in what happens because my betrayal led to his death too."

"If he could be here," I said, pausing midsentence till the kid looked me in the eye, "the Sarrum would tell you that he didn't blame you for any of that."

"No offense, but I think you've lost your mind," Charlie muttered, lowering his head to hide the tears welling in his eyes.

Damn near close to tears myself, I shook my head. "They knew you'd inform Godric that Emma was in the Light Kingdom."

Charlie's head snapped up. "What the hell are you talking about?"

"The boss wanted to let you in on everything, but things wouldn't have worked out as planned if he had. They expected you to give Emma up to Godric because he was controlling Rose, which meant that he'd most likely gain control of you too. Letting you know where Emma was allowed them to lure Godric there without raising suspicion. The plan was to stun him with the sight of his dead sister—thanks to Mia's shape-shifting—and get him to listen to his sister's dying message by having Clay show him the boss's memory of it. They just didn't anticipate Godric's backup plan. None of us had any clue that Doc stood with the enemy, and that sure as hell wasn't your fault. The Sarrum would tell you that himself if he were here."

A tear slid down Charlie's cheek, and he hurried to wipe it away with his shirtsleeve. "So what was this conversation he wanted to have with me?"

"The Sarrum had a vision for the future of Draumer that was pretty different from the way things have always been done. As you know, a pure democracy would never fly in Draumer because too many creatures' actions are guided by unfettered bestial impulses in this world. The only way to keep order is to have a monarch who's powerful enough to put any soul who breaks the law in their place. That position is being passed on to you," I said with a grin. "But the Sarrum wanted to talk to you about taking things even further than he did, and creating a democracy of sorts that'd work to govern this world behind the scenes. You with me so far?"

"Yeah," Charlie said, "and I like what I'm hearing. I love the idea of not carrying the entire burden of ruling this world all by myself."

"You'll never be all by yourself," Isa replied with a maternal grin.

I took my soul mate's hand in mine, then turned back to the kid. "The Sarrum set things in motion by having the most trusted members of his inner circle weigh in on selecting you as his successor. That's how he envisioned things working in the future, with a privately appointed ruler aided by a council of trusted advisors."

Charlie propped his arms on the table and leaned forward. "Who would my advisors be? Has that been discussed yet?"

"A little," I said. "We all need to sit down as a group and figure out who'll be appointed where, but I can provide you with a list of souls who've expressed interest. How does this all sound to you?"

"It sounds perfect, but there is one position I'd like to offer right now." With that, the kid pushed his chair back from the table and got down on one knee in front of Rose's chair. "Rose, I am so sorry about the unforgivable things I said on the battlefield to break the spell Godric had you under. I've already explained my reasons, but I want you to know that I will never stop trying to make it up to you. It killed me to make you feel like a consolation prize because you are my soul mate. I treasure you with all my heart, and I always will."

Tears glistened in Rose's eyes as Charlie took her hand in his.

"I've been a little too busy lately to go ring shopping," he said, smiling as we all chuckled at that, "but I can't wait another minute to ask you to be my Queen. I want to rule this kingdom along with you, and I want to spend every day for the rest of our lives showing you just how much you mean to me. Rose Salazar Talbot, will you do me the honor of becoming my wife?"

"Yes," she whispered, tugging him up from his knees and kissing him. "With all my heart, yes."

43

ROSE

I stopped feeling numb the instant Godric's hold over me was broken. Everything he'd locked away had come bursting forth in a maelstrom of bewildering emotions. Love and gratitude whirled around inside me amidst equally boundless portions of grief and remorse—turning my stomach and making me dizzy—till I had no idea what to feel.

Isa stepped from the Waterfall on the other side of my bedroom dressed in a pale-blue satin gown, and an empathetic grin spread across her face as she met my eyes. "Are you ready?"

I tried to smile back, but couldn't muster the sentiment to make it convincing. "I'm not sure."

My mother's brow furrowed as she crossed the room and sat down on the bed beside me. "Rose, I know I'll never be able to make it up to you, for leaving you in England to be raised by that wicked woman. But I intend to spend the rest of my life showing you how much I love you, and how sorry I am for everything you went through because of my inexcusable mistake."

"I don't blame you for anything," I said, shifting on the bed to look her in the eye. "If things had been different, I might not have ended up here with Charlie as my fiancé. Besides, I have no business judging anyone's actions after all the unforgivable things I did while I was with Godric and Louise. So please don't spend the present regretting choices you made in the past. Just be here with me now."

Isa's eyes filled with tears as she wrapped her arms around me. "I'll be with you until my last breath, Rose."

"Good," I whispered, hugging her back.

Across the room, Benjamin stepped from the Waterfall and smiled at the two of us. My mother was right; dressed in his formal uniform as commander of the Sarrum's army, her soul mate was every bit as handsome as he was intimidating. "My gorgeous girls," he said. "Let's go pay our respects to the fallen, and start the next chapter of our lives."

"Let's," I agreed, forcing a smile as Isa and I stood up and crossed the room to him.

Benji crooked both his arms. My mother and I each linked an arm with him, and a merciful sense of tranquility washed over me as the three of us entered the Waterfall together.

The moment we stepped from the Waterfall entrance into the great hall of the Sarrum's palace, my eyes were drawn to my husband-to-be. While Isa headed to her seat up front and Benjamin stayed by the Waterfall, I smiled at Charlie and started down the center aisle toward him.

I was keenly aware that both sides of the aisle were lined with a multitude of spectators because I could sense their presence and hear the beating of their hearts, but my eyes never strayed from my fiancé's. Charlie looked so regal and handsome dressed in his fine black clothes. I'd never considered myself particularly attractive; but as his flame-filled gaze wandered over me, I couldn't help feeling beautiful in my black silk chiffon gown beaded with countless flecks of diamond to resemble the magnificence of our late Sarrum's wings. My fiancé's brazenly lustful grin— regardless of all the eyes on us—brought a rush of heat to my cheeks, and every other part of me that ached for his touch under the heat of that gaze.

I responded with a seductive smile that widened as I sensed its effect on him, while I climbed the black marble steps to his throne and my seat of honor beside it.

I stopped next to Charlie, so we both stood a step below his throne. Then I turned and looked out at the multitude of Dark and Light creatures who'd come to join us on this momentous occasion.

Charlie lifted his hand, and a chorus of unseen angelic-voiced creatures began singing as the members of the royal guard marched down the aisle toward us in their formal black dress uniforms. Benjamin was in the lead, followed by Brian and Tristan, with Addison behind them; and they each carried wreaths of floral arrangements adorned with ribbons of black and silver silk. Behind them, an army of soldiers followed at a respectful distance.

When Benjamin reached the base of the steps to the throne, the rest of them stood at attention facing us while the Darkness ascended the steps, stopping a few below us.

Charlie nodded as Benjamin handed him a massive wreath of black dahlias, combined with an assortment of other black flowers, tied with black and silver ribbons. Then Benji handed me a wreath of the same size with a lovely array of lilies of the valley and various other blossoms, all with the pure whiteness of new fallen snow, adorned with ribbons of silver silk.

As Benji turned to face the crowd, the singing stopped and a heavy silence descended over the hall. "Thank you all for joining us on this joyous occasion." The Darkness's deep voice echoed throughout the cavernous room. "The war has finally ended. Peace has been restored to this world, and we are all about to witness the coronation of the next Sarrum of Draumer." Applause broke out and the Darkness waited for the noise to die down before continuing. "But this is also a somber occasion. We lost many noble souls to this war and we are gathered here to honor not only the souls represented by these wreaths, but all the creatures who lost their lives in the efforts to restore peace to our world."

A nauseating pang of sorrow gripped me as I looked out over the teary-eyed faces in the audience. I had played a major part in many of the deaths we were gathered to mourn, and one of those beloved soul's blood was directly on my hands. Yet, no one looked at me with fury or contempt. Many of them had also done horrific things while under Godric's influence, or had watched a loved one self-destruct after bowing to his will; they understood that my actions had been beyond my control. But despite the circumstances, I knew the unforgivable things that I'd done would haunt me till my dying breath.

Addison's eyes filled with tears as she moved to the base of the steps, holding three wreaths in her hands. I choked back a sob as my eyes fixed on the one that was smaller than the other two. Addison climbed a few steps and handed that one to Benjamin, and he placed it a few steps above him.

For a moment, the Darkness just stared at the wreath in silence. Then he cleared his throat. "Melvin Wise, who was otherwise known as Pip, was one of the earliest soldiers to lose his life to this war. He may have been small in stature, but he was brave beyond measure and loyal to a fault. I have no doubt that he holds a place of honor in the afterlife. And if our fallen brother's heart is what determines his size in the great beyond, he will forevermore be larger than life."

I could barely see through the tears in my eyes as Benji took the next wreath from Addison. His Dark eyes shone with compassion as they briefly met mine while he bent and placed that wreath next to Pip's. "We also honor the memory of Nellie Godric today. Nellie suffered Godric's cruelty in ways that most souls couldn't begin to fathom. You might consider her one of the would-be-king's earliest victims. That's how I would've described her after meeting her in the hospital, shortly after Godric tricked her into killing their child and then convinced her that her mental illness was entirely to blame for it. However, that poor broken woman was not the same Nellie Godric who sacrificed her life during this war. The Nellie who we mourn here today died in a selfless act of love— valiantly sacrificing her own life to save the lives of her comrade's family—and that is how Nellie Godric will always be remembered."

Tears spilled down Addison's cheeks as she stepped up beside Benji, clutching the third wreath to her chest. "We are also here to honor the memory of the most noble, kind-hearted, selfless soul I've ever known," she said, her voice firm but thick with tears. "Robert Cassleman has always held a place of honor in my heart because he sacrificed his entire life in the waking world to rescue me from the men who kidnapped me and my brother when we were children. He succeeded in getting us safely back to our mother, but he was shot in the head in the process. So that brave wonderful man spent the rest of his adult life in a long-term care facility, unable to remember his past or control what popped out of his foul mouth." Addison paused a moment, a faint smile on her lips as those who knew Bob chuckled at that.

"I grew up under Bob's protection in this world," Addison continued. "The Unsighted knight took me in, unaware of what he'd done for me in the waking world. All he knew was that I'd been traumatized and mistreated, and I was terrified and all alone. Bob gave me shelter. He offered me comfort and protection. When I was ready, he listened to me and helped me unburden myself of some of the pain. Then he taught me how to fight like a warrior so that no one could ever make me a victim again. When I grew up, I left and joined the nomadic knighthood, using the skills he'd taught me to protect the Unsighted inhabitants of the fringe. But quite recently I was blessed with the opportunity to meet up with that selfless knight in shining armor from my childhood again. I got to fight beside him, and show him what he'd helped me become. I can't begin to express what an indescribable honor that was for me. During our last mission to retrieve my Unsighted family—before Godric could get to them—Bob's life ended in one final act of honor, bravery…and selfless love. He stayed behind with his soul mate, Nellie, and the two of them sacrificed their lives in order to stop the hellhounds who'd been sent to kill my husband and children. I would give anything to speak to Bob one last time," Addison muttered, her voice cracking, "and tell him how much I love him, how much he always meant to me. I owe him everything, and I plan to spend the rest of my days doing my best to make him proud."

Tears streamed down Addison's cheeks as she lifted Bob's wreath to her mouth and kissed it before setting it down next to Nellie's. Her hand lingered there a moment, unable to let him go, until Benjamin took her free hand and drew her into a hug. For a moment, the silence in the great hall was vast enough to swallow up every last one of us.

My heart throbbed with self-loathing at the sight of Benjamin and Addison's tearful embrace because I was to blame for all three of those deaths.

Sensing my heartache, Charlie reached out and gave my hand a squeeze.

It was all I could do not to break the silence and draw everyone's attention to us by sobbing out loud. Charlie knew exactly what I was feeling. The two of us had spent countless hours together since our return to the palace, mourning the deaths we were responsible for, and doing our best to talk each other through the unbearable guilt that would haunt us both for the rest of our lives. We were determined to spend our reign doing everything in our power to make amends for all the devastation and agony we'd caused while under Godric's control.

As Addison descended the steps, Tristan and Brian stepped up and took her place.

Tristan was holding a wreath of flowers close to his heart. For a moment he just stood there, deepening the ache in my heart with his silence. Then he turned and sat the wreath down next to Bob's. "We are also here to honor my fallen brother today. Ezekiel Gaumond wasn't my brother by blood, but we grew up together in the same orphanage. We were sent to the same work camp, where we always had each other's backs, and we remained close even after we parted ways in this world. Zeke might've been a scoundrel in his earlier days, but he spent the second half of his life rescuing captive souls from the Purists' slave auctions. He housed more Unsighted souls in his safe haven than the Purists ever took in a single raid, and he lost his life trying to save one more Unsighted soul before the Purists could get to her."

Brian put a hand on Tristan's shoulder. "I will always be grateful to Zeke for having my brother's back in this world when I couldn't. Zeke devoted his life to saving innocents because I asked him to after I rescued his Unsighted sister from the Purists. Zeke loved his little sister fiercely. He would've done absolutely anything for her. I know you can't hear me, Zeke," Brian said, stopping a moment to clear his throat, "but I promise you, your sister will always be safe. I intend to see to that personally. Rest in peace, brother."

Brian and Tristan took a moment to place a candle at the center of each one of the wreaths on the steps. Then the two brothers descended the stairs. Tristan took the empty seat next to Mia, and Brian stepped back to his place at the front of the army as Benjamin stepped up to me and Charlie.

Benji nodded to us both as he took the large black wreath from Charlie and placed it on the step above the others. "I bound myself to the Sarrum back when we were in college and I still had a full head of hair." He paused a moment as a ripple of hushed laughter echoed through the hall. "The Sarrum was the most awe-inspiring creature I have ever encountered. He taught me what it truly meant to be part of a family. Because that's what we were, and it's what those of us who remain still are—and will always be—thanks to him. I am a far better man for having known him, and I'm a far greater shadow for having bound myself to him. I will honor our bond until my last breath."

Benji's pitch-black eyes fixed on the Sarrum's wreath for a few heartbeats. Then he turned to me, took the snow-white wreath from my hands, and placed it beside the Sarrum's. "I also had the honor of watching over the Queen of Draumer since the day of her birth. I protected Emma Talbot for most of her life. We spent our earliest days together having tea parties with stuffed animals, and embarking on imaginary adventures in her clearing. When she grew older, I watched over her during her lessons, and I taught her how to defend herself. I watched her grow up and become the loving, caring, selfless wife of the Dragon King, and I watched her take her place as Queen of the Light Realm to look out for the Light creatures during this war. We lost her to this fight, and she left a gaping hole in the hearts of all who loved her." Benji paused a moment to clear his throat as his Dark eyes filled with tears. "Losing the Sarrum makes me feel like I've lost a brother, but losing the Queen feels as if I've lost a child. They will both be missed more than I know how to express. My only comfort comes from the fact that they left us the same way that they did everything: together. I feel certain that's exactly how they'll remain in the afterlife. Together." With that, Benji placed a candle in the center of both the Sarrum and the Queen's wreaths.

Charlie breathed gently on Pip's small candle, lighting it. Then he did the same to the others. When he reached the last candle at the center of Emma's wreath, his breath caught in his throat, and he stopped and looked out over the crowd. "I owe the Queen of Light a debt of such magnitude that it guts me to my core. She and I met in the waking world…and I believe we saved each other there. I watched out for her and made her feel safe, and she introduced me to a world that I'd always been told existed only in my unbalanced mind. If it weren't for Emma Talbot, I would still be locked up in a mental facility in the waking world, and I'd be afraid to let the fringe out of my sight here in Draumer. It was because of her friendship that I came into all of this. Her husband took me under his wing, and although he terrified the ever-loving shit out of me at first"—he paused until the laughter died down—"he provided what had always been missing from my life. He had his finest men teach me all the things I should've learned as a child. He taught me how to be a better man by his own example, and he taught me what it truly means to be a dragon. I will be forever in his debt, and his Queen will always hold a special place in my heart." With that, he lit Emma's candle as a tear dripped from his cheek down to her wreath.

Then he straightened and took my hand in his, and we both took our seats.

44

CHARLIE

Despite the size of the crowd gathered in the great hall, there wasn't so much as a cough or sneeze to mar the silence as we watched the candles of our fallen loved ones burn. A mix of conflicting emotions warred within me as I stared at the flames, until I didn't have the faintest idea what to feel.

As much as I wanted to apologize to the assembled crowd—and the rest of the Sighted world—for all the things I'd done while under Godric's control, Benjamin had warned me not to in no uncertain terms. There were a great number of souls in Draumer who lived their lives without any regard to ethics or laws, and many of those creatures had willingly pledged their loyalty to my birth father. If I were to apologize for my actions during the war now, those creatures would interpret it as a sign of weakness, and they'd lose interest in following me no matter whose blood flowed through my veins. The Sarrum of

Draumer did not apologize for anything *ever*. Our world's newfound peace was dependent on my adherence to that mantra, so I forced myself to focus on other things.

The sight of Rose in that gown that fit her like a second skin, and shimmered like a star-speckled sky, filled me with more joy than I'd ever felt before. We had gotten her back. She'd forgiven me for all the hurtful things I said on the battlefield, and she was going to be my wife. Alone, I would be terrified about my impending coronation, but I wouldn't be alone. Rose would be with me from here on out, and so would Benjamin and Isa.

Incredible as all of that was, there was a heaviness in my heart because of the souls we were gathered to mourn and the part I had played in their deaths. All three of my dear friends from the mental facility were gone now. Emma, Nellie, and Bob had all lost their lives to this war, and their deaths hurt all the more— not only because I'd had a hand in them, but also because I never got the chance to say goodbye. On top of that, I had lost my mentor. David Talbot had seen my potential when I honestly didn't believe I was worth much of anything. In spite of my smartass attitude and juvenile sense of humor, he invited me into his family and took me under his wing. He taught me how to be a better man, he showed me what it truly meant to be a dragon, and he did it all by his example. After all that time I'd spent judging him for what I wasn't yet capable of understanding, I never got the chance to thank him and tell him how much I admired and appreciated him.

My coronation ceremony was a massive blur of pomp and circumstance: Brian presenting me with sword and scepter…countless soldiers pledging their undying loyalty to me…Benjamin placing a jeweled golden crown on my head. It was such a far cry from where my life had begun that it almost felt comical. After that, I formally announced my engagement to Rose. Following a bit more fanfare, Rose and I led the procession while the royal guard followed us to the hall's main entrance where we stood for one last round of applause. Then we took our leave.

Rose and I let out a synchronized sigh of relief as we stepped from the Waterfall into the banquet room, and a coy grin spread across her lovely face as she walked to the throne-like seat at the head of the table and pulled it out for me. "I believe this is your chair, Sarrum."

Benjamin stepped out of the Waterfall next, raising an eyebrow as I unceremoniously plopped down in my new seat. "I take it you've had enough formality for one day?"

"I think I've had enough for a lifetime," I muttered, eyeing the feast that was spread out on the table for us.

Rose nodded as she settled into the chair on my right. "I'll second that."

Benjamin shook his head, but there was a faint hint of a smile on his lips as he took the seat to my left.

Relieved to have the freedom to conduct my first meeting in as casual a manner as I pleased, I took the heavy crown off my head, hung it on the back of my chair, and placed the sword and scepter on the floor beside me. Then I leaned back against my new seat's sumptuous cushions to watch the rest of our party file into the room from the Waterfall.

Brian and Tristan were the next ones to step out. Tristan winked at me as he dropped into a chair halfway down the table. "Royalty looks good on you, dragon."

Brian settled into the seat across from his brother and kicked him under the table. "Show some respect, Tristan. That's the Sarrum of Draumer you're talking to."

"Right," Tristan murmured, cranking up the charm as he turned to me. "Royalty looks damn good on you, my King."

The way he said *my King* was enough to make me squirm in my seat—or rather, it would've been if I still let that sort of thing affect me. I grinned at Mia as she entered the room. "Tell me you plan to keep your soul mate in line after he joins my council."

Mia's cheeks flushed with color as Tristan stood up, pulled the chair beside his out for her, and pushed her chair up to the table like a perfect gentleman. "I'll certainly try my best, Sarrum."

Clay let out a rough chuckle—in response to something Isa had said, by the looks of it—as they stepped into the room together. Clay took the seat next to Mia, and Isa sat down between him and Benjamin. Addison was the last of us to enter the room, and she took the seat next to Brian. As soon as everyone was settled, all eyes in the room looked to me.

"Right," I said, clearing my throat. "So I guess it's up to me to lead this meeting?"

Benjamin nodded. "We'd be glad to help if you want, but this is your show to run now. You might as well get a feel for it."

"I suppose you're right." I looked at the faces in the room, hoping something brilliant and regal would magically pop out of my mouth now that the crown and the comfy chair were mine. But as I looked over their smiling faces—rife with emotion over all we'd been through together—I realized I didn't need to be brilliant and regal all the time. This was my home, and these souls were my family. The only thing they expected me to be was *me*. "Well, most of us have already talked about what's going to happen from here on out. So this meeting is really just a formality. Why don't we all relax and enjoy the food before it gets cold?"

Tristan helped himself to a turkey leg, sunk his perfect teeth into it, and tore off a succulent chunk of dark meat. A rapturous moan rumbled in the base of his throat as he wiped the juices trickling down his chin away with his free hand. If this were anyone else, the lax table manners would've seemed vulgar; but because it was Tristan, the whole display was so damn erotic that we might as well have been watching porn. I doubt there was a soul in the room who didn't secretly long to be that turkey leg for at least a second or two. With every set of eyes in the room now glued to him, Tristan shrugged and turned his attention to me. "I think you're supposed to formally appoint the members of your council first."

I let out a laugh as he took another bite. "Then why did you start eating?"

"I respect the crown," Tristan muttered around a mouthful of turkey. "When my King tells me to dig in, who am I to argue with him?"

"Amen to that," Clay said, helping himself to the potatoes.

A satisfied grin spread across my face as I watched them all fill their plates and start eating. It'd been a while since we'd all been together like this, and who knew when it would happen again? Maybe I could make some sort of royal decree that we all assemble for a shared meal every few months. *Mandatory trimonthly Thanksgiving feasts.* Would that be considered an abuse of my power?

Benjamin leaned back in his chair, picked up his wine glass, and downed a sizable sip. Although the Darkness wasn't big on outward displays of emotion, the twinkle in his pitch-black eyes conveyed how pleased he was to have us all together like this.

So, maybe he'd be all for the trimonthly feast idea.

The Darkness raised an eyebrow at me over the lip of his glass, making me wonder whether he could still read my thoughts despite how adept I'd become at keeping them guarded.

But I was guessing he couldn't, since he hadn't clobbered me for the thoughts that went through my head when I looked at his daughter in that starry-night-inspired dress.

Again, his eyebrow lifted as he set his glass down on the table. "You should probably get on with it and formally invite the advisors of your choosing to join the royal council."

"Right," I muttered, clearing my throat at the way his narrowed eyes suggested he absolutely could read my thoughts. "Benjamin, I'd be honored if you would accept my formal invitation to join the royal council. I'd like you to stay on as my right-hand man, in addition to continuing your position as commander of the royal guard."

"I accept, Sarrum," the Darkness replied, picking his glass up again. "It would be my honor to serve you."

"Sweet," I muttered. "Uh, I mean splendid."

Benjamin shook his head. "You don't have to talk like a fucking douchebag just because you've got a crown now. Did your predecessor sound like a pompous asshole to you?"

Yeah, sometimes. Benjamin scowled at me, and I straightened in my seat. "No, of course not," I said with an apologetic frown. Although in all honesty, I was glad he didn't plan to treat me any differently than he always had. "Isa, you've already agreed to stay on as royal sorceress, but I would also like to formally invite you to join my council."

"It would be my honor, Sarrum," Isa replied, lifting her glass as if to toast the invite.

"Clay," I said, pausing a moment while he put down his fork and met my gaze, "I wish I'd gotten to know you years ago, but I am truly grateful to have you in my life now. You'll be a great addition to our family in your new role as royal healer, but I'd also like to invite you to be a member of my council of advisors."

"Me?" Clay asked in a gruff whisper. "I'm not exactly royal-advisor material."

"If I'm Sarrum material," I said, grinning, "then you sure as hell are royal-advisor material."

Clay nodded as he shifted in his seat, clearly uncomfortable with all eyes on him. "Well, then...I accept, Charlie. Thanks. I'm honored."

Next I turned my attention to Mia. "Mia, you and Clay both played a crucial role in the ending of this war. I can only imagine how difficult that must've been for the two of you, given your histories with Godric. We are forever in your debt for setting the wrongs that were done to you aside to help restore peace to Draumer, and I would be honored to have you join my council."

The changeling's cheeks flushed with color as Tristan and Addison smiled at her, both of them beaming with pride. I knew exactly how they felt. It was remarkable how far she'd come from that broken victim Tristan had carried out of the Purists' cabin in the woods. "I would love to, Sarrum. Thank you."

I nodded, then fixed my eyes on Tristan as his pearly-white teeth bit off another chunk of that turkey leg. "Tristan, in addition to joining my council, I'd like you to oversee the training of all new recruits to the royal guard from now on."

Tristan dropped the turkey leg to his plate. "That's my brother's job."

"Yeah," Brian replied as his brother's eyes fixed on him, "about that..."

45

BRIAN

A contented smile spread across Davina's face as we pulled into the parking lot of Sinful Pleasures Coffee & Books. As I parked the car, I couldn't help grinning at the twinkle in her eyes. Making her smile was a far greater thrill than any victory on the battlefield had ever been.

I shut off the car and shifted in my seat to face her. "You really love this place, don't you?"

Her eyes drifted to the shop's sign for a second before they fixed on me. "Yeah, this is my happy place."

"I can see that," I said, brushing a wisp of hair back from her face with my fingertips.

Her breath hitched at the contact, and I couldn't quite bring myself to pull my hand away. I didn't want to break the connection between us. I wanted to pull her into my arms and never let her go, but letting myself fall for Davina would be unforgivable.

Oh, who the fuck was I kidding? There was no *falling* involved. I'd been in love with her since the day I rescued her from the Purists in Draumer all those years ago; but this was the waking world, and Davina was Unsighted. If I acted on my feelings for her, I'd be no better than the incubus who fathered me.

It was despicable enough that I'd been too weak to control myself after I barged into her life to protect her from Godric's goons the other day. I'd shown up fully intending to get her out of harm's way and keep my feelings for her to myself, but I'd also expected her to look at me like I was a stranger. I sure as hell hadn't been prepared for the reaction she actually greeted me with. The lust in her eyes had floored me, and the scent of her arousal had done a spectacular job of erasing every last scrap of decency from my thoughts.

Davina didn't know she was a succubus in the waking world, but she still instinctively knew how to use her charm. Of course, I didn't have to let her charm affect me—since I was half incubus—but in the heat of the moment, I didn't have the slightest inclination to fight it. Wrong as it was to give in to temptation, I'd been so relieved to find her in time to save her that I let my emotions get the better of me.

It was a selfish impulsive mistake, and I didn't intend to let it happen again. There was no way I was going to fuck up Davina's life—hurting her, the way my dad hurt my mom—by trapping her in a relationship she wasn't fully capable of understanding. I'd sooner jump off a cliff than do anything that'd make her feel the sort of anguish and resentment I used to see in my mother's eyes every time she looked at me.

"You know," Davina said, snapping me out of my contemplative silence, "my happy place would be all the better if you stuck around."

"Davina," I whispered, "you don't even know me."

She smiled at me and tilted her head, resting her cheek against the palm of my hand. "Yes, I do. You are literally the man of my dreams, Brian. Can you honestly tell me you don't feel the electricity between us?"

"No, I can't," I admitted, stroking her cheek with my thumb and pretending not to notice the way she shivered at my touch. "But you don't know the whole story. It wouldn't be right for me to trap you in a relationship."

"Trap me? I'm the one who's begging *you* not to drive away when I hop out of this car. I think I actually *might* trap you, if it was the only way to get you to stay."

"Sounds like a plot for one of your books," I said, tracing her lower lip with my thumb, despite the fact that I meant to do the decent thing and get the hell out of there.

A rush of air escaped her lips as they parted for me. "It could be."

Damn it. I needed to go before I did something just as unforgivable as my dad would have. "It's getting late," I said, a lump already forming in my throat at the thought of leaving her. "You should go check on your shop."

"Come with me," she whispered, her breathy plea and hypnotic eyes melting my resolve.

If I waited much longer, I might not have the strength to do the right thing. "Davina, doesn't it freak you out that some imaginary guy you've been dreaming about for years just happened to show up out of the blue when you were wide awake the other day?"

"Just in time to save my life? No, it makes me think I should never let you go."

"You could do a lot better than me."

"Better than the man of my dreams?"

Still unable to pull my hand away, I drew a deep breath and slowly exhaled it. "Yeah, much better. I'm no good for you."

"What are you basing that on?" she asked, eyes shimmering with tears. "Because I've imagined us coming together a thousand different ways, and all the scenarios that have played out in my head tell me you'd be *very* good for me."

"Then you're letting a fantasy cloud your judgment."

"So let's make one of my fantasies a reality," she replied in a seductive whisper. "Then you can tell me what you think."

"I think...that if I touched you again, I'd never be able to leave."

"Then touch me."

"Damn it, Davina," I muttered. "I'm trying really hard to do the right thing here, but you sure as hell aren't making it easy."

She reached back to open the passenger door without taking her eyes off me. "I'm going to get out of this car and go check on my shop now, but don't you dare leave without saying goodbye. Come inside with me."

Unable to stop myself, I brushed my thumb across her bottom lip again and stiffened at the hushed whimper that escaped her. "It's time for me to go,

Davina," I said as I watched her slide out of the car and step back, breaking the electrical connection between us.

"Follow me inside," she replied in a throaty whisper.

I shook my head.

"Don't break my heart." She smiled at me as she shut the passenger door. Then she turned and started walking toward her shop with such a confidant sway to her hips that I might have been irritated, if I wasn't so damn turned on.

I watched her unlock the front door and step inside, and a groan rumbled in the base of my throat as she disappeared from view, leaving the door wide open. *Well, it wouldn't be right to take off and leave the door to her shop hanging open like that.* It was a flimsy excuse, but the electrical pull drawing me toward her was too intense to resist. I opened the driver's side door, stepped out, and slammed it shut with a sigh of defeat.

The lights in the shop were off. As I shut the front door, the only illumination in the place was what filtered in between the slats of the closed blinds. In the dim lighting, I felt a little too much like a predator tracking his prey.

She wasn't in the main room. The electrical pull drawing me toward her wasn't strong enough.

As I headed down the hall toward the back of the shop, I found myself wondering about the scenarios in her books. *How exactly had she pictured us coming together?* Although I'd never admit it to Tristan, a small part of me regretted shutting him up when he started to tell me about her stories, but it had nothing to do with lack of confidence or fear that I wouldn't measure up. It was about wanting to surpass her fantasies rather than rehash them.

Salivating at her nearness to me, I stepped into her office. The lights were off in there too, but the last traces of daylight spilling in through the window bathed the room in a fiery glow. Davina was seated at a desk with her back to me—framed by the view beyond the windowpane—as the sun slipped toward the surf, leaving a trail of pink clouds melting in its wake.

When she heard me step into the room, Davina swiveled her chair around and smiled at me. It was a cat-that-ate-the-canary sort of smile—victorious, giddy, and *hungry*—and it made me forget all the reasons why I was supposed to be leaving.

It didn't matter that I'd never read a single page from any of her books. I wasn't the prey in this scenario, and I could sense her desires well enough to know damn well she had no interest in taking the dominant role.

I sauntered toward her with a far more predatory grin than her canary-eating-kitten smile. Stopping directly in front of her, I leaned forward and gripped the arms of her chair, caging her in. "So, how did you picture this scenario playing out?"

The smile slipped from her face as she tilted her head back and met my eyes, flooring me with the heat of her gaze. "However you want it to play out, as long as it doesn't involve you leaving."

Her playful reminder that I should be making my exit hit me like a slap to the face, knocking me back to my senses. "Davina," I muttered, tightening my grip on the arms of her chair, "you should tell me to get the hell out of here."

"Why?" she whispered, searching my eyes. "What is it that makes you think you're no good for me?"

I let go of her chair and took a step back. "It's a long story."

"I love stories," she replied in a velvety whisper as she stood up.

I shook my head and took another backward step toward the door. "This isn't a very good one."

She closed the distance between us and took my hand in hers, sending a surge of electricity sparking between us. "Then stick around, and let me tell you mine."

46

DAVINA

The thought of Brian leaving me flooded my veins with adrenaline. This was a fight-or-flight situation, and I needed to fight to get him to stay. Emboldened by desperation, I'd closed the distance between us and taken his hand in mine, and an electrical current had surged between us the instant we connected. The notion of losing this—of losing *him*—filled me with dread.

Afraid that the look on my face might convey how desperate I was for him to stay and spook him, I met his eyes with a coy grin and tugged him toward the door. "Come with me."

Brian shook his head but let me guide him from the room, his keen eyes never straying from mine. Contrary to the playful look on my face, there was nothing lighthearted about his expression. His stare was grave and intense, and I couldn't seem to shake the irrational fear that he could *feel* how fast my heart was beating.

I tried to focus on taking deep steady breaths as we moved toward the front of the shop, but my heart wouldn't stop racing.

"Where are you taking me?" Brian asked, the gruff whisper of his voice rasping in my ears like a match striking sandpaper, igniting a fire inside me.

I braced my palm against his broad chest to stop him as we reached the front desk, and a thrill coursed through me at the way he shivered in response. Grinning to myself, I grabbed the photo album I kept tucked behind the desk. "Save your questions till the end of my story," I replied in a much throatier voice than I'd intended as I straightened and met his eyes.

"Yes, ma'am," he muttered, his gravelly voice another match striking inside me, adding more flames to the fire.

I tugged him to the nearest booth with the photo album clutched to my chest. As he slipped into the booth beside me, the heat of his gaze told me he knew exactly how being this close to him affected me. I drew an unsteady breath, then set the album down on the table and opened it.

He lowered his eyes to the first picture—of me and my brother dressed in our Halloween costumes when we were kids—then he looked up at me with an apologetic frown. "I'm so sorry for your loss, Davina. Zeke was a good man."

I shook my head and pressed my index finger to his lips. "No comments till the end of my story."

"Right. Sorry," he said against my finger, the deep rumble of his voice sending a shock wave straight from his mouth to my core.

I tried to smile as I pulled my hand back from his lips, but I doubt my expression conveyed anything other than the all-consuming lust I was feeling. "Zeke and I were always inseparable," I muttered, dropping my eyes to the album as I turned the page. "My brother was eighteen when our mom died, and I was nine. He promised me he'd never let anyone pull us apart."

A tear slid down my cheek as I looked up at Brian, and the tenderness in his eyes as he brushed it away flooded my insides with warmth.

"Zeke was supposed to head off to college that fall," I said, turning the page. "But after our mom passed, he took a local job as a mechanic and devoted his life to raising me. He never once complained about what he gave up, and he never failed to be home for me every night. It was his bedtime stories that first inspired me to become a storyteller. Zeke used to tell me these elaborate tales about another version of himself who lived in a magical dream world full of mythical creatures. Most of the stories were about his adventures with a fictional brother named Tristan."

Brian's eyes filled with tears, but he refrained from commenting like I'd asked him to.

"When I was a teenager," I whispered, flipping the page without really noticing the pictures, "I fell into a pretty deep depression, and I tried to kill myself by swallowing a bottleful of pills. Zeke was devastated. He sat down at my bedside in the hospital and begged me to tell him why I'd done it, but all I could say was that everything just felt wrong with the world and I needed it to stop."

Brian didn't speak, and I didn't take my eyes off the page, but I could feel him watching me.

"Not long after that, I had my first dream about you," I said, voice cracking as I looked up at him. "When I mentioned the dream to my brother, he said it was more than just a dream. He told me the dream world in his stories was real and we all visit it at night when we sleep, although most of us don't remember it when we wake up. Ezekiel told me he sent you to save me from the monsters who'd abducted me in the dream world because he couldn't get to me himself. He assured me that I could trust you—because you were the most honorable soul he'd ever met, and he couldn't imagine a better man for me to end up with in either world."

"Davina…"

"Of course, logically I knew he was just saying what he thought I needed to hear to feel safe, so I'd snap out of my depression," I said with a wistful smile. "And when you showed up here to save my life the other day, I figured I was either dreaming or having a mental breakdown. Then you drove me to that private beachfront mansion where you said I'd be safe. Imagine my surprise when I met Tristan there. *Zeke's* Tristan. Brian, your brother told me about your mom and the way she treated you. Tristan said you're a noble soul—who'd do anything to help anyone—but your mother warped your opinion of yourself and your worth."

"My brother's an idiot," Brian said, shaking his head; but the affectionate grin that spread across his face at the mention of Tristan belied the insult. "I'm not worth much."

"I think you're just proving his point," I said. "You saved my life, Brian—and not just here a few days ago.

When I was a teenager, you saved me from feeling so hopeless that I saw no way out but to end my own life. If *you* aren't worth much, then I must be worth nothing."

Brian cringed as if I'd hauled off and slapped him. "What makes you say that?"

"If you hadn't saved me back then, I wouldn't even be here."

"That just proves I did something right," he said, dropping his eyes to the photo album. "It doesn't make me worthy of your affection."

He was about to pull away from me again. I could feel it. Desperate to keep him there with me, I shifted sideways on the bench, put a hand on either side of his face and tilted his head to make him look up at me. "If you go, you'll be leaving me all alone."

Brian smiled, but it was the saddest smile I'd ever seen. *A goodbye smile.*

"My brother is gone now," I said. "I don't have anybody else, so don't you dare leave me. I know you're worthy—even if you don't—because Zeke told me you were, and he never thought anyone was good enough for me."

Brian just shook his head.

I slid closer and touched my forehead to his. "You are not your father, Brian, and I'm not your mother. I *do* know about the dream world—maybe not in the same concrete way that you and Tristan know it, but enough to be certain you could never hurt me the way your dad hurt your mom."

The longer Brian sat there staring into my eyes without moving or speaking, the more the feeling of disconnect between us terrified me.

"If you leave," I muttered, "I'll have to assume there's something fundamentally wrong with me because—"

"Davina," he said.

"I need you to stay, Brian," I whispered, ignoring the interruption. "I need you as desperately as I need air."

He closed his eyes and let out a slow exhalation that washed over me, sending a heated shiver down my spine.

Overcome with emotion, I leaned into him and brushed my lips against his.

Brian's eyes opened on a groan. "Davina, I can't."

"Please don't push me away."

The longing in his eyes sent a rush of heat pulsing through me, and he hissed as if he'd actually *felt* it. "What are you doing to me?" he whispered, cupping my face in his hands.

"Begging you not to leave."

When whatever it was that was holding him back snapped, it snapped *hard*. I saw it in his eyes as he drew my head closer while his lips lunged for mine.

I pivoted on the bench and swung one leg over both of his, straddling his lap; and he responded with a growl that was more feral than human as he kicked the table behind me back to give us more room. The unexpected jolt of his body beneath me, coupled with the resounding thud as the table hit the opposite bench, drew a startled whimper from me.

He stilled at the sound and drew his head back to meet my gaze. For a moment, I was afraid he was going to pull away again, but the lust in his darkened eyes put my fears to rest. "I've wanted you since the first second

I laid eyes on you, Davina. You have no idea how many times I've fantasized about making you mine."

I barely had time to process the thrill his words sent coursing through me before he lifted me off his lap and flipped me onto my back on the bench. For a few pounding heartbeats, his eyes wandered over me as he stood and took a step back. Then he leaned forward, bracing his hands on either side of the bench as he hovered above me. "If we do this again, I'm not sure I'll ever be able to stop."

Desperate to close the distance between us, I arched my back. "Good, because I'll never stop wanting you."

Difficult as it'd been to convince him that this should happen, he certainly wasn't shy once he committed to it. "Yeah?" he murmured as his lips whispered their way down my neck. "Where do you want me?"

"Anywhere," I whimpered as his mouth moved lower. "Everywhere."

He lifted his head, and eyed me with a wicked grin as we hastily shed the layers of clothing between us. "Tell me you're mine, Davina."

"I'm yours," I said, punctuating the words with a moan as he thrust himself deep inside me.

"You're mine," he growled, staying perfectly still as the heat between us pulsed hotter.

My God he was beautiful, and our bodies fit together with an inexplicable perfection that was unlike anything I'd ever experienced, or even imagined, before. This was so far beyond my wildest fantasy that I might've feared it was just a dream, if I were still capable of rational thought. *This* was where I was meant to be—locked mind, body, and soul—with this beautiful man who had no idea how truly perfect he was.

"I love you, Davina," he said in a hesitant whisper, like he was testing the feel of the words on his tongue.

Tears filled my eyes as I gripped him tighter. "I love you, Brian. Don't ever leave me."

"Don't worry. You're stuck with me now. I'm all yours."

An explosion of ecstasy burst inside me at his words as the two of us began moving as one, and I knew without a doubt that I would be his until my last breath.

47

ADDISON

I'd been pacing back and forth along the winding path through the courtyard of the Sarrum's palace for over an hour, although I had nobody blame for that but myself. I was just too antsy to sit around waiting inside.

Brian had asked me to meet up with him in the great hall because he wasn't quite sure when he'd return from the waking world. I couldn't fault him for that. He was driving Zeke's sister back to her shop, and Davina was Unsighted. Brian couldn't exactly tell her he needed to get going because he had business to attend to back in Draumer. If anyone could relate to that, it was me. My husband and sons were Unsighted, so I knew what a feat it was to keep the two worlds separate when your loved ones were unaware of the other world's existence.

I stopped pacing and drew a deep breath of the humid night air as I wiped the sweat from my brow. You would think after all the years I'd spent living a nomadic life in the knighthood, I'd be used to the Dark Realm's stifling heat. I could tolerate the conditions in the Darkness well enough when I had to, but I was a creature of Light. I'd be lying if I said the oppressive climate never got to me.

As I stood there pondering my aversion to the temperature, every nocturnal sound in the courtyard came to a screeching halt. Shivering in the unsettling stillness despite the heat, I turned toward the entrance to the courtyard and found Benjamin walking down the path toward me with a half smile on his lips.

The Darkness dipped his head. "Good evening."

"Yeah, I suppose it's good enough," I said. When he raised an eyebrow, I shook my head. "I'm sorry. Good evening, Benjamin."

The Darkness let out a contemplative sigh as he stepped off the path and sat down on a bench beneath a tree with thick black bark and fragrant bloodred blossoms. He leaned back against the bench and crooked a finger, motioning for me to join him.

I had way too much nervous energy coursing through me to sit still, but I didn't want to be rude. So I sat down beside him and started drumming my fingers on the armrest.

Benjamin's pitch-black eyes dropped to my fidgeting fingers. "Don't sweat it. Brian will be here as soon as he can."

"I don't doubt that," I said, making a conscious effort to still my hand. "I just don't want to show up late for my first day on the job."

The Darkness grinned at me. If I didn't know him that grin probably would've sent a shiver down my spine. But despite his inherent terror-inducing aura, I knew the smile was genuine. "I think you're forgetting something."

I turned toward him. "What's that?"

"You don't have to worry about being late when you're the boss," he said as his focus drifted toward the courtyard's entrance. "Meetings start whenever you get there, and everybody else will patiently await your arrival."

I followed his gaze, and let out a sigh of relief when I saw Brian walking toward us. "It's more than just a case of the jitters over being late. I'm also anxious to get back to James and the boys."

The Darkness nodded. "I get that, but they'll be fine till you get there."

Brian flashed me an apologetic smile as he reached our bench. "Hey, sorry I'm late."

I shook my head as Benjamin and I stood up. "No worries."

Without another word, the three of us started down the path toward the Waterfall at its end. The night sounds remained curiously muted as we moved toward the exit. But I couldn't tell whether the pounding of my heart was drowning out the background noise, or the nocturnal creatures were too busy watching us from the shadows to go about their usual business.

As we stopped at the Waterfall, Brian and I turned to say goodbye to Benjamin.

But Benjamin smiled and shook his head. "Don't go just yet. There's somebody else who wants to see you off."

Before I could ask who he was referring to, Charlie stepped from a Water portal that appeared just a few feet away from us. The newly appointed Dragon King raised a hand in greeting as he closed the short distance between us. "You weren't planning on leaving without saying goodbye, were you?"

"My apologies, Sarrum," I replied with a sheepish grin. "I guess I was too distracted by my eagerness to see James and our boys to think about being diplomatic."

"Fuck being diplomatic," the new King said, "and call me Charlie. After everything we've been through together, you've earned the right to be on a first name basis with me."

I let out a laugh. "Well, I can't argue with that."

"Besides," Charlie continued, "if you call me Sarrum, I'll have to address you as Queen. And that just feels a bit too stuffy and formal, don't you think?"

"Absolutely," Brian said, taking a step toward our King. "I'm really gonna miss you, Charlie. It was a pleasure and an honor to serve as your first guide. I couldn't be prouder of the dragon you've become."

"Thanks," Charlie muttered as the half-incubus pulled him into a hug, "for everything."

Brian nodded. "You know where to find me if you ever need me, my friend."

"Sure do," Charlie said as they both stepped back from the hug. "In fact, I thought I'd escort the two of you to your new home."

Brian raised an eyebrow. "Why the heartfelt goodbye if we're not parting ways yet?"

Charlie shrugged. "This felt like too personal a conversation to have in front of an audience." A grin spread across the new Dragon King's face as he turned and wrapped his arms around me. "I'm gonna miss you, Addison, but there is no one I'd rather have as my ally in the Light. I have no doubt that you'll do a remarkable job."

As Charlie and I dropped the hug, I grinned at Brian. "How could I go wrong with one of your finest commanding my army?"

"It's probably time to get going," Benjamin said, surprising me by pulling me into a hug. "Bob would be so damn proud of you, Addison."

Too choked up to voice a response, I squeezed him back.

The compassion in the Darkness's eyes as he released me told me there was no need to say anything. "You two ready?"

"Ready as I'll ever be," I said, blinking the tears from my eyes.

"Ditto," Brian muttered as he pulled the Darkness into a hug. "I'm really gonna miss having you around to piss off, Benji."

"Fuck off, pretty boy," Benjamin muttered, the tenderness in his voice conveying an entirely different sentiment. "Listen, don't worry about that baby brother of yours. I'm gonna keep him in line."

Brian chuckled as he stepped back. "I don't doubt it. If anybody can keep Tristan in line, it's you."

I frowned at that. "Speaking of Tristan, don't you want to say goodbye to your brother before we take off?"

"Already did," Brian said. "We're good."

I stole one last glance at the Sarrum's palace. "Well, then I suppose it's time to take this show on the road."

"I think I'll tag along too," Benjamin said, stepping into the Waterfall ahead of us.

Charlie smiled at me, then followed the Darkness through the Water.

Brian dipped his head in a slight bow. "After you, my Queen."

"That's gonna take some getting used to," I chuckled as I stepped through, with him following close behind me.

I expected to step out into the meadow at the edge of the Light Kingdom's border. Instead, I found myself right outside the entrance to the courtyard of the Light Queen's palace.

A pang of doubt gripped me as I turned to the Darkness. "Are you absolutely sure I'm the right soul for this job? I'm not even a fairy."

A wistful grin tugged at the corners of his mouth. "It doesn't matter what I think. The rightful Queen of the Light Kingdom chose you as her replacement before she…"

"Right," I whispered.

Freya, the Queen's primary attendant, came flitting out through the gate with a beaming smile on her adorable little pixie face. "Greetings, my Queen. Your guests are all waiting in the courtyard to welcome you home."

I wasn't sure if I'd ever get used to the royal treatment, but I was definitely sure I was ready to see those guests she was referring to. Grinning, I followed Freya into the courtyard with Brian, Benjamin, and Charlie behind me.

Relief washed over me at the sight of my husband's smiling face while our two sons gleefully chased each other around the courtyard behind him.

And I knew I was home.

48

CHARLIE

Addison seemed about as comfortable with her new title—Queen of the Light Realm—as I felt trying to fill the Sarrum's shoes, but I knew we'd both adjust in time. A dopey grin spread across my face as Addison's husband came rushing across the courtyard to welcome her home with a hug, and my smile widened as Brian headed toward Davina and the other refugees from Zeke's mirage.

The instant she spotted him, Davina went racing into his arms. Brian scooped her up in a loving embrace, lifting her off the ground and spinning her around.

For a moment my smile faltered, and I breathed a sigh of relief because I was so damn thankful Brian had saved Davina from the fate I'd condemned her to while under Godric's control. But I couldn't help smiling again at the passionate way the two of them were grinning at each other.

When I turned to Benjamin, even he was smiling. "We should probably take off," he said, dropping the grin, "and let these creatures get started on their happily-ever-after."

As I nodded, my eyes drifted back to the hypnotic sight of my half-incubus friend locked in a passionate embrace with the succubus of his dreams. The chemistry between them was so intense that you could *feel* it across the courtyard. Witnessing their reunion made me feel like I was watching the opening scene to some bizarre, otherworldly, slightly pornographic nature documentary. I could practically hear the voiceover in my head: *Today on Discovery, the Mating Rituals of the Incubus and Succubus, Draumer's Most Captivatingly Erotic Creatures.* Voyeuristic as it felt, they were just too mesmerizing to look away from. *Wait…why was I nodding?* Shit, they were distracting. *What was it that Benjamin just said to me?*

"We should take off," the Darkness repeated, with a bit more volume and a bit less respect for me in his tone, "and let them get started on their happily-ever-after."

Reminding myself that I didn't have to let the charm radiating from those drop-dead gorgeous creatures affect me, I peeled my eyes away from them and turned to Benjamin as I replayed his words in my head. *We should take off, and let them get started on their happily-ever-after.* "Yeah, while we go back to ours."

The Darkness shook his head. "Not just yet."

I stole another sideways glance at the lovebirds. "Okay, then what did you have in mind?"

"I feel like stretching my legs for a bit."

"Right," I said as we waved goodbye to Brian and Addison, then turned to make our exit, "because there's nothing you love more than a nice stroll through the Light."

Benjamin shrugged as we stepped out of the courtyard and started down the path to the border. "It's starting to grow on me."

"Uh-huh," I muttered, shaking my head as he veered off the path and headed into the trees.

For a long while, I followed Benjamin through the forest in silence. The farther we walked, the more the Light Realm's sunlight stung my eyes. Disconcerted as I was by the pain, Benjamin kept on walking as if it had no effect on him.

If the Darkness could tough it out, I sure as hell wasn't going to wimp out and whine about it.

Eventually, I lost track of how long we'd been walking through the Light forest, but I was pretty sure it'd been days. My eyes were now all but useless in the blinding light. My feet were wrecked with blisters and sore as hell. My mouth and throat were bone dry, and my stomach was grumbling loud enough to terrify every woodland creature in the realm into a watchful state of muteness. Despite all of that, I toughed it out— because if Benjamin could handle it, so could I.

But I'm embarrassed to admit that as we headed out of the forest into the blinding sunlight of the foothills without a single source of shade anywhere in sight, I was inching dangerously close to my breaking point.

By the time the weathered stone cottage perched atop the highest hill came into view, I was convinced this was all some sort of test Benjamin had concocted to determine whether I was truly worthy of my new title. I lifted a hand to shield my eyes from the sun as I considered the cottage and the Waters below. "Well," I muttered, turning to Benjamin, "did I pass the test?"

Benjamin narrowed his eyes at me. "What the fuck are you talking about, kid?"

Normally I would've felt like a weakling for shielding my eyes from the sun, since the Darkness clearly didn't feel the need to, but I didn't really care anymore. "This whole torturous trek through the Light Realm," I said, feeling more like an idiot with each word that left my mouth, "it was some sort of test of my fortitude, wasn't it?"

Benjamin shook his head as we walked toward the cottage. "Nope. But if this'd been a test to make sure you're not prone to paranoia, you'd be failing miserably."

"Thanks," I muttered. Then I realized where we were, and felt like an even bigger moron for not recognizing it sooner. "This is Commander Mackendrick's place, isn't it?"

"Yeah," Benjamin muttered as he stopped moving.

As I stopped beside him, my eyes were drawn to the Water far below at the base of the hill. It was the exact same vibrant shade of sea blue as Mackendrick's eyes. The last time I'd looked into those eyes he was tossing me into the Waters, insisting it was up to me to save Emma. Tears filled my eyes as my throat constricted, and I cleared my throat. "Should we go up and knock?"

Benjamin's Dark eyes fixed on the front door of the cottage. "Nah, I'm pretty sure he would kick both our asses for disturbing him so soon after everything that went down."

I let out a maniacal laugh. "Then what the fuck did we hike all this way in the blistering sunlight for?"

"Closure," Benjamin replied with a shrug.

Ribbons of amber smoke began to seep from my nostrils as I snarled, "Well, that's just awesome. Next time you feel like taking a two-day hike through the Light Realm over a bunch of steep-ass hills just to get some fucking closure, feel free to leave me the hell out of it."

The Darkness studied me through narrowed eyes for a moment before replying, "Will do."

His even-keeled response to my hysterical outburst pissed me off even more. Flames filled my eyes as I turned my back to him and the cottage with a growl of frustration, and started to walk away.

Benjamin didn't follow.

In fact, he stayed behind for so long that I stopped moving and turned around to see what the fuck was keeping him.

He was just standing there motionless, staring at the cottage.

In all the time I had known the Darkness, I'd never once picked up so much as a stray scrap of thought from his mind—not even about what an idiot I was during the most embarrassing moments of my training. But as I turned and started to walk away again, I heard his thought loud and clear.

We did it, Boss. The war is over. Peace has been restored to Draumer, and both realms are in good hands.

49

DAVID

My shadow's presence was a merciful, albeit brief, distraction. For a moment, Benjamin's parting words even managed to put a smile on my face.

I suppose I should've gone outside to speak with him and Charlie, especially since they had traveled such a long way to visit. I'm quite certain the new Sarrum would have appreciated a bit of encouragement from his predecessor, or at least to be let in on the secret that I was not entirely out of the picture. But I wasn't ready to step outside the cottage. Perhaps one day I might ask the Darkness to bring Charlie back so we could talk, but not yet. I had too much on my mind to welcome visitors.

As I stepped toward the picture window that overlooked the brilliant blue Waters at the base of the hill, I replayed the events that'd followed Emma's poisoning over in my mind for the umpteenth time…

…Seconds after I caught sight of Emma sinking through the Waters below me, a blow to the back of my head

incapacitated me. Rage consumed me as my vision dimmed.

Then everything went black.

The instant I woke, I sat up and blinked my surroundings into focus whilst the moments that'd preceded my loss of consciousness slowly came back to me. Disoriented and enraged, I sprang to my feet with a feral growl.

I hadn't the slightest inkling why I wasn't dead. All I knew for certain was that I was still in the Waters. Someone had encased me in a pocket of air, similar to the one I'd placed Isa in—after Emma stabbed her—until we were able to bring her back. This was madness. If there was even a miniscule chance that Emma could still be saved, I needed to escape this aqueous prison to search for her. Perhaps it hadn't been all that long since I'd lost consciousness.

"It has been several hours," an infuriatingly familiar voice informed me.

"You're the one who rendered me unconscious?" I snarled as Mackendrick materialized inside the bubble he'd imprisoned me in. "So help me, I will tear you limb from limb, you—"

"I did not knock you out, Talbot," he replied, cutting me off midthreat, his unhurried tone and relaxed posture angering me all the more. "I am the one who came to your aid and destroyed the Water creature who was rather intent on making you pay for your past crimes."

"What crimes?" I growled. "You were the one who killed their monarch to save Emma, not me."

"Aye, but since I am the true ruler of these Waters, they could hardly fault me for that, could they?"

"So they blame me instead," I said, although I could not have cared less what the Water creatures thought of

me. *"I saw Emma before that simpleton rendered me unconscious. Let me out of here so I can look for her."*

Mackendrick shook his head. "Too much time has passed since your witchdoctor poisoned her."

His composure in the midst of my ruin was maddening. "Why the hell should I believe you?"

"What reason have I got to lie about it?"

"You have always despised me for taking Emma."

"That's true enough," he said. "Still, I cannot deny that you did an admirable job of raising her."

"Save your empty compliments," I snarled. "Did you find Emma?"

Tears shimmered in the Water dragon's ancient eyes. "No, and too much time has passed to save her now. If you don't return to the surface soon, the same fate will befall you."

"I don't give a damn what becomes of me."

Remorse momentarily flickered in the commander's eyes.

"You are hiding something," I said. "Why would you have wasted precious time saving me instead of searching for Emma?"

"Because she would have wanted me to save you."

"No," I growled, stepping so close that the salt-water stench of his breath filled my nostrils. "There is more to it than that. You know where she is, don't you?"

"Your wife is dead, David. Her heart no longer beats in the waking world."

"In the waking world." The way he phrased that gave me pause. "And what of this world?"

"We are not in either of your worlds," Mackendrick replied. "The Waters are an entirely separate entity."

"Semantics," I growled. "You are hiding something."

He pushed away from the wall of Water and stuck his face even closer to mine. "And what if I were?"

My nostrils twitched with fury. "What the hell are you playing at?"

"What if I were able to revive Emma's soul, but her body could no longer contain it?"

A flicker of hope sparked from the ashes of my ruined heart. "Did you revive her soul?"

"Aye, but it will take every bit of my power to sustain her without a physical form to return her to."

"Let me help with the burden," I pleaded, desperate to see her again. "Perhaps together we can bring her back."

"You kept her from me all her life. Why the hell would I let you near her now, when I can have her all to myself?"

A snarl reverberated in the base of my throat, but I held my tongue because I had no viable argument for that. Mackendrick had every right to keep her from me. Ensuring Emma's safety was the only thing that mattered now, whatever the cost. "If you were to drain my magic, then use it to heal her, and strengthen her with my blood, could you revive her enough to re-inhabit her physical form?"

The commander narrowed his eyes at me. "Why do you ask?"

"I never had any right to take her," I muttered. "If Emma had grown up in the Light with you, she would never have fallen victim to Godric's fury. Be that as it may, neither of us can rewrite the past. The only thing that matters now is Emma's future well-being."

The commander took a step back from me, crossed his arms over his chest, and leaned back against the wall. "What exactly are you proposing?"

"Take your revenge," I said, hoping with all my heart that it would be enough. "End my life. Then use the blood you spill, and the magic that seeps from me, to heal her."

He pondered that in silence for a moment. "Why would you ask me to do that?"

"Since the moment I first looked into Emma's eyes, every choice I made was driven by my desires, and look where that got us. If there is even a chance that killing me can save her now, what are you waiting for?"

"Is that what she would want?"

His passive tone made my blood run cold. Perhaps there was nothing left of her to heal and he was simply toying with me, prolonging my agony to exact his revenge. "Why don't you ask her?"

"She is not conscious at the moment."

I balled my hands into fists at my sides. "Then what makes you think she ever will be?"

A faint smile tugged at the corners of his mouth. "Emma's will to live is strong. Tell me something: If I gave you a choice—between reviving her briefly so you could spend a few more days with her, or ending your life without ever setting eyes on her again to heal her completely—which would you choose?"

"Why the fuck are you wasting time asking me stupid questions?" I replied through gritted teeth. "If you have the means to save my wife, end me now and heal her for God's sake."

Mackendrick's smile just widened. "What if I could promise you another year with her?"

A puff of smoke escaped my flared nostrils, a wordless declaration of my rage. "What the bloody hell are you going on about?"

"Answer my question, you selfish son of a bitch," the commander snarled, a crack emerging in his calm façade.

"Don't make yourself out to be some honorable martyr. If I offered you an entire year to be reunited with your wife, do you deny that you would take it?"

"Not that it is any of your business," I growled, "but no. I would never choose my happiness over her life."

Mackendrick tilted his head to the side, appraising me through flame-filled eyes.

If there was even the slightest chance that groveling before this fool could save my wife, it'd be well worth the indignity. There was no price I would not pay to restore her health.

"I always intended to send Emma to her rightful place in the Light when she reached maturity, but she forced my hand and refused to leave the Dark. My love for her..." Tears stung my eyes as I stopped to clear my throat. "However you wish to spin our story—the way I treasured her above all else...my greed...my obsession—my desire to keep Emma with me shortened her life. So if my death can buy her more time now, kill me and put my blood to good use. She has you to keep her safe, and Draumer has a new Sarrum. My absence will scarcely make a difference to anyone."

An instant after I finished pleading with him, everything went dark.

And I drifted off, grateful that my death could prolong Emma's life...

...Instead, I'd woken to find myself in Mackendrick's cottage. He hadn't taken my life, and my wife was still gone. I might as well have been dead for all my withered heart could feel.

There was no reason for me to return to the Dark Realm. The throne had been passed to Charlie, and it was better for all concerned if I remained in solitude. The company of a bitter old dragon who'd lost his dearest treasure was a hardship no one should have to bear. I was painfully aware of that, since the only parent I'd grown up with was a father who had spent every day since my mother's death mourning the loss of his beloved.

I shook my head as I crossed the room and sat down on the couch, my eyes still fixed on the Waters where I'd caught my last glimpse of my fairy bride. Were I not devoid of every emotion but rage, I might have found the irony amusing. I understood them now—my father, and Godric. This was what they were left with after my mother's death: a gaping hole where their heart had dwelt, and the excruciating agony precipitated by the memories of what they'd lost.

There was no point in lying to myself any longer. At every point in my relationship with Emma—with each new instance of trauma or heartache—I'd always known deep down that given the chance to do things over, I wouldn't have changed a thing. The thought of parting with a single moment I'd spent with her was too unbearable.

Now, I'd trade every last breath in my body—and retract every moment of my life since her birth—to turn back the clock and do the right thing.

I lied to Mackendrick, and he knew it. It was Emma's choice to remain with me in the Darkness when she reached maturity, but the fault was mine nonetheless. If I had never taken her, there would've been no danger of a future where she chose to shorten her life—by remaining in the Dark with me—rather than taking her rightful place in the Light.

I knew.

On the day of her birth, when I went to the hospital to determine whether she was Sighted, I knew damn well that taking her was an unconscionably selfish move. This newborn fairy princess had a bright future ahead of her. She was the heir to the Light Queen's throne, and there was a Water dragon who had already vowed to lay down his life to protect her. Mackendrick was an ancient being, capable of far greater magic than I was. Despite what I had always claimed, I knew there was no justifiable reason for me to take her. Yet, I told myself—and anyone else who dared question my actions—that I took her to protect her.

But she was already safe, arguably quite a bit safer than she would be with me.

It didn't matter.

The instant those gorgeous green eyes locked with mine and shined for the very first time, my heart was hers; and the notion of parting with my heart was too devastating to contemplate. So I took her, and I threatened to start a war if the rightful guardian her grandmother had selected to raise her made any attempt to retrieve her.

Unlike me, Mackendrick had made the selfless choice. He refrained from provoking a bloody fight that might've endangered the infant princess, and he walked away praying that I would keep her safe. It was right that Emma's soul was now under his protection, as she was always meant to be. This agony was exactly what I deserved for the choices I'd made.

I stood from the couch and moved back to the window, drawn by the view of the Waters where my heart now resided. "I am so sorry I failed you, Princess."

A sudden blinding burst of light outside the cottage gave my ruined heart a jolt, and I rushed to the door to find out whether Benjamin and Charlie had been injured.

As I opened the door and stepped outside, my eyes were all but useless in the brilliant sunlight. Shielding my eyes with a hand in a futile attempt to regain my sight, I started in the direction Benjamin and Charlie had headed.

"Aren't you going to say hello to me?"

My heart throbbed at the sound of that voice. "How?" I whispered as I moved toward her, certain that the loss of my treasure had finally driven me mad.

"What do you mean?"

"How are you here?" I whispered, trembling at the inexplicable feel of her hand taking hold of mine. "Have I lost my mind? If that's the case, I welcome the madness. I never want it to subside."

Her other hand caressed my cheek, lessening the blinding brilliance of the light so that I could see the impossible specter standing before me. "You aren't mad, David."

I drew her into my arms, desperate to savor every second of this hallucination before the madness subsided and left me in ruins. She dropped her head to my chest, and her body melted against mine with a contented sigh as her arms wrapped around me.

With her in my arms, our surroundings finally came into focus. We were standing in the center of our clearing—or rather, a new mirage fashioned to look identical to it—and it wasn't as sunny as I'd believed it to be. The light wasn't coming from the sun in the sky above. The light was emanating from a brilliant pair of gossamer wings, shimmering like new-fallen snow on a winter morning.

I traced a fingertip along the delicate edge of Emma's wing. "How is this possible?"

"Lochlan," she replied, grinning as she watched my finger trace over her wing. When I responded with a frown, she said, "He healed me all the way back to my original factory settings. Then he used my memories of my happiest days to re-create our mirage down to the last detail, and he returned me to my home."

"This isn't really home," I said, although I couldn't have cared less where we were standing. "It's a replica of our clearing."

She tilted her head back to meet my bewildered gaze without leaving my arms. "The clearing was never my home, David. *You* are my home. Wherever you are, that's home to me."

"How can this be real?" I whispered, lifting a hand to her cheek. "Powerful as Mackendrick is, no dragon is capable of this grand a miracle."

Tears glistened in her eyes as she smiled at me. "He used every bit of magic in his immortal being to accomplish this."

My chest tightened at her words. "What?"

"The commander sacrificed his life to bring me back to you, David."

"He loathed me. Why on earth would he do that?"

"He saw how miserable I was without you, and he was moved by your offer to sacrifice your life to heal me."

I brushed a wisp of hair back from her face and planted a kiss on her forehead, lingering there a moment as I savored the feel of her flesh against my lips. It was a blissful pleasure I'd never expected to feel again.

"Lochlan wanted me to tell you that your offer inspired his decision. He said he already had his happily-ever-after with my grandmother; and when he realized my happily-ever-after was with you, the choice to move on to the afterlife and be with his soul mate was the easiest decision of his life."

Overcome with gratitude, I tightened my hold on my wife. "You feel more whole and healthy than you have in years."

"I do," she whispered, "but only here."

A lump formed in my throat as I realized what she meant. Her soul had been restored, but there was no body for her to return to. "You cannot return to the waking world."

She shook her head. "I'm confined to this mirage for good, but I don't care. I'm with you, and that's all I've ever wanted. I can amuse myself well enough while you're in the waking world or attending to business back at the palace."

I traced my thumb over the petal-soft flesh of her bottom lip as I shook my head. "I am in a coma in the waking world, and Charlie has taken the throne."

"I'm so sorry," Emma whispered as her magnificent green eyes filled with tears.

I'd been willing to turn both worlds upside down for her after just one glimpse of those eyes. "There's no need for tears. I have no desire to be anywhere but here with you."

Emma's brow furrowed as a thought occurred to her. "Who's caring for you in the waking world? Our last few doctors didn't exactly prove to be trustworthy."

"Benjamin, Isa, and Clay are keeping a careful watch over my body; and the doctor who helped Charlie's mother escape Godric's men when she was pregnant is seeing to my medical care. Godric's blood is no longer controlling anyone's actions, so there's no need to doubt the doctor's intentions—especially since Clay can gauge his sincerity by viewing his memories."

"How do you know all this?"

A smile spread across my face. "Benjamin came to visit me, and he assured me there was no need to worry. They have everything under control."

Emma nodded. "My body isn't there anymore, is it?"

"No," I whispered, tearing up despite the fact that she was right there in my arms. "They cremated your remains, and had a memorial service for us both."

"But you're not dead."

"Benjamin is keeping that under wraps from all but a handful of souls."

The corners of her mouth took a downward turn as another thought occurred to her. "What will happen when you die?"

A wisp of blue smoke escaped my nostrils. "In the seconds I had before I lost consciousness in the Waters—when I saw you sinking below me—I tethered your soul to mine in the hopes of retrieving you when I woke."

A tear slid down her cheek as her pupils dilated in response to my scent. "But I was too far gone by the time you woke up."

"Yes," I said, brushing the tear from her cheek, "but your soul remains tied to mine. So when my time comes, you will go with me."

"So, our side won?"

"Yes."

"Then why are we standing here talking about death?"

I answered her with a sinful grin. "What would you prefer to be doing?"

Emma's eyelids lowered as those magnificent eyes of hers darkened. "Celebrating."

My smile widened as I lifted her in my arms. "Yes, we have much to celebrate."

As I started toward the entrance to our cave, she shook her head. "Put me down right here, David. I've been daydreaming about being back in your arms beneath the stars in our clearing for far too long to go inside."

"It is broad daylight."

A coy smile spread across her lovely face as I lowered her to the ground. "Yes, but I know a dragon who can change that."

I winked at her as I lay down on the grass beside her, extinguishing the light and scattering a multitude of stars across the sky above us. "Not just *a dragon*," I replied, pulling her body flush against mine, "*your dragon.*"

"My dragon once told me," she whispered as my lips traced their way down her neck, "that he would burn both worlds to ash to still time for us if I asked him to."

"And he meant it," I said, lifting my head to look into her eyes. "But it seems there is no need for that now. Those worlds will go on just fine without us, and you and I have all the time in the world."

The End

If you enjoyed this story, please consider leaving a review, giving it a shout out on social media, and/or telling your friends about it.

To learn more about the author and her books, visit her website: erinajensen.com